SISTERS

of the

SOLSTICE MOON

GINA MARTIN

WOMANCRAFT PUBLISHING

Published by Womancraft Publishing, 2019
www.womancraftpublishing.com

ISBN 978-1-910559-44-4

Sisters of the Solstice Moon is also available in ebook format: ISBN 978-1-910559-45-1

Cover design and typesetting by Lucent Word, www.lucentword.com
Cover art by Iris Sullivan
Map illustration and design by Jonathan Millar, with thanks to Malcolm Martin Simpson for initial concept and research.
Pronunciation guide by Eliza Martin Simpson

Womancraft Publishing is committed to sharing powerful new women's voices, through a collaborative publishing process. We are proud to midwife this work, however the story, the experiences and the words are the author's alone. A percentage of Womancraft Publishing profits are invested back into the environment reforesting the tropics (via TreeSisters) and forward into the community: providing books for girls in developing countries, and affordable libraries for red tents and women's groups around the world.

PRAISE FOR
SISTERS OF THE
SOLSTICE MOON

In Sisters of the Solstice Moon, author, teacher and priestess Gina Martin has woven together visions of the mysteries of the Sacred Feminine from the past, present and future, with an evocative and sensual urgency... Lush with rich, descriptive language that carries the reader into the cultures and rituals she dreams into being, one has only to let oneself be carried deeply into the heart of these rites and the important spiritual messages they contain.

Sharynne NicMhacha,
scholar and author of *The Divine Feminine in Ancient Europe, Celtic Myth and Religion*, and *Queen of the Night*

Sisters of the Solstice Moon is a generous offering of heart and spirit, expertly crafted as it envelopes the reader in its sweet embrace and has us caring deeply for the women on their journey, with all their qualities – both human and divine. Filled with wisdom and insight, this tale of love, healing and magic is a powerfully moving and transformative story for our time, as we reconnect with our own inner wisdom and knowing. I loved this book.

Celeste Lovick,
author of *Medicine Song*

Gina Martin weaves a magical tale of possibility. Parting the tides to bring forth a new/old understanding of our shared past; A past in which the goddess – and therefore all life – is held sacred. And that is exactly what we need right now.

Jessica M. Starr,
author of *Waking Mama Luna* and *Maid, Mother, Crone, Other*

Sisters of the Solstice Moon is a visionary tale of women coming togeth-er with a singular purpose... the survival of Mother Earth. Evocatively written, Martin draws us into an epic story that follows thirteen Priest-esses on individual quests that lead them to the star-filled skies of Egypt. Along the way, we are immersed in ancient Goddess rituals and instructed by these powerful women on living in harmony with nature. Feminist, futuristic and unabashedly Matriarchal, Sisters of the Solstice Moon is a story for this moment in time.

Lisa Levart,
author/photographer of
Goddess on Earth: Portraits of the Divine Feminine

Gina Martin's mesmerising tale carries us across water, fire, earth and air to the realm of the ancient Priestesses of the Goddess. As fiction blurs with memory, something stirs deep inside. We are pulled into the weave of the Sisterhood, and summoned to remember the wisdom bubbling beneath the surface, ready to re-emerge.

Nicole Schwab,
author of *The Heart of the Labyrinth*

Take everything you have learned of history and throw it away. And then, come, sit and listen to a tale of herstory, not a time when women 'ruled' but of Goddess cultures where they listened to the earth and the stars and guided with courage, strength and bravery. What a beautifully written book! Gina Martin writes lyrically and sensually, weaving the stories of matriarchal cultures coming together to prepare for dormancy so that the stories of the Goddesses could quietly live on in each cell and bone of our bodies until She could return, bringing balance to a world desperately in need. I do believe that time is now...

Karen Moon,
creatrix of 'The Divine Feminine' app

Homer move over! Gina Martin's Sisters of the Solstice Moon is a timeless, astonishing and visually captivating tale of the origins of female worship of the Divine Feminine that carries us into the land of Egypt during the era of the Pharaohs. Expertly and divinely inspired it is a remarkable journey complete with a super savvy elephant and a spirited sea creature who save our determined travellers from certain death. The characters are delightful and the words dance off the page!

Kristi Zea,
film producer, director, production designer

In Sisters of the Solstice Moon, Gina Martin has created a novel that is epic and intimate, mythic and maternal. Reading this book feels like remembering a legend I've known all my life, buried deep in my bones, but like the thirteen sisters themselves, long ago forgotten. Martin breathes narrative details into the embers of this story that make it crackle to life. Beautiful, engrossing, and dreadfully relevant, this book will remind you of the latent power of Women. At a time when the radical right and authoritarianism are on the rise all over the world, it's a great comfort to remember that hope is not lost; it's only hibernating.

Jeanine Cummins,
bestselling author of *A Rip in Heaven* and award winning novel *The Outside Boy*

Calling all priestesses! If you are a priestess, long to be a priestess, deep in your bones remember being a priestess, Sisters of the Solstice Moon is for you. Gina Martin's powerful, lyrical novel will bring you face to face with priestesses of thirteen diverse, ancient traditions – as well as their friends, consorts, and animal familiars. Join them on their perilous and beautiful quest as they answer the timeless and timely call of the Goddess.

Elizabeth Cunningham,
author of *The Maeve Chronicles*

Both in life and now in the pages of her timely and inspiring book, Gina Martin, brings women, who stand for sisterhood, together under the same moon. In Sisters of the Solstice Moon she offers the soul threads of thirteen women, following the call of the Goddess, weaving together new and forgotten myths to hear and remember ourselves. With urgency she holds for us an imagining, a mirror, imploring us to honor and protect the Divine Feminine as She waits for us to meet her within our own hearts and in our lives.

Deborah Kampmeier,
award-winning filmmaker

Written word that uses fiction to tell a story of reality can best be written by goddess-inspired Wimmin. Gina weaves a story that echos the events of our grandmothers lives. Beautiful and magically she reveals the stories long covered up by centuries of oppression and patriarchal fear. Hers is a story that will make you think and consider seriously the path that we as Wimmin need to reclaim to insure a future for our generations to come.

Beverly Little Thunder,
Lakota pipe carrier and author of *One Bead at a Time*

DEDICATION

*T*his book is dedicated to the Reverend Dr. Lee Hancock, Presbyterian Minister, Priestess of the Goddess, founding mother of Triple Spiral of Dún na Sidhe, soul sister and my Alama, smiling on us from beyond the Veil.

ACKNOWLEDGMENTS

Virginia Wolf said every woman needs a room of her own; I say every woman needs a writing group. From the incomparable Jeanine Cummins who gently and expertly held the tiny chick that was this story, to my fellow scribes, Linda, Judi, Naaz, Jess, Adelma, Ann, Cheryl, who listened and laughed and cared – this book wouldn't have emerged without your precious attention and wisdom.

I have been blessed with many teachers of worth and note. Sister Joseph Eileen, Sister Dorothy Louise, Mrs. Snyder, Mrs. Phillips – you all told me I was a smart girl and encouraged that intelligence. My teachers in adulthood – Sensei Reggie Ceasar, Dr. Jeffrey Yuen, Elizabeth Nahum, Beverly Little Thunder, Sharynne NicMhacha, ALisa Starkweather, Starhawk, Adhi Two Owls and so many more. My sense of the wonder of the world keeps expanding because of you.

I have the deepest gratitude to:

All the women, girls, boys and men of Triple Spiral of Dún na Sidhe, past present and future. We come together to stand in Circle and remember. You all have inspired every word.

My fellow travelers in the Priestessing Practicums – you have been the models for the reclaiming of our powerful heritage.

Lucy Pearce who decided to break her own rules to publish this book.

Laura Delano, soul sister and eternally optimistic first reader.

And my family – Rick, Eliza, Malcolm, my beloveds, who never doubt my abilities, even when I do. You are my greatest gifts.

PLACES AND CHARACTER PRONUNCIATION GUIDE

ARYA AND THE GODDESS KALI MA

[ˈɑːə̯jɑ] / AR-ee-yah/ and the Goddess [kɑːli mɑː] /kah-lee MAH/

Maia – the living embodiment of Kali Ma	[ˈmaɪ̯jə] /MY-ya/
Savi the elephant	[sɑːvi] /SAH-vee/

THE ROOF OF THE WORLD AND THE GODDESS LHAMO

The Goddess [ˈlɑmoŭ] /LAH-moh/

Tiamet – devotee of Lhamo	[ˈtiəmɪt] /TEE-a-met/
Yan and **Shema** – her servants	[jɑn] /YAHN/ [ʃimə] /SHEE-mah/

SUMERIA AND THE GODDESS INANNA

The Goddess [ɪˈnɑːnɑ] /ih-NAH-nah/

Parasfahe – Priestess and twin sister of	[pɑə̯əˈsvɑheĭ] /par-ah-SVAH-heh/
Erhenduanna – High Priestess of Inanna	[ɚhɛnˈdwɑnə] /er-hen-DWAH-nah/

THE SEA WITHOUT END AND THE GODDESS SEAL WOMAN

Autakla – a selkie	[aŭˈtɑkˈlə] /ow-TAHK-lah/
Feyl – mother of the tribe	[feĭl] /FAY-eel/

THE MYSTERY SCHOOL AT CALANAIS AND ITS PATRONESS THE GODDESS BRIG

The Mystery School at [ˈkælɪnɪʃ] /KAL-uh-nish/
and its patroness the Goddess [bɹiʒ] /Breej/

Brighid – High Priestess of
Brig, later known as **Celebi**
Silbara – one of the nineteen
priestesses of Brig
Malvu – Chief Observer
Dalia – the Egyptian scholar

[ˈbɹiʒid] /BREEJ-hid/
[seˈlebi] /seh-LEH-bee/
[sɪlˈbaɚa] /sil-BAR-rah/

[ˈmælvu] /MAHL-voo/
[ˈdɑliə] /DAH-lee-ah/

ALONG THE TIN TRAIL AND THOSE WHO REVERE THE DARK MOTHER

The village of the **Basquela**

[bɑˈskeɪlə] /bask-EL-ah/

LAND OF THE HUNTRESS, THE TEMPLE OF ARTEMIS AT EPHESUS

The Temple of [ˈaɚtəmɪs] /AR-te-mis/ **at** [ˈɛfɪsɪs] /EH-feh-sus/

Io – maiden of the Wild Hunt
Pel – a dedicant of Artemis

[ioŭ] /EE-oh/
[pɛl] /PEL/

THE SEA OF GRASSES AND THE GODDESS EPONA

The Goddess [iˈpoŭnə] /ee-POH-nah/

Kiyia – a Guardian of Epona
Misi – the pig herder
Smith Younger and Older
Yollo – the weaver

[kaɪˈjiə] /kai-EE-ah/
[ˈmisi] /MEE-see/

[ˈjɑloŭ] /YAH-loh/

THE MOTHER GROVE IN THE GREAT NORTH WOODS AND THE GODDESS NEMATONA

The Goddess [ˌnɛməˈtoʊnə] /neh-meh-TOH-nah/

Eiofachta – a student and seer,   [iˈfɑktə] /ee-FAHK-tah/
later known as Driftwood
Alama – the First Among Equals   [əˈlɑːmə] /ah-LAH-mah/

MALTA, THE OBSERVATORY OF THE SEVEN SISTERS FROM THE PLEIADES AND THE GODDESS GAIA

The [ˈpleɪəˌdiz] /PLEH-a-deez/ **and
the Goddess** [ˈgaɪjə] /GAH-yah/

Ni Me – one of the Seven   [ni meː] /nih MEH/
Ni Ma,   [ni mɑː] /nih MAH/
Ni Mae,   [ni meɪ] /nih MAYEE/
Ni Mi,   [ni miː] /nih MEE/
Ni Mo,   [ni moʊ] /nih MOH/
Ni Mou,   [ni maʊ] /nih MAWOO/
Ni Mu   [ni muː] /nih MOO/
– the others of the Seven

YUCATAN AND THE TEMPLE OF THE GODDESS IX CHEL

The Goddess [iˈʃɛl] /ih-SHEL/

Uxua – the Living Ix Chel   [uˈʃuə] /oo-SHOO-ah/
Talo – her twin brother   [ˈtɑːloʊ] /TAH-lo/

EIRU AND THE GODDESS THE CAILLEACH
['ɛə·u] /EH-roo/ and the Goddess ['kɑli ˌjəq] /KAHL-ee-yahk/

Badh   [bɑ] /Bah/
– the Keeper of Wild Spaces
Domnhu – her servant   ['dɑːmnu] /DAHM-noo/

WESTERN SHORES AND THE GODDESS YEMAYA
The Goddess ['jemaĭ ˌjɑ] /yeh-maee-YAH/

Awa – girl of the lineage   ['ɑːwə] /AH-wah/
Ndeup – her mother   [nˈdʊp] /en-DUP/

EGYPT AND THE TEMPLE OF THE GODDESS ISIS
The Goddess [iˈsis] /ee-SEES/

Atvasfara – High Priestess of Isis   [ətˌfasˈfaə·ə] /aht-vahs-FAR-ah/
Medrona   [mɛˈdɹoʊnə] /meh-DRONE-ah/
– She who was Pharaoh
Maisoun,   ['maĭsun] /my-SOON/
Maysa,   ['maĭsə] /MAY-suh/
Petrinh   [peˈtɹɪn] /PEH-trin/
– daughters of Medrona

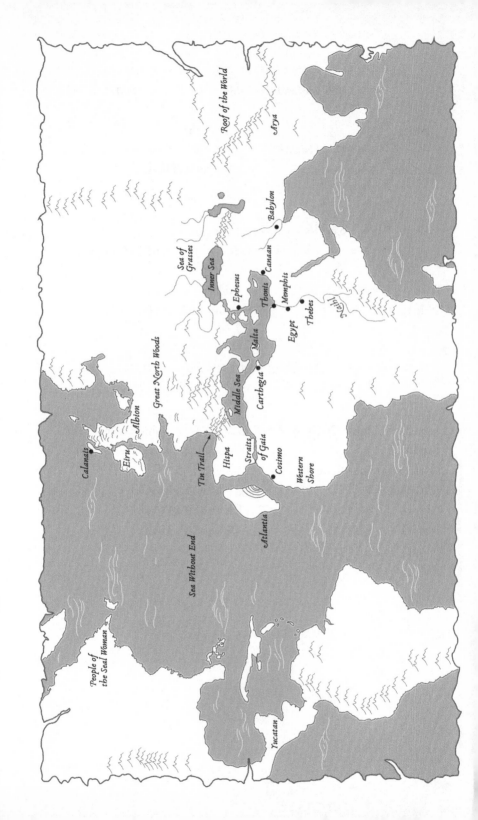

THE QUICKENING

The women are coming
From the misty north and west
With the sands of deserts
Rich with spikenard and amber
with diadem of crescent moon
torcs of gold and copper.
The women are coming
From Artemis and Kali Ma,
Epona comes with Isis,
Nematona, Cailleach, Inanna,
Nut, Ix Chel, Brig.
The women are coming
Walking the threads of time.

*T*he full moon spills light across the sapphire and jade, the topaz and pearl of the Earth, on this the longest night of the year. Around the world all the peoples celebrate with song, with dance, with prayer, with fire… asking for the return of the light, for the lengthening of days, for life to be reconfirmed.

This night of the Winter Solstice is a magick night. This full moon a powerful one. Their alignment creates the cauldron of transformation. Poised on the edge of the beginning of an end, the Earth holds her breath.

Across the planet thirteen women receive the same vision. Some are suspended in ecstatic trance. Some are gripped by nightmarish fever dreams.

All see what is to come.

They know they have been called.

And they know they will answer Her.

THE MIGRATION

THE DANCE OF KALI MA

We are pulled far to the east, where the night is beginning. We see desert, then ocean; we are flying too fast to see clearly what lies beneath. And then, there it is: the vast, moist, fecund jungle. A teeming source of life that assaults the senses with a wave of sound made by millions of birds and the smells of leaves unfurling and fallen tree trunks rotting. Birth and death and everything in between. The jungle is mottled in the moonlight with shades of gray and fern and midnight black. As we move closer, we see thousands of lights scattered through the dense canopy of leaves, a mirror image for the canopy of stars that blanket the sky. Some small fires spiral like the Milky Way into a moving swarm of smaller illuminations. Moving closer, we see it is a procession, a parade of lanterns and torches that make a serpentine river of light in the darkness. The drumming drives the footsteps as the people of Arya, the people below chant...

> *"Kali Ma, Goddess of the Fire!*
> *Kali Ma, Mother of the Bones!*
> *Kali Ma, Mistress of the Dying!*
> *Kali Ma, Daughter of Reborn!*
> *Kali Ma!"*

*T*he refrain soared above the crowd and into the emptiness of the night. Several thousand devotees had gathered on this auspicious full moon to dance and chant and drum till dawn. The bonfires scattered across the Temple grounds made the shape of the constellation of the Water Bearer, the symbol of the Goddess herself, the Giver and Taker of Life. At one fire was a cluster of the sick waiting for healing. At another, the dying waiting for release. At a third fire, richly pregnant women patiently swaying and laboring together. There was the fire for the warriors looking for a blessing, and a fire for the haunted asking for absolution.

The procession, many hundreds strong, was led by the Divine One, the embodiment of Kali Ma. Wreaths of frangipani and orchids hung around her naked body with strands flowing from breastbone to ankles. Her skin, the color of the jungle floor, was moist with sweat and the anointing oils of sandalwood and frankincense. On her head, above the slash of bright eyes rimmed in kohl, she wore a headdress standing three feet high woven of silver and gold, studded with rubies and sapphires, and rimmed with small, lit candles. She was ablaze with trance and drum and fire from within and without. Her hips swayed gently sometimes and fiercely at others. She danced and danced around all the fires the requisite nine times as the thunder of the drums grew, and the chanting splintered into waves of ecstatic sound and weeping and laughter. She danced and danced beyond all endurance, carried by the fervor of the people and the knowledge that this was her last Solstice as the Divine One. One last night to give all she was, all she had, to the people and the Goddess. Visions came and she declared them. Those waiting for death took their last breaths and she swung her arms skyward to release their souls. Cries ripped the night as one, two... twelve babies were born while the Divine One danced around them.

As the wind died down in the last hour before dawn, she came to the middle of the constellation of fires. The chanting was at a fever pitch, with raw voices calling on the Kali Ma, the Destroyer and the Creator. Ankle bells and finger cymbals clanged till bones thrummed. The drumming had sped up and become so fast that it was now a constant wall of sound, pulsing and beating against the body of the Divine One standing at the center, feet planted wide and arms stretched above her. She was shimmering and shivering, all life trembling within her. She drew a deep breath and all the people together gave one last orgasmic cry that split the night.

Hearts racing, the only sounds their ragged breathing, the people waited for the Divine One to return to herself, lower her arms and break the intensity with her devastatingly sweet smile of victory for the night's work.

The silence thickened. Still they waited. No one dared approach her. *Perhaps the Goddess had overtaken her completely tonight.*

Babies began to whimper and were quickly brought to breasts. And still she didn't move. The six attendants, including the young woman who was to be her successor, exchanged glances and gently inched forward. No one could touch the Divine One when she was filled with the Kali Ma. To do so brought instant and irrevocable madness. Only those disciplined by years of training could hold that power for even a second. Her body began to shake, her head thrown back and flung from side to side. It looked as if her very bones would fly apart. Could any human body hold all this power? Her mouth opened like a gash in the earth and she rent the sky with a scream of rage and terror.

She lowered her gaze and the people saw the traces of kohl running rivulets down her cheeks as she ripped off her headdress and the wreaths of flowers. She stood before them naked, wild eyed, with her oiled hair sticking to her body, looking like snakes on her back and legs. The Kali Ma had gone, and the woman before them was middle aged, with a soft belly and drooping breasts. No otherworldly majesty, only human frailty with a core of dignity that was achingly beautiful.

Her attendants rushed toward her, but she waved them off and turned to walk under her own power to the Temple at the back of the clearing. The six followed, motioning to the people to wait there. With worried faces and hushed voices, the people began to attend to the dead and the living. A milky light seeped through the leaves. Embers from all the fires were raked together, and wood was added to make the cremation pyre for those who had passed over, and the newly born were swaddled against their mothers' chests. But all had one ear tilted, one eye attuned to discover what was going on in the Temple.

Maia, who had served as the Divine One since her twentieth summer for a full thirty turns of the wheel, clasped the arms of her chair to lower herself down. She refused to falter on her last day of service.

The color of her face was dry and ashen, like the earth before the monsoons came.

"Dearest Ones. As you know…" her voice cracked, "as you know, today is my last day holding the Goddess in my body. The moon no longer pulls the blood from my womb, and so the power must pass to another. When the sun is high, I will pass the staff and ring to my chosen successor. You will serve the next Divine One well, I know."

Tears poured unbidden and unnoticed down her cheeks. Her attendants called for bath water and gently led her to the copper tub. As she sank down into the warmth, they washed her hair and worked out the snarls delicately. They brought her tea and mango, but she ate very little and said even less. They all sensed something was wrong, but allowed her to keep her dignity, assuming that she was overwrought by thoughts of the coming transition of power.

But Maia held the secrets of her final vision to herself. It was a terrifying vision, filled with danger and destruction. It was her mystery to unravel, and for the first time in thirty turns of the wheel she thought of herself first, before the needs of everyone else. As the sun rose higher in the azure sky, the attendants wrapped her in robes of scarlet and saffron, slipped goatskin slippers on her feet, and applied her ceremonial face markings of spirals and tear drops with great care.

Maia stood and walked precipitously out of the chamber toward the central courtyard. Her chosen successor, a talented and lovely, soft petal-skinned girl of eighteen turns of the wheel, stood, also draped in scarlet and saffron. The two women locked eyes and Maia passed the staff of office to the younger woman. The young one felt the total power of the Kali Ma travel up her arms like thunder and settle in her chest like a leopard wrapping its legs around her heart. She rocked on her feet, startled by the enormity of this surge, and then grounded down. With a slight nod, Maia took off the sacred ring – a ruby the size of a night beetle rested in the eyes of the gold serpent ouroboros – and pushed it not too gently onto the other's thumb. The young woman felt a bolt of energy like lightning shoot from her yoni to her crown. And with that simple set of actions the transfer was complete. No words were needed, no elaborate choreography, just one woman letting go, and the other catching the weight of responsibility. As the attendants moved in to surround the new Divine One, Maia turned and hurried, unseeing and unseen, out of the courtyard.

A short time later, changed into simple traveling pants and short cloak, Maia slipped out back to the animal pens. She carried a small pack of belongings and wore a curved knife on her belt. She unknotted the thick rope that kept Savi in her stall. The elephant gently wrapped her trunk around her mistress' hips and swung her up onto her back and out into the jungle. Maia heard an internal whisper, a guiding beacon, and urged Savi to the west toward the mountains and the lands beyond.

The people were all gathered at the front of the Temple, singing and welcoming the new Divine One. They did not notice the pair's exit, the bells around the elephant's feet ringing in descant with the finger cymbals of the Temple dancers.

Maia felt a strange sensation bubbling in her chest. Panic? Anticipation? Exhilaration?

Freedom!

This is what freedom felt like.

THE ROOF OF THE WORLD

We move rapidly over landscapes. Jungle, forest, mountains. And still we climb higher. We are far above cloud cover and the light of the full moon is painfully brilliant. Ahead we see a human-made structure that looks to have grown out of the side of the mountain, like lichen on a tree. The light directs our gaze to the veranda near the top of the formation carved from the living rock. A woman, draped in the skins of a white wolf, stands with her arms outstretched, and we hear her thin voice singing, drawing down the moon. Her shadow spills behind her on the brick floor, making her look three times taller than she is. Entranced, she sings.

*T*iamet was old. Impossibly old, many thought. She had lived here in the Temple of Lhamo longer than anyone's memory. Some of the younger sisters in the Temple actually believed the stories that she had been alive forever. Her skin was deeply bronzed, and she had the vivid scarlet cheeks that bloomed as people aged here at the Top of the World. Her face was crisscrossed with crevasses so deep as to appear bottomless. She was almost blind, her sight stolen by the countless years of staring at the sun and moon, here, where the air was so very thin. Year after year she stood on this veranda and drew down the moon, as the life of the Temple swirled and eddied around her.

She was respected for her age and for her position, but feared for her temper and avoided by all who could. All except the two young novitiates assigned to her care as a spiritual lesson in patience. These girls strove to calmly await the day when their time with her was over and the next team arrived to take on the task.

Yes, Tiamet was very difficult. She would sit in meditation for two or three days at a stretch and her attendants would bring sustenance to her every few hours. Mostly she would ignore it. But woe to the attendant the one time she forgot: that was exactly when Tiamet wanted her food. Her needs were few, but specific to her, and a mystery to everyone else. The attendants slept in the one room with her on pallets on the floor. She was seated most of the year on her bed frame, looking out the window to the never-ending horizon, night and day. The room was warm by Temple standards, but close. Any sound – the shuffle of a slippered foot, a dropped spoon – might send the Old One into a tirade that lasted till ears were blistered. She might ignore her attendants for weeks and then berate them for hours. A spiritual lesson in patience, indeed.

Time here was counted from shortest day to shortest day. And so, tonight was to be the last day of service for Yan and Shema, the two young attendants who had their belongings folded and packed, ready to move on. They stood on the veranda in the shadow at the door leading into Tiamet's room, shifting from one foot to the other. Yan, almost a foot taller than her fellow novitiate, was rubbing the fabric of her cloak constantly between her fingers, trying to keep the feeling in them. Shema, whose round face had given her the nickname Moon, was already numb.

"The Old One is going on longer than usual," Yan whispered in a not too quiet voice. Shema shot her a sideways glance and both girls started to giggle. It was shameful really to laugh at the Old One, but by the Goddess, she was trial. No matter, later today they would be free!

Tiamet, the impossibly Old One who was standing terrifyingly close to the edge of the veranda, turned suddenly and directed her nearly sightless eyes at the girls. It was unsettling how she always knew exactly where to look.

"You two. Gather my things. Get some real boots on. And follow me!"

The two girls raced into the room bemused by her command. *Follow her where? She hadn't left this room in decades. She never went anywhere.* Tiamet was not to be questioned, only obeyed. But where were they going? Before they could clarify their destination, she was already out the door and into the corridor. They could hear her starting down the staircase with a repeated growl as each almost vertical step assaulted her ancient knees.

"What should we do?" Shema squeaked. What if the Old One took a tumble down those stairs?

Yan looked startled for an eye blink of time and then giggled, "I think we had better put some real boots on."

Within moments the two had laced their boots, found Tiamet's prayer beads and head piece, put the cover over the brazier, and, with a final look around the room, grabbed their already packed belongings. They hurried out into the corridor and down the steps, following the distant sound of Tiamet's growls that now sounded more like a bear than a dog, deeper and more irascible with every descent.

Five stories down they could no longer hear the grunts, but followed the murmur of voices. Tiamet was standing in the Abbess's antechamber, raising a ruckus. As Yan and Shema erupted into the room, they saw the very sleepy Abbess and her two attendants trying to interrupt the avalanche of words.

"You had a dream…," the Abbess began, "… sorry, a prophecy…"

Tiamet kept the roll of words flowing, speaking without taking pause for breath or any attempt at punctuation. The give and take of conversation had never interested her, and tonight her vision and the mission it foretold were paramount in her mind.

The Abbess, who had achieved her position through a wealth of diplomacy and patience, sighed deeply and began again, "Of course, we will do whatever is…? *Now*? This very moment? Do you not first want to…?"

Tiamet turned and, with unerring accuracy, stormed out of the antechamber, snapping at Yan and Shema, "You two, you're with me!"

The two turned to the Abbess, who gave them a look that was pity mingled with relief at her own relinquishing of responsibility. She nodded, and the two novitiates followed the impossibly Old One. As they descended, they passed many more sleepy faces. Women in hastily wrapped shawls watched this curious parade in the flickering shadows thrown by the butter lamps. Ahead, the sound of Tiamet's tortuous journey and ancient knees. Behind, the whispered conjectures of the Temple's women. And with a sinking feeling Shema grumbled, "I have a suspicion that we aren't done with the Old One yet this morning."

Yan stopped on the step below, and looked over her shoulder at her friend. The tiny half smile that marked genuine amusement lifted her lips, "At least we have real boots on." And the staircase was filled with laughter as the two followed the trail of audible breadcrumbs down the stairs.

At the lowest level of the complex spread the village that existed to support the Temple and its inhabitants. The cooks and weavers and artisans and tanners all worked on this broadest platform of land, with the Temple itself perched above them like a finch in a tree. The mountain to the east now had a peach-hued rim. Tiamet stood, surrounded by men and yaks, directing them as to what provisions she needed. Everyone moved quickly, with automatic obedience, but shot curious glances at the Old One. She was the stuff of legend. No one here in living memory had ever seen her, let alone heard her voice. But there could be no doubt who she was.

The white wolf cloak, symbol of the highest level of reverence, was hanging from her shoulders to the ground. Only those women of the Temple of Lhamo wore white fur, starting with vole and rabbit, and progressing to fox and yak and bear. But only one had achieved the status of the white wolf. And here she stood!

Yan and Shema were gaping at this sight some thirty feet away when Tiamet's voice ran out like a branch cracking, "Get over here, you two, and tell these idiots what we need!" The girls scurried over and exchanged puzzled looks. *What did they need, indeed?*

Yan, always the braver, said, "Most Revered, what do we need... and for what purpose?"

"Have you two not been listening? We leave on a journey to save the knowledge of the Goddess. We need food for the trip down the mountains."

"For how many days, Most Revered One?" asked Shema, always the most literal.

"How in the name of the Earth and sky should I know?" Tiamet's voice revealed a slight tinge of uncertainty. And when she was uncertain, she was even more cranky.

By the time the sun had risen above the tip of the mountain to the east, all three women were seated upon yaks, and a cluster of porters with all the provisions that anyone could imagine would be needed were poised behind. Yan and Shema were petrified at the swaying of the beasts below them. Suddenly, the reality of this adventure hit them both. They were leaving the Temple, leaving the Land of Lhamo perhaps. They would not be relinquishing their service to the Old One today, or for an untold number of days to come. Shema began to cry softly, and Yan turned pale.

The now fully dressed Abbess, with her cloak of white bear, had gathered all the women of the Temple to bless the journey. As the Abbess approached the yak upon whose back Tiamet seemed precariously perched, she saw how tiny and frail the Old One looked out of the Temple in the daylight. She reached out to touch Tiamet's thigh as a farewell.

"I will never return, you know," Tiamet's throat was gripped so tight that the words came out like a creaky leather hinge. "You had better miss me!"

Tears filled the Abbess's eyes and she chuckled. A wordless blessing was passed from one to the other. Perhaps she would miss her after all.

AT THE RIVER

One day stretched into the next as Maia, formerly the Divine One, She who holds the Kali Ma, rode west atop her friend. The jungle took on different personalities as she daydreamed, rocking gently on Savi's back. Small streams crashed down rock-strewn gullies, and each day brought birds and creatures she had never seen before. For three days she wove through the deepest foliage where the folk lived in the trees, high in the highest branches. After the first week, Maia came into territory that had more farmland, with houses made of daub and wattle. She traveled along valley bottoms and through small villages. The farther west she went, the more cinnamon and cyprus trees she saw, so slender and aromatic compared to the palm and mahogany of her homeland. As she and Savi climbed higher the smaller the flowers became and more pastel in hue. Down into the next lowlands, more wonders unfolded with a richer intensity of colors and a grander size of blossoms. In her lifetime of profound experiences Maia had seldom been as moved as she was now by a splash of fuchsia across a hillside.

It had been many years since Maia had needed to think about feeding herself or finding shelter. These tasks were challenging as she traveled through mile after mile of jungle, but oddly thrilling. She was free of expectations, free of responsibility. Some nights she shared a fire with fellow travelers, on others she stopped in a local village, and some she slept between Savi's legs on a rough pallet of palm fronds. These two moved as the day moved, east to west, with space for thoughts and non-thought. Maia found herself enjoying washing her own clothes and cooking her own food. She knew herself well enough to know that this novelty might expire and she would look back fondly on her time of exalted status. But for now, in these formless days, she reveled in the sun and the rain and in her no-oneness.

After a span of one moon she found herself on a widening road. Women and men carried bundles on their heads, children ran along side or slept in the wagon beds. The gathering stream of people and carts was converging at a river crossing ahead where a ferry waited to transport those walking or riding in small wagons. Donkeys could be ferried across, but horses, and of course, elephants, needed to swim. Savi began to quicken her steps, smelling the water ahead and looking forward to a bath. Maia eagerly anticipated a bath today, too, after several days of dusty roads.

As the road widened further and the river spilled out before them, the sounds of screeching and wailing reached a crescendo. Two young women stood with heads bent, the recipients of the direct blast of a sound like, well, unlike anything Maia had ever heard. Maybe the sound of a tiger and an elephant quarreling over the same meal. Or the sound of jackals in full-blown battle with village dogs. But there were no big cats, jackals or dogs anywhere to be seen.

The source of the racket appeared to be a tiny, shriveled human draped in the fur of a very large white animal, the likes of which had never been seen in this region. A few yards past them in the direction of the river was a small caravan of strange, hairy, cow-like creatures, with the people clearly assigned to lead the beasts pulling and cursing and yanking at them to force them into the water, with no success. Every one of them, human and beast, looked hot and miserable and ready to weep.

For these travelers, their journey from the Top of the World had seemed like a descent into the bowels of the Earth. For an entire moon they had been funneled down dramatic mountain passes, leaving behind the sweet, thin air of their home. Now, their clothes were too heavy and cumbersome, and the air felt like they were breathing soup. Yan and Shema dealt with the increasing irascibility of Tiamet, whose mood had disintegrated with every mile. The heat, such intense heat, made the yaks sluggish and intractable. As the final inequity, yaks feared moving water and couldn't even be tempted to drink from it. And to swim across this torrent? The nightmare of nightmares.

Maia nudged Savi forward and the elephant trumpeted a hello. At the sound, the two young women whipped around, startled, and let out a skelloch to burst an ear. The shorter one fell to her knees and began sobbing in fright, and the taller bravely stepped in front of her companion. The very old, shriveled person took a step back with eyes as round as a full moon and abruptly stopped her screeching.

"May I be of some assistance?" Maia asked in the common tongue.

The Old One opened and closed her mouth like a fish on shore. Maia wondered if perhaps this person, who she could now discern was a woman, only spoke a local dialect. She had assumed that the little person was of high rank because of the richness of the fur she wore, and with rank usually came education and the benefit of the common tongue for commerce and exchange of cultures. After that pause the tiny woman brusquely replied, fluent yet thickly accented, "These two idiots are useless. Mayhaps you know how to get the yaks across the water. The ferrymen refuse them passage. Ridiculous!" Her face looked ferocious, but her voice quavered at the end.

Maia surveyed the knot of humans and animals. One of the hairy cows was up to her chest in the shallows of the river, thrashing and bellowing in sheer terror. The man pulling her harness was floundering, pulled down by the weight of his heavy and now wet clothes. There was a stunning cacophony of shouts and bleats and muttered and forceful exhalations, and the scene was quickly deteriorating to a riot. Maia stood with a graceful hop up to Savi's neck and used her priestess voice to garner attention.

"BE QUIET AND STAND STILL!"

And they were, and they did.

Before the shock could wear off and chaos ensue again, Maia slid down Savi's trunk, walked through the melee to the water and grabbed the yak's harness, bringing the animal and the nearly drowned man back onto the shore. She quickly determined that not all the caravan drivers spoke the common tongue, so she gestured for them to

16

link all the animals together in a long chain and shooed the drivers onto the waiting ferry while the already boarded passengers laughed uproariously. Then, with some ceremony, she herded the Old One and her two companions toward the elephant, and gave the hand command so that Savi swept them all onto her back with seemingly little effort. Not waiting for the remonstrations or yelps of fear from her passengers to subside, Maia urged Savi forward into the river, and leaned down at the last moment to clasp the lead of the first yak in her right hand. With a giant and stately dignity, Savi led them all into the water, and the yaks followed after only the tiniest of hesitations. Soon the line of beasts was a black procession of muscle and hide that arced across the water like the path of a falling star. On the opposite shore, the people gathered to watch the spectacle, and broke out into a cheer as the parade emerged onto dry land again.

As the caravan drivers rushed forward to help their three dignitaries slide off the elephant, Maia stood again on Savi's back. With arms raised she tilted her head back to the sun and laughed like she hadn't since her childhood. "I haven't had such fun in years!" she exclaimed. "Thank you!"

The old woman, Tiamet, was still cradled by the caravan driver. From within his arms came a sound like the rocks of the Earth grinding against one another in an earthquake. It began low and rumbling and began to build till all who clustered on the riverbank heard it. Tiamet, the Old One was laughing with a mirth that was so rusty as to be calcified. The caravan driver cracked a smile and then joined in the laughter. The giggles and cackles and woops were contagious, spreading until all those present were holding their sides and wiping tears off their faces. Yan and Shema alone of the company shook their heads at the silliness. *What was the world coming to?*

As all the laughter died down, there only remained a wizened wheezing sound coming from Tiamet.

"Glad to know you, Grandmother," Maia called down. "Where are you headed?"

"Egypt. Wherever *that* is."

"By the Goddess, so am I! Want to ride along?"

Tiamet gestured crossly to the driver to put her down, but before she stepped away she turned, smiled sweetly at him and rested her gnarled fingers gently on his cheek. With that she walked toward the elephant. Maia gave a quick command, and Savi, ever so gently, lifted the Old One up onto her back, her long white wolf cloak floating behind her. With a kick of her heels, Maia sent them off down the road. Shema and Yan scrambled onto the backs of the saddled yaks. The other porters and drivers quickly followed suit, and soon there was only the dust of the beasts' footsteps to prove that they had been there. The long line of animals, like a strand of extraordinarily large black pearls, moved west, toward the Land of the Goddess Isis.

BABYLON

We see a rich land below us, shimmering with layers of green and copper. Two rivers form a V. As we glide closer toward the land, the rivers' waters flicker silver and slate, oscillating like the scales of a powerful swimming fish. We descend further until a city and the outlines of a vast complex of buildings come into stark detail. Marble walls look blue in the full moonlight, and red clay roof tiles look like blood. The only sounds are fountains in courtyards rich with jasmine and pomegranate. On this longest night of the year the suspension of activity purchased by sleep is shattered by screams.

*P*arasfahe was awoken by the screaming… before realizing that it had come from her. Bare and frantic feet crossed the marble floors to her chamber, and she felt, more than saw, the lamplights as her sister and the attendants rushed in. She was wrapped and twisted in the bed covers; her heart was racing, and she was afraid, no, terrified to open her eyes. She heard voices, soft, worried, edgy from the startle of sudden wakefulness. She felt the hands touching her, probing for injury or pain or fever. And she felt paralyzed to move through the oily fog of her fear.

"Please, Sweetness, what is wrong?"

The patient voice of Erhenduanna broke through. Parasfahe, the elder of the twin sister priestesses by two minutes, struggled with the silken bed wrappings, and carefully pulled herself upright. The pain in her joints was searing. She leaned forward and poured what she had seen into her sister, the High Priestess' ears. They were a study in contrast, with their two heads tipped toward each other like lilies on bended stalks. One had streaks of gray and the other had glossy sable hair. One's face showed the ravages of pain and illness while the other's skin shone translucent with vibrant health and vigor. Both sets of eyes were deep and molten brown, but one was framed in worry and hesitation, while the other looked with steady confidence and authority. One was crippled; the other ruled their world.

Erhenduanna, High Priestess of Inanna, the Incarnation of She of a Thousand Names, listened with eyes closed as her sister described her nightmare. She heard of men with rictuses of rage on the backs of horses, slashing death-bringing long swords, of priestesses herded and shackled, led out into the mountains to die. This was the orchestrated decimation of women, all women, no, women of power: the violent birth of a new and ugly world order. The anguish and tumult of the dream was greater than anything the High Priestess had ever experienced, and she burst into tears. She heard the rustle and worry of the others in the room, sounding like those tiny finches in the bushes when trouble was near. No one had ever seen Erhenduanna weep. Ever.

The attendants, that carefully chosen thirteen, stood close together, with sleep-mussed hair and varying degrees of dress. A bare shoulder, a pillow creased cheek. The pomegranate silk bed curtains barely moved in the pre-dawn quiet. The eldest attendant staggered, and, without taking her eyes off her mistress' face, committed the heretofore unheard of breach of sitting in Erhenduanna's presence at the foot of the bed. The only sounds were the sounds of gentle weeping and the exhalation as the Earth let go of night.

The two sisters, one filled with great sovereignty and power, the other tortured by twisted joints and self-doubt, interlaced their fingers and locked their eyes. This foretelling was too horrible, not possible to grasp, and yet, in their hearts, they knew it was coming.

$$) \bigcirc ($$

"I can't do this! I can't and I won't!" Parasfahe wailed.

She sat in her chambers on a low divan with her legs stretched before her under a thin linen blanket. The twisted line of legs could be seen under the wrap, and her sister's heart broke for the millionth time as she witnessed Parasfahe's suffering. But Erhenduanna, swathed in the vivid robes of Inanna, blue and gold, continued her pacing around and around the room, as if by sheer force of will she could walk her sister's fears away. She was a woman of small stature with delicate bones and a sharp, pointed chin adorned with a wide and surprisingly sensuous mouth. She had impeccable carriage and the air of one whose every command is instantly obeyed. "Sweetness, you received the vision. It is clear what must be done and that you must be the one doing it!"

They had had this same argument every day for more than a moon cycle. Erhenduanna smelled damp in the breeze blowing in through the doors that opened onto the veranda, that breeze slightly moving the long panels of bleached muslin hung to keep out any harsh light. The room was soft with the muted hues of late afternoon. Everything in this room was softer and more subdued than the surrounding Temple decor. Six small braziers scattered around the room worked to keep the mid-winter chill at bay. Parasfahe's quarters faced east toward the rivers and were cooler in the summer than the rooms that faced the setting sun. Heat caused her pain. Cold caused her pain. Damp caused her pain. Being alive and drawing breath caused her pain. This room where she spent most of her time was richly appointed and yet sparse: a bed, the divan, some stools for attendants, and the freestanding tub, long enough to stretch out in, a tin bathing tub that offered some privacy and a respite to the feeling that her joints were filled with shards of glass.

"Sweetness, there is rain coming. Let me have water brought for a bath to ease your pain." She motioned to a servant girl to send for water. Erhenduanna, High Priestess of Inanna and ruler of the Land of Sumeria was at her wits' end. Her sister, Parasfahe, after a life of making no demands and acquiescing to everything, was making a stand and refusing her destiny. Both women had been marked as Goddess-born. Twins always were. And they had been brought to this sumptuous Temple here in Babylon at the age of three. They had no memory of their parents: the Temple and all who dwelled within were their only family. The bond between the two sisters had always been close, but as they grew and as Parasfahe's illness became apparent, they depended on each other. Their private kinship deepened when Erhenduanna was chosen to replace the last High Priestess. They trusted each other as confidants; no one else understood their secret longings or dreams. But when Erhenduanna became the High Priestess and Potentate of the mighty lands on the Tigris and Euphrates rivers, Parasfahe became more isolated, staying only in her rooms. Erhenduanna had always made decisions for the both of them. Truth be told, Erhenduanna made decisions for all of Sumeria. But now, after forty sun cycles, Parasfahe had found her voice.

An attendant, a bright and competent woman of some fifty-four sun cycles with sun-streaked hair stepped into the room and took in the charged scene. She brought with her the scents of frankincense and myrrh, the aroma of cumin and the midday fish and lentils on the sapphire and saffron of her robes. Everyone in the Temple had been aware of the conflict between the sisters, and the attendants had been talking constantly about what could be done to help. No one had ever had to intercede between the sisters before, and it felt like walking on the thin crust of ice that covered village ponds in winter to step into the mix and offer any solutions or advice.

"Exalted One, there are two women who say they are Priestesses of Lhamo and Kali Ma in the Great Hall. They ask to speak with you. They said they received a vision and are on a grand journey. They arrived on an elephant!"

The attendant's sandy eyebrows were lifted almost to her hairline, and she shot a quick glance to the side to see how Parasfahe was taking this news.

Erhenduanna paused for only a moment before replying, "Please make our honored guests welcome. Show them to rooms and arrange for baths. Tell them my sister and I will greet them in the Great Hall at sunset."

The attendant nodded her understanding, and as she turned to leave the room, she heard a gasp of outrage and the beginnings of rising voices.

"I am *not* going to the Great Hall! I don't want to meet *anyone*."

"You *will* go, if I have to carry you myself!"

Parasfahe threw one arm over her face and turned onto her side, away from her sister. Erhenduanna sat gently on the divan at her sister's hip, hesitant to touch, and finally yielding to the need to stroke Parasfahe's hair, "Sweetness, what is it really? We two have served the Goddess all our lives. Why do you not heed Her now?"

"No, *you* have served Her! It has been *you* She has chosen."

Erhenduanna felt something rip open inside her, some secret fear that she had plastered over for decades. "It should have been you! You have the gifts! You were first-born. If you hadn't been ill…"

"No!" retorted Parasfahe. "You always believed me more blessed in order to not accept your own gifts. It is not me. It has never been me. I don't have the courage, I cannot, I simply cannot leave these walls and do this task. What if I fail?" Her voice was swallowed in waves of tears, her thin shoulders heaving until sheer exhaustion brought peace.

"Sweetness, if you fail, then the world is lost."

The sound of an elephant's trumpeting split the air and was surrounded by the lowing of yaks in a herd. And far in the distance, in the foothills of the snow-topped mountains, there was a blue fog of smoke from the campfires of an unknown peoples waiting at the outskirts of Sumeria, waiting, waiting.

THE TEMPLE OF INANNA

*T*he sun was setting, throwing long silver shadows in the hallways, as the two sisters processed down to the Great Hall. They had been dressed in their ceremonial finery: layers and layers of silk in sapphire blue and saffron yellow like the petals of a rose, their hair in tight coils and pinned up into the honeycomb style worn by the highest ranks in the Temple of Inanna. And as the diadem of High Priestess was settled on her head, Erhenduanna felt resolve and responsibility soak in to her bones. She had been as good as her word and had literally lifted Parasfahe up under her armpits and dragged her to the sedan chair. The scream was an ear-slicing blend of pain and outrage, "You can't make me!"

Met with an equally furious, "Oh, yes I can!"

The four attendants in the room looked frightened and hesitant to intervene, like the onlookers at a dogfight, fearful of getting bitten in the fray. They ran to lift the sedan chair and it tipped precariously to the right as the young woman in front momentarily felt her grip slip.

"Aaaaahhh!" That scream was pure pain as Parasfahe was jostled. Every instinct in Erhenduanna to protect and shelter her sister rose up, but she hardened her heart and took on her most commanding priestess voice.

"We go to meet our guests!"

The journey down the corridor and the wide steps to the Great Hall was interspersed with moans and mutterings from Parasfahe and a total locked-jaw silence from Erhenduanna. The group emerged into the Hall, to find it brightly lit from the torches placed every arm-stretch along the wall. Erhenduanna ascended the three steps to her throne on the dais, and the attendants gently placed the sedan chair on a raised small marble square directly next to the throne, leaving Parasfahe at rest as they cautiously slid the carry poles out and stepped away.

Erhenduanna, the Exalted One, the High Priestess of Inanna, let her gaze softly fall on the group of travelers standing at the bottom of the dais. Many peoples traveled and traded through Sumeria, but even with that exposure to all types, to her this group looked particularly ill-matched and motley. A woman of middle years with deep brown skin and slightly slanted almond eyes stood with feet planted wide, and a look of wary anticipation on her face. Her hair, the color of bear fur was as long as she was tall, twisted into a rope that she had slung forward over her left shoulder. Her clothes were simple and unadorned, pants that fell to mid-calf, a rough short tunic, and small half sandals tied around her ankles. She was dressed like a poor and insignificant person, but no one who looked into those eyes could mistake her for anything but a ruler of people and places.

Next to her stood a figure swathed from crown to foot in a white animal fur cloak and hood. All that was visible outside the fur were two crabbed hands and two eyes like burning charcoal. Behind this figure were two young women also draped in animal fur, one tall and wearing an air of defensive hostility, the other short and round faced, with perspiration dappling her upper lip and shallow breaths that moved her cloak to a flutter. They were clearly waiting for the tiny figure in front of them to do or say something.

Those two figures in the front, the strong woman and the tiny person drowning in fur looked like they came from totally foreign worlds, but something in the way they stood, separate, yet aware and connected to each other told Erhenduanna that they were a partnership, companions of some undertaking, no matter how strange their union might seem to others.

"Welcome, travelers, to the Temple of Inanna. The Goddess of Heaven and Earth gives you shelter, if you come with goodwill." Erhenduanna spoke in the common tongue in a low and commanding tone, offering amiability wrapped around a core of iron. Hers was a voice that expected and received total and immediate compliance, and she looked composed and serene. Inside she seethed with frustration, anger and a little guilt. She had rough-handed Parasfahe. She had hurt her, and she hadn't felt bad in the doing of it. In truth, she had felt a little delicious thrill at having that kind of power over her sister. Guilt, anger, confusion – all warred within her so loudly that she barely heard the muffled reply of their guests.

"Ha! We have little but goodwill with us, as you can see," the brown-skinned woman, Maia, once the Living Incarnation of Kali Ma responded. "We follow a vision and a voice in our heads that steers us right, left, or forward. That tiny voice, like the chirping of an annoying nesting bird, told us to come here and meet with you… and so we did, and so we are."

Maia directed her remarks to Erhenduanna who was most definitely the one in charge, but her eyes strayed to the frail woman seated to the right of the throne. Her eyes strayed and were arrested there, as the woman in the sedan chair stared back with a rebellious, and damn-you-all glare.

Tiamet stepped forward and spoke directly to the insolent Parasfahe, "We have come for you, little sister, and you know why, yes? Cheer up, it may only mean the death of us all!"

A stunned silence filled the Great Hall, and Erhenduanna struggled to get on top of the wave of emotion filling her body, filling the room, threatening to fill the world. *The death of us all!* For as much as she had believed her sister and the vision that she had suffered, it wasn't until this moment that the enormity of what was to happen, and the fact that it was going to happen to them here in this Temple occurred to her. Her beloved Temple, all the women of Inanna who were so precious to her, all of it. *The death of us all.*

"Clear the room!" Erhenduanna commanded her attendants, and women swept from the room like fog burning away at first light.

With a gesture of her hand, she motioned that the two young companions of the impossibly Old One, were gently maneuvered out of the Great Hall as well. Only the four remained, and Erhenduanna invited the two travelers up onto the dais to sit on the bench positioned to her left. Parasfahe had begun rocking forward and back, moaning quietly. Maia took Tiamet's hand and helped her up the steps to the bench, and the Old One accepted the assistance without ever once taking her eyes off Parasfahe, rocking, rocking, rocking.

These four sat in a motionless moment, poised before catastrophe, each waiting for the others to begin. Finally, Maia spoke and told the story of her vision, the meeting with Tiamet and her young companions, and the insistent inner voice that had steered them here to Babylon. Tiamet interjected from time to time, still never dropping her gaze from Parasfahe whose rocking had become more insistent.

"We who know the Goddess best, know that the cycles must revolve, know that the Wheel of Existence is inexorable, but this level of destruction bespeaks a whole new world, and it is one I fear," Maia concluded.

"My sister has had the identical vision. But what causes this abruption in the fabric of our world?"

"I saw a giant wall of water," said Tiamet.

"I saw flooding and famine," said Maia.

They all turned to look at Parasfahe for her piece of the puzzle.

"It will all be ashes and pain," she gritted out between her tightly clenched teeth. There was a long silence.

"And why to Egypt?" asked Erhenduanna.

"We have discussed little else over these last few days. We think… perhaps more accurately, we have a knowing, that we aren't the only ones called, that a gathering of women will come together and…"

"And do a work of magick!" Tiamet finished the thought. "What do you know of this… Egypt?"

Erhenduanna paused to give an enigmatic response, and then decided to toss diplomacy to the winds. If there ever was a time for brutal truths, this was it.

"We have many dealings with the land of Egypt, in trade and scholarship. It is a viper's nest, a den of jealousy and envy, a place that seems to breed petty behaviors and back-stabbing intrigue. I would wish you need go anywhere but there." Another long silence fell over them.

Tiamet's gaze went inward, her eyes rolled up, her chin tipped downward, and she began to speak in a voice not her own.

"The place of discord and dissonance. The container of heat and friction. The vessel of alchemy. Great magick requires this."

Erhenduanna spoke under her breath, "Well, if it's discord you need, you'll have it in the tonnage there."

Erhenduanna's eyes were wet, yet she didn't allow the tears to fall. She could see her sister out of the corner of her eye, see her rocking with a ferocity that she had never seen before. Where was that sweet compliant woman? Where was her best friend and confidante, the one person she could share the burdens of leadership with? This person rocking and moaning to her right felt like a stranger; she missed her sister, her wombmate, with a piercing slice, like a spear to the heart. But whatever else Erhenduanna was, she was a High Priestess first, and the Goddess had spoken so loudly here that to deny Her command would be to deny the breath in her own body. She took a long stuttering inhalation, "The Temple of Inanna and all her dedicants will do all that is possible to facilitate your journey. And my sister will accompany you."

And with that Erhenduanna felt the tear, the rending of that umbilical bond, as Parasfahe wailed like a beast caught in a trap.

$$\text{)} \, \text{O} \, \text{(}$$

The night before they were to leave for Egypt, the travelers and all the women of the Temple stood in the chill air after the moon had risen in the east and was visible a quarter way up the blue silk sky. They processed in silence down into an enormous cavern directly below the Temple itself. This had been, in the days before remembering, the holy place of the First People, the ones who worshiped She Before She Had a Name. Over the ages, the Temple had been built above the cave, but the doorway to it, a small and unassuming wooden door at the edge of the Great Hall, was still the entrance to the most secret and deep mysteries. On this night, as torches threw high shadows, the travelers watched as the story of Inanna's Descent into the Otherworld was re-enacted.

The air was thick with the smell of copal and myrrh. Priestesses created a spiral shape by forming two twisting lines, and Erhenduanna personifying Inanna and more richly dressed than they had ever seen her, journeyed around and down the spiral, taking off symbols of status and identity, as Inanna had done, to become bare and unadorned. She came to stand in the face of her Shadow, her divine sister Ereshkigal, portrayed on this night by her real-life sister, Parasfahe. Off came the diadem of her rank, then the jewelry of her wealth. Next, she removed sandals, then girdle, breastplate, then tunic and breechcloth. Naked and vulnerable Erhenduanna/Inanna had drunk all the herbs in the large silver chalice, a potent mixture concocted to send her into a death-like trance. As she slumped insensate, the women caught her and suspended her body in a harness on a hook that was attached to the rock face. The voices of the women rose and rose, shimmering off the walls of the cavern. Their sounds held dissonance and power, invoking, demanding that Erhenduanna, in the role of Inanna, come back to life.

Lady of all the divine powers,
Resplendent light,
Righteous woman clothed in radiance,
Beloved of An and Uraš!
Mistress of heaven, with the great diadem,
You are the guardian of the great divine powers!

To the travelers it truly appeared that Erhenduanna was dead. She was still; no breath moved in her chest. The singing built and built and built, and the rock sang the high overtones and the cavern became a world of sound as three hundred women's voices sounded like three thousand. Finally, after a handful of moments, or perhaps a handful of hours, Erhenduanna/Inanna jerked her head upright and gasped for air. She looked wild and unmoored, blank-eyed and so very, very ancient. The women erupted in ululation that seemed to make the rock walls tremble. Erhenduanna/Inanna was lifted from the wall and carried deep into the darkest recesses of the cavern, and completely submersed in a small lake. Then they carried her body, gently toweled it off, and dressed it in new clothes, before placing her on her feet. All the women of Inanna, joyous and triumphant, celebrated the struggle, the surrender and the victory of life by initiating a beautiful and intricate dance, the dance of rebirth, which wound through the cavern and up the staircase until it spilled into the Great Hall of the Temple. The dancing went on long into the night leaving the travelers to eventually slip away to grab what rest they could.

$$\text{)} \bigcirc \text{(}$$

The next day was the one appointed for their departure, and Maia with her Savi, and Tiamet with her young servants awaited the signal for their journey to commence. The scene in the Grand Plaza was chaotic and colorful. High atop Savi the elephant was strung an elaborate contraption that looked a little like a hammock. There were upright braces and a beautiful woven awning, as well as a suspended platform that would stay stationary as the elephant walked and swayed side to side. This design would enable Parasfahe to ride west to Egypt with the growing caravan of mis-matched travelers.

Tiamet, the impossibly Old One, from high in the highest mountains, stood, still draped in her white wolf cloak despite the warmth of the day. Deep in the creases of her face, deep like wild mountain crevasses, her eyes had a far away look, seeing her homeland with inner vision, missing the cold, crisp, thin air with an unexpected stabbing pang. With a deep breath, she said a final goodbye to all that had been before, and opened herself to drinking deep of what was to come: a new day, a new adventurous life.

At her shoulders stood Yan and Shema, the two young women who had been conscripted into being on this journey with her. They now wore the loose, flowing tunics in bright sapphire and saffron that were worn by the priestesses in Sumeria. If they had their wish they would stay in Babylon, having found friendship and warm welcome in the Temple of Inanna. They had spent hours learning the sacred temple dances, giggling with their new friends as they fumbled with the steps, emulating the flowing graceful arm movements of the women of Inanna. In turn, they taught them the Moon Dance that the women of Lhamo did at each full moon, and looked on gleefully as the elegant Sumerians tried to follow them and stomp the moon down into the Earth. The elaborate baths and lovely time spent brushing and braiding each others' hair had also been a revelation. At the Top of the World, hot baths were a rare luxury. Here, every woman felt it her daily right. Home felt so very distant to them, and yet, with the courage of youth, they had settled into enjoying this adventure, even with the frequent explosions of need and grumpiness from Tiamet.

Maia, formerly the Divine One, the Incarnation of Kali Ma, stood with feet planted wide, hands on hips and a wide, bright smile illuminating her face. She too now wore the blue and yellow of Inanna, but she had taken a knife to the lower half of the tunic, so it hung at midthigh, leaving her brown, sculpted legs free to jump on Savi's back and sit astride that beloved neck. She had taken the same knife to her hair, which for her role as Kali Ma had never been cut and had fallen to her ankles. Now, freed of the burdens of weight and responsibility, it made a cap of glossy obsidian curls all around her head.

Maia felt itchy at the need to be on their way, while feeling regret at leaving the beauty and comfort of the Inanna Temple. This place was so very different from her home. Here, there was cool, cultured dialogue and hours spent on prayer and meditation. Here, she sat for hours in shaded chambers watching the fine and intricate rituals to honor Inanna. Here, she had moved in and out of a subtle doze as the priestesses sang the stories of their Goddess. At home she had either been up to her elbows in the everyday needs of her people or lost for hours in ecstatic trance. This Goddess was as demanding as Kali Ma of Her dedicants, but it all involved much less sweat and human mess. It had been revelatory for Maia: dedication to the Goddess without getting dirty.

In the crush of people in the Grand Plaza two figures stood alone and as motionless as statues, oblivious to all around them. Erhenduanna clasped the tightly held body of her sister, Parasfahe in her arms. Parasfahe had not spoken to or looked her sister in the eye since Erhenduanna had, as High Priestess, ordered her to make the journey to Egypt to fulfill the vision she had received. Under duress Parasfahe had been carried down to the Great Hall to receive the visiting priestesses from the mountains and the jungle. She stayed mute through the many days of consultation and preparation for their now conjoined mission. It had been Maia's idea to design a floating platform that would reduce the rigors of travel. It had been Tiamet who commiserated on the ordure of leaving home for the aged or infirm. And even Savi had helped by kneeling down and making her sweet presence available for connection and communication. Parasfahe endured all of this with a modicum of grace. But to her sister, her constant companion from the womb, she gave not a glance or a whisper of tenderness.

Now, at the very minute of their parting, she refused to yield, standing frozen with her arms down at her sides.

"Sweetness!" Erhenduanna begged. "Forgive me! Look at me one last time!"

But Parasfahe, rigid with rage and fear, would give her nothing. Abruptly she turned out of her sister's arms and moved to join Maia and Tiamet at the head of the procession of animals.

Maia looked at Erhenduanna with oceans of compassion in her eyes. Tiamet brusquely shoved Parasfahe in the small of her back, "Say goodbye to her, you idiot."

But Parasfahe was unbending. As all the Priestesses of Inanna began to sing the song of grace and blessing, Savi gently swooped Parasfahe and Maia up with her trunk, and Maia helped settle Parasfahe onto the floating bed, gently patting and shushing her moans of pain. Tiamet and her young servants swung onto the yak saddles, and the caravan began its slow procession out of the Temple grounds, down the sloping hillsides of Babylon and west, west to Egypt.

The wrenching wail that tore from Erhenduanna ripped at the ears, like flesh separated from skin. "Parasfahe! Parasfahe! Parasfahe!"

It continued long past time, when the sound should not have been able to reach the caravan. It haunted them long past time, when the caravan had moved beyond the edges of the city and sauntered past fields and farms. It lingered like the cobwebs of dreams, long past time.

"Parasfahe!"

High atop Savi's back, gently cradled in her floating bed, Parasfahe reclined, stony faced, pulling tears inward to tamp down the inferno of rage that threatened to devour her.

And long past time she still could hear the ghost of sound.

"Parasfahe!"

THE NEVER-ENDING SEA

As we travel over a vast ocean the air grows colder. We push against the prevailing winds that try to steer us east, and we struggle to stay on course going north by northwest. Directly below we begin to see ice floes and white-peaked waves. The full moonlight makes gray shadows in a mirror image of the ice. We swoop lower as we approach the meeting of land and sea. This is a rocky shore with dangerous waves and currents creating a funnel into a smooth silver bay with a sandy beach. Along the beach are tossed a handful of stone huts with roofs of woven reeds. Dark figures move across the beach and the water. One sleek shape moves urgently through the shallows and up onto the sand. Attempting to stand, she takes one step forward, and collapses to her knees as the water laps her feet.

Autakla, a thin maiden with a heart-shaped face and eyes swiftly changing from brown to hazel, grabbed for her chest as the breaths that felt like jagged shells tore her open. *Too fast! Too fast, this transformation! Skin emerging and cold, sharp air!* All around her she felt the eyes of her people, the Seal Woman People, watching from land and water. Behind her the seal women who had heard her cries of distress and followed her landward, their brown pelts streaming with steam as water met air. Before her, the worried faces of those in land-form hurrying toward her. Her father called for help and people rushed from their huts to help move her toward the fire. In the bay dozens of round heads watched with concern. Her own pelt was draped around her slight shoulders, and her baby sister brought a gourd cup of seaweed broth to warm her. Her skin was gray and chalky from fear and cold.

"Drink, daughter. Slowly now. Slowly." The gentle, patient voice of her father warmed her the most. Autakla looked into his eyes, surrounded by a fine network of lines from laughter and weather. Her father, and all the men descended from the Goddess Seal Woman, were landbound and their skin and bodies aged quickly. They hunted, fished, and tended children and the fires.

The women, the daughters of Seal Woman, began their lives as shapeshifters when they reached menarche. Time worked very differently for them. A woman might spend one moon cycle or thirteen in the sea at a stretch. She might live through the lives of two or ten mates. She returned to the land to mate, give birth, tell her stories and to teach her children how to swim. When, after many decades of sun cycles, she became a crone, she had the choice to return to the land or remain in the sea. These women, these shapeshifters, these selkies, particularly loved the moonlight when they raced the wind and played with the shadows. It was their gathering time in the deep, black water and on tiny outcrops of slashing granite rocks. None of them ever willingly came ashore when the moon was full. But tonight they had sped in to follow Autakla, pulled by the tide of her pain.

The consternation was great as the land folk huddled around Autakla. Speech was difficult for the selkies as they transitioned between their worlds. Moving from one state of mind to another, the gathering of human language around them again, the attention needed to use fingers and arms. It all took time. So no one hurried her to say what was the matter. Her mouth moved as if to speak. Nothing. They all rested on haunches on the cold sand and waited.

There was sound like whales breaching from the bay. The people turned as one and saw all of the selkies in the shallows rolling their bodies landward, transforming as a tribe. In the history of the Seal Woman People this had only happened once before, when the selkies arrived all together to tell of a giant wave approaching and to help the people move inland to safety. That tale was told around fires to weave the children into their history, and to reinforce the sense of the community as one being, one destiny, no matter what shape.

The Mother of the tribe was woman of middle years named Feyl.

She moved like water with strong thighs and a decisive air of authority. Like all the selkies her hair was short and tended to look like fur rubbed backways when on land. She stood at the front of the formation of shapeshifters like the point of a wave breaking on the shore. The women following behind her ranged in age from young maidens to elders with white streaks amongst the deep brown. They found their feet, felt gravity pull them heavy, and walked slowly toward the fire.

With one voice, the land folk began the welcome song, the song of gratitude for the sisters and mothers who have returned from the sea. The song built and swelled like the waves behind them, telling the Seal Woman that her daughters were safe. The verses of the song overlapped like the tide as it rushed in. The voices, female and male, melded together to make the container of sound that held the People. As their voices returned, the newly shifted women joined in until all the people sang together, sang their history, sang their wisdom. Space was made close to the fire for all the returning women, and men went off to gather more wood, for it looked that the People, all as one for only the second time in their history, were uniting to learn what was to happen.

This longest night was thick with wood smoke and brine, covered by a sky like beadwork studded with stars. Autakla's mother, with a baby at her breast, knelt down on her daughter's right and leaned in gently to share her warmth. Baby Sister sat on Autakla's toes to bring the feeling back into the newly emerged digits. Her father wrapped his arms around her from the back and gently swayed in time to the singing. This was his girl, his sweet Autakla, of the freckled cheeks and mischief dimple, now fifteen sun cycles, but still the baby of his heart.

With fear rising like the tide in each heart, the fire stoked high and the returning women warm and fed, the People readied themselves for the story to come. Was it another giant wave? Minds were already sorting which supplies could be bundled quickly if they were moving inland soon. It was winter and the hunting would be sparse. Dried fish and berries would travel well, hides for sleeping and for shelter. Caribou could pull sleds fast over the frozen rivers to the high ground. Babies fussed and were quieted; children fell asleep in parents' laps.

Finally, Autakla lifted her eyes from the fire which danced in them as she spoke, "I had a vision."

The People drew a breath inward. These were the words at the beginning of the sacred stories, the tales of the Goddess Seal Woman and first People, the stories of how the world was made.

"Is it the wave, daughter?" her father spoke soft in her ear.

She shook her head, "No. Not the wave. Fire. I had a vision. Of rage and hatred and fire… So much fire."

Glances passed back and forth across the fire. Seal Woman had made the world in fire. Was this a new beginning? A new world?

"I saw land-folk hunting seals," her voice strangled, "for food."

These last words were said in an ashy whisper that held no breath, too awful for breath. This was incomprehensible to the People. Not the beginning of a new world, rather, the death of the old world. But Autakla's voice swelled with strength and hope.

"I saw women, land-folk, rushing to come to a place of heat and little water. Rushing to bring the cords of their wisdoms together, and weave a net to catch the world as it falls into a place of darkness. Weaving a net, weaving a net…" her sweet high voice trailed off. With a tearful look over her shoulder at her beloved father she said, "I need to try to save us all from that darkness. I need to bring our wisdom to that place of heat and dryness. It is very far. I don't know if I will ever make it back."

Around the circle of the People the faces were wet with the salt water of tears. The light from the east above the ocean went from deep mauve to pearl, and the shadows became magenta in the little light that would be on this shortest day of the sun cycle. There was too little sun to warm the sand that day, and the air had a heavy, almost oily quality. Throughout that time of shimmer and half-light the People, led by the Mother of the tribe, talked softly and deliberately of what was to come and what was needed. As always with the People, thoughts were weighed, measured, spoken slowly. And every thought was given time and space. A thought. A pause. A question. A pause. Words were precious to a people for whom language was only sometimes possible. It was decided that a deep, dream journey to the

Seal Woman was needed, that the People, all together, required Her wisdom and strength.

As the dimming happened and the long night approached, there were bowls of stew and then cups of mugwort tea to help the Dreaming. As one, the People entered into a deep trance led by the drumming of the shaman, a very old woman who had chosen land-form in her crone time. She held the frame drum in her left hand and beat gently, insistently, with the gnarled fingers of her right. Deep into their collective knowing, the children of Seal Woman dove and dove to meet Her, the Maker of the World. They dove deep between the worlds. They found their Goddess in their Dreamtime journey.

She, Seal Woman was seated on a mound of shells, basking in the light of the moon. Half human, half seal, She turned her liquid eyes upon them, her children. The People poured out their fears to Her; they showed their trembling inner selves. And Seal Woman bathed them in Her love.

When the drumming became louder and more demanding, the People slowly returned to the fire, to their earthly bodies, to their tribe. The shaman tilted her head back and sang the song of making, the oldest sounds known to the People. The tribe was wrapped in crystal, frozen in time, held between the worlds. And again, the moon rose in the east.

Autakla stood and the women all stood with her. Feyl, the Mother of the tribe, led them as they walked toward the water, and as one turned to look at the men and children and grandmothers on the beach. With hearts aching they slipped into the water and shifted shape. Arms and legs melded into powerful, pelt-covered bodies. Within just a few moments, the shallow water was roiling with the intensity of their feelings. As one they lifted their heads toward the shore to see the fire and the human forms still encircling it. As one they turned to dive out into the sea. They would travel with Autakla as far as they could and still be able to come back home. And then, they would leave her to make her way onwards through the distant and immeasurable waves.

CALANAIS

We move east, pulled by the magnetic lines of the earth. Land, then sea, then land again. And still north and west. Finally, we see an outline shaped like a jawbone, jutting with impudence into the western sea. As we move closer, we see many giant circles and shapes formed on the earth by human will. Forming a half moon shape to the east sits a vast complex of buildings nestling close to the giant patterns, like pups nudging in close to the mother's teats. Closer still, we are directly above a double circle of giant stones with four projections, one in each direction, like massive columns laid upon the ground. We see nineteen cloaked women facing the east, still as statues. Suddenly, one of them, a young woman tall and slender as a rowan sapling, crumples to the ground with an ice shard shriek like a lost fox cub.

*T*he remaining eighteen Priestesses of Brig heard the shriek, and the dull thud of a body bonelessly hitting the ground. No one moved. They had all been trained in the absolute priority of the astral observation. And so, when, from time to time, one of their number fainted from cold or heat or hunger they stayed on task. Watching ever minute as the full moon traveled the sky on this longest night of the year. Locating its exact position against the horizon, waiting without thought of time for the rising sun to precisely note its location and relationship to the setting moon.

It was only later, after sunrise and the silent recalling and absorption of all the information into memory, that they noticed that Silbara was still lying, long body twisted like a braid on the cold ground. The women hurried to her, rolled her over and saw her eyes wide open, gray and opaque, not blinking.

They frantically called for help. The sounds of feet rushing in response, cracking the blades of frozen grass, were like the splintering of shards of glass.

Silbara, at twenty-three cycles of the sun one of the junior priestesses, was gently placed on a blanket and a group of men picked her up and carried her away from the Stones toward the living area of the Mystery School. They walked swiftly past the cluster of buildings housing the students, teachers and visiting scholars. The architecture of the quarters reflected the terrain here at the edge of the world, with blue-gray granite slashed with quartz for walls and twilight black slate roofs. The men rushed up to the main building in the women's quarters. They exchanged worried glances. Silbara was still motionless, wide-eyed and as pale as new milk. As they approached the wide double door they were granted permission to enter by the senior priestess and moved together into the large common room.

"Lay her here, close to the fire."

This direction came from the highest-ranking priestess, the one given the honorary title of the Brighid. No one else spoke. It was as if all knew that this was a portent, a sacred action, and not an everyday fainting spell. With a sideways thrust of the head by the priestess closest to the door, the men silently left the Women's House, but stood close by outside, waiting.

Inside, the nineteen Priestesses of Brig formed a constellation with Silbara, in the center, and the others, ranging in age from maiden to crone with their foreheads marked by the crescent moon, encircling her as if to protect and warm her by their closeness. She was covered in blankets and warm rocks were placed at her feet. And they waited.

They waited through that long day. None had eaten since early the day before and they had stood all night for the observation. So, little by little, the servants brought changes of clothes, and took the damp wraps away. They brought soup and tea and warm tubs of water for feet to painfully thaw out.

Their pallets were brought to ring the still motionless Silbara, her shallow rapid breaths the only sign that she lived. Her eyes had closed and her cheeks had a scattering of freckles that stood like stark bits of ash on the snow white field of her face. The priestesses slept fitfully, then woke and sat and stared mutely once again at the fire and their sister priestess. Silence reigned. And they held vigil through the next even longer seeming night.

At dawn on the second day, Silbara began to mumble and stir. Leaning close in, the High Priestess, the Brighid, could hear words forming but understood none. The same fragment of words kept repeating and repeating. Silbara didn't seem to be conscious of anyone or anything except the frantic need to repeat her message. One of the youngest priestesses, a linguist, leaned forward, "I know that language!" she said. "Get Dalia!"

A rustle, a command, an impatient waiting, and shortly the visiting scholar entered the main hall. She was a tiny woman of middle age, no taller than a child, with sun-bronzed skin and sharp black eyes like slashes of obsidian. She was so profoundly bundled against the cold and damp that the women in the hall couldn't hazard a guess as to her exact shape. But this round tumble of wool and leather crossed the floor with a seamless grace and stood next to the young woman on the pallet before her. She listened for a moment and then sat down effortlessly on the floor, legs crossed as she tilted forward to hear more clearly. She began to translate, brief tangles of words.

"She says," the small woman began translating into the common tongue in an accent of flipped r's and soft vowels, "that the burning of the sacred places… the burning will roll across the world… the sacred women are torn up? … no, torn away… mysteries forgotten… no one will watch the stars!" she continued to bring forth the stuttering story and her eyes began to reflect the light from the fire as they filled with tears. Abruptly she sat back and looked up into the intense focus of the Brighid, "She says she must go to Egypt!"

☽ ○ ☾

Later that day there was a meeting of all the senior scholars and observers. Nothing ever happened here at the Mystery School at Calanais without a meeting, or two, or twenty. This was a culture that praised poetry and oratory; a place where stories could take all night. The oral history of the world lived here, and was always given a good hearing.

The great oval table of burnished oak was positioned in the center of the largest lecture hall with its high, vaulted ceiling, the beams forming the eight-pointed star of the Goddess. Seated at the table, Silbara now looked composed, if wan. Her hair, the color of ripened grain, was thick and expertly restrained into multiple braids and fashioned into a long cable down her back. She had no color in her cheeks, but her lips were the deep raspberry that came from chewing them, as she always did when nervous. It was the only sign that she didn't have the complete composure expected of the Priestesses of Brig. Next to her sat the scholar from Egypt, Dalia, still inordinately bundled against the weather in spite of the braziers blazing in every corner of the hall, spilling the scent of apple branches and balm of Gilead into the air. On Silbara's other side was the Brighid, so still, so focused, that it didn't appear that she even breathed.

Several thousand women and men from every part of the globe lived and studied here at the Mystery School. They came to know the world and all the science of its people. Out of that number about sixty of the highest ranking had gathered in the Great Hall and stood in small groups talking with no evident anxiety or concern, as if this was just another meeting in the Great Hall. When the many were settled, the Brighid stood and began to tell the story of the events of the last two days and the vision as experienced by Silbara and translated by Dalia. Her language was the formal and poetic manner of speech that was esteemed here in these halls of learning. But underneath the flowery descriptions and mythical metaphors her voice held an iron core of intensity and warning.

As she finished the last breath of the tale there was an immediate and raucous outburst of talk and overtalk. Exclamations. Questions. Doubts. Suspicions. And wonder. Now there was anxiety and concern. The noise began to fill the hall, like thunder in a summer storm.

"Enough!"

In a voice trained to carry over wind and rain and mist, Malvu, the elder Observer shouted and brought an immediate silence in the room. He stood and let his dark gray eyes touch each person there: Priestesses, Observers, scholars.

"We will proceed with decorum and the intelligence that is reputed to be present in all of you."

People took their seats again, a few blushed, and the Brighid allowed herself the swiftest flicker of a smile. It warmed her eyes as she looked at Malvu, her oldest friend, and the years they had studied along side each other melted away. She saw the tall, overly confident boy with the untamable thatch of black hair that he had been. And he saw the lithe girl with the blazing mind and translucent green eyes the color of gooseberries. Their partnership had been forged by debate and countless hours of memorization and astral observation. The deepest of friends, they might have been lovers if they weren't dedicated to this scholar's life. They understood each other as well as two people could. She knew he could steer this meeting toward some semblance of calm and consensus, so she exhaled and sat back ever so slightly. Her look, with an almost imperceptible flash of glee, conveyed the unspoken: *Proceed, and good luck, my friend!*

Malvu had opened his mouth to speak again when Silbara stood suddenly, and held herself with the poise expected of the Priestesses of Brig. Tall and lean with the soft edges of a scholar, she spoke quietly with the precise diction required by her position. She was an expert in astral observation and meditation, quiet practices that suited her perfectly. Even so, her voice didn't tremble, though she had never spoken in a Great Hall meeting before.

"I have been given the vision that it is necessary for me to travel to Egypt. I have been given the vision that I need to arrive before the Summer Solstice. And so, with all due deference to the order of all things, I would assume that means I need to leave soon."

With those words her newfound courage in public speaking escaped her and, hidden by the table, she grabbed for the hands of the Brighid and Dalia the Egyptian. Poise be damned.

AT THE MYSTERY SCHOOL

I t had been one complete moon since Silbara had collapsed with
the vision of what would befall her world. The initial meeting
had birthed several generations more meetings, and discussions
and arguments. Those women and men, Priestesses, Observers, visiting scholars, that held composure and sensibility in high esteem
were, to a one, rattled by the portents of how their world would
change. Silbara, the bearer of the terrible tidings, vacillated between
utter panic at what was in store for her, and frantic edginess to be
gone and away from the endless discussions and discord.

On this day, after yet another interminable planning session, she
had escaped from the Mystery School halls and, wrapped in a cloak
and shawl, slipped over frozen ground downhill and the two miles to
the bay. A ship waited there to, eventually, carry her to Egypt.

She stood on the shore, the wind tugging tendrils loose from her
braided hair, and stared hard at the fragile craft that was supposed
to carry her over oceans. About forty feet long, it held two sails and
a small cabin in which to shelter during bad weather. *What was she
thinking? All the weather would be bad! Winter travel on these seas…
it was madness!* The ship looked like a small fishing curragh dressed
up in its mother's clothes. *Madness!*

And yet, the very blood in her veins was pulled as if by the tide
to be gone over the waves and to the Land of Isis. Silbara had spent
much of this last month with Dalia. She had learned of the land of
her birth, the expanse of sand and heat, the temples and pyramids,
the Goddess Isis, the Mother of All Creation, Goddess of Rebirth,
Protector of the Dead. Here at Calanais, all forms of She of a Thou-

sand Names were honored and revered equally, with the Goddess Brig being the patroness of the Mystery School. Silbara was intrigued with this notion of any one divinity being supreme. It seemed silly and reductionist. But the academic in her dutifully gathered and stored the knowledge that would be useful in her murky future. She was terrified to paralysis and antsy to move, back and forth, back and forth, in the space of one breath.

As she stared unfocused at the bay, Silbara noticed a small round wave, then another, then another, till the water looked like a boiling pot with bubbles popping up and disappearing again. Transfixed, she walked closer and closer to the sea foam, until one of the small round waves came into focus with the large deep brown eyes of a seal. And another, and another. Selkies! Silbara opened her arms in greeting, and in the common tongue called out to them, "Welcome travelers!"

A chorus of deep resonant barks came as reply, as one by one the sleek sable bodies crescendoed toward the beach. Pelts slid backward, foreheads emerged. There were now long noses and thinning necks. Flippers elongated to arms and the powerful tails delineated into legs. They began to stand, this tribe of shapeshifter women, stretching upright against the drag of gravity, knee-deep in the pale green water.

Silbara looked with open-faced delight and with an inarticulate cry of pleasure rushed forward, speaking with words tumbling over each other, "Welcome! Oh joy, welcome! We… the Priestesses of Brig… we… Oh joy!" She took a breath to gather her wits, and her training slipped into place. "We, the Priestesses of Brig and the Mystery School of Calanais, welcome you. We extend the hospitality of our hearths and the generosity of our people. Please come to our halls and accept our heartfelt protection."

This formal and ever-so-correct greeting was received with silence. Silbara waited several moments and began again. "May we grant you shelter and sustenance, as we are honored by your presence."

More silence, but the woman standing at the front of the cluster of shapeshifters began to turn up one corner of her mouth in a smile. As if pulling the knowledge of how to speak from a very far distance, she slowly formed words so faint that Silbara had to lean forward to hear her.

"We... are... grateful."

With that, Silbara ushered the selkies to the small driftwood shelter on the beach that was used to store nets, then she hurried up the zigzag of the cliff and raced back toward the Mystery School, to summon help.

Soon wagons arrived and people rushed to wrap the pelt-draped shapeshifters in blankets and assist them in walking up the cliff. A short ride later, the Brighid in her vivid azure cloak stood at the gates of the Mystery School, surrounded by her fellow priestesses and phalanxes of the curious. She strode forward and delivered a long and eloquent paean of welcome and hospitality. Again, this speech was met with silence and a small lop-sided grin by the head selkie.

Finally, in a voice crusty with disuse she began, "I am Feyl, of the Seal Woman People."

As if the floodgates had opened, the Priestesses of Brig flowed forward to help the Seal Women out of the carriages, walking with them to the women's quarters. The selkies gradually found their voices, and in a strongly accented version of the common tongue began to talk and giggle with their hosts with a ratio of about two words to every twenty spoken by the priestesses. Tea and broth were passed around and the selkies' pelts were stretched over beams to dry.

There was a startling visual difference between the two groups. The Priestesses of Brig had long hair ranging in hue from corn silk yellow to deepest auburn all woven into elaborate multiple braids and cascading like ropes down their backs. They wore layers of flowing tunics and overdresses, and all had the upturned crescent moon sigil in the center of their foreheads. The selkies had thrown on the borrowed tunics provided by the priestesses, but eschewed any leggings or shoes. Their hair from shiny black to ash white was all shorn short and stood up in irregular swirls on their heads. They had three vertical lines tattooed from lower lip to chin with patterns of blue dots between the lines that seemed to dance when they spoke. But in spite of the differences, comfort was found and friendships were formed.

The day was half gone when the selkies came ashore, and a few hours later as the daylight faded, lanterns and candles were lit. As if a signal had been given, Feyl the leader of the selkies, and another woman, a girl really, stood. The older woman spoke in a deep voice that held seawater and deep mysteries, "One of our sisters, this girl here, Autakla, has had a vision."

No one blinked, no one even breathed as a long pause held. Silbara began to tremble with a fine tremor that lifted the wisps of hair the color of sand curling around her face.

The Brighid stood and motioned to Silbara to come to her feet as well. In a voice that had been trained for decades to speak the most ancient stories and poems of her people the Brighid said, "Our daughter too, this young woman of our lineage, Silbara, Priestess of Brig and watcher of the stars, she too has had a vision. I am given to know that these visions are conjoined and that our futures are woven together."

The two young women, the receivers of the dubious distinction of a gift of a vision, stared at each other. Hazel eyes met dove gray, and the rest of the world fell away. They spoke directly to each other's minds, the women surrounding them in the hall oblivious. Quick, back and forth, the horrors they had seen were passed back and forth.

"I still hear the screaming."

"I can't sleep. When I do, I hear it all again."

"I am frightened."

"As am I."

"It only helps when I can see the stars."

"Let's go!"

And as all the others poured words out like water falling over high rocks, the two young women slipped outside. Silbara took Autakla's hand and they skimmed over the frozen ground till they reached the center of the Center in the great stone circle. Surrounded by thirty-foot stones and held in the vibrating web of the Earth's lines of force, they looked skyward. In the biting night air, they breathed in the starlight, and drank in the starlight, and pulled power from the starlight. Spread across the midnight black silk sky they saw the millions of diamond sparks illuminating the dark. And for now, it was enough.

$$) \bigcirc ($$

The arrival of the selkies seemed to have broken the logjam that had held the community of Calanais in indecision. It felt as if, suddenly, forward movement was imperative, so the quibbling about who and when and how evaporated, and the day was set. In three days' time, the boat would sail southeast, carrying in it Silbara, Dalia the Egyptian scholar, and Autakla. Both young girls had begged their elders to come on the journey with them. But the Brighid, the High Priestess of Brig and the head of all the Mystery School in Calanais, as well as Feyl, the Mother of the tribe of the selkies had been adamant. If violent change was coming in the world, and it seemed clear from the girls' vision that it was, then they needed to be with their people, to try to hold the center in each of their communities, as the rest of the world spun into pieces.

The Brighid was seen in impassioned conversation with Malvu, the Chief Observer and her friend since childhood. She had always been able to turn to him as a sounding board, but now she seemed to be arguing with herself, and he looked more and more worried with a deep bruise of the heart that was visible in his eyes. The two were walking up to the Great Stones, far enough away that no one could hear their conversation, but Dalia the Egyptian, who had come to love them both, watched their progress with focused interest, as the Brighid shook her head violently and raced away, leaving Malvu directly beneath the north portico. Dalia, massively bundled against the light sleeting rain, hurried up to stand beside him.

"Have you told her that you love her yet?" she asked.

"She is not mine to have, you know that. She has always been dedicated to the Goddess," Malvu muttered in reply.

"I know that if you had ever asked, she might have been yours. I do know that," came the response. "And I know that we can all be dedicated to more than one thing at a time, you proud fool. Did you fear that she would reject you? Is that what has held your tongue for these long years?"

"It's too late for that now. We are not people ruled by our passions, but rather we are ordered by our duty."

Dalia snorted and trundled away. "Fool!" she threw back over her shoulder.

$$☽ ◯ ☾$$

The morning of their departure broke with rare blue skies and a soft wind that held a tease of spring. The departure was set for one hand past sunrise to catch the morning tide. The two young travelers and their mentors held deep and wrenching conversations of guidance, advice and farewell.

Feyl sat squatting on her heels on the beach staring with mingled suspicion and longing at the ship that would carry Autakla away to her destiny. The older woman had her sealskin draped over her shoulders and shivered slightly in the early chill. She still wore the sleeveless mist-colored tunic gifted to her on the day of their arrival, but her powerful thighs were bare and her toes, rimmed in silver, dug into the cold wet sand. The sea birds were vocal this morning, swooping and making sigils in the clear and capricious blue sky, signaling each other about the shoals of small fish in the shallows. This was Feyl's element, the smell of the sea and the call of the waves. And she had lived her life floating back and forth across this liminal space between the ocean and the land. But this morning, it all felt very, very wrong. *Madness, absolute madness! How can I send this child off to who knows what, for what possible purpose? I should stop this.*

And yet, even as she formed these thoughts she knew them to be sheer vapor woven of fear and guilt. The fear was massive. If this vision that Autakla and the wispy girl, Silbara, had was true, then more destruction than was fathomable was on its way. The guilt was crushing. She, Feyl, should be the one to take the risks, not the sweet dreamy Autakla. What chance did the young one have of steering the currents of humankind? *I am all that stands for this child,* she thought, *in the place of her mother and her father, as the Mother of the Seal People, I am all that stands between her and the immensity of the chaos to come.* Trapped in the tangle of her own thoughts, Feyl was slow to realize that this very Autakla, the dreamy and immeasurable sweet Autakla had come to crouch down beside her.

In the way of the Seal People, words were rare and treasured, but touch was free and abundant. Autakla leaned in to Feyl's left side and wrapped her arms around the older woman's waist. She nuzzled her head into Feyl's neck and made low soft whimpering sounds, giving and asking for comfort. Feyl rubbed her cheek against the soft bristle of Autakla's dark brown hair, and turning slightly she clasped the girl in her arms and held on as if in a storm.

"The tide calls," said Feyl, her voice barely audible and strangled in her throat.

"She is turning," whispered Autakla in reply.

"Remember..." Feyl trailed off.

"Everything you have taught me," Autakla finished.

They stood wordlessly together, and Feyl took one last look at the girl. She was dressed in the long silver tunic of their hostesses, with ropes of amber and pearls strung around her neck. Her thick wool cloak dyed a shimmering sea moss green, was held together with an elaborate copper clasp of three spirals, more gifts from the Brighid and the community at Calanais. Her face was pale and the three vertical lines and dots that ran from bottom lip to chin stood out stark and vivid deep blue. Their eyes held and Feyl's spoke all the volumes that her words could not. *Be wise. Don't lose yourself. Don't be too brave. Trust no one. Come home.*

And Autakla's eyes responded: *"Don't forget me."*

With that the girl spun away and walked down the beach to the curragh, reaching for the hands and folks waiting to take her out into the bay to the ship. She faced backward so she could see Feyl as they rowed her out deeper. And once aboard the ship, she came to stand in the stern, staring as Feyl and the other selkies began to shift shape, wrapping their pelts around themselves, rolling into shallow water, leaving the beach strewn with discarded tunics like the empty shells of cicadas. The waters churned, and the selkies swam up next to the ship. Autakla knew they would follow her as long as they could before they turned to go back to their village. Those eyes, so beloved, watched her as the selkies lifted and dropped with the soft waves in the harbor.

While the selkies had their parting, the entire community of Calanais, all of the Priestesses, all of the Observers, all of the visiting scholars, and the local fishing and farming folk, gathered on the cliff overlooking the beach to say farewell to Silbara, one of their own, and Dalia, the daughter of Egypt.

Silbara stood tall and thin with her wheat colored hair elaborately braided lifting back in rows and patterns from her hairline to fall in shapes like ogham down her back, her crescent moon sigil on her forehead shone with otherworld intensity. Those soft eyes swept back and forth over all the assembled as if to drink in the sight in anticipation of a long drought. She wore layers and layers of silver fabric from palest moonlight to deepest dusk, swathed in tunics and overtunics and shifts and a thick cloak lined with rabbit fur held closed with the triple spiral symbol of her community. She held herself together with all the discipline gathered by her years of study, while her heart raced in her chest.

Dalia knew that she would miss these people and this community at the Mystery School with a great ache, but she felt a deep longing for the heat of the sun bouncing off desert sand. On the night after the selkies had arrived she had received a vision dream of her own. The voices of the Goddesses of her homeland, speaking in unison, had said, in no uncertain terms, *"Daughter, it is time to come home."*

Facing them was the Brighid, the High Priestess of Calanais, and the remainder of the Priestesses of Brig standing in a formation like a flock of geese in flight. The Brighid felt numb, as if there was an echo inside her mind, and her shell of a body just kept moving her to the correct places and saying the correct things. To Silbara she said, "You travel on a great and mystical journey with our blessing and our prayers. You carry the wisdom of our ancestors. Make them, and us, proud." Then she turned to Dalia, "We entrust our Sister into your care. May the Goddesses of Egypt hold you both safe."

And all the while, in her soul she was screaming. Every single bit of her was fighting like a wounded and trapped animal to break free from who and what she was. She was the Brighid, and her place was here. All of these people and the heritage of study and knowledge depended on her and the maintaining of order. She was in her place; this life was the one she was destined for. And yet, a great force within her was pulling and demanding and ripping her from that certainty. She, the Brighid, the pinnacle of power and control, was flying apart.

The company processed down the cliff, onto the beach, and to another waiting curragh. As Silbara turned to look at her Sisters, a single tear traced down her face. Dalia flung arms out of all her coverings and embraced the Priestesses of Brig, and several of the Observers, waiting till the last to draw Malvu, the Chief Observer and her special friend, down for a long hug and a not-so-gentle kiss on his cheek. His eyes filled, and he took the edge of his cloak to wipe the tip of Dalia's nose.

"Save her, you proud fool," she said into his ear. Startled, he looked into those intelligent brown eyes and blushed.

"She is not mine to save."

"She has always been yours, and you have always been hers." Dalia cupped his cheek with her hand and whispered, "Fool."

As Dalia and Silbara stepped into the curragh and the rowers pulled it out into the harbor, the internal scream broke out of the Brighid. She wailed and plunged into the water, struggling with skirts and cloak and shifting pebbles under foot. Her face was frozen in total panic. Somehow she had to get herself onto that ship! She flailed and stumbled and struggled again and again. Malvu ran into the water after her, catching her as she slumped down, and he held her tightly.

"Hush, my beloved, hush. I am here, and I am with you. Hush."

The Brighid sobbed and turned into him. Her eyes, soft green like spring apples, acknowledged what he was giving her, and what she was giving away.

"I love you beyond measure, and I have to go."

She pulled away and dragged her body out past the breakers as the curragh turned, held, and arms reached over to drag her in. Malvu stood in the shallows, buffeted by waves, his eyes never leaving the sight of the Brighid as she became smaller and smaller. As she and

Silbara and Dalia climbed onto the awaiting ship, all the remaining Priestesses of Brig began to sing the high multi-part harmonies of the stars and the moon. The music soared and reached the heavens, and the stars sang back the descant. The women sang with every fiber of their beings, long after the ship was gone from sight, singing their Sisters to Egypt.

And still in the sky hung the Goddess Star.

THE TIN TRAIL

*T*hey had traveled for a full moon cycle and more, and the lengthening days leaned in closer and closer to the Spring Equinox. The first days out from Calanais had been cold and wet, moving along the western shore of Albion, the homeland of the Moon Watchers. For Autakla, the world of the selkies had always been short on words and long on feelings. As shapeshifters, the women of her people had always split their time, and split their experience of life between land and water. At the beginning of this journey down the coast, she found that every few days, the compulsion, the itch, to be of the water was overwhelming. She could share this with Silbara, who would go with her to the aft deck and hold her clothes as she transformed, then wait and watch as Autakla joyously swam along with the ship. Sometimes others would come from the deeper sea and join Autakla. Families of dolphins would dance alongside her for hours. Another time a small pod of whales appeared and made water rainbows for her to jump through. And as the daylight diminished, she would come right alongside the ship and Silbara would have the small curragh lowered to allow the selkie to be pulled back up on deck and complete her shifting back to human form. As the days progressed the words came back to her faster and more easily, and the need for the sea lessened its grip. Now she would share her joy in new discoveries not only by grabbing Silbara's hand and stroking her face, but with words. She and Silbara deepened the bond formed by their shared vision, and never ran out of things to share and discuss, stories to tell, dreams to reveal.

Silbara found that, free of the formality of Calanais, she devoured the new horizons and sites. Through all her years of training she had learned how to sharply observe and then describe the natural world and the dance of the celestial bodies. Now she found herself verbalizing her experiences less and enjoying them more. To simply *be* in the moment of sunrise catching hoarfrost on blades of sheep nibbled grass was a delight. Neither she, nor her teachers, had ever felt her to be especially gifted, but she was diligent. She worked longer and harder than her more talented classmates, and had only ever aspired to be competent. Now, by nature of her unsolicited vision, she was extraordinary, and that set her free from her perceived mediocrity in some unexpected ways. She spent most of her hours on deck unbound by duty, and the winter sun brought peach to her cheeks, scatterings of freckles across her nose, and white blond streaks of color through the wheaten hue of her hair.

Every few days they would come to another Stone Circle, another community of Priestesses of Brig and Observers, all laid out carefully in eons past to best monitor the celestial bodies and keep the people balanced with the powers above and below. They always received a fulsome welcome and warm food and dry beds. At each stop the people were amazed that the Brighid, the first amongst all of them, was embarking on a journey away from Calanais, away from her Mystery School, away from the pinnacle position that she held. These communities knew of her august scholarship, and though they were gracious and giving, they held her in awe. The two young women with her, Silbara, also of Calanais, and Autakla of the Seal People, were more easily embraced into the laughter and conversations around meals and late-night fires.

For Dalia, this journey was a reverse of the one she had made four years earlier when she had traveled to deepen her studies at Calanais. Her time abroad had been simple for her: study, sleep, study, eat, study and enjoy the simplicity of being an outsider with few obligations and no deep emotional ties. But she knew that to return to Egypt was to be plunged into the complexities of her family and the Temples. When she returned, her heritage would be inescapable, and as always, messy. Now she frequently stood in the prow of the ship, a small bundle of furs and hides, nose lifted, as if she could already smell the juniper and tamarisk of the desert. The Brighid would join her and let the salt spray douse her face and hair, as if making this all more real.

"In all the years you lived among us, I never asked about your homeland, did I?"

"Well, you were usually very busy," Dalia responded with a slight tinge of sarcasm.

And with nod of acknowledgment and straightening of spine to remind them both of her former status, the Brighid replied, "I don't appear to be very busy now."

So, day after day, hour after hour, the two women stood looking ahead and discussed what might be in store.

Once they had left the land of Albion, and braved the channel of open sea to the Tin Trail, the woman known as the Brighid lost some of the aura of command and status, and started joining the others in jokes and tales. Mile by mile, day by day, the Brighid seemed younger and younger, more and more accessible, until finally she insisted that the other women call her by her given name, Celebi. Autakla gave over easily to this new nomenclature, but Silbara stumbled over it every time. She rode and slept next to her mentor and teacher, but to call her casually, and not by her title, still felt brash and rude.

☽ ○ ☾

In time they landed on the coast of Hispa, and began to ride their newly acquired mules up into the mountains along the tin trade route. Their plan was to follow it overland to the Middle Sea and then, by boat cross to Egypt avoiding the dangers of the Straits of Gaia at this time of year. The peoples of Albion had traveled and traded with the Middle Sea folk for many generations, so the way and the contacts were quickly found.

The girls rode side by side when the trail obliged, and to Celebi's eye they looked like two young fledglings, chattering and chirping in their nest, awash with the newness of life. In her deepest heart, she knew that the impulsive move to join these two in their quest for Egypt had been the right thing for her to do. But she missed her friend Malvu like a limb and there was still a filmy disguise around what her purpose was in this mission. Was she chaperone, teacher, student…?

They had been welcomed to a small village, high in a mountain pass and met the Basquela, a people who revered the Dark Mother, the Goddess of the Cave and the Night, whose faces carried the stories of their ancestors with scarring and tattoos. The people of the tribe lived in caves that dotted the sides of the steep ravine, and they guarded the pass against thieves and the massive animals that lived in these mountains. Gigantic cave bears and powerful mountain lions roamed in the high altitudes, and the Basquela women and men were fierce defenders of their home and the Tin Trail. With generosity of hearth they had welcomed the travelers, marveling over the crescent moon sigils on the foreheads of Celebi and Silbara, shyly touching the vertical lines and blue dots on Autakla's chin, proudly displaying and explaining their own facial art.

Silbara and Autakla, arms around each other's waists, sat on a log around the central fire learning the songs of these mountain people. Frame drums and pipes played along as the girls laughingly stumbled over the sounds of this mountain dialect, enough like the common tongue to be understandable but with strange throat-clearing consonants that both found challenging and humorous. *Stream* sounded like *schreeem*; *river* came out *hrrrreeever*.

It was a glorious night. The lapis lazuli sky was filled with millions of stars, and the pattern was reflected by the small fires at the front of the myriad caves that wound up the steep sides of the ravine. It was dry and the late winter chill was not bitter. On this night, Celebi sat across the fire from her two young companions and envied their ease. A grandmother of the tribe sat next to her and handed Celebi a horn of mead, "Drink, daughter, and let yourself love this life."

With a start, Celebi felt a lightning bolt of revelation. Was this true? Had she held herself off from loving her life? Or mayhaps, this was just a figure of speech here, like a greeting or blessing?

In short order, the Grandmother's meaning was made clear as Dalia came up and sat on her other side, "You found your purpose in your purpose. You knew what you did well, and you found contentment in doing those tasks really well. There is no harm in that, Celibi, but perhaps no great joy either."

"I have always done all that was asked of me," Celebi said, a note of wounded honor in her voice.

"Yes, as the Brighid you have. But as Celebi, have you always done all that you might ask of yourself?"

In a moment of pique, Celebi stood abruptly, wrapped her traveling cloak tight around herself, and walked into the darkness, away from the fire and the people and the niggling thoughts Dalia had put in her head.

She had only been gone a few minutes when the people heard a high pitched shriek and a deep grunt. All the dogs of the Basquela began to bark and howl at once. Looking around themselves for the source of the commotion, the travelers around the fire noticed that Celebi was missing. Was that her in distress? With a practiced order, women and men picked up knives and short spears that lay close to hand and the elders gathered children in close together near the central fire.

Another scream from the inky black.

"Bear!"

Several of the larger hounds ran out past the light and started braying. The smaller herding dogs formed a pack of noise and tumult, snapping into the blackness. Blinded by the abrupt shift from light to dark, Celebi had walked full tilt into a large creature of musty fur. Now panicked, she stumbled backwards into the firelight and pointed into the night.

"I ran into a bear! It's just there in the dark!"

A man's voice emerged from within the cacophony of barking and snarling. "Get back! Get back, I say!" Then an almighty yelp as teeth met flesh, "Help! Help me! In the name of Brig, have someone call off these hounds!"

Celebi's face turned from fear to surprise, "Malvu?... Malvu, is that you?"

The warrior chief of the Basquela, a solid woman of some forty sun cycles with ritual and battle scars across her face and chest, looked to Celebi for confirmation.

"You know this man? He is to be trusted?"

"Yes!" Celebi replied, her voice a tangle of laughter and tears. "I know him, and I trust him with my life."

And with that, she ran out into complete darkness again, as voices called dogs back to heel, and the women travelers from Calanais looked to each other in mingled confusion, befuddlement, and dawning delight. They looked and saw Celebi, with tears streaming down her face, glowing as if lit from within walking beside a shaken and weary Malvu who was draped in a long fur cloak of questionable heritage. He had two sleek lurchers still snapping at his heels.

"What on earth? Are you hurt?" exclaimed Celebi as Malvu staggered into the firelight, blood dripping from him. There were two long gashes on his forearm and he limped rather badly on his right foot.

"Beside the fact that my ear is shattered by your screams and the hounds are a most efficient band of protectors, I am better than I have been in a very long time."

He looked at her with the blooming realization that what he had thought impossible had now materialized. He had found her! And everything else would be sufficient unto the day.

Food, safety, salve, bandages and the warmth of the fire did their healing work. Soon it was only Malvu and Celebi left by the central fire.

"You have done the craziest thing I have ever seen you do by following me alone and unarmed," Celebi said quietly with a trip of a sob in her voice.

"Followed as a close second by your plunge into the ocean and running off to Egypt," he replied with a wry twist to his lips and the understanding of thirty years of friendship between them.

"We are a confusing pair, indeed. Who are these impetuous and unreliable people we have become?" she queried.

"Well, I am hoping we are the ones who have realized their souls are mated before it was too late."

And their lips met as slowly and as inexorably as the tide pulls the waves on shore. They stayed by the fire for much of the night touching, kissing, talking of deep thoughts and tender endearments, until shortly before dawn Celebi led him back to her cave. As they fell into cloudless slumber in each other's arms she thought she heard him mutter, "I *am* the luckiest fool."

$$\text{)} \bigcirc \text{(}$$

When Celebi and Malvu woke, several hand widths after sunrise, shyness floated like a leaf on a stream across their faces, and then broad smiles spread like that sunshine reaching into all the shaded spots of the ravine. They gathered themselves and walked down the switchback ramp to the canyon floor and the central fire. There they were met by a cluster of curiously embarrassed and yet stalwart individuals comprised of Silbara and Autakla, arm in arm, and Dalia almost hidden behind the broad shoulders of the Warrior Chief. The Grandmother who had jolted Celebi with introspection the night of Malvu's arrival stepped forward as spokeswoman for the group.

"I have been given permission by the Grandmothers Council to offer you our deepest Mystery. It was given to us by the Goddess to aid those who require the presence of the Black Mother. You," she said, gesturing to Celebi, "as the High Priestess of your people, and you," shooting a sharp glance at Malvu "as her consort may perform the Sacred Marriage in the Womb Cave of our people."

She stopped speaking and had a look of completion, as if all she had said was all that needed to be said. The deep crevasses on her face blended with the patterns of the ritual scarification so that her face was a map of ley lines and animal tracks and star patterns. And she waited.

Celebi felt as if her mind was wrapped in wet wool. She assumed she should know what the Grandmother was talking about, but instead she sought out Dalia and Silbara's eyes for support and illumination. Dalia's gaze of impish good humor flowed on an ancient knowledge of fate and destiny. *Yes? No? Decide!*

Silbara's hair, all the colors of grains and unbraided for the first time since childhood was blown by the wind across her eyes, making their message sparkle interrupted like stars on a cloudy night. *Yes? No? Decide!*

For Celebi, the Brighid, the mantle of leadership was hard to put down, so she responded as if she knew how to respond and to what she was responding.

"When?"

"Tonight," the Grandmother replied. "It is the dark moon tonight, the time for the most sacred mysteries."

Malvu slipped his hand into Celebi's. He cleared his throat and deferentially asked, "Grandmother, what *is* the Sacred Marriage? Are we to be given to know?"

"Well, it wouldn't be a Mystery then, would it?" the old woman snorted. She looked at Celebi and formed aloud the words that had been crashing though Celebi's mind.

"Yes? No? Decide!"

Celebi turned slightly to see Malvu's eyes. They were clear and as deep gray as water running from the mountains in granite-strewn streams. They met her pale green eyes with love and patience. He squeezed her hand. Encouragement? Assent? Deference? She took a deep breath.

"Yes."

$$\text{☽ ◯ ☾}$$

High in these mountains, when the sun set, darkness fell quickly with none of the long lingering shadows and liminal light of Calanais. And on this night of the dark moon an overcast sky let no starlight through to temper the blackness of the night. Nine women, Grandmothers of the Basquela, with their silver hair flowing over their cloaks of animal skins, stood at the entrance of a cave, a yawning mouth higher than seven people and wider than eight. They stood with one lit torch for each, and in total silence they began their descent into the Womb Cave. Following behind were Celebi and Malvu, each wrapped in white hides of sacred elk, adorned with the same symbols and patterns that were dyed and scarred onto the faces of the Grandmothers. They had been given no torches so they followed right on the heels of the women before them into a darkness that defied dark, a black deeper than any other, into the absence of all light. There was no singing, no drumming, no chanting to fill the widening space of the cave, just the sounds of breath and heartbeats loud in their own ears.

With each turn deeper into the darkness, they felt more and more the weight of the earth above their heads, the compression of all the life above, the distillation of self to the sensations of feet on rocks and breath mist rising up against the face.

Before this night's Mystery, Celebi and Malvu had been taken to separate caves to prepare their bodies and spirits for what lay ahead. Much of that time, in all honesty, most of that time, had slipped beyond memory. They had been given a sweet and musky decoction to drink, and then, the day seemed to have passed and they found themselves standing in this procession with only a residue of thickness on their tongues to harken back to the last hours. Now, with no time given for them to share, neither knew what the other had been experiencing, but they could feel the fine tremor running through each other's bodies when their hands brushed in the dark. This ritual was old, older than the rites of Calanais, older than the distinction of peoples and languages and cultures. This ritual was as old as the very first people, and Celebi and Malvu felt the vibration of that lineage in the very marrow of their bones.

They traveled down, around sharp turns, through narrow corridors and into vast spaces in which the torches threw enormous shadows onto reflective walls. Whenever they came into a large chamber the light from the torches slashed and splintered at the eye. And then, in the narrow and descending tunnels, the torches disappeared ahead and the light was only a memory.

At long last, half a night, many nights, a hundred nights later, the Grandmothers walked into a dome shaped chamber and formed a circle of shadow slanted faces and dancing torchlight. Celebi and Malvu were led into the center of that circle and positioned facing each other. As if a silent signal was sent, the nine Grandmothers toned a high single note, as high as a hawk's cry. The sound ran around the walls of that chamber, stampeded along the walls, circling moonwise and gathering speed till it came crashing into Celebi and Malvu who fell to their knees, knocked down by the power of that sound as the hides covering their bodies fell to the cave floor. They looked at each other in the broken, jagged flashes of light, and saw that their bodies had been painted with the same symbols and patterns that adorned the sacred hides, the same as adorned the faces of the Grandmothers.

"Ah!" Celebi sighed at the sight of him.

The soft sound floated toward Malvu, and as it reached him it lit up the pattern of symbols around his mouth, on his chin and down his neck. Zigzag lines of deep cobalt illuminated slowly, as if someone was running a torch above the surface of his throat and chest. The jagged lines became spirals that curled over his shoulders like snakes draping around his body. And brilliant scarlet waves cascaded over his arms down to his fingertips. As each pattern became visible and alight, the sensations over his skin and reaching deep into his muscles and sinews tickled, then stretched, then pulled, running along that boundary between pleasure and pain.

"Oh!" Malvu uttered low, almost a moan.

And his breath, his utterance, arrived at Celebi's skin and initiated the awakening of patterns and color that sent ripples of gold ellipses and quivering lines from her eyes, tripping down her throat, and circling her breasts. An arrow of deep moss green shot down her torso from the base of her throat to disappear in the soft patch of hair at the meeting of her legs. And as with Malvu, each illuminated segment of skin became exquisitely awake and teetered at the edge of too much sensation.

The toning of the Grandmothers shifted. It split from a single high tone fracturing into nine distinct tones that made a shape, a structure, a cocoon around Celebi and Malvu that seemed solid. It was as if they were held in a chrysalis of sound that was matter. The two took one step closer to each other, pushed forward by the tones and some deep inner knowing that only when they reached the other would the aching end.

"Goddess," Malvu whispered.

"Beloved," Celebi replied.

As their arms wrapped around each other, and their mouths met in reverence and delight, the symbols on their bodies came alive, took full shape and began the dance of creation and expansion and death and rebirth. And the sanctity of that life cycle was amplified by the tones, and the cave, and the purity of focus from the Grandmothers and the woman and man in the center of that circle. The energy grew and grew till the mountain around them began to tremble with the fullness of life, and in the explosion of climax all the life above and below received the blessing.

At long last, half a night, many nights, a hundred nights later, Celebi felt herself sift down into her own singular body. One by one her senses returned. She heard the thump-da-thump of Malvu's heart under her ear. She felt the twinge in her right hip from the position of her leg draped high over his thigh. She smelled the smell of Malvu, green and dark like waterweeds. As she stirred he groaned slightly as he felt himself slip from her body, and the sharp poke of rock against his spine. He instinctively wrapped his arms around her, to keep her close, to remember where they were, to keep her safe.

One torch remained in the domed cave, and all the Grandmothers were gone.

"How long... ?" Celebi started.

"I have no idea," Malvu finished the thought.

"Your heart is racing," she said. "So, mayhaps we haven't been here so long."

"If we stay like this much longer, I can vouch that my heart will race even faster," he retorted.

Celebi chuckled quietly as a feeling of peace and completion and power as she had never known before spread from her toes to her eyebrows. She wiggled up to kiss his lips. He flinched as the puncture wounds on his calves felt the cold rock beneath his legs. As the benefits of the ceremonial potion wore off, he was feeling every mile he had traveled and every indignity he had suffered from the guard dogs.

"Ouch! But perhaps we look for a bed of leaves or moss? A sacred cave leaves much to be desired as a sleeping place."

"Oh, so it's sleep you are after?" Celebi teased. Malvu sat upright abruptly and pulled her onto his lap, lifting her gently and lowering her down onto him.

"Sleep later, I think. After we try this again, just as us and not as the Goddess-filled."

"Just as us," Celebi breathed.

$$) \, \bigcirc \, ($$

Sometime later, as ragged breathing slowed, Celebi whispered sleepily, "That torch is burning low. We should leave soon, or we will be lost forever here in the dark."

"Hmmmmm," Malvu responded.

They were wrapped around each other, her in his lap with arms and legs encircling him and head on his shoulder. He knew he had lost the feeling in his legs, and he didn't care.

"Malvu?"

"Hmmmmm?"

"We should go soon."

"Mmhmm."

The torch sputtered, and they both looked up as the very real possibility of being forever entombed in the deepest cave became real. They clumsily stood up, clasped hands, and Malvu held the torch as Celebi led the way out of the cave, up and out. Along the way, the remaining eight torches were positioned in sconces in the cave walls, a path marked for them by the Grandmothers. They eventually emerged into the vast cave opening and saw daylight reaching almost to the back wall. How long had they been in the belly of the Goddess?

THE WILD HUNT OF EPHESUS

*We move swiftly over the Middle Sea, so clear and calm tonight
that it reflects back the full moon light. The sky above is black silk,
and the stars dim in the brilliance of the moon. As we are pulled
east, beyond the rim of tawny sand and villages of clay, we see a
forest of giant trees, the Forest of the Source. We can articulate the
small clusters of buildings and markets that surround a circular
structure of marble and tree trunks with a conical roof. Hundreds
of figures, women and girls, stand on broad steps slightly swaying.*

☽ ○ ☾

The Wild Hunt is running.
The Wild Hunt is running.
The Wild Hunt is running. She is here.
The Wild Hunt is running.
The Wild Hunt is running.
She is here.

*T*he sound of the chant sung by several hundred women
floated clear and bright as the full moon lit the woods. Nine
girls of long legs and narrow hips whose shadows look like
young tree limbs ran swiftly in that illumination, farther and farther
from the singing, till the only sounds were their breath and the soft
thuds of footfall on the loamy forest floor. Measured breaths, four
counts in, four counts out with one stride for each count. This sacred

night was the longest night of the turning of the wheel. A sacred night that marked a new beginning. The Wild Hunt always ran with the full moon, and for that to happen on this night was indeed auspicious.

Nine girls ran on this, their first Wild Hunt. Nine girls who had each been born on a full moon and marked as Goddess-born. Nine girls who had lived for nine turns of the wheel, been dedicated to Artemis, and still felt the sting of the blue sickle moon tattoo on their foreheads. Their training had been severe, with everything pointed at this night and the Hunt. The Nine had no thoughts, no human concerns, just the run, the moon, the pack, and the prey. Four counts in breath... four counts out breath. They ran steady and sure in a formation like a flock of geese in flight. They didn't feel the cuts on their feet or the cold as it swirled mist-like sand devils between the trees. The moonlight lit the woods like midday, but threw long shadows, and the bracken looked like tall hunchbacked men. And they ran on through the sweetness of linden and the tang of cedar.

They came to a creek bed and slowed, silently slipping into the icy water, numbed feet clutching on the rocks with bruised toes. On the other side of the creek, the girl on point raised a clinched fist, swung to go to the back of the pack as the girl at the front of the right wing stepped forward to run point. The hounds that ran with them stood with front paws in the water and quickly lapped to quench thirst. All the girls listened with heads tilted, listening for a clue. A sharp acrid smell? No, that was a fox. And then, there it was! A crack of a twig off to the left and forward. The girl at the point lifted her left hand high, the Nine took a deep breath together, and the Wild Hunt was off again.

Four counts in breath, four counts out breath. Knives at their belts, bow and quivers slung over shoulders. And they ran on. The stag ahead felt the Wild Hunt gaining on him. He had three arrows in his right flank, and was losing the battle between fear and fatigue. More trees, more gullies, another creek. The Nine could smell the stag, smell his blood and musk, smell his surrender. They came upon him in a small clearing with the moon directly overhead. His sides heaved with the effort of breath and pain. But his head was held high, and the points of his antlers looked aflame. The Nine unfolded from the running formation and encircled the stag. They could see each other clearly, damp faces and bright eyes. With a single motion they drew their knives from their sheaths and walked toward the king of the woods. With a single breath they fell on him, and the night was raw with his dying cry and the flush of heat that poured from his body with his blood. Nine girls ablaze with the power of Artemis, filled with the Goddess of the Hunt, wild with their own wildness.

One of the Nine was called Io. She was tiny, smaller than any of the others, with a mass of fine curly hair the same color as all the different hues of honey. She was tiny but fierce, and all the other girls had learned quickly that they needed to keep up with her in their training. She ran fast and forever. Her knife was always thrown true. She fought to win. And she wanted no friends. The other girls looked for companionship and warmth, missing their families and villages. But Io was a lone wolf cub, a wounded badger, a suspicious soul. Her teachers admired her and feared for her. Her pack mates looked up to her and were afraid of her. And what Io thought, no one knew. But at this moment she felt a peculiar peace, a belonging, a connection to the others that she had always secretly wanted but avoided at all costs. They had done it! The Wild Hunt had run with Artemis. She had indeed been with them and in them.

The Nine looked at each other with blood spattered on their faces that looked black in the moonlight. They saw the victory in the other's eyes, smiled, and threw back their heads to howl like the successful pack they were. The song for the soul of the stag was begun, to sing his spirit free from his body and thank him for the gift of the hunt. With the hounds whining at the outside of the circle, the Nine began to field dress the stag, throwing the offal over their shoulders for the dogs. Then came the song for the lifting of the hide, the song for the quartering of the meat, the song for the freeing of the antlers. All done to honor the stag. All done to honor the Goddess. All done as they had been trained.

Suddenly Io picked up the severed antlers and placed the horns on her head. The other girls were several heartbeats slow to see what was happening and were startled. No one had taught them to do this. Was this a secret rite? Was Io performing a Mystery that the others weren't gifted to know? Or was this a sacrilege? Only the priestess who invoked Artemis at the Temple wore the stag horns. Lightheaded from the aftermath of trance, the eight stood frozen, unsure what should or could happen next.

Io began to speak in a deep voice, the voice of a very old woman. Her eyes were fixed straight up at the moon, opaque and never blinking. She spoke in the common tongue, a language formal and temple trained with no hint of her own hill country accent. She spoke of blood, of the horrors of destruction and carnage. She spoke and spoke until the sound of her words stabbed at their ears and their knees folded under them. One girl cried softly into her friend's lap. Another whimpered into the fur of her hound. One tucked her thumb into her mouth for comfort. These were now just little girls, frightened and without guidance, deep in the forest.

The hint of dawn slid gray pearly light between the trees. With a shudder, Io broke her locked gaze and the girls saw that it was if she had floated back into herself. She lowered the stag horns and looked at them bewildered. She saw her pack mates staring at her with a mixture of awe and a loathing born of terror. Her throat felt ripped and hot like she had a fever.

"What happened?"

Her voice was again the high, light sound of a child with the slight lisp of the hill folk. She was met with silence. None of her pack mates would meet her eyes. All they could think to do was to run fast and panicked back to the Temple and the safety of the women there. But their training won out. They shot swift low glances at each other and made nervous motions with their hands at the hounds. The girls quickly packed up the meat, antlers, and hide, distributed the burdens, and took off with an easy lope back toward the Temple. Their stride was easy, but their hearts were not. The sweet delicious thrill of their Wild Hunt, the power of their being one with Artemis was gone. Now they were just frightened little girls strung together by habit and ritual. Io hung back with only her hound for company.

She spun on her heels and vomited, retching up bile from deep in her guts. As she straightened up and wiped her mouth with the back of her hand, the memory of the message she had been given slithered into her mind like an oily fog. It was all there, every last detail, every dire warning, every image of her world ground to dust. She threw back her head for the second time that night, but this time her howl was shredded with pain. The hound beside her joined in the howl, and even the moon wept.

Up ahead, the other eight heard the sound and their stride stuttered, pattern broken. Uneasy, they shifted the packages on their backs, and looked to each other to see what they should do. As if with one mind, they closed their eyes, lifted their chins and joined the pain chorus. Io's pain was their pain, the pack, the Wild Hunt girls of Artemis, and they returned to fold her into the group and help carry her vision. With Io amongst them again they headed home.

The painful paean of girls, dogs, spirits of the trees, and the spirit of the sacrificed king of the Forest, all rose toward the wisps of blue and mauve clouds now visible in the new light of day. The sound was carried on the wind toward the Temple and the villages that surrounded and served the Dedicants of Artemis. People hurried out of their homes, horses brayed, children woke with night terrors. Deep in the center altar room of the Temple, a jagged crack appeared in the plinth that held the Sacred Flame kept burning eternally for Artemis. For a brief shudder of time, the Flame wobbled and curled inward as if to go out. And then the Flame settled and grew bright and steady again. Priestesses, linked by the hive mind of their craft, hurried toward the central sanctuary and began the preparations for the journey that must be taken. Trainers and Dedicants were summoned, and each bent to her work.

The sun had risen three hand widths in the sky when the Nine wearily returned to the Temple courtyard. All the Priestesses, Trainers, other age groups of Nines, and bands of Dedicants grouped by age from eighteen to thirty-three stood arranged on the wide, marble steps that led up to the Temple complex. A caravan of horses and mules stood waiting. Io walked toward the head of the caravan as if moving through mud. She took the arm of the Dedicant on the lead horse, and was swung up behind her onto the horse's back. This Dedicant, a powerful young hunter of eighteen turns of the wheel named Pel, with the seven-strand braid of one who has taken her vows, looked over her shoulder at Io with a look equal parts pity and excitement.

"So, it's to Egypt, is it?"

Io grunted assent, Pel gave a forward command, and the caravan headed south and east to follow the coast of the Middle Sea. As they rode away, they could hear the sound of several hundred women singing and singing and singing till the sound was so faint as to be the internal sound of their blood moving through their bodies as they swayed atop the horse.

The Wild Hunt is running.

The Wild Hunt is running.

The Wild Hunt is running.

She is here.

THE SEA OF GRASSES

There is an inland sea below, a dark midnight blue with the sharp pointed waves of winter east winds. The sea is vast with a pinch in the middle like a bee's waist. As we swing lower, we are pulled to an earthen sea, another series of waves, waves of rolling plains and undulating grasses pushed over by that same east wind, waves that extend farther than the horizon in every direction.

Directly below, near the power place where the earth and water meet, we see a massive fire shooting seventy or eighty feet into the air, fed by grandmother trees, surrounded by several thousand small figures dancing and singing. Fanning out like the spokes of a wheel are wagons and tents and yurts. Dotted around are smaller clan fires and herds of goats, and horses, thousands of horses. All the People of the Sea of Grasses have come together for the Fire to protect them through the longest night. In the midst of all the movement, one figure stands as if carved in stone. Abruptly she draws her sword and then storms off into the darkness.

"Why am I in a boat?" Kiyia's head slammed against the rib of the small vessel again and again with the rocking of the waves. "Ow! Why in the name of thunder and pain am I in a stinking boat?"

She opened one slightly crusty eye that blazed green fire to discover that she was sprawled against the back end of said vessel in a puddle. Four people huddled at the front of this rocking, creaking, smelly, piece of goat turd boat. Their faces looked familiar, like she had dreamed them up after too much elderberry wine. She had a vague memory of dancing round the big Solstice Fire, and drinking, perhaps, a bit much… Suddenly a larger than expected wave rocked the wooden craft, and Kiyia's head took another good crack against the side.

"I swear by the Goddess of the Horse and all her warriors that I will knock a few skulls if you don't tell me WHY I AM IN A BOAT!"

The four who sat shivering together were wet and terrified and had no idea why any of them were in this boat. This woman, this six-foot-tall beast of armor and muscle had 'urged' them at the end of her sword down to the bay and into this vessel. They had put to sail just before dawn and were now a good half a day out to sea. Since this beast woman had threatened their wellbeing if they didn't acquiesce, none of them had dared to turn back to land when she had fallen into a drunken snore-filled sleep. A man and his son, both coppersmiths, a woman who was a weaver, and a girl of thirteen summers who kept pigs, all sat frozen now in fear, as well as brine.

Kiyia attempted to stand, thought better of it, and slumped back against the stern. She drew a deep breath, but before she could bellow again the girl, Misi, who had faced down angry sows and thought this woman of equal ferocity, sputtered a staccato reply.

"You said… *get in the boat*… so we did."

When she saw how the Beast's face turned a shade of purple like a deep bruise she immediately reassessed her comparison. This woman was far more frightening than an angry sow.

"You said… *sail the boat*… so we did?"

Her voice turned upward as if to placate the now trembling Beast. Misi had the short-cropped hair of a woman, newly made after her First Moon. But hers looked as if she had sawn it off herself with a short knife, which she had. She was an orphan with no family, no one to make the ritual for her, so last night she had stood in front of the Fire, hacked off her own hair, and proudly declared herself a woman. A mug of wine later, a few dances with damp strangers, and she had moved off away from the fire to rest, sitting down next to a friendly, fragile looking woman of middle years by the name of Yollo, who wore an elaborate plaid shawl. They had barely exchanged three sentences when a whirlwind of leather and pelts burst from the darkness with a full-throated battle cry and sword pointed directly at them. She, the Whirlwind, the Beast, rounded them up along with the two men seated nearby and had marched them all down to the water's edge, muttering incoherently under her breath. Misi had caught a few words – temple, Egypt, and slaughter – the last being the only one of the three she had understood. It was enough to keep her moving and staying away from the point of that sword.

The four captives helped each other as they staggered through the dark, farther and farther away from the crowd and the fire. The older man kept one arm under the elbow of the woman in the beautiful shawl who had staggered repeatedly and was struggling to catch her breath. The younger man kept track of Misi and helped her over several rocky outcrops. They exchanged terrified glances, and Misi wondered if her first night as a woman would be her last. The Beast had pushed them into the boat, told them to set sail, and stared daggers at them as they did so with the occasional burst of slurred words and a flailing sword.

With the sun now directly overhead, the elder of the two men, the father, hazarded a supplication, "Please, Guardian, may we look for a place to make land? We have no water or food."

Misi's breath caught like a rope had been thrown round her middle. A Guardian? By the Moon and all She rules! A Guardian? Of course, she should have known that anyone that brawny and armed had some special standing. A Guardian of Epona! A breed apart, the Guardians were trained from the time they could walk to ride and fight and show no mercy to the enemies of the People. They were rough, could be crude, but were pledged to protect and guard. If two clans were in dispute about the use of a well, Guardians of Epona came to settle and soothe. If outlanders threatened the flocks, Guardians arrived to drive them off. They solved problems with brawn and justice, often in that order. They worked under the premise that blackened eyes and loosened teeth might very well deter some idiot from a larger altercation, thereby avoid anyone's rage from accidentally committing the ultimate taboo: the taking of another's life. In keeping the peace, a Guardian might break a few fingers, but People would, should, never kill People. These women were brash and bruising, but devoted protectors of life in all its forms, from all enemies human and animal. This particular Guardian was looking at them now, from under fierce red eyebrows, her green slits of eyes boring holes in them, as if *they* were enemies of the People.

"No," said the Guardian. "We sail till nightfall." Her words fell into the silence of the boat like hailstones. And with that she tilted back, slouching down against the wooden rails, and closed those terrifying eyes.

As one, the four captives let out a breath and faced forward in the direction they were sailing. The younger man of about eighteen summers, looked as if he would speak, but his father shook his head sharply and the young man closed down again, his chin with sparse blond whiskers sinking into his collar. The two men looked so similar as to be comical: same face, same posture, same pale blue eyes, just twenty summers difference in their ages. The father's hair was more gray than yellow these days, but both men had the sinewy forearms of a smith, with hands covered in tiny scars and burns. Next to them sat Yollo, the woman with the beautiful shawl, her black hair shot with white and plastered to her skull by sea spray showing the sharp cheekbones and haunted eyes of the constantly hungry or ill. The four shifted their bodies quietly, found less uncomfortable positions, and settled down like broody hens to wait out their fate.

Kiyia allowed herself to doze in that vigilant way in which she had been trained. *One eye open, one ear ready*, her instructors used to say. The rocking of the boat was even and rhythmic and tempted her into a deeper state. Bits of memory came flashing back to her, tiny fragments of vision and sound. She now clearly remembered *seeing* the total destruction of shimmering white temples and hearing the never-ending screams fueled by rape and torture. She heard again the message, no, the order from the Goddess, to race toward Egypt and guard what might be saved. She had a recollection of watching herself as if from above as she reeled with sword held high and dashed into the darkness. Kiyia cursed it all to cinders. *Oh, by the Horse! Was this a bloody vision?* She hated all the mystical trappings and trance nonsense that others enjoyed. She was a warrior, plain and simple. Why did she have to have this inconvenient vision now? She was on her furlough, had come to the Gathering for a bit of relaxation before she had to report back to her unit. Couldn't she just get to go out, have some fun, and bash something about?

From deep in her past rose up the remembrance of the shaman in her clan emphatically insisting that this girl, this Kiyia, would be a mystic. She had resisted the notion then as fanciful and frightening. Today, as she knocked back and forth in this stinking turd of a boat, she wished she had smashed a hand over the old woman's mouth before she had a chance to utter that prophecy. For with the People, the word, once spoken, became the Word that must be. As distasteful as this vision of destruction and its path for her to go to Egypt was, it had been spoken by powers of the Otherworld, and so it must be. She was a warrior and would face the battle before her without question or retreat.

When the sun was one hand's width above the western horizon, Kiyia grunted and waved her sword toward the shore to her right. The father Smith and the girl were still awake as their companions slept. He turned the sail and she grabbed the pole to help steer the boat as they came into shallow water. The boy and the woman struggled to lift from sleep fog, and slipped over the side to drag the boat on shore. There was a small stream with ferns and cress lining its banks and a tiny fingernail of beach. While Kiyia stood with arms crossed looking menacingly at them, sword still attached to her hand as if it grew from her arm, the four gathered firewood, fixed a snare for fish and brought armfuls of grasses for sleeping.

Night fell over their shoulders like a blanket. The air was sharp and their small fire did little to warm and dry them. They shivered steadily as they ate the partially cooked fish and laid down to rest. Only Kiyia showed no discomfort. She displayed no signs of struggle with either the spirits of wine or spirits of the ghostly kind from the night before. She sat cross-legged and upright with her cloak about her and the light from the fire only illuminating her mouth and chin. She had both eyes open and both ears ready tonight. She was on guard. She was a Guardian.

THE VILLAGE OF
THE SHAMAN

S even days had gone by and it was clear to all the inhabitants of the leaky, stinky boat that the woman in the beautiful shawl was very sick. The four captives had found a rhythm as they huddled together for warmth at night and struggled to obey the commands of Kiyia, the Guardian of Epona. The fierce contempt in which the Guardian held the four captives was still achingly apparent, but even she could feel pity for the sick woman.

Of the four, the young girl, Misi, was the most forward, and asked now for their day to end and help to be found for their comrade. She, like the others, looked bedraggled with matted hair and stains from damp and sweat on her clothes. Her cheeks had multiple insect bites and her lips were chewed raw in spots.

"Guardian, Yollo is feverish and her cough is so much worse. Might we pull ashore at a village and ask for a healer?"

"Not her name! Don't tell me her name, young idiot. She is dying. Can't you see that?"

For Kiyia and the others had indeed seen the scarlet stain from the woman's cough and the chalk white face with crimson patches of color on the cheeks. She had the Final Cough, the disease that always killed. And to Kiyia's way of thinking, if you knew her name it just made it that much harder when it came time to bury her.

Misi's face flushed with fury at this response, but she was yanked back by her shirt to sit next to the younger Smith. The father and son exchanged glances that spoke full thoughts, and blessedly, the woman in question had fallen into a fever slumber and hadn't heard her own death pronouncement.

And at that, after days of worry and privation and seasickness and having to pee over the side of a boat while the others politely looked away, Misi reached her limit and began to cry. This, the girl who hadn't even shed tears when her parents and brothers had died of the bloody flux, who had simply found a way to keep food in her belly and avoid trouble. After all that, now she wept. It was all just one death too many, one pain too great to bear. The tears rolled down her face and she began to sob big, whelping sobs that sounded like strangled geese while snot raced over her upper lip.

"Alright!" Kiyia bellowed. "We'll stop at a village, but it won't make a bit of difference. She's still going to die!"

With that she turned the sail toward the shore and the threads of smoke rising from fires that told of human habitation. *I'm not showing mercy,* she told herself. *I could use a stretch of the legs and maybe some new supplies.*

They had traveled over deep water and through the narrow straits from one side of the Inner Sea to the next. The days had slipped into more and more light as they sailed south and west. The egrets and herons that had dappled the shoreline at the start of their journey were now replaced with eagles snatching fish in explosions of water and power. Here the forest came right down to the water with no sight of grain fields. Aspen and birch with white marbled trunks raced each other to the shore. The cold had eased a bit as they headed south into the Middle Sea, and Kiyia could smell the saltier water. For her, the absence of wind was disconcerting. At home on the earthen Sea of Grasses, the wind was a constant presence, a singer of all the Earth's songs. Always the wind, sometimes roaring, sometimes crooning. Here, the sounds of birdsong and the scuffle of small creatures in the fallen leaves sounded brash without the muting of Mother Wind. Kiyia was out of her element and not at all happy about that. *Yes, time to get supplies, and perhaps bury the sick one. By the Horse, why must I drag these civilians with me?* But to that, there was no forthcoming answer.

As the boat slipped easily toward the village the travelers could hear drumming and chanting. With increasing clarity, they began to see the people gathered, brightly dressed in what could be supposed to be their best, facing away from the shore with arms raised toward a small wooden structure elevated a few steps above the ground. *Idiots,* Kiyia thought grumpily. *I could storm in here and rob them all. Some people are too stupid to deserve to live.*

The Smiths, elder and younger, moved to tie the boat to the pier while Misi wiped her face on her sleeve and the sick woman moaned in her sleep. The chant was in an unfamiliar language, but the one name "Artemis" was recognizable.

"You, boy!" Kiyia jutted her chin at the younger Smith. "You come with me. If you," and she bore her eyes into the father, "try to get away or do anything stupid, I have a dagger in his ribs. Understood?"

Misi and Smith the father gasped. The Guardian wouldn't actually hurt the young man, would she? For reasons still not understood by Kiyia or her captives, she refused to set them free, no matter how cumbersome or difficult it was to keep them. Misi stood to follow, but a sharp sideways jerk of Kiyia's head was all that was needed to keep the girl in the boat. Kiyia leapt onto the pier and the younger Smith scrambled to follow. Father and son had decided days ago that the safest way to stay in one piece was to do exactly what the Guardian said. Kiyia strode ahead and the younger Smith looked over his shoulder at the boat and its inhabitants dusted with the golden light of late afternoon.

The village shore, a pebbly beach of small, round, pale yellow stones smelled of the charcoal used to smoke the fish for storing. The Guardian grabbed the young man's belt, and he felt the small prick of metal in his side. They looked companionable enough, like mother and son, if the mother was a six-foot war machine with her head shaved on the sides, a single long braid the color of a fox falling down her back, and narrowed eyes the color of spring greens that held no warming glow. They stepped to the back of the singing crowd, and Kiyia could see two girls dressed in identical fawn-colored tunics and leather leggings standing on the highest step in front of the small structure that was painted with silver spirals, crimson yonis, and black snakes. Of the two girls, the younger was a tiny thing with a wild mass of curly hair all russet and amber and gold that glinted in the late daylight. She didn't look at the crowd below, and indeed, looked all done in, paler than the inside of an oyster shell. The elder was tall, well muscled, and twice the age of the little one, with wheat colored hair in a warrior braid and a forced smile below a high bridged nose and sapphire eyes. At long last the chant came to an end.

"We are grateful for your ceremony," the older girl said in the common tongue.

An old woman with necklaces made of snake vertebrae and dreadlocked hair down to her ankles, clearly an important personage, perhaps the shaman of the village, began to translate into the local dialect for the others around her.

"We will accept your hospitality for tonight, but we must continue on our mission tomorrow. And now, my companion needs rest," the older girl said.

The villagers muttered and grumbled as this message came to them. Only one night! They had hoped to impress the Dedicants of Artemis from the Mother Temple with many days of feasting and song and dance. Perhaps even a hunt in their honor? But the younger girl swayed on her feet, and the elder caught her by the shoulders. Immediately the shaman lifted her staff topped with a snake skull, silence fell, and the way parted through the crowd as the two emissaries of Artemis were led to the shaman's hut. Kiyia and the young Smith fell in behind as if they belonged.

"You will have food and warm water for washing brought to you," began the shaman, when a shadow fell over her from behind. With the sun at her back, the shadow loomed as large as cave bears and creaked of leather and armor.

"And for us, as well," said Kiyia in the voice that had commanded battalions.

The young woman with the warrior braid sprang around and pulled her sword from her scabbard with a ting like a high bell. Kiyia lifted her dagger into the light behind the old woman's shoulder and sneered, "Want to have a go, girlie?" And the shaman fainted dead away at their feet.

The tiny one with hair all the colors of the sun and a small smattering of freckles across her nose started and stood erect. She locked eyes with Kiyia, and gave a single nod of recognition. With that the Guardian stepped over the prostrate body of the shaman, the tiny girl bolted forward under the raised sword of her companion and flew into the waiting arms of Kiyia. The two heads bent together, and the very, very soft sound of weeping came from one of them.

$$\text{)} \bigcirc \text{(}$$

A while later, the shaman's hut had settled into a deceptively domestic scene. Io and Kiyia had recovered from the impact of their souls' recognition and were seated close together at the back of the central fire sharing food from the same wooden plate. They spoke seldom and so low as to not easily be heard by the others, but the occasional word or phrase floated through the hut as if framed in crystal. *Visions... priestesses tied like cattle... Temple of Isis... the women are coming.*

Two others sat across the fire, nearer and to the left of door. Pel, the Dedicant of Artemis and guard for Io, and Smith the Younger had found an easy companionship as well. They were sharing the story of their respective journeys, the frightening visions received by Kiyia and Io, the total lack of discussion and the haste by which they were compelled toward Egypt. They described the uncanny way that the two across the fire would tilt a head and listen, to what they didn't know. But then, it would be as if a voice had been heard, and some decision would be declared, and the route adjusted as if they had received direction from the Otherworld. To Pel and Smith the Younger no other explanation made any sense to explain the craziness of their last few days. Steered by the Goddess they were, which lent some small measure of grace to their travails.

On Kiyia's command the young man had brought his fellow travelers up from the boat, and the village healers had swooped in like starlings to tend to Yollo. She had been carried into a nearby hut from which healing songs and incense smoke of cedar and motherwort wafted. On the other side of the door from Pel and Smith the son, Smith the father and Misi sat slumped together. The hut was close and slightly smoky, and the girl was warmer than she had been in over a week, fervently glad to be out of the boat and under a roof. They had eaten, and Misi's eyes had floated shut as she leaned into the elder Smith's shoulder. He put his arm around her, and it seemed to comfort them both.

The shaman squatted close to the fire looking through it, and her faded blue eyes never left Io and Kiyia. She knew that they were emissaries of the Goddess; for what purpose she knew not and cared less. For her, a lifetime of service to the people and the Goddess had resulted in this gift: the sight of these two, gilded by the Goddess' touch. She watched and listened and absorbed this miracle, folding it all in close to her heart.

$$\text{☽ ○ ☾}$$

In that time of deep night when the Earth turns from inhalation to exhalation, one figure silently lifted the hide covering at the door of the hut and slid like fog out into the night. This woman, Kiyia, a Guardian of Epona had talked long into the dark with the tiny Hunter of Artemis, Io. Kiyia had never felt such belonging, such a sense of being a part of someone else before, even with her sister Guardians, even in all her years of training to serve Epona and protect the People. Always before she had felt some odd disconnect, like some slight misstep between her and the walk of others. But meeting this tiny girl, was like coming home to a place within herself she hadn't even known existed. They shared this vision of what was to come, and they shared a destiny too.

So, as Io had finally fallen into the deepest of slumbers, Kiyia had slowly dragged her arm out from under the girl's head, stepped over the bodies scattered around the hut in sleep, and escaped out onto the stillness. Without even knowing it was happening, her feet turned toward the healers' hut and she walked with an undefined purpose, striding silently like the warrior she was. One almost indiscernible clack of bone against bone, and Kiyia slapped her left side and pulled the dagger that lived there as she whirled on her heel and wrapped her free arm around the neck of the shaman, pressing the old woman's snake vertebrae necklace into her skin. "If you weren't so old and near to dying, I'd take you down right now."

"For walking the night walk of the very old in my own village? Or for getting close without your knowing?"

"I knew you were there the entire time."

But Kiyia had the honesty to acknowledge, at least to herself, that her thoughts, and her awareness had been a thousand miles away. Indeed, the ancient shaman had gotten much too close without her even noticing.

"You are headed to see your bondswoman in the healers' hut," the shaman said calmly, rubbing her throat, making it a statement, not a question.

"Well, why not?" Kiyia brusquely replied.

The two women bent to enter the low door to the hut, and the shaman nodded to the healers gathered around the body of Yollo. One healer was wringing out cool cloths and replacing the ones on Yollo's forehead, cloths that seemed to become steaming hot way too quickly. Another was dropping tiny drops of a decoction of willow, elderberry, and meadowsweet from a rolled-up bay leaf between Yollo's pale lips, then gently stroking her throat to encourage the febrifuge down.

Kiyia stood with feet braced wide, two deep furrows between her russet eyebrows, and stared down at her captive. The shaman asked the healers about Yollo's condition, and their replies were soft and murmured with quiet pity. Though their answers were in a dialect unknown to her, Kiyia could tell that their report was far from favorable. The shaman turned to her with a world of sadness in her eyes. Before she could tell the news, Kiyia spoke quickly and tersely.

"She has what our people call the Final Cough. Over the last few sun cycles, more and more of the people have contracted this, and they all die. Our healers are helpless. See, she has the bright red cheeks and whiteness of face. And when she coughs, there is blood."

"You care for her."

"I couldn't care less!" And Kiyia whipped around to leave the hut. The shaman placed one brown hand, knobby with age, on her arm.

"You may lie to me, but what is gained by lying to yourself?"

Kiyia brought her face down low to look directly into the shaman deep-set eyes, faded and pale in the firelight. Her voice was frighteningly quiet and trembling with ferocious control.

"I have dragged this woman, these others too, with me into what madness I cannot say, and I have no reason why! I have brought this woman far from her people, to what? To prove that I could? And now she will die alone, and without the proper rites of our people. What kind of Guardian am I? I have broken every vow I took to protect and defend."

The shaman took Kiyia's hand, fragile bones warm and dry like parchment slipping into the powerful calloused hand of a swordmistress, and she drew her outside the hut.

"Tell me," she quietly commanded.

So, the two, one tiny and bent, one muscled and towering, paced around the village of small cone-shaped huts, and out to the outermost dwellings of animals and food storage, and then back again, making the circuit of the small cluster of structures over and over again. The goats and sheep in the paddock rustled at the sound of their quiet voices, and the horses that had carried the young women of Artemis came to the fence, hoping for an apple or a small handful of oats.

Because they were side by side, and because they were in the dark, and because the shaman had the voice of an ancient and the patience of the rocks, Kiyia was able to pour out her story. The vision that had felt like a wine-induced nightmare, the kidnapping – for what else could she call it? – of her four servants, the urge, no, the absolute compulsion to push hard toward Egypt and the stubborn refusal to let her captives go.

"I could have let them go that first day, they could have found their way back home. And every day after. But it feels, they feel... like the threads of their lives are so wrapped up in this mission, this madness, that I cannot sever them from it... or from me. I think..."

"Yes?"

After a very long pause, so long that the shaman had believed she would not receive an answer, Kiyia's voice dropped so low as to be almost like the whisper of crickets, raspy and broken.

"I think I am afraid to let them go, for then I will be alone."

The shaman stopped and turned toward Kiyia, reaching her hands up to press gently against the tall warrior's cheeks.

"Many generations ago, this place was a center of power, a place for study and healing, a portal to the Source. There were tall buildings of stone and elaborate societies of healers and magicians. One devastating earthquake, and all of that was gone. A few survived, my ancestors. And as was right, my people stayed, connected to the power here, and pledged to save the wisdoms. We appear humble now, but we still possess some ancient magicks, some healing mysteries. We may be able to save your Yollo."

"She's not my Yo…"

"Hush!"

Kiyia was shocked into silence.

"If we perform our ritual, it is in the hands of the Goddess. She may give life, or She may take. We only open the portal to the Ancient One, She before She Had a Name, She who came before your Epona, before Artemis and all the other Goddesses. Something elemental will happen when that portal is open. We cannot know the outcome; we can only surrender to the Great Mother. Do you wish us to do this?"

"Me decide? Why me?"

"You have said this woman is woven into your story. Perhaps you brought her here so she could live."

Everything fell silent around Kiyia but the hum of the first bird song floating through the pre-dawn dark. She felt the shivering reverberations of those words ripple through her body. That there was some bigger purpose to all of her inexplicable actions these last wild days! How magnificent that would be. Could she be the agent of such primal wisdom?

"We should ask her. If there is a danger, it is she who should say yay or nay."

"She is fever-deep, she will not wake again without intercession. You are a Guardian. You must take the full responsibility for her life: yes, or no?"

As the Goddess star rose above the horizon in the east, Kiyia, the Guardian of Epona did as she had been trained to do. She shouldered her burden.

"Yes!"

$$\text{) O (}$$

"Io! Io, wake up!"

Pel stood over her young charge and not-so-gently nudged her with a foot in a thigh. She had been trying to wake the girl for what felt like half a day, but what had been actually only the time it takes a gourd of water to come to a boil. Io was sleeping so deeply that she barely breathed, her thin chest not visibly rising and falling. When Pel had first come to her in the pearl half-light before dawn, she had felt under the child's nose to see if she could feel her breath. When she confirmed for herself that the girl was still living, relief and the heavy press of responsibility warred within her for ascendency. Relief eventually won out.

"IO!"

And with that a small flutter of eyelids, and the color started to return to Io's cheeks making the constellations of freckles across her face stand out in stark relief.

"Wake up, Io. That crazy woman is busy, drawn away. I think one of her servants may be dying. Anyways, we can slip away and be done with her before anyone notices. Hurry now!"

Io felt herself gather her wits back to her, strands of dreams and whispers of memories. She pulled back to her all the knowledge of her vision, and the sheer relief of having found Kiyia, a someone who was living the same madness as she was. The bits and pieces of herself were like the unraveling threads of a cut blanket, and she grappled to re-weave herself. She sat up, struggling briefly with the furs that covered her, and focused on Pel defiantly. "She isn't crazy! I will travel with

Kiyia from now on. You can return to the Temple if you want to."

"I can't just leave you!" Pel was stung. "The priestesses gave you to my care. I cannot leave you alone with that woman, she is as wild as a hare! Even her servants have the sense to be afraid of her."

"Well, maybe I am crazy then, for she seems perfectly sane to me!"

Their voices were rising and heating up as the shaman stuck her head under the deerskin covering the door to the hut, the snake vertebrae necklace around her neck clacking and swaying.

"Ah, finally awake, eh? Best come quickly, there is a healing ritual about to begin." She looked straight at Io and said simply, "Kiyia will need you there." With that she turned on her heel and was gone.

"Come on then. Let's go see what your precious Kiyia is up to now."

Pel grabbed Io's elbow and brought her abruptly to her feet. The girls left the hut with dueling glares and mutterings under their breath.

Across the village, at a distance from all the other huts was the healers' dwelling. There were dozens of people standing outside the hut, quiet and bristling with anticipation. Kiyia stood near the door of the hut with arms akimbo and a murderous look. Misi, and the Smiths, father and son, were at her left side with their usual demeanor of sullen fear. The shaman stood on the other side of the door, and pounded her staff with its skeletal snakehead into the ground three times as she saw the girls approach. She threw her head back and began a chilling ululation, long and piercing. And then another. And then another.

The drummers began a quick sharp, snapping rhythm and all the villagers gathered started a chant with the men's voices uttering a deep, long, rolling melody and the women's voices floating high and swooping like starlings in a murmuration.

Io and Pel watched as the village healers wearing necklaces of braided healing herbs and their helpers carried out the body of a woman, Yollo, the fourth of Kiyia's servants. They hadn't seen her the night before, and with all the meeting and intense conversation they had barely been aware that someone, this woman apparently, had been brought up to the healers' hut from the bay. Kiyia had muttered something under her breath about somebody not dying soon enough for her liking, but Pel and Io, the young women of Artemis, hadn't known what she meant or to whom she was referring.

Now they saw Yollo and a look passed between them conveying shock at how very ill she seemed. She was wrapped in a beautiful shawl, intricately woven in deep ruby and amethyst. One healer held the woman's head, and others braced crossed arms under her body whilst another waved eagle and hawk feathers over a small gourd with plumes of smoke rising from it. The girls recognized the smell, resins of myrrh, copal and dragon's blood, powerful incenses used for deep trance in their Mother Temple. As Yollo was carried out into the center open area of the village the singing and drumming increased in volume and intensity. Io and Pel, trained in the halls of Artemis, could understand about every fourth word being chanted, but the meaning was clear. The Great Mother, the Source of all life, the Maker of all things was being summoned and asked to bring health… or death for the suffering woman. Vitality or a merciful end to suffering.

Kiyia stepped forward, drew the small knife that lived in her boot, and lifting her hands to the sky said in a voice loud enough to be heard above the drumming and chanting, "I offer my life blood for this woman here! She is under my protection! I ask for intercession! Come Great Mother, come!"

And with that she sliced across her left wrist and let the drops of blood fall into a waiting cup held by the healer who then dipped her finger into the cup and made symbols on the ill woman's forehead and lips and heart. Two helpers gently tilted the woman's head back and the healer tipped the cup toward her so that some of Kiyia's blood ran into Yollo's mouth.

All of the villagers began to stamp their feet on the earth in rhythm with the drums, and the beat sped up faster and faster. The smoke wafting from the incense reached now to the outer edges of the people chanting and stomping. Time was suspended, and Io and Pel found themselves joining in the chanting, letting their spirits sing the words they didn't know, but did, in the deepest sense, understand. Io looked across the crowd and saw that Kiyia's servants, Misi and the Smiths, were also stamping and chanting with eyes closed. She saw that Kiyia was standing stoically, arms raised in supplication, eyes fixed on the ill woman. The crowd became a single organism, a moving, pulsing body of prayer. The shaman was on her feet, pitched forward as if leaning into a strong wind. There was a rope tied securely around her waist held taut by several helpers to keep her from traveling too far and being lost in the Spirit World as she journeyed to hunt for the missing pieces of Yollo's spirit. Only if those pieces were found could the woman heal.

After some time, or no time, Yollo began to convulse. It looked as if her body was being shaken from the spirits of the earth below, and her limbs started to writhe violently. At this, the crowd, the prayer body, raised the volume of the chanting and drumming. Sound was solid. Movement was liquid. Time spun out and out.

With a final crescendo, Yollo's body was jerked upright and she screamed. Blood gushed from her mouth in rivers of dark red. And then she and the shaman collapsed back onto the ground. Everyone fell silent; no one moved.

A healer leaned over Yollo, gently touching eyelids and throat. And for an eternity, no one dared breathe.

"Her fever is broken! She is healed! She will live!"

The healers' helpers tenderly lifted Yollo up and carried her back into the hut. Several rushed to gently assist the shaman to her feet and help her too into their hut. Some villagers laughed softly, some fell to the earth and said quiet prayers of gratitude to the Great Mother. And Misi and the Smiths, father and son, noticed that Kiyia was swiping tears away from her cheek.

))O((

The sun was at its zenith, a bright light for mid-winter with an odd filmy haze around the orb. Kiyia sat upon a fence post, feet dangling into the paddock talking to the horses of the young women of Artemis. She was a creature of the plains, a woman of the Horse Goddess, Epona, and these last days without the feel of the gliding rhythm, forward and back, of horse covering ground had left her feeling bereft. Now, on this troubling day, she sought solace with the horses and put her dilemma to them.

"What to do, what to do? Shall I leave them here, those poor pitifuls that I have dragged far from home? I could leave them the boat and travel overland with the tiny girl."

These horses were more delicate than her companions back home on the Sea of Grasses. These, both mares, had long narrow necks that arched like swans, with narrow chests and delicate leg bones. One, black as jet, had come up to Kiyia's outstretched hand and bumped it in commiseration. The other, the bay, whinnied softly and flicked one front hoof against the earth raising a small puff of dust, *"You worry for them."*

"I'm not worried," Kiyia replied to the silent statement from the bay. "It is a matter of honor and duty. It's not as though I like those folks, not at all. Don't think me gone soft!"

The bay proceeded to nibble the tops of Kiyia's boots. *"Liar!"*

"Well, I don't!"

"Don't what?" came Io's voice from nearby. Kiyia jerked and nearly fell off the fence post.

"You have some hunting skills, little one. I only barely heard you approach."

And now the black nibbled at her boots as well. *"Liar!"*

Io slid between the cross bars of the fence and began stroking the face of the bay who had immediately switched her focus from Kiyia's boots at the sight of Io. The girl's hand barely reached up to the chestnut forehead, and the horse nudged her softly and repeatedly, the girl giggling as the horse pushed her back to the fence.

"You don't what?" Io repeated.

"She denies caring about her servants," said the shaman, who seemed to have appeared standing full formed behind Kiyia, rising from the earth itself.

"I wish, by all the powers of the Horse, that you all would stop popping up like this!" Kiyia snapped.

Io and the shaman exchanged mischievous looks and stepped closer to her, one on either side. "What are your plans next? You and this little one travel together, yes? And what of the others?"

"What I would really like is to drink a gourd of wine and wake up next moon," Kiyia snarled.

The shaman and Io waited with good humor, feeding blades of hay to the horses. Kiyia rubbed the newly healed cut across her wrist until the blood began pebbling up on her skin. Indecision was not a natural state for her, but she felt paralyzed by all the unknowns before her.

"Grandmother, what do you know of this Egypt?"

The shaman took her time and marshaled her thoughts. To say all she knew might change the course of events. To say too little felt like a betrayal of the trust placed in her by this warrior woman.

"Egypt is a mystery wrapped in a fog," she replied. "The Goddess Isis is powerful there, and Her Dedicants own true wisdoms. But there is a coiled serpent of envy and jealousy that seeks ascendance like we seek water to drink. They allow few foreigners, as they call all those not of Egypt. All travelers are required to have an official guide from the Pharaoh's court. Watch yourselves very, very carefully there, so as to not be the object torn asunder in the struggle between Temple and Court."

"Why, in the name of thunder and rain, are we called to that place then?"

Kiyia sounded irate. The sky above looked as storm-tossed as her face, and wind whipped up, only moving the very highest branches of the trees.

"Great magick requires great sacrifice, daughter. Are you prepared for that?" The shaman cast a sidelong glance up and high to see Kiyia's eyes.

"When am I not?" Kiyia snorted. "I have to check on Yollo!" And with that she walked back toward the healers' hut, Io and the shaman rushing along behind as hail began to pelt down on them.

☽ ○ ☾

Later that day, after the storm had passed, as evening light softened the edges of all things, Kiyia stood in the healers' hut with Misi and the father and son Smiths. Yollo was wrapped in multiple blankets on a low platform nestled near the fire. Earlier she had conferred with Io, all the while Pel standing at her shoulder and frowning mightily, and decided that they would leave the village the next day, traveling overland to Canaan where she had learned that guides were available to help traverse the Naihl river.

Pel had made occasional interjections and suggestions. "What about horses? We will need a mount for you." But Io and Kiyia had paid her little heed. "Why do we need a guide? I have done the work of plotting our travel so far."

They had ignored her.

"Could someone listen to me!"

Kiyia and Io slowly turned their heads and directed identical looks of vaguely veiled impatience at Pel.

"We need a guide, for the Land of Egypt will not allow visitors without a pass and an escort. It seems they don't trust outsiders." Kiyia had lifted one ruddy eyebrow, as if to stifle any further questions from Pel, and turned back to low conversation with Io.

Now Kiyia glared at her captives as if they were troops under her command. She made a gesture with her forearm toward Yollo.

"This woman will, it seems, recover. At the very least, I won't have to bury her. I don't know why you all were along for this journey. It is a mystery to me why you are here at all. But enough is enough." Kiyia cleared her throat. "So, I am giving you the choice to remain here in this village, or to find your way back to the Sea of Grasses. I will leave the boat. You can steer your way back simply enough if you follow the coast."

Stunned into silence, the three captives contemplated the unimaginable. They had been hungry and tired and afraid and numb for so long now that their world was Kiyia, and Kiyia was their world. But a future of their own devising?

No one was more surprised than they when their decisions rose fully formed, like sea creatures breaking from the hidden depths to appear glistening in the sunlight.

The elder Smith spoke first, "I will stay with Yollo, and when she is well, we will decide together where we go." His son shot him a startled glance, and received a look of permission and bittersweet farewell in return.

The younger Smith and the girl, Misi, clasped hands. They turned and looked at each other in a split second of perfect understanding.

"We go to Egypt with you," said Misi.

"Only the Goddess knows what kind of trouble you would get into without us," added Smith the Younger as a slight surge of red rose up his neck and to his cheeks. Misi snorted, and Kiyia looked abashed.

Yollo spoke with a ragged whisper, "You may not have to bury me just yet, but you are not shot of me as easily as that. We all go to Egypt, for only the Goddess knows what She has in store for us all." She reached for the hand of Smith the Elder, and squeezed it with more strength than seemed possible in one so recently delivered from the lifted veil to the Otherworld. "All of us, Guardian. We all have parts to play." She laid her head back down, but held Kiyia's gaze without breaking the stare.

Kiyia felt the world as she knew it turn upside down once again. *Captives taking charge and giving orders! What next? Puppies ruling the world?* She cleared her throat of some sudden obstruction and barked a few orders.

"Well, what are you all waiting for? Let's get ready to go and see what Egypt has in store for us!"

THE GREAT NORTH WOODS

We are high above a colorless sea, and the land that kisses it is the deep green and blue black of ancient trees. As we descend, we begin to see openings in the dense woods. Flashes of moonlight reflect off the snow and tiny slivers of brooks are threaded through like quicksilver. There. There is a grove of trees and a complex of wood and stone buildings nearby. The biggest building has walls of stone and a peaked slate roof. Around it are smaller dwellings shaped like beehives with thatch roofs and daub walls, each with tiny ribbons of smoke ascending through the center hole. Only one figure is moving, racing from a hut toward the Grove, along the path brilliant white with snow in this full moon light. We hear a high-pitched keening as she tears through the woods and falls at the foot of an enormous beech.

When Eiofachta came to she was huddled at the base of the Mother Tree in the Grove. She was in her sleep shift and shoeless, clasping the roots of the ancient tree as if she were drowning and it her life-rope. She felt hollowed out, and floating above the self that had tree bark and snow ground into her cheek. Gradually, quietly, the other Sisters of the Grove came to encircle her, standing solemn and still in the cold, damp night. *Who were they? Who was she? Where was she?*

She floated back into her body as those Sisters, the Priestesses of Nematona came into focus. In a clear, bright voice that carried to the back of the crowd she said, "The end of our time is coming…"

Soon they would know the details of the young seer's vision, but in their bones, they already knew it was true.

From among the crowd one woman, tall and graceful, stepped forward, and the others fell back like flower petals falling open to the ground. She was Alama, The First Among Equals, and Eiofachta's mentor. She had lived thirty-five circles of the sun, and had deep auburn hair, a long, high-bridged nose and sharp blue eyes that saw through fools. She had taken the time to wrap her thick green woolen cloak around her, but she was shoeless, and the snow stabbed tiny darts into her feet. She looked calmly at her protégé, the full moon light bouncing off the white ground making each detail day clear. She saw the young girl standing tall and reed thin, with her pale gray eyes, so pale as to be almost translucent, wide like owl wings. Eiofachta was a seer, they all knew that. She had the marks of the Goddess constellation on her left shoulder blade. But in the ten sun circles since she had been recognized at the age of four by the Crone Counsel, the youngster had seldom expressed any eagerness to prophesize. She would skip lessons, run and hide during ritual, and most frequently was found high in the branches talking to the trees, whispering in their language.

Many, many generations ago, the Shining Folk, the Fey had watched the emergence of the human people. They had seen and appreciated their curiosity and cunning, their capacity for generosity and creativity. But the Shining Folk had also witnessed the humans' rapacious movement through the world with little regard for the other living creatures. And so, with much deliberation, the Fey began a long-span strategy to protect all the living things. They approached and befriended certain human clans, and learned how to teach and love them. Eiofachta, like most of the priestesses here was a mix of Fey and human, a combination that allowed them to bridge the worlds and protect all the peoples of the Earth. But Eiofachta was more Fey than some, and she had avoided her seeing talents like a field of nettles.

This night's seeing had been forced upon the girl, Alama would swear to that. The girl was trembling from cold and vision and her skin seemed to shimmer with a light coating of sweat and moonlight. "Let's go into the Mother House and hear your telling," Alama said, voice pitched low and even. She felt as if she was calming a startled wild thing.

"I will tell you all I have seen," Eiofachta replied in a high thin tone. "But it must be told in the open so that the wind and the trees and the water hear it too. I cannot..." and her voice caught. She took a breath and continued with more force and strain. "I cannot speak of it in a structure made by people. It cannot be contained thus. And once spoken, I can never speak of it again."

The girl seemed to waver, edges dissolving, as if her body was disappearing. But she pulled energy from the Earth and her form solidified.

"Please, Mistress," she said, looking directly into Alama's eyes. "Please hear me here, witnessed by moon and starlight. Please."

And so, orders were given for stools and blankets to be fetched. And all of the Priestesses of Nematona settled in to hear how their Grove would be burned, their bodies plundered and their Goddess forgotten. It was visceral, this telling. Each woman felt the hands grabbing her flesh as the stench of smoke coated the back of her throat. They heard the sounds of horse hooves crushing the clay pots that held offerings. It would be the obliteration of sacred space in the memory of the living. The telling lasted till the first hints of mauve flushed up from the east.

At last Alama, First Among Equals spoke, "We have heard your vision and we believe you. But why must anyone go to Egypt? And why must it be you?"

Eiofachta's ears with the nibbled edges of the Fey were pink from cold and a sudden embarrassment. Why indeed? It must be done. Of that she was certain. But why must it be done by her? There were others, any of the others, truth be told, that were wiser, braver, and more reliable than she. She had shirked every ounce of training and discipline that had been offered her. And now, unequipped as she could see that she was, what could she say that would make the others see this truth? And where... and what was this Egypt?

"There is a way that all will not be lost," she said simply. "The Goddess said to me, *'You have been called'.*"

The women uttered a collective sigh. That was the wording from Nematona that all waited for. *'You have been called!'* Some of the priestesses had heard these words, some only longed for them. But as they rose stiffly to their feet they joined in one voice to reply, "And you shall answer!" With eyes closed, they joined hands in the circle around her, and began to sing together the song of praise to the Goddess.

Eiofachta took her opportunity, slipped out under their arms and back to her hut. There she put on her stoutest boots, wrapped a shawl around her head and took off on foot, heading south out of the village by herself.

When the paean was ended, the women raised their hands and opened their eyes, to see the circle was empty. Alama looked around and saw the girl's footsteps in the snow.

"Quickly! She's heading off on her own! By the Goddess, that child will be the death of me!"

The women gasped as one and all heads turned toward her. All faces ran pale as the snow at their feet. Her fellow priestesses huddled around her with tears streaming, but she gently pushed them back and ran to the Mother Tree. She felt her heart skip a beat as she placed the palms of both hands, her forehead, chest, and womb space against the Tree, sending out the message to all the forest and the Shining Folk who dwelled within.

"Watch out for Eiofachta, please! I am on my way."

) ○ (

Much later that day, Alama was sitting on her favorite horse, the sweet and brave chestnut roan that had been her companion and familiar for sixteen sun circles. With a spare horse for Eiofachta on the line and three horses following with food supplies and protective gear for the weather and sleeping, the convoy had been moving through the deep woods for several hours. Alama had dismounted periodically and greeted the Protector Tree of each section of forest. She had received updates through the trees on Eiofachta's progress and lack thereof. The girl had started off at a decent clip but had been slowing down and was, by the most recent report, stumbling and had lost her head shawl on a thorn branch. The light was thinning from its mid-winter short burst of brightness, and fat, wet snowflakes had started to stick to the roan's mane. The cold was inexorable.

So it was with a sigh of relief that was underlaid with exasperation, that Alama, with the lost head shawl in one hand, came around a bend in the path and saw the shivering bundle sitting on a fallen log with head bent. Her long thin legs poked out from beneath her tunic and her skin looked blue from cold. The girl started when she heard the muffled sound of hoof steps, and she glared at Alama with a mixture of defiance and relief. The snow and cold pressed all the sounds and shapes and colors of the forest into a heavy, dense blanket of sensation, and the trees sent out a chorus of gratitude.

Alama swung off the horse and her right shin, the one that she had broken last spring, complained at the sudden weight. She set about to make camp, unloading dry wood from one of the packhorses, and leading all the horses to the nearby stream for water. Within a short time, a fire was happily pushing back some of the cold and Alama had a pot with stew suspended over the flames. She sat, rubbing her shin bone and watched Eiofachta on the nearby log. The girl still sat, glaring at her mentor, but as the thin light became thinner, and the sound of the forest's night hunters could be heard, slushing through the snow banks, she finally gave up and moved closer to the fire. The pearly clouds filled with snow blocked the moonlight, and the small circle of heat and light was silent sentry against the dark. As the snow hit the fire it hissed and whispered like the ancestors telling a bedtime tale. The young girl resented the rescue and yet silently wept inside in gratitude.

A sense of shadows taking form, a compression of the very air, and then three of the Shining Folk stood at the edge of the light thrown by the small blaze. Startled, Alama and Eiofachta jumped up, took in the dress and deportment of their visitors, and fell to their knees. These were not just any three of the Fey, but clearly of the royal family, with cloaks made of rainbows and moss, and stars woven through their hair. They stood three across, but the woman in the center was the leader with an air of authority that defied question. She stood twice as tall as Alama with cinnamon hair that fell to the ground in ringlets and eyes that seemed to slip color from amber to green to black to deep blue as the flames threw shifting light.

"Much rests on your slender shoulders, Eiofachta, daughter," said the Queen in a voice simultaneously deep and childlike, *"and you will accept Alama's help, and will be gracious about it."*

The last was said with the barest hint of a smile. She leaned forward and placed a kiss like a benediction on each of their mouths. With that, the three Fey turned soundlessly, took one step away from the fire, and disappeared.

☽ ○ ☾

With the dawn, the two travelers began the painful process of moving fingers and toes in the frigid air. They had been warm enough in the bedding of furs and blankets, wrapped around limbs and wrapped around each other as close to the fire as they could safely lie. But food and hot tea would demand crawling from this cocoon, and flesh met snow as they inched into the day. Both Eiofachta and Alama were strangely quiet. Eiofachta because she never quite knew what to say to anyone, and Alama because the message she had received last night from the Fey had kept her wakeful all night and was foremost in her thoughts now. In that tiniest of moments between the Fey Queen's kiss and her disappearance, she had sent a message straight into Alama's mind, a knowing of what was to come.

One part of Alama, the human, of the Earth, pulsing blood part wanted to throw herself onto her mare and race back to the Grove and her community and her sanctuary of self. She felt her heart give several painful thumps. The horse, sensing her disquiet gave a soft wuffle, and Alama walked over to her and buried her face in the powerful and yielding neck. "Friend, friend, friend. I want to run!" The roan shifted her weight from leg to leg, ready to take off in the space of a heartbeat. She began to pick up the tremble that wafted from her human, the two old companions in a tight embrace of fear and fate. From the forest, a morning hymn to the rising sun began, sweet, tender, eternal. Gradually Alama and her horse settled, until both had found their center, their rightness in this time and in this life, their rightness in the fabric of all that was unfolding.

Eiofachta had been standing watching this silent interplay, aware on some level that the next few moments were profound in the path of events. She started singing along with the forest morning song, ever so softly under her breath. This time, this moment when the sun re-emerged and the day spun forward was one of her favorite suspended points of gratitude, points of gratitude strung throughout the day like drops of rain along a tree branch with rainbows of light trapped in each one. And it was whilst she was held, supported in this sacred moment, that Alama turned to her, with turquoise eyes flooded with a serenity that grasped and took the breath and said, "We move onward, toward your destiny, with a fullness of heart, and the kiss of the Fey Queen as our blessing. But right now," with a bittersweet smile, "it's food we need."

Eiofachta moved to stir up the embers and add fresh wood onto the fire, little fir twigs to catch quickly and slender apple and elder branches from the supplies Alama had brought. Soon tongues of flame reached upward and tendrils of warmth soothed her fingers. A quick reheating of last night's stew and water on the boil for elderberry and nettle tea. The girl looked to her mentor and saw none of the earlier anguish on the older woman's face, only calm steadiness. And with that return to normalcy, the girl's world settled as Alama combed her thick deep auburn hair into a braid and with a lifted eyebrow suggested that Eiofachta do the same with her tangled curls. A flash of irritation moved like thunderclouds across Eiofachta's face at what she took to be the implied criticism of her grooming.

"We need to hurry," she scowled at her mentor.

Alama sighed.

That day set the pattern of many to follow. The women rose early with the first promise of light, broke camp, and traveled farther and farther south. Whenever they entered a new section of forest, Alama dismounted with easy grace, settled the folds of her thick, green cloak and made acquaintance with the Protector Tree, asking for permission and protection in their journey. She would place both palms, forehead, heart and belly on the trunk and send her thoughts directly to the tree, while Eiofachta waited chuffishly on horseback.

"*Dear Protector. I am Alama of the Mother Grove. We humbly seek passage and succor in these woods.*"

"*Welcome, Alama. We have had word of your coming and will see you safely through.*"

The voice of each Protector Tree was singular, and yet there resided the undertones and overtones of all the trees connected to it. And every few hours the Fey folk would appear. Sometimes one clear figure swathed in moss and dew. Sometimes three vague forms comprised of shimmer and gossamer. And twice, five Fey holding court and passing along blessings and messages, "*The Mother Grove sends their love and wants to be sure you keep your feet dry, Alama.*" The voice of rocks and water and the Otherworld was amused. "*We have alerted the Fey of the oceans to be on the lookout for your arrival.*"

Every couple of days the constant and mutable songs of the forest would intensify until the specific song of a Grove came into focus. These Groves, scattered like the stars in the sky across the forest of this land, were all connected to the Mother Grove in allegiance and sisterhood. The priestesses in each Grove had spent time training at the Mother Grove before they were assigned a Sister Grove to love and serve. Whenever they heard a Grove song rising above the general chatter and murmurs of the trees, Alama would insist that they leave their path and detour to visit these Sister Groves. Eiofachta would grumble about time wasted, snapping like a hungry cur. At each Grove, priestesses eagerly sought Alama's counsel and blessings. She stood amongst them, tall and beautiful with hair glossy, the color of wild chestnuts, pulled back from her widow's peak, a woman in the prime of her power. She would gently kiss each woman and girl on the forehead before she and Eiofachta departed, and the trees would joyfully spread the news, "*The First Among Equals was here!*"

The spruce and larch of their northern woods gradually gave way to cedar and alder. The ground pack of snow disappeared, and the leaves that had fallen held the shimmer of summer sun and warmth in layers of vivid gold and russet along the forest floor. Occasionally Eiofachta would pause as they reached a fork in the path, tilt her head to the left as if listening, and lead her horse along the choice that led to their fate. Alama would follow.

The two women and their line of horses moved steadily south and east, being funneled through the forest into a deep gorge nestled between high limestone cliffs with caves sprinkled along like freckles. Thin strands of smoke rose from the caves, home to families and small clans of humans since the beginning of remembered time. The river that formed the gorge was wide, the color of granite, and no longer the frozen expanse it had been in their home part of the forest. With the chatter of non-migratory songbirds and the smell of thick and musty loam, the woods around them imprinted on their senses. This was a new and hauntingly beautiful wood, painfully different from home.

As the days passed, they began to talk, sporadically at first, and in an almost constant stream. Alama told the stories of their people and the Fey, the mysteries, the hidden wonders that would have been given to Eiofachta much later in her training if things had been as ordinary. The girl was only fourteen, but this was most definitely an extraordinary circumstance, so the transmission of wisdom continued. Eiofachta always acted as if she had no interest in the stories, with a mulish scowl on her face, but Alama patiently persevered.

"So, Rionach, the Queen of the Fey, chose a mate amongst the people. When her child was born, she delivered the babe to the man's village and commanded that the child live with the people for seven circles of the sun, and then with the Fey for seven circles and so on, and so on. This child, a girl child, Niose, became the first of the First Among Equals."

"When was this, Alama?" Eiofachta sounded eager to know.

"Far, far back in the mists. And then the Fey began to visit the people, and many babies were born, all with that same life arch of living in both worlds."

"Why do we now live only amongst the people? Can I go live with the Fey? I hear them... louder and louder..."

Alama's face lit briefly with a genuine happiness to be able to share this with the girl.

"This was their plan, that we be the Bridge between the Worlds. It is a gift, daughter, to hear them as well as you do."

"But it makes me so lonely," Eiofachta said wistfully. Then, in a sudden embarrassment, kicked her heels into her horse, raced ahead, and sped up their pace down the path.

Alama sighed and berated herself. She, the First Among Equals was a teacher, mentor, ritualist, and leader. Her role was to nurture and inspire. And here she was with this brilliant, prickly child who always seemed so tantalizingly out of reach. Alama wanted to like her, but she just couldn't. She could love Eiofachta as a child of the Goddess, but like her – that was proving to be, also, just out of reach.

$$\text{)} \bigcirc \text{(}$$

Their journey continued for a full moon-cycle. The bitter cold had gone, but each morning held a lingering fog that seeped deeper and deeper into their bones. Alama developed a cough that had a cloth-tearing sound. Her already pale face was becoming whiter and almost translucent. There were times when the simple action of saddling her horse left her short of breath, and she could feel her heart lurch against her ribs. She told fewer stories, and Eiofachta began to miss the sound of her voice that had become like a warm steady stream of honey through her soul. The independent feisty streak in Eiofachta's nature started emerging in small and petty ways, complaints, contrariness, like a feverish toddler. The girl totally refused any attempts at grooming, and her dun colored curls were forming long tails of snarls. She looked pinched, wan, bedraggled, and much younger than fourteen.

"It's too early to stop for the night! I want to keep going!"

Alama's body ached from the days on horseback and the pressure in her chest and the fear in her spirit. It was late in the short day but as was consistent with her nature, she responded with calm reasonableness.

"We can proceed for one more hand's breadth only. The horses will need to rest then." She broke out in a spell of rough coughing, and Eiofachta had a moment of guilt before she raced ahead, leaving Alama to follow slowly with the line of packhorses behind.

Little sun shone through the milky clouds, and the air was chilly and damp. The river was out of sight, but gradually, a sound like the distant stampede of big hooved beasts began to build and build to a roar. Alama came around a bend that took them slightly uphill and to the north. Eiofachta was there, standing next to her horse, gazing at the fierce, turbulent river before her. The water looked churned and whipped, shades of black and silver, with small chunks of ice tossed and thrust upward. Narrow branches and big logs crashed together. The distant bank was as accessible as the moon. Alama felt her heart give several stuttering thumps against her chest as Eiofachta turned to her, gray eyes wide and panicked, "We need to cross this river! I need to get across now!"

"Impossible, daughter. We can camp here and follow downstream tomorrow to find a ferry or a narrow crossing if you feel we must journey to the other side."

"No! Now!"

"Eiofachta, listen to me. It isn't safe here. We have followed this river for ten days. We can find a way to cross tomorrow." Alama felt her temper fray.

"No! It has to be now!"

The trees began to whimper and urge caution.

Alama shouted over the wall of sound from the river for the girl to step back from the edge of the riverbank. But all Eiofachta could hear was the voice of the vision like a swarming of bees, driving her forward with an urgency that precluded all sanity. She shook her head violently and her right foot slipped out from under her. In an eye blink, she was in the river and the cold squeezed all the air from her lungs. She twisted around with one arm to reach for Alama, to grasp for help, but the current had already pulled her downstream.

Without a moment of thought, Alama pressed her horse forward, down the short, slippery slope, and crashed into the river.

All was bone-snapping cold and screeching chaos. Alama struggled to stay on her horse as they were both swept down, crashing between branches and rocks, turned upstream and then down, like leaves on the water. It took every ounce of her waning strength to cling on to the reins. *"All the spirits of Water and Air! Help me!"*

She scanned the surface of the water for a hand, the girl's cloak. Nothing. Just the water and the rocks. Eiofachta was gone. Gone. Her heart lurched and she let out a wail, "Oh Goddess!"

The current rushed at them, sweeping them around the bend. Alama, shocked by the icy water was fighting to breathe. The roan struggled in vain to find its footing as Alama called the girl's name, over and over, her words swallowed by the thundering torrent. She scanned the river again and again to no avail. The girl was lost. Lost. And then as she scanned once more, she saw what at first seemed an eddy of debris caught behind a large branch... could it be? Yes, there was the tousled hair, matted like last year's straw. The girl's twig-thin arm was clinging to a broken branch barely attached to the tree above. The current pulled at them with fierceness like a mountain lion pulling at the legs of its prey. The horse finally found purchase under foot, and Alama fought their way to the struggling girl. With a final surge of effort, she reached out and hooked Eiofachta under the arm, pulling her up across the roan's back, belly down.

The three made their way up onto the narrow muddy bank, shivering and gasping. The two women slid off the horse and Eiofachta fell to her knees into the mud. Alama stood and turned slowly, looking at the trees in exquisite detail, seeing the Fey standing in their multitudes, all watching them with boundless affection. In that moment, she heard a loud internal pop as all other sounds disappeared. The great vessel leading from her heart ruptured, and she felt split apart by the beauty of the worlds. As her body spiraled down and her spirit spiraled up, she rejoiced, *"In deepest gratitude. In deepest gratitude. In deepest gratitude."*

The trees began to sing the great Song of Passing, building in crescendo as the message passed through all the forest. The Fey built on this song and added their paean to the First Among Equals, sung only at moments like this. The beauty of the music lifted Alama's soul and, as had been foretold, she was enfolded into the realm of the Fey.

Eiofachta wailed and wailed like a wounded animal, as the chestnut roan wept.

THE SONGS FROM THE STARS

Below us is the Middle Sea, and from this distance she looks like an opal in a verdigris setting. The specks of color in the opal are islands, and one island is a pebble kicked off the toe of the foot-shaped landmass. We swoop in closer to see the bands of bronze and green, ribbons of grapes and grains that circle the island created by the terracing of humans. Above them rests a ring of fog perpetual. Atop the central mountain, like the nipple of the Goddess' breast, is a round building of huge stones rippled with quartz and aquamarine. In the rounded dome that spans the building an opening like an eye, lined with pure quartz, is aligned with the east-southeast horizon. We see six figures streaming toward the central building as if pulled by a magnet, soft lavender robes flowing behind them. All six are singing a single tone, high and fraught.

"Ni Me!"

As the six sisters ran into the observatory the single tone became the two tones of her name.

"Ni Me!"

The seventh sister, Ni Me, was crumpled on the floor with one arm thrown over her head. The enormity of what she had just seen had overthrown her consciousness. As the others encircled her, she began to stir and her eyelids fluttered. The air was thick with the smoke from the candle that she had knocked over as she fell and the layers of myrrh and spikenard from the incense brazier. Beeswax candles were clustered near the Observer's chair, where each sister took turns to receive and interpret the information that came in from the Mother World. The room filled with the tones of their language as they helped Ni Me up to sitting and brushed her pure white hair back from her face.

Like her sisters, Ni Me was pale and long of bone and face. They all possessed the amber eyes of their people with hair that ranged from gray to white to tawny, pale gold. The humans who lived on this island thought them beautiful and divine. The Seven Sisters never disavowed them of that opinion, for it served their purposes to be held in esteem and have their needs tended to. Over the past millennia, there had always been Seven Sisters on this island to watch the humans, report their development and receive their instructions from the Mother World. Every seven years a new Seven arrived, and the women they replaced could decide to stay on Earth or return home. Most went home, but every cycle one or two walked down the mountain to the villages below and began their lives as people of the Earth. They were drawn by the exquisite beauty and endearing innocence of this Earth. These women never divulged their origins, never shared the secrets that lay beyond the ring of fog perpetual. But with mystery and glamoury they joined the human families. Throughout the centuries, the humans of Malta had acquired height and fair hair, and those disturbing amber eyes. They excelled at astronomical navigation and higher mathematics, and their language held a particular tonal quality that made them sound like they were singing all the time. And the people below the mountain continued to revere the Seven at the peak.

On the wall opposite the entrance the symbols in the quartz wall were startlingly bright and frantic as they raced over the surface. The eldest of the Seven, called Ni Ma here on Earth, stood and raced over to the wall. Her eyes flicked back and forth, trying to keep up with the information and data as it skittered across the receptor wall. In their language of tone and pitch she began to report the news. One by one the other Sisters stood and moved, as if floating, over to join her. One Sister lifted Ni Me up from the ground and held her by the elbow to steady her.

The details of the nightmare that had been visited on the twelve other chosen women all over the Earth were spun out. There would be hordes of ravaging men. There would be total destruction of the

Forest Houses and Goddess Temples. The very names of the Goddesses would be wiped from human memory. And the deities of war and punishment and anger would arise.

"This is what we have known would come, Sisters. This is the beginning of the end of this era. We should begin to collect our things and deconstruct this place before our transport arrives to take us home."

Ni Ma, as the eldest, was used to having her statements taken as fact with little or no discussion. But tonight, she was shaken by the sudden and strident arguments and distress of her Sisters. They had indeed always known that this day would come. This is why their ancestors had built an Observatory over two thousand Earth years ago: to be able to watch the humans and plot their evolution. It had been foretold that the tides would turn, that gods would overtake goddesses, that the Great Mother would be subsumed.

But what the Wise Ones at home in the Pleiades had neglected to take into account was that after watching these creatures for two thousand years the Seven Sisters had slowly developed a liking for them. Each new tour of Sisters grew more and more fond of the little ones. And as some of their Sisters had mated with them, the humans had actually become intelligent and capable of higher thought. This team of Sisters heard the call from the nightmare vision. They heard the appeal for help. And they wanted to answer.

Throughout the rest of the night they argued. Two camps emerged. Ni Ma and her confidante, Ni Mou, were fervent in the need to hurry and leave before the darkness fell. The other five wanted just as fervently to follow the call for help, and go to Egypt to assist their human sisters in an attempt to save something of what was now so beautiful.

As the light of dawn spilled peach and violet into the Observatory no way to compromise had been found, so the five, Ni Mae, Ni Me, Ni Mi, Ni Mo, Ni Mu, their names an ascending pentatonic scale, pleaded one last time.

"They need us to complete the circle!" Ni Me insisted. "Without all the wisdoms coming together they can never make a spell strong enough to last this destruction. Five thousand years must be endured."

Her voice was tight and raw from the hours of talking round and round. The quietest of the Sisters, Ni Mu, had spoken very little in this battle. She shared her thoughts very sparingly, but when she spoke the others listened with respect. She gently cleared her throat and silence fell.

"If our Wise Ones sent us here two thousand years ago only to observe we would never have been allowed to interact or stay or mate or live amongst the humans. Our presence has changed this world. We cannot now pretend we have no responsibility for what befalls the Earth."

There was a small yet profound silent click as the Sisters came into alignment. Their hearts rested as they came into agreement, for discord among them was physically painful. As one, they stood and moved, gliding out of the Observatory and down the mountain through the ring of fog perpetual, to the villages below to speak the truth of who they were for the very first time. Ni Me stayed behind to send the message to the Mother World that the Seven Sisters, now the Seven Daughters of the Earth, would be breaking protocol, disobeying orders, and remaining on Earth.

$$\text{☽ ○ ☾}$$

Over the next moon cycle there was a constant flow of activity between the villages and the mountain peak. Earlier Sisters who now lived below and the descendants of others from ages past came up to the Observatory to begin to take over the tasks of maintenance and observation. There were elaborate plans for the methods by which the present Observatory would need to be covered over in four hundred years to establish the correct elevation to be able to continue communicating with the Mother World. Star charts were made to explain how the orientation of the Observatory would need to be shifted by three degrees to adjust for the changes in the planetary positions.

Hours and hours were spent in often tense consultation with the humans of Malta who had actually left the island and had knowledge of the world around them. The Seven were taught the human language, the common tongue, to be able to communicate with outsiders. Much discussion was given as to how the Seven should act and dress. Should they present themselves as divine? Should their origin be revealed? Should they wear the diaphanous robes of Mother World fabric or subject themselves to the scratchy coarse linen that humans wore? The Seven and their allies, both human and Pleiadian, were grappling with the tumult these changes would make in their lives. Now that the secret was out, no more groups of Seven would be arriving from the Mother World. That had been made excruciatingly clear by the fury of the Mother World's response to their disobedience. The humans were now going to have to maintain the connection to the Pleiades. And these Seven were now Earth-bound; there was no going home for them.

At the end of one particularly trying day, Ni Me sat on the hillside looking out at the Middle Sea. She saw the boats in the harbor and wondered on which one they would sail. The sky was hazy and the sun barely visible, but Ni Me knew it was close to sunset. The air held a threat of rain as she pulled a thin branch of rosemary through her fingers. This task before them was laden with uncertainty and danger. No Seven Sister had ever left this island. The knowing that she had felt in her bones of the rightness of their mission now was ephemeral and as distant as the smell of hyssop and rue in the spring meadows.

She heard a sound behind her and a woman came to lower herself down beside her with a small exhalation of effort and pain. She was an Atchi. This was the honorific for *big sister* on the Mother World and the name given to all the Sisters who had remained on Earth when their tour was over.

"You look troubled, Sister." And the Atchi put her gnarled hand on Ni Me's. "May I give you a blessing?"

With that the Atchi took a small handful of soil, mixed it with the rosemary, and blew her breath into it. She leaned over and anointed Ni Me's forehead between her eyebrows, the site of true seeing, "You are blessed by this Earth and the Goddesses who live on and in Her. May your journey and your task be wrapped in golden light. May you live forever in the memories of all the daughters of the Earth."

Ni Me leaned into the crook of the Atchi's shoulder and silently and completely fell apart.

ON THE BEACH

A nother moon had turned and was at the half by the time all the preparations had been made for their departure. The Seven Daughters of the Earth had, after exhaustive discussion, decided to continue wearing their pale lavender robes. They stood on the pebbly beach waiting to board their ship. Seven robes pushed backward by the wind. Seven billowing heads of hair like strands of silver and moonlight. Seven voices entwined in song, bidding farewell to this island and beseeching good fortune from the Sea Goddesses. Their song was an orison for intercession and protection. It wove together with the sounds of waves and wind and gulls till the island itself began to hum and vibrate, lifting up inches higher than before. The crowd behind the Seven, a sickle moon shaped cluster of former Sisters, the Atchis, and their descendants joined in the song. The music rose and rose. The island rose and rose as well, pulling the sea toward it.

It was in the midst of this thrall that a small fishing craft with one sail floated silently into the shallow bay. On board were two weathered fisherman with eyes wide at the world of sound they had sailed into, and a young woman with dusk colored hair and enormous pale gray eyes. She had deep mauve shadows under those sad eyes, and seemed to be wrapped in a cloak of grief so profound that she barely noticed that they had arrived.

The song built to its final crescendo as the small boat's bottom met the sand. The three in the boat waited, hesitant, unsure of the protocol and of their welcome. As the song ended and the island settled down like a broody hen to its original position, the waves kicked up in response and turned the small boat over, tipping its inhabitants into the water.

The Seven Daughters of the Earth turned as one and looked, silent now, at the upturned craft and the three humans standing bedraggled in the shallows. With all of her dignity and most of her hope lost, the girl staggered against the waves, and standing thigh deep began to sing her own song, the song of her forest, the song of the Fey, the song of her loss and the ones who have crossed over. It was bitter and beautiful, this song, and tears ran unchecked down the girl's wind and sun-roughened cheeks. This girl, Eiofachta from the Land of Nematona and the Mother Grove, was only a half moon cycle older than when she had suffered the loss of her mentor and friend, Alama. But she felt eons older, brittle in bone and weary in heart. She poured all of her pain into her song as she held herself up for inspection by these women.

The Seven listened, and began to add their voices in harmony and descant. The girl's song was transmuted into the song of all pain, of all loss, of all human frailty. The former Sisters, their descendants and all the humans scattered along the beach wept, and the world added its tears as a soft rain sifted down from the low-lying clouds. Time stretched and suspended until those sounds rippled out across the island, across the water, to all other bodies of water. And the Earth felt grief.

Ni Me stepped forward, and in the common tongue said, "Welcome, little one. Your message of suffering has been heard. How may we ease your pain?"

The girl seemed to wake from her sorrow dream, focused on the very tall woman with arresting amber eyes before her. The shallow waves knocked her forward. She staggered, found her footing and then walked up onto the beach. She trembled from cold or trepidation. "I beg you… take me to Egypt!" And she melted down onto her knees with hands outstretched, only sheer will holding her together.

Women surrounded her, enfolded her, like the wings of a giant bird closing around her. They lifted her gently and brought her farther up the beach to a place where a fire had been built. With a look to the tide and a quick reappraisal of time, Ni Ma, the leader of the Seven, softly gave orders for the ship to be secured till the next outgoing tide. The Seven would wait until this girl's story had been heard, and then the sea could pull them on their way.

It was just past midday, but the sun was weak and the light rain had left a chill. More branches, driftwood and wind-gnarled juniper, were piled onto the fire, as the Seven, their relations and then the outer ring of humans all settled in like wave after wave of migratory birds, to hear the story of this wan woman-child.

The girl had layers of clothing, tunics of different lengths, leggings and scarves of browns and tan. Over it all she wore a deep green woolen cloak that was a bit too long for her, and dragged along on the beach with stain upon stain of seawater and mud and leaf mold. Her hair was brown and gold, like the scales of a mountain trout, with long snarled tails pulled back into a single cable down her back. She smelled of sweat and sea, and horse, and mourning. She started to speak and her voice was parched. Someone handed her a cup of sweet water that she took with a quick upward flash of gratitude in light gray eyes. Again, she began to speak.

"My name is Eiofachta. I come from the Great North Woods and the Mother Grove in the land of Nematona. On the Solstice, at the full moon I had a vision…"

She told the story of the same nightmare vision that had been visited on Ni Me, and which had precipitated all of the tumultuous and unequivocal decisions and changes here on Malta. Of how she had swept, thoughtless, down the path to Egypt without plan or provisions or permission. She told of her mentor, the First Among Equals, Alama who had been her companion and guardian. Of how she had bucked and kicked and resented Alama's help and wisdom, until, too late, she discovered that the older woman had been her friend, and like a mother she had never truly known. She shared with deep sorrow how Alama had sacrificed her very life to save Eiofachta's. And how with her passing, the raw hole in Eiofachta's heart seemed to pump out her own life's blood and will. About how she had stood by as the flesh that had been Alama was absorbed by the very trees of the forest as they sang her praises. And how then she, Eiofachta, pummeled by grief, had sent Alama's chestnut roan back to the Mother Grove as she had continued down south and east to the Middle Sea, trading her horses for passage in this fishing boat, whipped forward constantly by the voice of the vision driving her here and to Egypt.

As she ended her story, she looked into the eyes of each of the Seven, with their long, sculpted, alabaster faces and identical amber eyes.

"I hate everything about this vision and the destruction it has wrought. But the best woman I have ever known gave her life so I could do this. I know... how do I know?" and with a head shake she continued, "I know that you plan to go to Egypt. Yes? Is this your madness, too? I humbly ask if I may accompany you. And if you deny me, as is your right, oh Goddess, I am a curse to those who love me. If you deny me, I will walk into the sea and let it do with me as it will."

The girl looked down into the flames, flashing blue from the driftwood, and all her will deserted her. The Seven started talking, singing over each other in their home language, the language of tone and pitch.

"We never said we would travel with humans!"

"She has seen the vision! She is called!"

"This entire endeavor is benighted; she says herself she is a curse. Let her find her own way."

"And she smells even worse than most humans."

"But she has been given the vision!"

The arguments waged on. The girl barely heard them. To her it was like being in a swarm of songbirds, and she only wanted to collapse onto the beach and escape into sleep.

The singing continued and Eiofachta fell into a daze, lulled by the warmth of the fire and the release of confessing her story. She saw snippets of faces and places. The look in Alama's eyes when she told the old stories. The smell of hearth fire smoke slipping out of thatched roofs in the Mother Grove. The feel of the Fey Queen's kiss on her lips, and the sight of her, tall and glorious with the wisdom of her world in those constantly changing eyes. The sound of keening trees and a weeping roan mare. With that, Eiofachta came to with a start. She sat upright and noticed that the singing women were now silent and staring at her with preternatural intensity.

"We have heard you, little one, and considered your request," Ni Me said in the slightly singsong accent of her common tongue. "As you said, this is, indeed, our madness too. We too have wrought destruction, the end of our ways and the way home. We will take you with us, little one, and let the vision whip us all forward into what may come. But first, as we wait on the tides, you must have a bath."

And with that, the Seven and the Atchis and their descendants swept her up to the village and the bathhouse, and the next stage of her journey. She acquiesced with good grace, letting her tattered clothing be stripped away, only clinging to the deep green cloak that had been Alama's.

JAGUAR TEMPLE

We sweep swiftly with the movement of the moon across the vast ocean. There are white lines of sea foam blown by westerly winds and the tiny dots of dolphin spouts leaping in the moonlight. We come to land. We come to the land known as Yucatan. The jungle is thick and impenetrable, rising up to mountains that look like giant green waves. Standing clear of the flat black night stands a complex of wood and reed huts around a four-sided monument of stone that rises higher than the highest tree. At its peak is a triangle of solid gold encircled with a massive serpent of emeralds and sapphires. Even the jungle is quiet in that sliver of time between the night hunters and the dawn. No sounds of speech or laughter or lovemaking. And then, a sound of fear.

Uxua was twitching in her sleep. Whimpers floated past her lips and hung in the frangipani-scented air. Her long brown thigh, draped over her lover's pelvis, twisted and contracted as if ready to run. Eyelids trembled and the whimpers deepened to growls, until she reared up from the waist and roared like a jungle cat. Her lover, a young man of extraordinary beauty but no head for alcohol barely stirred from his sleep. But her totem, the jaguar lying at the foot of the sleeping platform, was wide awake, on all four feet, with the black hair down his spine bristled up and green eyes wide.

Uxua, too, was now wide-awake. She was coated in a fine shimmer of sweat and breathing hard. The remnants of her nightmare clung to her like cobwebs. She peeled her thigh off the slumbering man beneath her with a slight sucking sound, and rolled to her feet, restless as the cat. The air was heavy with the vestiges of last night's rain and sweet with wet bark and nicotiana. Uxua paced around her hut, her footfalls soft on the rush mats. She heard the sounds of women's bodies slapping against wet leaves as they ran through the still black night toward her. Naked and glorious, the color of amber, she went to the doorway to meet her worried attendants.

"Exalted One!"

"Are you safe?"

"We heard you scream."

"Is there danger?"

Voices, still disembodied, rushed at her from the dark. Down the path from behind them, her brother Talo came running with a torch. He pushed past the frantic women and hurtled up the four steps of her hut. He stopped short when he saw Uxua and her jaguar framed in the door.

"Sister!"

As the flames of the torch threw jagged flashes of light across her face, he took a quick step back, stumbling down a step. The torch jerked, then steadied, and the women below saw Uxua, smooth and iridescent as if carved of wax. Her face a blank mask, her right hand rested on the jaguar's head, and the serpent tattoos that wound around her arms and torso looked as if rimmed in starlight. She was magnificent. She was the embodiment of Ix Chel.

And then she fainted.

Talo dropped the torch and caught his sister as darkness fell again with the spitting sound of the flames meeting the wet ground. She had fallen face forward and was half over his left shoulder with her feet on the step above. He struggled to keep hold of her body, slick and heavy as water. The confusion behind him quieted as he carried Uxua up into her hut, the jaguar matching him step for step. Several attendants hurried in, rushes were lit, and the barely conscious lover was unceremoniously rolled off the sleeping platform and bustled away.

Talo laid Uxua down on her bed as her eyelids fluttered. In the space of two heartbeats, she, the woman who was never less than totally in command, realized that she had been seen at her most vulnerable. The succession of awareness, embarrassment, humiliation, and rage flashed across her wide face and tightened the skin over the high arching cheek-bones. She lifted her head and shoulders to upright and the jaguar's low growl caused everyone to take a step back. Even Talo knew to sit back and pretend that nothing untoward had just happened.

"Water…" she struggled to push the word past her strangled throat. "Water!"

This second time the sound was firm with that sharp edge of imperiousness that was the norm. An attendant scurried forward with a cup, stopped short, and veered to the other side of the bed so as to not cross between Uxua and the jungle cat. Another woman brought a wrap to cover her lady's body but was brushed away with an abrupt gesture. And the jaguar, like a coiled river of muscle, jumped onto the bed and sat beside his lady facing the crowd. Now two sets of green eyes looked haughtily at those assembled as if daring a single one to say that anything out of the ordinary had happened. The silence held. And held. And held.

Finally, as if she had called them all there for the whim of a moment, Uxua cleared her throat and began the telling of a tale as absurd and horrifying as any of the monster stories told to children to get them to behave. Stories like the five-headed python that threatens to swallow the world, or the tiny evil forest spirits that eat children's feet if they wander off. This story had fire and destruction. It was an end of the world tale filled with abduction and slavery and a thing called snow. Uxua had retrieved her regal composure and told this with the slightly amused air she had when speaking to lesser mortals. But Talo, who sat at the bottom of her bed, could see how shallow his sister's breathing was, and how dilated her pupils were. He alone was not fooled by her performance. This was the first time since they were tiny children that he had ever seen his sister frightened. And that was enough to terrify him.

Talo was three minutes younger than Uxua, and had come with her when they were six sun cycles old to the Temple compound to be trained in temple arts. Their parents had been sad to see them go, but the honor of having not one but two children chosen, not to mention the substantial gift of land and gold, had softened the blow. Two children with the eyes of the jaguar, Goddess blessed and destined for a sacred life. The two children had been each other's safe haven in those early days at the Temple, and they remained each other's confidants and best friends. When Uxua had been selected as the next High Priestess, only Talo had seen her cry when the ceremonial tattoos were applied. Only Talo had held her when the sacred plants made her wretch. And only Talo knew that she often felt lonely and caged. To the rest of the world she was Uxua, the Exalted One, the living Goddess Ix Chel. She was short tempered and sharp. She could win a heart with a half-smile. She would choose a lover with a crook of her finger, and not notice how broken he was when she dismissed him. She would remember an attendant's sick parent and send special medicines. She was unpredictable and tempestuous. She was adored.

Uxua finished her story with a tiny shudder and waved them all away with her hands. As everyone moved to leave the hut, she motioned to Talo to stay behind.

Brother and sister looked as alike as twins could look. Tall and lean, they had skin the color of hammered bronze with high, wide foreheads and full lower lips. Their hair, soft and slightly waving, the color of raven's wings, fell down to their waists. They walked alike with a roll and a grace from thousands of hours spent in temple dance. He now stood a head taller with a nose slightly marred by being broken in combat training. She now had furrows at the bridge of her nose from frustration and the weight of command. Talo's strength of body was met by Uxua's strength of will. Together they were an insurmountable force.

Talo waited till all the others had left and then moved up on the bed with his sister. The woman, the man, and the cat filled the bed with curved spines and flowing hair looking like fern fronds at water's edge. The night quieted again, and all three creatures relaxed. As his flushed face softened, the starburst pattern of ceremonial dots on Talo's face looked stark against his skin. And with the flickering of the light from the rush torches, the snakes on Uxua appeared to move and writhe gently with her breath. In this time before dawn the air was thick and damp with little breeze and the mixture of orchids and musk and rain clung to the bedcovers.

"Brother, I am frightened," she whispered the words even though no one else could hear, as if to say the thoughts aloud would be the final sign of weakness.

"We are together, sister. We will always be together."

The twins talked until the raucous sounds of first light birds made speaking a challenge. Their plans were made. Talo sat on the edge of the bed until Uxua finally drifted off to sleep, and the jaguar's eyes slipped half closed. And then he went to set everything in motion.

$$☽ ◯ ☾$$

Three days later a procession left the Temple compound and headed toward the ocean. There was a ship already loaded with provisions and casks of fresh water, waiting for them to leave at the tide. The chanting followed them through the jungle as they wound their way down through the green sea of trees and vines. This fecund world of wet and heat and sound wrapped around them and they breathed it in deeply. There were women attendants and sailors alongside the phalanx of male warriors deemed necessary for such a journey into the unknown. At the head of the procession walked the jaguar with Uxua on his back and Talo striding beside. The gold of their head-pieces struck sunlight as they emerged from the jungle to the beach. With one last look over her shoulder, Uxua could see the top of the Temple pyramid with its pinnacle flashing gold in the sunlight. She turned to her brother with a spark of panic in her eyes.

"Talo, do you think there is anything so magnificent in Egypt?"

THE WILD SPACES OF EIRU

We see an island below with projections of land to the south and west like the fat toes of babies' feet. The southern-most toe is covered with deep purple shreds of clouds. As we move lower, we see a patchwork of pewter and green with mountains marked by the veins of streams flowing to the sharped-edged sea. At the end of a spit of rock-strewn jumble there is a figure leaning way out over the water as if not bound by the laws of gravity, poised on one foot, the other foot lifted like a heron. Her long hair of amber and white and her cloak of the same colors are shot back away from her face and body by the eternal wind. A strangled, breathless, wheeze-like scream spins thinly from her mouth. We see the back and lower legs of a man crouched on his knees behind her, clasping onto her hem, and a massive silver wolfhound behind him with teeth clenching the hem of the man's tunic. All the figures are motionless, pummeled by sea spray.

"Mistress! Mistress!"

The young man gentled his tone to the one used to calm a runaway horse. He was lean and well-knit with chestnut curls plastered to his skull by the wave mist. His hands clenched tightly onto the bottom of her tunic, and a fine tremor ran through his body, as if she were ground lightning and he was unable to let go. "Mistress!" he tried again.

"What?"

And she snapped as if that was not a question, but rather an expression of annoyance. Gradually the pinprick focus of her eyes widened, she felt the sting of the spray and began to wobble. The sniff of soldered bronze that always accompanied her walking dreams stung the back of her nostrils. And bit by bit she came back to herself, to being Badh, the Keeper of Wild Spaces. She slowly placed her right foot down on the uneven surface, and it landed on a lower rock. She staggered, and found herself unhappily on her bottom, tugged rudely backwards by that confounded boy.

It was still dark with the only light coming from the setting moon and the stars slipping away as dawn crept closer. She could hear his ragged breathing, and realized that it wasn't just the rocks she sat on, but also his fists, that were still retaining a death grip on her tunic. He connected those thoughts at the same time, and they both scrambled to pull flesh away from flesh. His cold fingers, and her chilled bottom. The contact brought a brushfire of red up to his face and she made a rumble of inarticulate sounds that expressed the melt of desire, the stab of rock into her right knee and a bit of her hair blown into her open mouth and down her throat.

As she jerked backward, frighteningly too close to the edge, Domnhu, that confounded boy, grabbed her again, this time by the wrist and stopped her inelegant descent into the bay. They sat for a time, staring at the other, as the light went pearly to the east. She saw him with his tawny eyes and the blush slowly fading from his cheeks stippled with the reddish bristle of a night's beard growth. His rough spun tunic with its stripes of dun and moss was drenched. He, like she, was shoeless, and the intelligence that he often shaded was blazing straight at her. Bit by bit, her dream became a separate and observable thing, no longer her, but a thing apart.

Her eyes shot sideways and she grudgingly said, "I believe I have you to thank for me not being swept out to sea right now."

He let go the breath he hadn't known he was holding. He had heard her leave her hut and followed softly behind, hoping that she wasn't just going to relieve herself. That had happened one time too often and his ears still burned from the tongue-lashings she had given him. But it was his job, his sacred charge, to guard and protect her. And if that meant standing back and hearing her make water in the distance, he would do that gladly. He had come here to this wind-blasted place two sun circles ago. He was the next in the long line of young men from his clan that went up into the mountains when the scarlet banner was sighted. She flew that banner when she was bored with her latest attendant, when she had seen the young fellow flinch one too many times at one of her diatribes. The banner flew sometimes once, sometimes twice and on a few occasions had flown three times in one sun circle. Badh's patience was a scarce commodity.

For fifty-five circles of the sun, the men of the Bearana clan had served the Goddess who lived amongst them, and had come home with stories to tell. Domnhu had lasted longer than any of the others. He stood fast against her legendary temper. He was like a sword in the forge, heated, tempered, and heated again, each time made stronger and more adept. She was puzzled by his tenacity, and intrigued by his perspicacity. He guarded and served, and she had, for once, let someone into her sphere. She found herself astounded that she actually cared about his wellbeing, that she watched to see if he enjoyed the roasted rabbit she had snared, that she was more and more aware of where he was. And she worked very hard to make sure he never knew that.

Tonight had been one of 'those times' that he had been warned about. Those times when she was taken by spirits and led to a vision. When she dreamwalked she had no sense of her safety or whereabouts. One time he had steered her to safety at the last minute as she went to step directly into the Beltaine fire. And another, when he had first come to her and was not as attuned to the sounds of her night movements, he had lost her for a day and a half. When he finally found her atop Beara Mountain, he swore he had lost years off his life from fright. He had been covered with burrs; his leggings were torn in five places, and a spider web collection of gashes spread across his face from the blackberry bushes he had crawled though. She, of course, looked no worse for wear. She was, as always, fierce and wild with windswept streaks the colors of all the metals of the Earth in her hair. She was hawk-eyed and knife-edged of cheekbone, she was timeless and sensual and ancient and vital. And he loved her with all of his heart.

"Mistress, where was the dream taking you?" Domnhu had found that if he asked little, simple questions after a dreamwalk, Badh would, bit by bit, gather her pieces together, and a narrative of the vision would emerge. After that she was usually starving. With some thought to what food would make a quick breakfast in the back of his mind, he realized he had missed what she just said. "You're going where?" he asked.

"Egypt," she replied.

$$\text{☽ ○ ☾}$$

A few lines of the sundial later, after a quickly cobbled meal of brose and venison jerky, Badh was feeling more coherent and in control. She rummaged around in her hut, grabbing clothing and stockings, shoving them into her bag. Domnhu stood at the door of the hut with a stubborn set to his shoulders, his bag already packed. "I'm coming with you," he said firmly for the fourth time.

"I am Badh, daughter of the Goddess Cailleach. I who was found at three days old draped in the caul, standing upright in a tidal pool, created by the union of Sea and Mountain – I am sovereign. I need no man when I say I need no man!" She shot a lethal look over her left shoulder and returned to forcing more clothing into the bag.

"It is as you say, Mistress. But I am coming with you."

With another inarticulate sound, this one of fierce wave meeting hard rock, she slung the bag across her shoulder, picked up her bow and quiver, shoved the small sword into her boot, and stormed out of the hut with the giant dog right on her heels, toward the bay to the east where she would find a sea-worthy curricle.

Three steps behind, Domnhu had provisions and cooking gear, along with the treated hide to protect them from rain as they slept, his bag of clothing, the waxed bundle of fire-starting kindling, dried wool and moss, the blankets, the rope-secured double handful of extra arrows, his treasured small harp, and Badh's cloak that she always said she didn't need but would be grateful for once at sea, all strapped to his back.

Halfway to the bay she turned on a heel, glared at him and said with quiet venom, "I don't need a man to accompany me, now, or ever."

Domnhu took a tight, quick breath and replied, "It is as you say, Mistress. But I am coming with you."

Badh whipped back face forward, and with an inarticulate sound that combined resignation and a sweet secret surprise, she headed down the slope to the waiting sea.

"I suppose you may be useful."

Three steps behind, Domnhu's face lit with a quicksilver smile that swept across like clouds moving rapidly across a hillside.

The path sloped down quickly for another half mile as the sun held position a quarter way up the sky. The small bay had a sickle moon shaped beach of silver sand and a few small fishing curraghs. A handful of Domnhu's clan folk stood staring at Badh, and then fell to their knees. One amongst them, a short, burly man who had once served Badh many sun circles past, stepped forward. Badh vaguely remembered him, not by name, but as the one that chewed with his mouth open.

"Mistress, how may we assist you?" His eyebrows grazed his hairline. This had never been seen before: the Keeper of Wild Spaces, here, like a person.

BECALMED

*T*he ship carrying Uxua and her brother Talo toward their unknown fate in the land of Egypt had been becalmed for several days. As long as they had moved steadily north-eastward Uxua and her companion jaguar had held their impatience barely under the surface. They paced the deck for hours of a day, like two black lightning bolts striding back and forth across the wooden planks. Sailors, warriors, attendants, all moved forward and back like billowing clouds to make way for the pair.

The ship was long and broad in the middle with a raised deck in the back and the wheel for steering. Stairs there led below decks and to the prime cabin, normally reserved for pilots, but on this trip the resting spot for Uxua, Talo, and the jaguar. One sail fore, two midship and one sail aft meant she could take full advantage of the winds that blew consistently from southwest to northeast. The normal trade routes hugged the southernmost edge of the prevailing winds to take goods back and forth to Africa. For this journey, the pilot was leaning on the northern side to steer to their first stop: the island of Atlantia.

The wind had been steady and warm for a moon cycle and half. But then, at the waxing half moon, the breeze had stopped suddenly. The constant accompanying rumble of wind in sails had become the silence of the deaf and the benumbing sensation of forward motion disappeared. The ship rocked uneasily side to side with the swells that rolled through waters of oscillating turquoise and silver. The sun became relentless without the breeze to cool faces. Attendants and warriors made makeshift protection with long stretches of palm fronds and fabric, and sat for hours reading their fortunes with the small white cowrie shells used for divination. The smell of salted fish became stronger, as did the smell of bodies bereft of daily washing. One day passed, and then another. With each becalmed hour Uxua and her jaguar felt more and more trapped, more and more quick to snarl and snap.

On the third day of no progress Uxua's patience came to an end. Talo made the mistake of suggesting that she sit down and relax.

"RELAX!?"

The sound of raised voices was heard from the cabin where Uxua had gone to escape the worried eyes of her fellow travelers, alternating high-pitched, angry, edgy bursts with lower, marginally calmer grumbles. The two tones got louder and louder, and began to tumble over each other into a snarl of unmeant and soon to be regretted utterances until all was split by the scream of a very large and very black cat. The jaguar had had enough.

Talo erupted up the staircase and onto the deck. His normal countenance of calmness and slight bemusement was gone. Flushed and stern faced, he took long, angry strides to the front of the ship, and clenched the railing till his knuckles whitened and his forearms looked like tightly pulled ropes.

A few moments later Uxua came up the stairs looking uncharacteristically sheepish, and the jaguar at her heels refused to look up at his mistress. All the people on deck suddenly found their own feet extraordinarily interesting. Uxua took several deep breaths and walked quietly forward to stand next to her brother. She wore a thin, indigo, linen tunic that came to mid-thigh and her thick black waves of hair were scooped up on her head with some strands tumbling down her back like a waterfall. She looked regal as ever, but penitent in front of the only person to whom she ever felt apologetic.

"Talo?" she reached a tentative hand forward, hesitating to touch that attenuated arm. "Talo, please. It's this voice in my head. I can't shut it out. It's maddening and insistent. I need to be there, and I would whip up a hurricane to get me there faster if I could."

She rested her hand on his arm near his wrist, settling gently onto him like a leaf falling from a tree. Talo didn't reply, but gradually his arms relaxed and his fingers softened their death grip on the railing. Side by side the twins stood looking at the vast uninterrupted world of water, finding their rhythm together again, finding their solace within each other as they always had.

"I can't hear the voice that is driving you mad, but I can feel your pain. I may help you if you let me."

Talo let his eyes drift over to his sister's beloved face. The strain of her internal messenger was showing in fine lines between her eyes and a tightness around her mouth. This was his Uxua, born to laugh and give orders and sing praises to Ix Chel. It weighed on his heart that he couldn't carry this burden of hers. As his gaze swept forward again, he spotted something new on the horizon. A whale? A small outcrop of rocks? Talo shouted back to the pilot and pointed toward the small brown shape in the distance. Twelve sailors jumped to work the six pairs of oars, and the ship turned slightly to port to come up on the mystery bundle.

There, in the narrowing distance, rocked a small craft, a tiny boat shaped like a walnut shell. At first there didn't seem to be anything moving in the boat. But as they got closer Talo could make out three shapes. People? Dead? Sailors threw over the rope ladder and made their way down to secure the little boat. Yes, two people and a giant shaggy dog the size of a fallen tree, all lying on their sides and not responding to the shouts from above. Talo quickly slid down the ladder and reached into the little boat.

"They are breathing! All three! Send down more ropes!"

In quick order the three were harnessed and lifted aboard. Space was made on the deck for them. There was a woman of middle years with hair all the colors of the earth, a young man with chestnut curls plastered to his face, and a silver coursing dog with a long spare muzzle, a massive sprung chest, and giant feet. The humans were severely burnt from the sun and their clothes were torn. The young man had one boot, the woman had none. Their breaths were shallow, but the dog roused first with a small whimper and then, one eye peeling open, a muted yet convincing growl. Uxua knelt next to the hound and spoke only to him. She gestured for a shell with fresh water, and gently dripped liquid into the dog's mouth. With the wisdom of familiars, the dog, at his mistress' side, lifted his giant head and draped it over her belly. The woman's hand rose instinctively and stroked the salt-matted hair from eye to ear, *"Cu Cu Cu,"* came a thready sound from the woman.

The hound responded with a solid thump of massive tail upon the deck. Uxua leaned forward and gently lifted the woman's head, dripping water against cracked and bleeding lips. A sputter. A cough. And then lids pried open from salt-caked lashes, and Uxua was pierced with a look from deep blue eyes.

"The boy?" Again, the voice was thready, but this time with a color of imperiousness and in the common tongue. "Where is the confounded boy?"

An hour later the three wayfarers were seated, resting against cushions and leaning against the railing on the deck. All had been given water and mashed bananas, and the humans had had healing salve brushed gently on the burns across their faces and shoulders. The young man seemed the worst off. As the story of their journey emerged, the massive storm that had blown them far to the south, and the young man's insistence that the woman have their remaining water, the woman, Badh, kept giving tender glances and gentle touches to her young champion, Domnhu. He called her "Mistress", and she called him "confounded boy", but whatever their relationship had been before it clearly had transformed into mutual respect and love.

As the half moon rose in the east, man and dog curled around each other and drifted into sleep. The woman stood, and slowly, easily, pulled her body away from her protectors. She looked around the deck and found the object of her curiosity. She held the railing to steady her weak legs against the sideways tip from waves, and walked with deliberation toward Uxua and Talo, standing at the bow of the ship with the jaguar between them. There was still enough light that their features were clear, and they were gazing at the river of phosphorescence spreading in front of the ship. The jaguar heard the woman first, turned his sleek black head around, and stopped her in her tracks. Uxua and Talo turned as well and the woman, Badh, was lanced with three identical pairs of emerald eyes. She gave a shout of laughter, and the twins flashed identical mischievous smiles.

"That usually works to set the right tone," Uxua said. "It helps to instill an appropriate amount of awe in people. But you, my wandering friend, are not awed." Talo snorted a swallowed laugh, and the jaguar sat back on his haunches.

"Awe is tiring," Badh replied. "And not my natural state."

"That is what I had surmised."

"You and I have much to discuss, I think. As to our destination, and the forces that drive us there."

Uxua gave a nod of agreement.

"I am Badh, Keeper of Wild Spaces, daughter of the Goddess Cailleach, formed in the union of Sea and Mountain."

"And I am Uxua, the Exalted One, High Priestess and Living Embodiment of the Goddess Ix Chel."

The two women held each other's eyes, met and measured. A small half smile lit Uxua's face and a crinkling of laugh lines on Badh's gave proof of the recognition and acceptance each found in the other.

Talo stood stock still for a moment, and watched as the two women of power began to exchange the details of their visions and the nagging urgency that kept them going. He felt a strange and unfamiliar feeling in his gut. It moved, and rose, and felt like it was strangling him from the inside. He looked away and realized what had him gripped: jealousy!

As the two women reached and clasped forearms, the wind suddenly rushed, the sails filled fully, and they moved inexorably east.

$$) \bigcirc ($$

On the second day of full westerly wind since the rescue, a curious sight presented itself midship. Black jaguar and silver hound, now fully restored to health, stood nose to nose, their combined length taking up much of the ship's width. The cat's ears twitched and rotated, the hound's nose moved emphatically. All the humans on board stood breathless, waiting to see what might explode. What the people couldn't hear was the silent conversation taking place between the two familiars.

"I serve her, and she serves Her."

"As do I, and as does she."

"I am glorious. She says so."

"And I am magnificent. So says she."

The feline and canine versions of chuckles ensued as the hound pulled his hips back into play mode and the jaguar moved slinkily around him swiping his face with the long black tail. They raced and chased each other up and down the deck, narrowly missing a water barrel.

At the prow of the ship stood Badh and Uxua. Both women focused, looking into the rapidly advancing future, willing it to happen faster. Since arriving on board the night before, Badh had barely left this spot. She peripherally took in the movement of people and creatures behind her, and with brusque grace accepted the food and drink that was brought to her at regular intervals. She had slept a scant four hours, curled up next to Domnhu and her hound on the deck. But then, even before first light, she was back at the prow, leaning slightly forward, squinting into the fierce sunlight. Uxua had joined her with the sun a quarter way up in the sky, and they had stood in easy companionship ever since.

With the resilience of youth, Domnhu had woken with the sun, restored and happy. He had spent the hours since talking to Talo and everyone else on the ship. His grasp of the common tongue had been academic, but his open, friendly ways led to eager conversations. With each hour he became more fluent and more in command of his new surroundings. People simply liked Domnhu, as opposed to the imperious presence of his mistress. The folks on deck steered clear of her. He now wore a linen tunic of amber and orange gifted to him by Talo. The tunic picked up the colors of his hair and beard, and he shone with good health and good humor despite the patches of peeling skin on his cheeks.

With the hound and jaguar in full play, and the priestesses at the prow, Talo took the moment to ask Domnhu up to the back upper deck. Talo, bronze and beautiful like his sister, had a single frown line between his eyes. He gave Domnhu a tight smile, looked sideways toward the prow, and cleared his throat. "You travel with the Keeper of Wild Spaces. What is… are you kinsman, servant…?"

"What am I to her? Is that what you are asking?"

"Yes. Forgive my boldness."

Domnhu gave a short bark of laughter, "My good man, until you have spent time with Badh, the Keeper of Wild Spaces, you will not truly know boldness or rudeness. I am inured to it all."

The sweet smile with which he said these words softened any sting, and the underlying tone of tenderness with which he spoke her name gave Talo some of the answers he sought. "I am her servant, her protector unto death. I carry her water and firewood. I stand strong in the storms of her furies. Amongst my people, there is always one who serves the Keeper, and I am now he."

Talo took another pause and asked, "And how should we make *accommodations* for you? What is the protocol…?" He pursed his lips, blew out a strong breath and plunged ahead. "Do you sleep together?"

Domnhu blushed fiery red from throat to hairline, "When she says so." He kept a calm gaze, tawny eyes straight into Talo's emerald. "And you and your sister… how do *you* sleep?"

Talo felt mindless rage flood up and bunched his muscles to throttle the young man, until he saw the look of mischief and slight defiance in Domnhu's expression. *Ah, there it was. The meeting of power with resistance in the most civilized of ways.* The verbal swords had clashed, and held, poised with equal strength. They were, like the jaguar and hound, sniffing each other out and finding the other man not an enemy, but not a weakling either. Talo's eyes narrowed slightly and he replied.

"Ever so comfortably. And of such like minds that when we sleep, one of four eyes is always open."

Swords met and parried. Roles defined and territories marked. And so it was that with an unspoken yet fully understood camaraderie, the two men walked forward and stood flanking their priestesses. Badh acknowledged the comfort of Domnhu's presence with a slight sideways glance and a gentle bump shoulder to shoulder. She was wearing a tunic of Uxua's in magenta and rose that fell to her knees and gently covered her sunburnt arms. She had made what was for her a considerable effort to tame the hair that was tangled and snarled from the days at sea. This was a vision of Badh that Domnhu had never seen, dressed in rich colors, somewhat coiffed, and attempting moderate behavior. But the smile that raced across his face with brilliant sunlit power flashed and then was, wisely, wiped away before she could see it.

The two familiars, jaguar and hound, sensing a kind of power summit in the making, walked up behind and stood, easy and yet observant next to their women.

"We would like to offer you the hospitality of our ship as we make toward Atlantia," Uxua said. She spoke with the formality of one sovereign to another.

And with equal dignity Badh replied, "We gratefully accept."

With a snort of irreverence Domnhu exclaimed, "Thank the Goddess! I never want to see the inside of that pea-sized boat of ours again!"

Badh gave him a sharp elbow into his ribs and continued, "We hope to return the favor of generosity when we arrive in Atlantia, before we part ways." She gave a sour glance at their small curragh that was being pulled alongside the sailing ship. "Or," with feigned nonchalance, "perhaps we could travel together to this Egypt. If you would desire that."

Domnhu opened his mouth to speak again and received another, sharper elbow jab in the ribs for his trouble.

Uxua, understanding the need for her new acquaintance's dignity, graciously tipped her head and replied, "We would be very pleased to have company on this journey, wouldn't we, brother? New friends are always a treasure."

She smiled. Badh smiled. Talo lifted an eyebrow. And Domnhu exhaled in relief. With that settled and everyone's pride still intact, the two familiars resumed their silent conversation.

"My name is secret."

"As is mine."

"To know my name is to have power over me."

"This is true for me as well"

"Perhaps, one day, I will tell you my name."

The hound rubbed his muzzle against the great cat's ears. The jaguar purred like the rumble of the earth when it quakes. And the wind picked up even stronger as they flew toward the east.

THE WESTERN SHORE

Below us there is a vast sea of green. Jungle and highland rainforest and pulsing rivers erupting over massive falls. This is the womb of the Earth, the origin of all the peoples of the planet. There are millions of acres of savannah crossed by countless animals, herd after herd, moving and eating and dying in the womb of the Earth. A hundred shades of green roll like waves as we move with the moon, traversing from east to west on this longest night of the sun cycle. At the far western edge of this continent we see a string of fires, all along the coast like a strand of pearls. There the people are gathered to honor the sun as She starts Her journey northward on the horizon. Listen, the drums are calling. Powerful songs of the life of the people are pounded on the drums, rhythms of elephant feet, rhythms of women's heartbeats as they birth their babies, rhythms of the footsteps of migrations for food and survival. All of life, sung by the drums. At the meeting of ocean and land there are lines of dancers, priestesses, moved by the drum and by the very forces of life. And one figure stands alone.

Awa had lived her life of sixteen dry seasons in silence. Since her birth she could feel the drums in the soles of her feet and along the lines of her bones, but the sounds of the world were not hers to hear. She heard no sounds and made no sounds. She stood alone in a column of moonlight with the waves at her back, watching the lines of dancers as they spilled onto the beach and wound back into the grove of baobab trees. The night air was balmy with the tinge of citronella and geranium from the oils that made skin glisten in the heat. The women were singing; she saw their mouths moving in unison. Each line held a lineage, a family of priestesses, and each line had distinctive headdresses to mark their affiliation. One line of women had crowns of cowrie shells strung on sinew that made veils of small white dancing spirals over their faces. Another line had towers of ostrich feathers standing straight up from the top of their heads. The host lineage of this celebration, Awa's lineage, had turbans of lion skin, each with a lion tooth hanging over her forehead. Lineages from several day's journey away had gathered here to mark this night, this rare alignment of the power of the full moon and the poised southern-most sun.

Awa saw her grandmother, mother, aunties and sisters, the women of the lion turbans, make the circle around the statue of Yemaya so black that it absorbed all light, and begin the circuit again back into the trees. Her mother caught her eye and nodded her approval at Awa's vigil at the statue: since dance and song were not possible for her with the line of relations, she could be the witness, the guardian, the One Who Sees.

As soon as her mother and the others moved out of sight, Awa sank back into the shadows closer to the ocean, back away from the fires. Her skin was as black as the statue made from star rock fallen from the sky. The women told the story of how long before the memory of anyone living now, a sound like thunder had brought the flaming rock from the heavens to the shallows at their shore. Smoke and steam and mist rose up hundreds of feet as the rock's heat met the ocean's cool. When the mist had settled the people had run to see, and found the shiny, black form of Yemaya, as tall as three people, waiting in the sea foam. She had been sent for them, the meeting of Sky and Sea, the Mother of Life. Her statue had been placed here at the opening to the sacred baobab grove, and a vibrant city had evolved around Her. Priestesses, artisans, farmers, teachers, drummers... all were called to serve Yemaya.

Awa couldn't hear the drums or the songs, but she could hear the ancestor spirits that lived in the trees. She could converse with the spirits that swam in the waves. She alone of all the people could listen to Yemaya who spoke to the girl from Her statue. And as the dancing and drumming continued hour after hour, Awa had long conversations with them all.

"Hello, Baby Girl. You look so pretty tonight."

"Thank you, Great Grandfather. It is a beautiful night. Can you see the dancing?"

"I'm dead, Baby Girl, not blind!" Awa giggled in her silent way.

From time to time she moved back into the firelight as her grandmother's lineage wove its way back around the front of the statue so that her mother could see her, and as soon as the coast was clear, she slipped into shadow, tilted her head to the side like a small bird and picked up her conversations where she had left off. She was slender with small high breasts and long legs ending in elegant feet with high arches. She looked like the long-legged herons that fished the shallow edges of the lakes. She had the unbound hair of a maiden that fell in tiny ebony ringlets past her hips as it cascaded out the back of her lion skin turban. One of the lineage, and yet apart. One of the priestesses, and yet never a participant. She was like the shimmer of light at dusk that held form, and yet disappeared if you looked at it directly. She was liminal, of this world, and yet not. And that suited her just fine.

Another pass of her kin, another dodge back into the light of the fire, and then the blessed escape back into shadow.

"Yes, Great Grandmother, I know all the weaving patterns for our baskets. I'm not a ninny!" Awa giggled. Her ancestor was short of memory and asked her almost every other day how her basket weaving was coming along.

"Remember girl, just because we are dead doesn't mean we got any smarter," came the acerbic voice of her great aunt Soua. These two foremothers could do this gentle bicker all day and night, and she found them delightful. Their voices came from the closest tree, a palm that held dozens of ancestor spirits. It was Awa's favorite place to be and chat and escape from the demands of the hearing folk.

"She may not have been smart, but she sure was a beauty," came the dry, smoky voice of her great grandfather. Their love affair was legendary amongst Awa's family. *"Yes, quite a looker,"* he chuckled.

And a flutter of laughter floated from the tree.

Then the deep commanding voice of Yemaya came from the statue, "AWA! AWA! MARK ME!" The ancestors quieted and Awa turned to face the statue.

"AWA, YOU NEED TO SEE WHAT I WILL SHOW YOU. YOU. MUST. SEE!"

The Goddess sounded angry. No, not angry… afraid. Awa nodded and closed her almond eyes to be able to see better with her inner eye. Images began to flash through her mind, of swords used to kill women and children, of buildings toppled and burned, of their own statue of Yemaya pulled from its base and rolled out into the sea.

And the girl who had never made a sound before now screamed. She screamed and screamed and barely drew breath to scream again. The sound split the night and pierced through the drums. The singers faltered and stopped in their places. The scream went on and on till only shards of sound came through her throat. The women of her lineage came running to her, and still she screamed with only slivers of voice.

"TELL THEM!" Yemaya demanded.

And so, this thin reed of a woman-child who had never said a word in her life, began to speak in the voice of the Goddess with tones of molasses and cinders, in a voice that everyone could hear above the waves as she stood illuminated in a column of moonlight.

Awa finished the telling of Yemaya's tale with the dawn and collapsed exhausted into her mother's arms. The people sat silent on the beach under a muted sky like an abalone shell. The breeze had died down, and the sea was flat and calm with purple-tipped swells. The tide had gone out, and the damp sand smelled of sea grass and crab.

As the sun rose higher in the sky, the head women of all the lineages formed a circle to begin to deliberate what needed to be done. Yemaya had been clear that someone needed to travel east to the North Flowing River, the Naihl, and find the women of Isis. Traders had told of this place, but the journey would be harrowing. How would it be? By river? By sea? Overland? Awa burrowed deeper into her mother's lap as the discussion went on into the heat of the day, and the women were brought fish and fruit on palm frond plates.

Several times Awa tried to slip away, but the voice of Yemaya from the black rock pinned her to the spot, "STAY! THIS IS YOUR DESTINY!"

Awa would sit down quickly, slide back under her mother's arm and plot how to evade notice. Each time she tried, Yemaya would demand she stay. Finally, Awa stood and in a thin torn voice that was indeed her own, she shouted at the statue, "I don't want to go! Pick someone else! A hunter, a priestess, anyone but me!"

All talk stopped and the women began to stand, first a few, then in twos and threes, till they all were facing the statue of Yemaya. Awa kept pleading with the Goddess in her shattered fragment of voice, "Please, not me! Others *want* to go. Pick someone brave! Please!"

And all of those women began, for the very first time, to hear the voice of Yemaya inside their minds. This gift was a sad and heartbreaking one on this day. Finally, their Goddess speaks to them, and She tells them to send their wounded bird of a girl out into danger. The harder they resisted the idea, the louder Her voice became in their heads.

And so it was that two days later, Awa stood in the rear of the flat-bottomed boat with her mother at her side, watching the people on the shore grow smaller and smaller, hearing the voices of the ancestors who rested for all time in the baobab trees grow fainter and fainter, until finally, when all were out of sight and hearing, she turned to face what was coming.

Egypt.

☽ ○ ☾

For days now the flat-bottomed boat had traveled north along the coast, never going out of sight of the shore. The women and men using the long paddles and small sails were the fisher folk who knew these shallow waters and never strayed out into the deep. Awa and her mother, Ndeup, sat with their legs tucked to one side on the front bench, while the others sang to keep the rhythm of the oars. Awa watched their lips and arms work in concert, and felt her body dance forward and back as the pull of the boat forward was immediately followed by the rest and return. Forward and back, surge after surge, hour after hour. The plan for their journey was to follow the coast until they reached the ferry port of Cosimo, then to find a larger vessel to take them through the Straits of Gaia and into the Middle Sea. This was a sound, if vague plan, and relied on the bits of lore and sailor tales that had made their way down the western coast.

When they approached Cosimo their small ship was dwarfed by hundreds of bigger craft all snuggled into docks, like birds roosting on branches for the night. They worked their way into an empty slip, and the captain of the fishing boat swung herself up onto the dock and went to ask for information for the next leg of the trip. Awa and her mother took the opportunity to climb the small ladder and stand on solid ground, happy and disconcerted to feel no motion under their feet. It was late afternoon and the sun was edging into the horizon with swaths of pink and peach and lavender. The docks stretched in either direction and were swarming with people and goats and chickens. Awa felt the trembling in the wooden planks under her feet, and felt it mirrored in her ribcage with the trembling of her heart. She was buzzing with anticipation, had been since the night of Yemaya's revelations. She drank up every new smell, sight and sensation. The fragile woman child had emerged from her chrysalis, and strained to gobble up every aspect of the world. Her mind was now a quiet place without the constant stream of conversation with the ancestor spirits, and she inhaled color and tasted salt breeze avidly, moving like a puppy from one new experience to the next.

Ndeup was not a good sailor, and had suffered constant nausea even in the gentle swells of the near waters. Her face was ashy, and she couldn't decide if she wanted to weep or fall to her knees in gratitude that the world was stable, even momentarily.

"M'am Ndeup?" said the captain, a powerfully built woman in her thirties with a rolling gait and long ropes of hair that she wound around her head fastened with strands of seashells, looking concerned as she approached Awa and Ndeup. "M'am Ndeup, I fear you must change your plans. I just learned that at this time of year the currents are too strong to enter the Straits of Gaia from this direction. You must travel west and north to Atlantia over open water, and there you can find a ship that will carry you through to the Middle Sea."

"We have to go over deep water?" Ndeup asked with a rising inflection that reached toward panic. Awa, who had been awash in the colors of the sky, could feel the tension in her mother's arm and turned to read her face. "Water so wide we cannot see the land?"

And now panic had been reached, and Ndeup's breaths became fast and shallow. Awa lifted her hand and gently stroked her mother's cheek so that Ndeup turned to look at her daughter. After a lifetime of talking with gestures, Awa's hands flitted like quicksilver finches, asking questions, giving comfort, and bringing a small smile to her mother's face. "Mama, I swam in the deep waters of your womb. We will be safe in the deep waters of the Great Mother, no?" Awa's newly forged voice was still thin and flat in intonation, but confident now and with a beauty that pierced her mother's heart.

"Safe, perhaps, but puking over the side the entire way, no doubt," said Ndeup wryly. Turning back to the captain, she pulled her shoulders back and with only a slight shake in her voice she asked, "Where is our next brave vessel?"

$$☽ ○ ☾$$

And so it was that the next morning the two were waving goodbye again, this time to the crew of the fishing boat, their last connection to home. Awa and her mother were heading north by northwest in a fat boat crammed with bales of cloth, people of every heritage, and so much livestock that human conversation proved impossible over the din. Awa looked in every direction, trying to see everything at the same time, while Ndeup clasped the railing of the deck with whitened knuckles and stared straight at the horizon, having been told that this would keep the seasickness at bay. The farther from Cosimo they sailed the myriad blues and greens of water turned to slate and pewter, and the tribes of seabirds that had followed them out of the port were replaced by porpoises playing tag along the sides of the boat as Awa skipped from port to starboard to watch.

A full day of sailing at the very edge of the powerful whirlpool current defining the Straits kept the ship timbers trembling, and that was followed by a full night of pulling north and west toward Atlantia with substantially less strain. Ndeup never left the railing of the port side, retching frequently and violently over into the bottomless waters. She was gripped in a cold sweat and fear of that very bottomlessness, *"Blessed Yemaya! Mother of Ocean and Sky! Let me live to feel Earth beneath my feet!"*

Awa, free from fear and alight with wonder, studied every person with undisguised curiosity. She received a tutorial in steering from the first mate, and helped to rescue a chicken that had flown high up onto the mast. Awa, of course, having spent much of her life clambering in trees and talking to her ancestors, found the climb exhilarating. If her mother could have spared her a glance, she would have barely recognized her formerly reticent child.

Soon after dawn, with the light expanding at their backs, the crew let out a shout of "Land Ho!" and Awa followed the gazes to the bow of the ship. Racing forward she spotted a flash of gold as daylight hit the gilded spires of the Atlantian Temple, and warmth spread down the black rock mountainside like honey. The city, layered and cut right into the volcanic rock emerged from sleep and shadow as if the sun was pulling off a blanket. The light hit the port and Awa gasped. If Cosimo had seemed expansive and overflowing with life, Atlantia's harbor was of so great a magnitude that it was almost impossible to fathom.

A harbor tender boat pulled by eight oarsmen sped toward them, pulled along ship, hailed the captain, and turned to guide them into the docks. Awa skipped to her mother's side and squawked with excitement. Ndeup was rinsing out her mouth for what felt like the one-hundredth time, and gave her daughter a small, weak, sideways smile: Awa's enthusiasm was infectious.

As their ship was steered into a dock slip, Awa felt a buzzing along her skin like ground lightning. The bustle of the crowd and animals around her seemed to slip into the distance and her eyes were drawn to the tall, long ship on the starboard side. Two women stood near the railing. One had skin the color of cocoa and wore an elaborate headdress of what looked to be parrot feathers and ropes of brilliant stones flashing blue and scarlet in the deepening dawn. She appeared deep in conversation, a rather heated conversation if the flashing hands and flailing arms could be a testament, with a tall woman with hair all the colors of the earth, streaks of rust and white and tin and ochre.

As if by given signal, the two high in the ship turned to look down and fastened Awa with their gazes, one set of emerald eyes, one set of agate blue. To the right of the human emerald eyes appeared another set, the same startling emerald in the sleek black head of an enormous cat. And to the left of sky-hued human eyes appeared a set of golden ones, in the long skull of a giant hound. All four pairs looked steadily, unblinkingly at Awa. And she could hear them!

"Well, would you look at that!" from the woman with the streaks of stone in her hair... or was it the hound? *"There's another one of us. This complicates matters splendidly."*

And the magnificent parrot feathered woman... or was it the cat... answered, *"This just gets better and better!"*

Awa threw back her head and laughed.

THE CONVERGENCE

ATLANTIA

Atlantia is a large landmass, an island of substance and girth. It looks like a rose with layers of opening petals, a black rose floating on a bed of iridescent blue and jade silk. The island is equidistant in its four quadrants, and in the eastern half the center of the obsidian flower reaches toward the heavens.

The layers of life carved into the volcanic mountainside flow all down the eastern slope like tapped tree sap, cascading toward the wide-mouthed bay.

In the bay, guarded by twin headlands at the far points of the opening, are thousands of boats, from tiny two-man curraghs to three-masted sailing vessels built to traverse oceans. Line after line of docks fill the port till it looks like a giant honeycomb. And flitting, moving, hastening from that beehive, the small harbor vessels guide travelers in and out.

East from the twin headlands gushes a current of water, wave after wave after wave of opal and tourmaline, all racing with the fierceness of amniotic waters gushing out of the birth canal. Here the ocean summons all her force to funnel through the narrow Straits of Gaia, and emerge into the Middle Sea, the Ocean giving birth to the Sea with the screaming and tearing and mind expansion of all birthings. It is the ripping of the veil between the worlds. It is the race to oblivion and the resolution to life, with Atlantia as the placenta.

The Atlantian shoreline is packed with warehouses, customs offices and shipping companies, all shoved together like a mouth of crooked teeth. The air here is filled with frenetic activity: the deafening rumble of shouts; animals voicing their impatience and displeasure; the smell of manure and livestock and unwashed people and spices and cut hay and clover; the palpable excitement of debarkation and new possibilities. Interspersed between the buildings, like the black gaps of missing teeth, are the jet-black staircases of pumice that lead to the next level of the city.

The market tier mirrors the gentle curve of the harbor in reverse, reaching farther around the volcano to the north and south. Here the crush of humanity still feels intense, but more directed. Captains come looking for return cargo. Heads of households shop for provisions. The smells are different too: broiling fish, steeping coffee, herbs, perfumes, cinnabar, and sandalwood. The sounds of barter and haggle, the squawking of poultry in wooden crates, the cries of a lost child. Small alleys wind between awnings and stalls like a nest of snakes. And again, the occasional and deliberate gaps made by the wide, deep staircases, that follow the ley lines of the Earth up and up to the summit, with steps worn smooth and glassy from a thousand years and a hundred million footsteps.

At the next layer of the terraced city there is less bustle at this time of day. Most of the people of Atlantia live here in homes and apartments carved into the living rock, looking out over the bay.

The next level up is the Scholars' City where the children of Atlantia live and study from the ages of seven to twenty-one. It is here, in long two-storied buildings with pillared porticos open to the bay, that the science and magic of geomancy have been cultivated since the beginning of remembered time. It is here that the knowledge of the Earth's great renting has been predicted. And it is from here that the people's exodus from Atlantia is being planned.

More staircases flow upward to a narrower strip of buildings of the government: embassies from all the corners of the Earth and the open circle of giant standing stones where the Atlantian Council meets.

Only two sets of stairs lead up to the highest level, the very pinnacle of the mountain, the rim of the volcano. Here, surrounded by a ring of massive columns of obsidian topped with gold, three people *are standing in a small circle. These are the Crones of Atlantia, the wisest women of this wise island, seers of the planet's fate. They stand with arms raised high, faces tilted to the streaks of crimson and mother-of-pearl, above, eyes closed, held in rapture between the heavens and the Earth.*

THE GREAT PORT

*T*he three Crones of Atlantia felt it at the exact same time: the subterranean rumble, running along the ley lines from the port to the pinnacle. Something was happening. They lowered their lifted faces, slid eyes wide open and nodded to each other in complete agreement.

"An audience must take place!"

The eldest of the three, a woman of over eighty sun cycles with gray hair the color of manganese, shouted over the top of the staircase for attendants to hurry to the port and fetch whomever or whatever remarkable thing had just arrived in Atlantia. The soles of the Crones' feet, bare against the lava rock, were tingling with information, hearing the language of the Earth and the creatures and plants on Her. And amongst all that data, there were the new and intriguing vibrations of energetic signatures of merit. Oh yes, this was new, and important.

Down six layers of the terraced city, a small group of travelers stood on the shore. Uxua was bending her head to address the slender girl with ebony skin and bright eyes before her.

"We," and here she gestured to the woman standing to her left, "feel that, perhaps, your journey coincides with ours. We would like to offer you and... your mother?... a meal during which we will share our stories." As she moved her hands to gesticulate, the snake tattoos on her arms seemed to undulate up into the feathers that comprised her cape, and disappear onto her torso.

The young girl, Awa, was simply dressed in a white tunic, her midnight ringlets stiff from salt water. She stood, effortlessly balanced on her left foot with the right gracefully resting atop the high arch. She watched Uxua's mouth move, and then looked with sharp attention to the jaguar. The cat's silent message repeated her mistress' words, and Awa heard it as clear as she had ever heard her ancestors' voices in the trees of her homeland. She nodded quickly, and then in her curious and endearing flat diction said, "My mother and I are far from our home and would welcome your hospitality," in the formality that such an invitation required. Then giggling, she added. "I'm starving! But my mother may decline food for a while yet."

As the assembled group turned their eyes to Awa's mother, Ndeup, the gray hue and the tight lines around her mouth gave credence to her daughter's comment. Awa radiated health and excitement; Ndeup looked ready for a three-day sleep under warm covers.

The other woman, the one Uxua had gestured to, stood with feet widely placed and arms akimbo. Badh, the Keeper of Wild Spaces, the Daughter of the Cailleach, wasn't sure about any of this new development. Her own clothing had been repaired so she was dressed as she liked to be, with a serviceable tunic of rough, undyed, woven wool, a cloak of the earth's colors that matched the colors of her barely contained hair, and copper bands with spirals and intricate woven patterns that clasped her muscular upper arms. She had made a quick wash of her face and hands in cool saltwater and felt herself duly presentable and ready for whatever was to come. But now, this girl and her mother! Did the girl not even hear?

It was bad enough that she, Badh, was beholden to the jungle priestess for saving her life and the lives of her servant and familiar. It was difficult for Badh to be beholden to anyone, and even more difficult for her to be gracious about it. But now it had been made clear that she, her companions, plus the feather-festooned one and her companions needed some special boat and pilot just to pass through the Straits of Gaia to get where they needed to go. Now, to add insult to injury, Uxua was acting the all-benevolent one and inviting the bird-like girl and her woebegone mother to come along. More people to accommodate and get along with!

Badh's servant, Domnhu, was standing at her right shoulder, trying very hard to hide the grin spreading across his bewhiskered face, tawny eyes sparking in badly contained glee at his mistress' discomfort. Badh's familiar, the enormous silver hound, had stretched her long neck forward to nudge and rest her nose in young Awa's hand. After an initial startle at the wet bumping her knuckles, Awa's palm opened and gently held the long muzzle, giggling her low, flat giggle when the hound slipped his tongue out to lick her fingers.

Their attention was distracted by a contingent of finely dressed and official looking personages calling for the crowd to part and make way. The three women who had received the Goddess' vision and their company turned at the sound and saw a wedge of older women edged with young girls and boys carrying banners approaching them. "Welcome to Atlantia, travelers! Our Wise Ones, the Crones of Atlantia, have requested your appearance at the pinnacle."

The woman at the front of the greeting committee was richly dressed in long robes of superfine linen the color of mustard flowers, with ropes of the small, white cowrie shells, the kind that Awa and Uxua recognized, draped over her hair and neck and waist. She looked about middle years, with skin the shade of sun ripened peaches and clear, green eyes the color of a tidal pool. Her request for them to attend the Crones sounded more like a command than an invitation, but she smiled and added warmth to the possible sting of an order.

As if choreographed, Uxua, Badh and Awa stepped forward as one, their companions arrayed behind them. With a gracious nod, a lifted eyebrow with an abrupt dip of the chin, and a sweet, eager smile, in that order, the three agreed and stepped out to follow their hosts to the summit.

From the port up to the market level they could walk twelve abreast up the wide staircase of ninety-nine steps. The activity there seemed frenzied with people shouting and piling up large quantities of goods. The woman who had extended their 'invitation' told them about the design of the city and the places they passed. Up another ninety-nine steps to the domicile level the stairs narrowed a bit and the company was now eight abreast. People scurried in and out of the buildings looking harried. Uxua continued to nod graciously and look calm and unimpressed. Badh scowled and looked more and more suspicious as they ascended each level of the city. And Awa couldn't seem to drink it all in enough, her eyes racing from sight to sight. The jaguar and the hound trod as close to their mistress' heels as they could, and Talo and Domnhu felt increasingly wary.

The next ninety-nine steps of the Scholars' City stairs brought them six abreast. Up the next staircase to the government level and the group walked four abreast. Uxua was used to the stairs in her pyramids. Badh was accustomed to climbing mountains. And Awa had spent most of her life scrambling up trees. Yet this ascent challenged them all. Steep, relentless, on and on, up into thinning air they climbed. Pride demanded that they not flounder.

At last they reached the stairs to the pinnacle. Their guides stepped aside and motioned for them to continue, looking down and aside as if afraid to finish the ascent. Clearly, this final set of stairs was not for the faint-hearted or uninvited. The air was thin and cool on hot sweaty skin, yet a current of heat ran down the staircase like a funnel. All the travelers felt the hairs stand up on their arms, and the jaguar and the hound lifted tails and hackles.

"You don't go any further with us?" Uxua asked with a slight edge of exasperation in her voice. But their guides had already disappeared.

THE PINNACLE

*T*ogether the travelers slowly climbed the final, almost vertical steps, thighs burning, chests tight and straining. As they rounded the top, they could see the massive black obelisks in a giant circle slightly off to the right. To the left was the lip of the volcano with steam and small explosions of sparks pouring from it. And right in the middle, on a raised plateau of polished lava rock, stood the Crones of Atlantia: three women of advanced years, one with hair as white as new snow, one with hair as shimmering as hammered silver, and one with hair the deep gray of manganese. Their hair was long, past their knees and to the ground, unbound and gently moving in the heat breeze from the volcano. Three women with all the wisdom of the Earth in their eyes, naked as the day they were born.

"Welcome to Atlantia!"

There was a moment of stunned silence while the Crones of Atlantia waited, and assessed the energies of their visitors as the vibrations traveled through the rock.

"Ah," they thought, *"here is a power triad. Here is prudence, and obstinacy, and open-hearted wonder. Clearly they have been brought together by the wise hand of the Goddess. But they will need the others' talents before their task is finished."*

The pause lengthened as the three travelers felt, rather than saw, their companions struggle up the last few steps and come to stand behind them. They were completely transfixed by the Crones, the bubbling lava and the strange sulfurous fumes that moved like wraiths over the surface. The jaguar came up on Uxua's left and slipped her head under her mistress' hand. The giant hound came to his mistress' right and leaned into her side.

Awa, who was one step in front of her vision sisters, felt enormous currents of energy shooting up her legs like a geyser. Suddenly, without warning, she began to spin, arms stretched wide open, spinning faster and faster. Her face tipped up, her hair flew back, and she began to laugh uncontrollably, a laugh that spread like wildfire through the group. Talo and Domnhu tried to move toward their women, but their feet were fixed to the lava rock with whispers of Earth power and it was impossible to pull free.

As the laughter erupted, the Crones began emitting a tone, then three tones, then the bottom drone of bagpipes until the entire pinnacle was visible sound. The shimmer of the tones met and swooped and overlapped and danced making a spectacular tapestry of color and light and vibration.

As the toning ended, Awa gradually slowed her spinning. Badh and Uxua regained control of their breathing. All stood still, suspended in time, with feet a-tingle, and hearts racing in the intense heat that wafted from the sulfur smoke billowing from the volcano.

"Step forward, if you please," said the Crone with white hair.

"We are eager to hear your story," said the Crone with silver hair.

"We haven't got all day!" said the Crone with hair the color of manganese.

The Crones moved and spoke in intricate interwoven rhythms like a well-rehearsed piece of theater. Their bodies seemed to shimmer, with edges blurring and fading like a mirage. Were they even human? To watch them too closely was like watching a flame, not solid, not liquid, but all heat and life. The travelers stood mesmerized.

Badh and Uxua exchanged looks. Something felt wrong. The apparent amiability and warmth of welcome seemed a thin veneer over some hidden agenda. Domnhu and Talo sensed it too and moved even closer, sidling hound and jaguar out of the way to be within arm's reach of their women. Only Awa and her mother seemed indifferent to the currents of energy and tension. In fact, Awa had silently slid between the Crones, tipping her head to the left as if listening to their internal dialogue. Ndeup was struggling to breathe, waves of nausea overwhelming her.

"We have had a vision," said the Crone with white hair.

"And you have had a vision, one that brings you here," said the Crone with silver hair.

"A vision that spells out destruction." And the Crone with hair the shade of manganese told how the gigantic plates of the earth would crash together and cause an earthquake of such intensity that the island of Atlantia would be split asunder when the volcano erupted from the subterranean chaos. She told them of how the earthquake would form a massive wave, and how that wave would wipe away cities and villages and fields. How lakes would become seas, and how seas would become oceans. And how Atlantia and all her wisdom would slip into the mists of time.

"We are organizing the people to begin evacuating the island within the next seven days. We will send our emissaries to all the known corners of the Earth and seed our knowledge in the hope it may help humanity. You arrived just in time. A handful of days later, and all here would be an empty shell."

"Where will you go?" asked Uxua.

"We will remain here," said the Crone, "and disappear like our island: all great magick requires sacrifice, and we will give ourselves to the earth that all others may escape. You, too, have been called to make this sacrifice"

Awa had been feverishly trying to follow this tale, reading the Crone's lips, and receiving the messages that her body told. As she understood the last sentence from the Crone she screamed.

"No! Noooooo!"

As she screamed the earth began a terrible roar, a ripping asunder that deafened the ear and caused bones to turn to liquid. The ground rippled beneath their feet, like bedding shaken out for airing. The volcano was screaming at them, demanding, ordering.

"The time is near," the Crone with white hair said.

"We need more time!" the Crone with silver hair said.

"We must feed Her!" the third Crone added.

Badh raced toward them and shook the Crone with white hair by the shoulders, "What do you mean, feed Her?"

And the three Crones of Atlantia looked at Awa, and to each other, and nodded.

They started toning one more time, sending the tones into Awa's body, telling her all their wisdom, and letting her know in her bones why they must do what they were about to.

"We must feed the Goddess in the volcano."

"We need to give the people more time to get away."

"Come, be that sacrifice!"

The familiars heard the message, and began to growl deeply. *These Crones wanted a living sacrifice! Never!* The Crones began to move toward Awa and the familiars, staring, never blinking their lashless eyes, eager to feed their Goddess.

Awa felt herself leaning forward, giving in, giving over, as if some part of her beyond her control was acquiescing, her feet moving without her volition. Eyes open, she walked calmly towards the spewing crater. Her mother ran toward her and was held by the Crones' ropey arms, wrapped like octopus tentacles around her torso as she began to scream.

The scream shattered the spell and the hound and the jaguar grabbed Awa's dress in their teeth, pulling her back from fiery oblivion and into the waiting arms of Talo and Domnhu. Uxua and Badh fought toward Ndeup and pulled her free, dragging her exhausted body behind them, with the three Crones of Atlantia fast on their heels.

As they sped over the lip to the staircase, the Crone with silver hair dove forward and caught Ndeup by the ankle. In a single heartbeat the hound was on the Crone, jaws clenched around her scrawny arm. The jaguar stood, feet braced, all teeth bared, holding back the other two Crones while Ndeup scrambled to her feet and spilled over the edge and down the stairs with hound and jaguar right behind. As the band of travelers raced down the flights of stairs toward the port, they could hear the toning from the Crones, vibrating, screeching, and mingling with the rumble of the volcano, trying to draw them back.

At each plateau, Uxua and Badh paused, and with rapid gestures drew sigils of protection in the air between their party and the Crones. Ndeup and the familiars sped past them at the first landing of the government buildings. Talo and Domnhu held Awa between them, and gradually the energetic hook in her middle pulling her back toward the pinnacle lessened, and she began to help them help her. They pushed themselves faster than their feet, tripping, cascading down, down, down till they reached the port.

"We need a boat!" Badh blasted.

Domnhu shouted to Talo to bring the women and familiars as he pelted toward one of the long narrow boats designed to brace the Straits of Gaia waiting at the end of pier. He shoved people aside, lifted one man by the tunic and tossed him into the water, and stood in the boat, feet planted wide, as it rocked wildly. Men and women leapt out of the way as hound and jaguar galloped to the boat followed by Talo and the women.

"Quickly!" Domnhu howled as he began to cast off from the pier.

The travelers tumbled in to the narrow spit of a boat, as the pilot stared at them with mouth wide open. Another heatwave of power flew at them from the pinnacle.

"Get us out of here! Faster!" Domnhu yelled.

Badh stood in the prow and lifted her arms high, summoning a fierce wind. Uxua placed herself mid-ship, raised her hands skyward and called a blinding rain. And Awa alone looked back and up the mountain, seeing three tiny outlines at the peak, swathed in smoke and flame.

The Goddess of Atlantia demanded a great sacrifice for great magick. So mote it be.

)O(

As the long needle of a boat shot out of the harbor like an arrow from a bow, Talo loomed over the pilot, his face a terrifying mix of fury and panic, "You will take us through the Straits of Gaia! Understood?"

The pilot mutely nodded. The boat picked up speed as Badh urged more and more wind to come to their aid. Uxua directed the rain to cloak them from pursuit. With a solid wall of falling water at their backs and the ferocity of the wind in their sails, they raced toward the narrow opening into the Middle Sea. Within one hand's width of sun they could hear a roar, a solid entity of sound created as an Ocean squeezed Herself through the birth canal of two continents and a Sea emerged. It was a roar unlike anything they had ever imagined. The pilot, white-faced, with arms strained at the tiller, mumbled prayers and invocations under his breath as he guided the boat to thread the needle of the Straits of Gaia. The travelers clung to each other and the sides of the boat, the roar too loud for speech between them, too loud for thought within themselves. It was a roar that compressed and stunned and obliterated everything but the next moment in time.

And then suddenly, they were through. Still racing rapidly forward, with the roar at their backs. Alive, whole, jettisoned into the Middle Sea.

IN THE MIDDLE SEA

*T*hree days had passed since the windswept waif, Eiofachta, had landed on the shores of Malta with her story and her plea. On that first day, on the long side of mid-sun, the Seven and their former Sisters and their descendants had swept the girl up to the village bathhouse for what they believed to be a much-needed and expeditious cleaning. The girl, more bone and sinew than flesh, allowed them to scrub and sluice her body. When she emerged from the rinsing pool, she looked several shades less gray, but with dirt embedded into nails and callouses, and all manner of woodland detritus still snarled in her hair. Ni Ma, the leader of the Seven sighed, ordered food and tea, and a repeat of the first bath. Past sunset, the women rubbed spikenard oil onto her feet and hands, worried combs through the tangle of strands of sunlight and forest shadow in her hair, and kept up a constant soft chatter of small talk and song to soothe the girl's shattered spirit. Ni Ma and the others of the Seven conferred.

"The girl is exhausted, like a small bird carried far in a storm."

"Shall we leave with the tide and let her stay behind?"

"She has asked for our help. Do we abandon her?"

"Well, I for one did not ask her to wash up like driftwood and disrupt our plans!"

"Our plans? You mean your plans? They are not carved in stone, more like written in the sand!"

And the singing conversation devolved into a cacophonous argument with five songs being sung simultaneously at a very high volume. Finally, Ni Me stepped into the middle of the huddle.

"Enough! The Goddess has brought this girl to us. I suggest we listen to the Unsung Message."

All the Seven took a step back, folded hands on their bellies, tipped heads down and closed their amber eyes. Three breaths they took together, and involuted into their inner silence, to listen, listen for the Unsung Message.

After a long moment, they lifted their gaze to each other and nodded in agreement. Ni Ma, the leader of the Seven spoke for them all.

"We shall wait till the young one is fit to travel, for more is to be revealed."

And all the Seven sang together, *"And so it is."*

And so it was that on the third day, not long after dawn, after a full day and half of dreamless sleep, the girl Eiofachta was ready to put on the new leggings and tunic provided for her by her hosts, allow her pristine hair to be braided and coiled, fixed atop her head by the copper pins used by the Seven, and walk down to the beach, draped in the newly washed green cloak that had been Alama's. All the people of Malta had gathered with much fanfare to create a fitting send-off to their beloved Seven and the girl, now called Driftwood, as Eiofachta had proven to be too difficult for the Maltese to pronounce.

"It is with sad and heavy hearts that we leave you, our loved ones. We know you shall be vigilant in your obser…"

A start of surprise, then alarm came from the people facing the western side of the half-moon bay. Everyone turned and saw a long, sliver-thin craft driving across the water with unnatural speed. It didn't slow as it came into the shallow harbor, and crashed at full pace onto the beach, jolting its motley crew in all directions. Stunned, the people of Malta watched in silence as slowly, inexorably, the boat began to tip, leaning toward the shore, till it came to rest at a jaunty angle. A jumble of people and creatures began to slip over the side of the boat and land in a heap on the hard-packed sand.

There stood four women, two men and the most enormous cat and dog anyone had ever seen – looking warily at the large crowd amassed on the beach. A sunbaked man with powerful arms and a chest covered in wave tattoos clung to the tiller and refused to get out of the boat when they gestured to him to get down.

"You people are crazy!" he shouted. "I want nothing else to do with you!"

The newly deposited group looked slightly abashed.

"Let us help you, friend!" said a young man with skin like polished bronze and black hair flowing past his shoulders. "Shall we push you back out?"

"NO!" the pilot shrieked. "Leave me and my boat be!"

The youngest of the women, a thin, tall girl with ebony skin, lifted her palms toward the pilot, a gesture of apology, friendship, and appeasement. His gaze softened at her and one side of his mouth lifted in a sweet grin.

"Pardon our dramatic arrival," said the oldest of the women, strong-limbed and wild haired, to the gathered folk on the beach, "but we have escaped from Atlantia with our lives, well, at least one of us was going to die. It wasn't going to be me. It was going to be that girl there. But to any effect, we escaped and have been driven by Goddess wind to your shore."

The people of Malta appeared stunned, and said not a word. The graceful woman with the bronze skin and what looked to be the remnants of parrot feathers in her hair looked with humor at her companion, and cut in smoothly.

"What my friend is trying to say is this: we need to get to Egypt, and now," with a graceful gesture sideways at the boat and pilot, "we seem to be at a loss for a boat."

She smiled widely at the people gathered before her, and the smile deepened as she heard the snort from the wild-haired one beside her.

Driftwood walked from the crowd and locked eyes on the women who had spoken and the young girl with them. And then Ni Me strode forward and found their gazes. They all had the same thought. *Now there were five of them! Five with the same vision! Five for Egypt!*

Ni Me turned and faced the other of the Seven. "We have more company," she said, barely containing the laugh that formed in her throat.

Ni Ma, the leader of the Seven threw up her hands, ordered fires lit again, food prepared again, and supplies to be shifted in their ship to make room for the new arrivals.

"Will we ever leave?"

CANAAN

"What do you mean I can't take the elephant!" Maia screeched. "Take your hands off her or I will curse you with all the fury of flood and fire!"

Heat and dust swirled as the swarm of guides who had been shoving and shouting to garner the job of taking these travelers into Egypt scurried back several paces and reassessed the situation. These guides were a motley bunch from many peoples and lands. Some were draped in garish colored silks with decorative turbans. Others were more poorly dressed and looked frantic and hungry. The central square was teeming with groups of travelers who had entered Canaan from the north and east gates, and loosely formed assortments of guides, shifting and surging around their prospective customers like flies. The edge of the square was lined with market stalls. The smells and sounds were overwhelming: camels, donkeys, hundreds of unwashed humans, all jammed together to be molded into caravans and funneled into Egypt.

Maia, the formerly Divine One, the Incarnation of Kali Ma, had jumped down from Savi's back, and was swinging her long mahogany stick back and forth to ward off the greedy guides. The day had started warm and thick, and now, by mid-morning, the heat had caused her cap of inky curls to lie flat on her head. She had a slash of crimson across her cheeks, more from rage than heat. "Nobody touches my elephant!" she shouted in tones that brooked no defiance.

A circle of open ground now surrounded Maia and her fellow travelers. Parasfahe looked down on the scene from her perch in the floating platform bed on Savi's back. Spotting some Sumerians in the rabble, she let out a yell, "Adei Inanna!" in a forceful volume that belied her fragile health.

With their Goddess invoked, the Sumerian guides stepped back farther and farther and bent at the waist to honor the priestess who had spoken the sacred words. Maia, feeling grateful that for once her passenger had roused herself to be helpful, shot a glance upward to see Parasfahe with her head peering over her platform. She yelled up, "Thanks! But I could use some more help down here!"

At that Parasfahe swung her legs over the edge, setting the platform to swinging. She wore the diadem of a High Priestess resting across her brow, and it caught the sunlight as she sat up, sending splinters of brilliance into the crowd.

"Adei Inanna!" she declared again, and an even greater space opened around them. The Sumerians knelt and the other guides began to quiet and settle. "We travel by the direction of the Goddess, and we require immediate transport, elephant and all!"

Stunned by this demonstration of authority, a Sumerian man of late middle years crept forward on his knees, nose nearly scraping in the dust, and said, "I am most privileged to serve you, Most High. Allow me to guide and protect you on your journey."

He dared a single-eyed glance upward, and was rewarded with a slight nod of assent from Parasfahe. He rose and turned, immediately shouting orders to women and men around him. Like magic, a path opened up to the south gate. Maia warily stepped forward, still gripping her mahogany stick tightly in her hand.

"All will be well now," Parasfahe said in a low voice, and then she seemed to melt back down and become invisible, hidden in the awnings and drapings of her platform again.

Behind Savi came the yaks carrying Tiamet and her young servants and the teamsters that had come with them from the Roof of the World. Just past the south gate the Sumerian caravan leader led the group to an expanse of hillside that flowed gently down to the river below. Pockets of olive groves were scattered down the slope, and river birds swooped into the water making tiny silent splashes. The guide, with eyes of light sable and hair with gray at the temples, looked up to receive direction from Parasfahe, but all he saw were softly rippling curtains. Assuming rightly that from now on he needed to deal with Maia, he said, "My Lady, we cannot take the shaggy beasts with us."

At the sight of her ferocious glance he quickly continued, "The elephant, yes! Yes, of course! The elephant can come! But the shaggy cows will never stand the heat of Egypt."

Maia had been concerned in recent days for the yaks. They were increasing easily fatigued. Several times their company had had to cut short the day's journey to allow the yaks to rest. She saw the wisdom of the man's statement, and with great reluctance and a bone deep sigh she turned to go speak with Tiamet. She looked back at him over her shoulder, "Well, don't just stand there. It will take a lot of convincing to sway the impossibly Old One to part with her yaks."

With a combination of curiosity about what an 'impossibly old one' was, and a sense that he was stepping into a river current that would sweep him off his footing, the guide, Uluf, followed Maia into the dust storm that was the yak herd. Coughing and waving the dust from her face, Maia stopped abruptly and shouted, "Tiamet! Tiamet! Where *are* you?"

"Here, my mighty Maia!" A tiny woman of indiscernible age put down a yak's hoof and straightened up from within a cloud of dirt and sand. "Ha! I found it! This stone has been paining this poor beast for the past five miles."

While Maia was of middle height, this Old One made her look like a giant, and she barely reached Maia's shoulder. Her small black eyes shone out of a face of a million creases. Her wide triumphant smile showed a cluster of remaining teeth in the front of her mouth, yellowed and long, but sturdy like tree trunks. In spite of the heat of the day she was swathed in a long white animal skin cloak that reached the ground and dragged piles of earth and broken twigs and plants behind her.

"I can tell by the look on your face, my Maia, that we have a new obstacle before us. Bring it to us! We have proven ourselves unstoppable so far!"

One of the strangest things that had happened on their very strange journey was that Tiamet, who had lived the last untold decades of her life as a hermit in the highest levels of their Temple, with years of so much internal meditation as to mostly lose her external sight, had taken to the outside world like a fledgling to flight, and her sight had miraculously restored, bit by bit, day by day. Now she saw the world through eyes that rivaled her young servants'. Each new place, each new situation had become a delight to her. The irascible venerable that had left the Roof of the World with Yan and Shema some moons ago had disappeared with her blindness. Meeting up with and traveling alongside Maia had seemed to make all the difference. She now had not one but two vision sisters since Parasfahe had joined them. She was eager to solve problems as they arose, open to conversations, and seemed to have a particular way of diffusing arguments that ended with all parties laughing and agreeing that this woman, this Tiamet, was so funny, so wise, that of course, they would do as she asked. Maia had learned that Tiamet could charm the fleas off a camel, and had left her to it, especially since they had left Babylon and were weighed down by their concerns for Parasfahe and her health.

As Tiamet's vigor and energy had waxed, so Parasfahe's had seemed to wane. She barely ate, moaned in her sleep, and never participated as they discussed their route, their decisions, their fate. Instead she seemed to shrink into her skin and retreat to a small ball of pain and revolt. Only just now, as she had interceded in the market square had she even noticed where they were or what they were doing.

"Tiamet, this is…" Maia said, as she turned to look at the guide.

"Uluf, most Revered One," he quickly supplied. He might not know where this Old One was from, but he could spot a priestess anywhere. "I have offered my services to guide you into the land of Egypt."

Tiamet met his gaze with a sharp and amused eye, "Most Revered, am I? Ha!" She began to chuckle in her way that sounded like boulders rolling down a mountainside. "Hear that, Yan and Shema? This downlander calls me 'Most Revered'!"

Yan and Shema, long-suffering and beginning to melt in the heat, smiled small smiles and nodded. They, like their yaks, found the lowlands filled with heavy, wet air and sweltering temperatures.

"Yes, Most Revered, we heard. How very clever of him," Yan answered.

With a tinge of suspicion that perhaps that was sarcasm coming her way, Tiamet turned back to the guide, "And I suppose you have a problem, eh, Uluf?"

Maia, the former incarnation of Kali Ma, gathered the courage of her Goddess around her like a girdle and said bluntly, "You can't take the yaks."

Total silence followed.

"Tiamet, did you hear me? The guide says the yaks won't flourish in Egypt. It's hotter than here with little water. Tiamet?"

More silence.

"Most Revered One," said Uluf. "It is the deepest wish of my heart to fulfill all of your requests. But indeed, the shaggy ones will not live in the heat of Egypt. I am most heartily sorry."

Maia was waiting for the explosion, but all that followed was Tiamet looking at Uluf with her head tipped slightly to one side and coquettish glance, "All right, my guide, it shall be as you say." He gave her a low bow and look of amusement and respect as he stood upright.

Yan and Shema exchanged slightly disgusted looks and shook their heads. Maia caught the unspoken message between Tiamet and their new guide, and bowed to the totally unexpected but seemingly inevitable scenario of Tiamet and Uluf sharing a tent.

"Excuse me? Did I hear you say Egypt?"

Maia whipped around and saw a tiny girl of eight or nine sun cycles with a mass of curls framing a sharp and discerning face. Close at her heels was a tower of a woman, armed to the teeth and sunburned to match her flame of hair.

Maia began to answer this question with one of her own, *"Who asks?"* but was brought up sharp as her eyes connected with the little one's, and then the warrior woman's. The twang of recognition deep in her heart was so strong as to be a pain, and yet. And yet, she knew these women to be ones who shared her own vision.

"Who are… ?" Tiamet began, and then she too made eye contact and felt the thrum of knowing.

And from high atop the elephant Savi, the floating, disembodied voice of Parasfahe said, "Welcome, sisters!"

MOTHER NAIHL

*T*he longboat from Malta approached the shore at dusk. The light was pearlescent with streaks of magenta and peach ribbing the western sky. A soft caress of breeze gently coaxed the boat landward till it came to rest on one of the many sandbars that stippled the shallow bay just west of the mouth of Mother Naihl, the river that birthed and fed the land of Egypt. It was a balmy night, and the travelers on board could hear the disembodied voices of the fisher folk laughing and jostling to end their work and hurry to their homes.

"Is this it? Is this Egypt?" Driftwood asked.

She had gained color back in her cheeks in the ten days they had been sailing the Middle Sea. Her braided hair had long since tumbled out of the topknot so carefully constructed on Malta, and the Seven Daughters of the Earth had prudently picked up the copper pins that had fastened it when they had fallen on the deck. She still refused to take off the green wool cape that had been Alama's. But she raced back and forth over the deck with abandon, and the Seven Sisters exchanged glances and breathed deep sighs of relief that the young one appeared to be taking hungry bites out of life. Her sadness would be with her a long time, and the loss of Alama would be with her forever. But she was focused forward now, and the Seven Sisters could relax into knowing that their Driftwood girl would choose life.

"Yes, young one, this is the Egypt we have sought." Ni Me's musical voice was soft at Driftwood's shoulder. "It doesn't look like much, does it?" she continued with her usual good humor. "We shall see what Egypt has in store for us."

The sailors began to lower the small rowboats down into the shallows and the assortment of travelers on board gathered their belongings, and waited to climb down the rope ladders to the crafts.

"Sisters, are you sure you want to go ashore tonight? It is getting dark. Where will you lodge?" the captain asked, concerned.

"We must push on," Ni Me responded. "We all feel the urgency to keep moving. Your concern is much appreciated, friend. But we all," and she swept an arm back behind her to indicate the group of vision carriers and their companions, "agree that we need to feel Egypt beneath our feet."

The captain gave a small bow and turned to facilitate the departure. The number of travelers now stood at fourteen people and the giant dog and cat. There were the Seven Sisters from Malta, the young Driftwood from the North Woods, Sweet Awa and her mother from the western shore of the land of Yemaya, Uxua the splendid beauty from the land of Ix Chel with her equally beautiful brother, and the wild Badh from the land of the Cailleach and her devoted Domnhu.

The jaguar stood near Uxua, and the massive dog swished his tail so hard that it smacked against the side of the boat. They filled three of the small boats, and landed on the shore in the half-light, one group right after the other in clumps and bumps, like apples falling from the trees at just past harvest. As the rowboats pushed off to return to the longboat, and the sailors raised arms in salutes to the Seven Daughters of the Earth in final goodbye, the sounds of drumming and song tussled with the sounds of the waves against the shore. In and out, in and out, they could hear it as their group moved farther up on the beach. They were drawn to the drumming and chanting like those lost in the desert crave water. They saw a large fire a way above the tide line, and the shapes of people dancing round it broke the light into fragments, dark and bright, dark and bright. A voice rang out clear, "Listen to this one! We sing it at the awakening of spring."

The young woman who had spoken grabbed the hand of the young man sitting next to her, and they began a dance with the rhythm of galloping horse hooves, as a giant woman with flaming red hair took a frame drum and echoed the beats. An older man with a pale woman tucked into the crook of his arm picked up the song, as other drummers followed along. Folks jumped up to try the steps with varying degrees of success, but all with much laughter.

The travelers from Malta stood and watched, just outside the line of the firelight, until, one by one, those in the circle of light felt their presence, stopped their singing, and turned to look, until only the crack of one drum beat sounded.

The tall, fierce red-head, a strong young woman with pale warrior braids, the dancing man, a lithe woman of deep brown skin and slanted eyes, and a man in the robes of Sumeria formed a line of defense against whatever it was that stood in the dark.

"Who goes there?" barked the tall woman with the cloud of red hair.

Within the circle of firelight, a woman, face carved by pain, limbs weak and fragile, stood and began to move forward with agony in every step. On one side, a tiny girl with a nimbus of curls, and on the other a tiny woman of age beyond description, took her arms and helped her move toward the line of defenders who parted as she limped through.

"We know you, don't we?" the crippled woman, Parasfahe, stated rather than queried, with a catch in her breath.

The giant hound and jaguar moved into the rim of light and shadow as multiple women's voice replied in unison, "And we know you."

FROM THE TEMPEST

On the day that Celebi and Malvu had emerged from the cave after the Sacred Marriage, Autakla and Silbara had stepped up as the leaders of their party. Up until now they had felt deference to the elders amongst them. But now they both felt a growing urgency and constant internal drive to arrive in Egypt. Up till now their journey had been steady and measured. But with the arrival of Malvu, all felt complete, as if they now had all the pieces they needed to push forward faster.

Their hosts of the Basquela had helped them pack and be off that very afternoon. The nine Grandmothers stood in a long row and solemnly smiled at Celebi and Malvu, as the party rode the pack mules out of the village.

"You travel with our deepest gratitude and all the blessings of our people!" the eldest Grandmother shouted. "Our people will survive what is coming, thanks to you and the rite you performed. We will hide, safe in the mists." And as the travelers moved down the Tin Trail, the people of the Basquela ran alongside shouting good wishes and handing up parcels of food and treasured bits of clothing.

"Thank you for the mist!"

"Go with our blessings!"

"Take this. It was my grandmother's!"

"Thank you for making our saving magick!"

After only a short distance the travelers looked back, only to discover that the village was now invisible in a fog so dense as to be solid.

"Where did it go?" Silbara gasped.

"I can hear the people, but I can't see them," Autakla replied.

Dalia stood up on the back of her mule and made sigils of protection in the air, to complete the disappearance of the Basquela.

Their concern drew Celebi and Malvu's attention, and they too turned in their saddles to look back. Now, and only now did the Basquela's purpose in asking them to make the Sacred Marriage become clear. After hearing of what was to come, the Basquela wanted to hide in their mountain aerie and let the tempest of the change come roll right past them.

"We worked some magick, beloved," Malvu said softly.

"May it hold them safe for five thousand sun cycles," Celebi said as she looked at him with tenderness. "A great magick, but no great sacrifice for us. Rather, a great joy."

"The greatest of joys," he said, so only she could hear.

) ○ (

With many more days of hard travel they reached the coast where ships sailed to the eastern shores of the Middle Sea. This was a busy port, with dozens of longboats sturdy enough to handle the sudden squalls that could erupt on these waters.

Autakla and Silbara rode ahead and, with much haggling by Autakla and much soothing of ruffled feelings by Silbara, a passage was set for them that left on the evening tide. Silbara made arrangements for the pack mules to be led back up into the mountains where the Basquela had reassured them that the beasts could find their way home. Autakla gathered their belongings and began to exchange stories with the sailors, some of whom bragged that they had actually *seen* selkies in the Northern Sea.

"For real?" she teased, "or did you just think it when you saw a dolphin?"

"No, little sister," the grizzled sailor responded. "There are such wondrous creatures. I only wish that I could see one in my lifetime."

"I shall give you a gift then. Watch carefully when we set sail, and I promise you shall see a selkie."

The old man laughed and chucked her under her chin, "Can you make such magick happen, little one?"

"It's a promise," she called over her shoulder as she walked down the dock toward the ship. Climbing aboard, she leaned toward Silbara and whispered in her ear. Both girls turned to look at the sailor who was now standing on the dock with his friends, laughing that the young thing had promised him a magickal sighting.

Come eventide, as their boat slipped away from the dock, Autakla stepped behind Silbara and stripped off her clothes. In an eye blink she shot herself over the edge of the boat and dove into the bay, twisting three times in the water to complete her transformation. The sailors on the dock shouted in warning and then in awe as a sleek, dark shape moved fast and effortlessly toward the dock, slicing the water as if it were air. Suddenly, a wet brown head popped up near the side of the dock, hazel eyes filled with mirth, as the selkie flipped and floated backwards in the water, yipping and barking with the message, "See! I promised!"

The sailor fell to his knees and rubbed his eyes. He raised an arm in salute as she turned to swim back alongside the ship as it sailed past the headland and out to deep water.

$$\supset \bigcirc \subset$$

And so it was that they were back in a ship once more, and racing full forward to Egypt. Celebi and Malvu stood, arms around each other's waist, in the stern watching as the land grew small, holding in their minds' eye the sacred cave deep in the mountains. Autakla, thrilled to be of the sea once more, joyfully dove under the ship time and time again. And Dalia and Silbara stood in the prow, leaning forward as if to will the ship faster onward.

After four peaceful days of turquoise skies and even breezes they had sailed due south and skirted the shore along the settlement of Carthegia. And then something shifted. The sailors stopped what they were doing and lifted their eyes and noses skyward. Dark, angry clouds filled the sky ahead to the east, as if conjured in an instant by a malevolent hand, Autakla swam alongside the ship and barked up to Silbara, who let the crew know to lower the small rowboat and let Autakla come aboard. As she shed her pelt, Silbara stood nearby with her human clothes, and, sensing some distress, hurried to help in the transformation.

"Quick! I need to speak to the captain!" Autakla rasped.

As the girls ran toward the captain, Dalia, Celebi and Malvu came to join them. The captain, a short and powerfully muscled woman of middle years with arms and legs covered in colorful tattoos of sea creatures, stood at the wheel and turned to hear their news.

"There will be a fierce storm within but a few minutes," Autakla rushed the words past newly human lips. "News from the waters to the east sends us warning of high winds and lightning, with cross currents all along this southern coast."

"News? From the sea itself?" the captain sparked. She was thrilled to hear directly from the sea, and yet worried that such news was a portent of the intensity of what was approaching them.

"Should we try to make a port? The nearest is some miles away, and a shallow one at that."

"No time!" Autakla replied. "I feel it building even now."

They all gazed forward and saw mountains of black clouds whipped by peak after peak of dark, churning winds. The sails began to twist and struggle, as if torn and wrung by giant unseen hands.

"I will return to the sea. I can best help from there!" Autakla shouted as she ran back to where her pelt was laying on the deck, and quickly tore off the human clothing once more. As she prepared to leap off the ship into the waves, she heard a thunderous crack and looked back over her shoulder to see the mast of the mainsail snap like a twig as the sail sifted down like flour.

"Tie yourselves together to the bottom of the mast!" she screamed, right before she pushed off into the churning tumult below.

Silbara ran to the rail and saw her friend twist three times in the water and then look back up toward her with her seal eyes. "Care for yourself!" Silbara shouted, but the wind slapped her words right back against her face. She slid across the deck to where Malvu was lashing the rope around each waist and then around them all as he crisscrossed the lashing to the mast.

The next hours were a blur of water and salt-stung eyes, of thrashing bodies and broken ribs. The ship tossed forward and backwards like a toy and as they tipped precariously by one of the largest waves, a sailor was swept over the side.

Silbara, Celebi and Malvu muttered a constant stream of prayers to Brig, while Dalia was strangely silent and composed. Her ochre face held a small smile, almost a delight in the fierce battle being raged between sea and air. It was as if Mother Egypt was welcoming her back with brass cymbals and horns.

The ship began to take on more and more water, and the exhausted remaining sailors were losing the race to bail and steady. When all looked lost, they felt a lift, a surge, a rightening of course and the ship began to steer itself straight east along the shoreline.

The captain spared a quick glance to the stern in confusion, making out gray and brown shadows by the hundreds in the water, converging on the ship, like geese in migration, literally pushing the ship aright. They raced along for what seemed forever until an explosion of quiet manifested, and they were catapulted out of the storm and into the peaceful sea beyond.

The army of helpers continued to guide them eastward, and as the sea calmed and the waters went from stormy slate and dun to achingly blue and clear, the travelers and sailors moved toward the stern to watch. Directly below them was Autakla in her selkie form leaning her shoulder against the wooden frame of the ship. She was surrounded by porpoises, dolphins, and giant fish only seen in sailors' dreams: a fleet of swimmers; an armada of the sea's inhabitants. With broken sails the ship was beholden to their swimming helpers. No winds held them back and they picked up speed, moving east until they were shoved toward a sand bar at the outer edge of a small bay.

The shore was filled with people by the dozen who had gathered to see the tempest farther west play out from the safety of the beach. The speed of the approaching ship startled this group and they scuttled up the beach, and then sifted down again as the ship came to rest right in front of the vision carriers. They began ululating in welcome, and the elephant trumpeted joyfully as the newcomers walked out of the waves.

Dalia wept as she stood on the soil of Egypt again after four long and precious years. She was under no illusion that this homecoming would be simple, or even desired by some here. But she was here, and the Goddess had prescribed it. And so it was.

Several of the Egyptian villagers at the rear of the crowd gasped in recognition and raced forward to kneel before her with foreheads in the sand. Her companions exchanged puzzled glances as Dalia graciously acknowledged those prostrate before her.

"Stand and receive my blessing," she said in the local dialect. The villagers stood, some trembling, some not daring to look upon her face, and she gently touched each one at the third eye of their foreheads. When she finished and the villagers had backed away, the vision carriers were there making a circle around her, Silbara and Autakla with their feet still washed gently by the waves. Maia led Savi forward so he could kneel and allow Parasfahe to peer over the edge of her floating bed and bear witness. Io and Kiyia moved to the right and Ni Me, Awa and Driftwood to the left. Uxua and Badh helped Tiamet to find her feet on the shifting sand. They all moved with a knowing, as if this had happened before, or would happen, or had always been happening.

And so it was that Dalia, half-sister of the Pharaoh and Priestess of Nut, came home to Egypt, and twelve of the thirteen vision carriers stood together for the first time and felt that their circle was almost complete.

THE TEMPLE OF ISIS

We see a land nestled below the Middle Sea. There is a wide-open mouth of river pouring into the sea, the current surging north through a vulva of intense fecundity, surrounded on both sides by desert. The River Naihl, the Mother of Life, roils and surges like the movement of an immense sacred snake, her scales brown and bronze. On the east side of the river, a jewel-like city of marble and sandstone buildings spreads out like an open fan along the river-bank, and glistens in the moonlight. In the center of the river sits an egg-shaped island, terraced and dotted with date and olive trees. As we move closer to this island, we can make out the central building with an open central courtyard, a covered portico, and pillars of chiseled marble columns around all four sides. In that courtyard, a statue of Isis stands, taller than any tree, Her head reaching above the roof and toward the sky: Isis, the Mother of Creation, the Maker of the Heavens, the Source of all. This is Her Temple. And at Her feet, on a dais, there is a tableau of women, one seated, and three surrounding her like fallen rose petals.

In the Temple of Isis, Atvasfara, High Priestess for these last four-teen passages of the sun, sat on her throne in the central court-yard in the darkest part of night. She was robed in wool, the braziers burned the space to a high noon temperature and her hair made tiny curls around her face, as it did in the heat. But still the trembling wouldn't stop. It was contained by the enormity of her will to an internal shivering, but those standing nearest saw the fabric of her cloak moving almost imperceptibly, like the movement of a hummingbird's heart.

From down the shadowed corridor the susurration of robes against the sandstone floor preceded the entrance of the Bardic Priestesses she had summoned into the moonlit courtyard. These women were trained from childhood over a course of nineteen sun cycles in the art of memory and recall, and were always required to document the prophetic dreams of their High Priestess. As with everything that occurred in the Land of Egypt, there were wheels within wheels and schemes on top of schemes. To avoid the Pharaoh's court from deliberately misinterpreting her prophetic dreams, Atvasfara had the Bardic Priestesses witnessed and observed by her own personal attendants. And the Pharaoh had her own eyes and ears within the Temple, to avoid the High Priestess from pursuing what she called "that Temple's own design." Trust was very scarce on the ground in the Land of Egypt, and no one ever followed a straight path to anything. The word of this dream had moved along the slithering conduits of telepathy and whispers to every actor in this power-hungry drama. So inured to these layers of purpose and loyalty was Atvasfara, that she barely registered the concentric circles of people arriving, some in full moonlight, and some appropriately, left in shadow. The Moon, viewing the scene from Her zenith, saw the assembled like a giant multi-hued gardenia, with Atvasfara at the center surrounded by her attendants, then the Bardic Priestesses, the ritualists, the teachers, the choirs, the "special guests" – observers from the Pharaoh's court – and, the last circle, the children and students of the Temple, hanging off the columns like limpets, leaning in to hear what momentous thing had called them all from sleep.

The High Priestess was a slender woman of middle years with hair the color of newly turned soil. She had a short little nose that had, due to the aesthetics of the times, labeled her to be no beauty. She had used this lack of physical coin to convince her parents that she was more valuable to them as a priestess than a matron of household, and she had entered her training at the age of twelve. Her prophetic talents were almost immediately discovered, and she rose swiftly through the ranks to her current status. The intrigue and manipulations of Court and Temple life were an irritation to her, but the dreams were almost always a dive into ecstasy. Each time, there was an unfolding of events and fates with dazzling color and dizzying speed. She cultivated herself by meditation and practice, and longed for her dreams as her reward for the burdens of her position and the inanity of mundane life. Tonight's dream, however, was a painful and massive deviation from her norm.

No one spoke as they settled into positions to see and hear the High Priestess. She began her telling of the dream as the torches caused ripples of light and shadow against the walls of alabaster and mother of pearl inlay. The wisps of copal incense made blue streaks across faces: more moving shadows. As the story of the dream unfolded, those faces grew grave and silent tears fell down their cheeks. Atvasfara's dreams always came to be, and they knew that that of which she spoke would come true.

The three attendants that always accompanied the High Priestess moved in close to her, an instinctive protection against this vision and what it might mean. The youngest, only eighteen and with the soft blurred features that were a prophecy of the beauty to emerge with maturity, knelt down and placed a hand on her knee. The other two, friends of the High Priestess since they all began their training together, rested their hands on her shoulder. And the silence held. No one wanted to break it by speech or weeping or railing against fate. The wicks on the lamps at the foot of the statue behind her were smoking slightly, burning low, and the statue looked alive in the liminal light, as if Isis Herself was holding Her breath, and tipping Her head in sadness. The horizon to the east was ochre with the coming day. And still no one broke the tableau.

Suddenly, Atvasfara stood abruptly and shook herself as if breaking free from underwater. Her voice was raspy and pitched so quiet that all of those present leaned forward to hear her.

"We must prepare for our visitors," she said. "They will arrive over the next few moons. We need housing and servants for each, and foods that will be familiar to them."

Her friends and confidants, those attendants that were her constant source of comfort and company, exchanged puzzled glances. *What*

178

visitors? Each of the three had a moment of worry. *Had she slept during the telling of the dream? What did she miss?*

Atvasfara laughed with a tight tearing sound like she had forgotten how to laugh.

"They are coming. There will be twelve of them from ice and jungle and fog-drenched mists. We have much work to do so that all will not be lost. These twelve – and I make thirteen – we together must make a magick so strong, so impenetrable, that the Goddess can live within for thousands of years, until it is safe for Her to awaken and return."

Her deep-set brown eyes cleared. She stood, and as always seemed so much taller than her stature might suggest. With all the power given her as the forty-second High Priestess of Isis, in the Land of Egypt, in the navel of the world, she let the words fall like drops of mercury.

"The women are coming."

And with that, groups of people broke off, and slipped away to their various cabals. The viper's nest that was the Court of the Land of Egypt began to writhe with the news.

The women are coming.

The three attendants gathered Atvasfara into their arms and glided from the Hall. The Bardic Priestesses formed a circle and began the word-by-word recitation of the dream as it had been told. The teachers darted left and right, rounding up the students, and herded them out of the Temple like a gaggle of goslings. The choirs and ritualists, divided by their own internal strata of high and low liturgy, moved out of the Hall in opposite directions, each group hurrying to compose appropriate songs, chants and ceremonies for the tasks that would be ahead. The observers, those special guests from the Court, slipped out of the Temple and stood on the front staircase, conversing in twos and threes as the sunrise cast dappled shadows over their faces and robes.

"What does the arrival of these foreigners indicate?"

"It might be a ruse, a way for Atvasfara to gain ascendency."

"Please, everyone, some decorum, she is the High Priestess Atvasfara!"

Some snickers and half smiles flitted across the faces of the close group huddled in the shadows. The constant, and lately it felt like daily, struggle between the Pharaoh and the High Priestess to achieve the loyalty of the people had fomented an incessant stew of rumor and veiled innuendo in the Court. All of this was bubbling up from the Pharaoh's insecurity and her awe of Atvasfara's powers of divination. The Pharaoh always felt as if the High Priestess could "foretell" a reason that she would tumble from power. The fact that Atvasfara had absolutely no ambition to do such a thing made her even more untrustworthy in Pharaoh's mind. Power and the acquisition of it were all Pharaoh understood, and her own inability, year after year, to birth a daughter made her feel the precariousness of her status. She needed a daughter to secure her position, but the Goddess had not given her any such life in her womb. Atvasfara, as High Priestess, needed no heir, nor could she procure position for any child of her body, and to Pharaoh a woman with no dynasty to cultivate couldn't be understood nor trusted. How could you predict the actions of someone with nothing to lose?

Back in her private quarters, Atvasfara motioned to her youngest attendant to come close. "Go see what the Court spies are saying. This dream and all it brings into being will be rich food for their gossip and fantasies of conspiracy."

As the young woman swept out of the room, Atvasfara leaned back on the divan and sighed deeply. As if the dream wasn't going to demand all she had to give, she was sure that Pharaoh and her swarm of sycophants would do everything in their power to obstruct and divert. As she fell into an uneasy sleep she saw faces, the twelve faces of strangers who felt like sisters from another life. The face of a tiny girl with a jumble of honey curls. The face of an ancient woman with hair as white as the fur cloak she wore. One face as black as obsidian, another as pale and translucent as wet papyrus. The faces floated in front of her mind, unknown and yet beloved.

I can do this for them, she thought. *We can do this together.*

DOWN THE NAIHL

Atvasfara came down the River Naihl in procession. Anytime she, the High Priestess of Isis traveled, there was much pomp and circumstance. But this particular procession outshone any that had gone before. There was a flotilla of river craft, barges and multi-storied platforms holding all of the highest of rank. There were awnings of silks and billowing draperies of finest cotton. Huge fans of peacock feathers were suspended overhead and spun gracefully in the thankfully gentle morning air. Atvasfara and her three devoted attendants rested on the top level of the most splendid of the barges, whilst below and around were positioned the Bardic Priestesses and the ritualists, all very careful and protective of their placement and access to the High Priestess.

All that brilliance was surrounded by a hundred small boats with single sails that carried the folk of the less exalted classes. Choir members and personal servants as well as cooks and mistresses of wardrobe were crammed into the small boats, all extremely grateful for the breeze and the coolness coming off the water. Yesterday had been hot, so hot that several women had fainted and needed to be revived. Today was looking to be less arduous as the temperature seemed more forgiving, and they were nearing their destination at the mouth of the Naihl.

Atvasfara was reclining and sipping chilled hibiscus juice as she thought over the news that had arrived yesterday evening when they had moored along the banks of the river. A breathless messenger on his way up the Naihl had stopped and asked to be given an audience with Atvasfara. When the young man was allowed entrance to her salon, he bowed and bobbed his way forward until he came to rest, nose to the ground, at her feet.

"You have a message for me?" Atvasfara urged him to speak.

"Yes, Most High. It is a blessing to find you here, for the Lady directed me to tell you first before I went on to Pharaoh. She said it was most important that you hear the news first." And the young man, sweaty and dust coated, fell silent.

After a long pause, Atvasfara nudged again, "And what is this 'most important news'?"

"She has come back!"

"Where?"

"She has returned to Egypt, Most High!"

"Who?"

'What, Most High?"

"Young man, look at me. Take a breath and tell me: who has come and to where?"

As he looked upward into the eyes of the Most High Priestess of Isis, the young messenger was surprised to see a glint of amusement in her deep-set brown eyes. She was actually smiling at him!

"It is Dalia, Most High! The Dalia that is of the Royal Court and the Temple of Nut. The Dalia that said she wanted nothing to do with power or the crown or Egypt. She is back, and with a group of outlanders, at the village of Thonis at the mouth of the river. It's an odd group, Most High. Strange looking peoples and some that don't even look like people and some very strange beasts as well. They were dancing and singing and celebrating. And she, Dalia that is, saw me and asked me to hurry to you before news of her arrival reached her half-sister, Pharaoh, that is. And I set out at once, and here I am." He finished this recitation with a look of complete triumph on his narrow face.

"Breathe, little brother," Atvasfara said with a glimmer. "You have done well to bring me this news. The return of our Dalia is, indeed, important and auspicious. I must ask of you that you proceed on your journey to Pharaoh's court with heavy feet, very heavy feet, feet so heavy as to demand that the journey take many days."

"You want me to… ?"

"Be intent upon each grain of sand along the way." And she looked at the young man with an added message in her eyes. *"Take all the time in the world."*

"Yes, Most High. Of course, Most High. I see the necessity of observing each grain of sand, and indeed, my feet feel most heavy."

"And after you deliver this joyous news to Pharaoh, if you find yourself being that same kind of careful observer, observe what is said and who does the saying. And if you then find yourself coming to the Temple of Isis with some speed, we would be most curious to hear of your travels. And grateful."

With those words, she looked at the messenger with a particular kind of intensity, and he felt an impression, like a thumbprint, pressing on his third eye. It made a slight stinging feeling that spread deep into his brain as he felt his perceptions expand rapidly. How glorious! Now he could see the colors surrounding and swirling around the High Priestess. Now he could see, or did he hear, the spirits of the river itself. How glorious this new way of seeing was, and how distracting: to see and hear and feel so much more!

"I understand, Most High. I *see* exactly what you require." He bowed deeply again and again and again, till Atvasfara chuckled and summoned a servant to take the young man for food and refreshment.

"Be on your way to Pharaoh tomorrow then, little brother. And we will look to see you at the Temple in the days that follow."

As she replayed this conversation, Atvasfara's mind was spinning with the repercussions of this news. Dalia, half-sister to Pharaoh, and the choice of many for that highest seat had, in a massive confrontation with her sister, publicly thrown away the battle for ascendency and made haste out of Egypt to study somewhere in the far North. Atvasfara stood abruptly and walked to the front of her protected platform, standing just inside the shade thrown by the silk curtains. She watched as the water of Mother Naihl, brown and amber at this point of the river, carried them with gathering speed down to the mouth, the village of Thonis, and what the messenger had said was the strange assortment of companions that stood with the returning Dalia. Atvasfara's youngest attendant came to stand by her.

"You seem troubled, my Lady. May I assist you somehow?"

"No, my dear, I need nothing. But I am troubled. Rather, there is trouble coming, and I can't see it." Atvasfara's brow formed a deep single line between her brows. "Why, when I need fore-vision the most, did no dream come to me last night to shine light on our way? I feel the pull of those other women. I know they are coming. But why... ?" Atvasfara shook her head as if to shake off a spider web. "Ah, now with Dalia in the mix, it is less clear. She always was the wild card.

"She had gone away before you came to the Temple, my dear. But Dalia had been the favorite of many within the workings of the court, had been seen as the most stable, dare they say, most sane one of the sisters entitled to receive the throne. When their mother, Medrona, She who was Pharaoh, had died, the second eldest daughter, Petrinh, ascended to the throne. She had died in her thirtieth sun cycle, in what some posited as suspicious circumstances. No one dared say aloud their deepest fear, the most horrible of possibilities: that a life had been taken deliberately. No, the thought was repellent, too evil to even contemplate. So, the court split into factions, rumors flowed like the Naihl itself, and continuance of life was not a certainty. In the midst of that Dalia had departed. What might it mean now that she has returned? Has she come back to claim the throne? Ah, it is nonsensical to ramble. We shall just have to see what is."

Shouts were heard from the barge at the front of the flotilla. The young attendant, sweet and with the promise of great beauty in her face, looked with tender eyes upon her Lady.

"We approach Thonis, my Lady. Shall you prepare to disembark?"

She helped Atvasfara into her ceremonial robes of gold embroidered onto gold, and attached the headdress of Isis with the beak of the raven atop her head. It seemed that Atvasfara grew in stature and magnificence as her official garments were laid upon her. Her aura shimmered in a vibrant deep magenta, and she radiated authority and celestial right.

They felt a low bump under their feet as the barge was moored at the riverbank. Atvasfara murmured a small thank you to the young woman and turned to find that her other two attendants, her friends since childhood, stood ready to process with her down to the shore. They saw her brace her shoulders and grace them with that flash of smile that said she was ready for anything. Like a flight of swans, Atvasfara and her three devoted attendants glided down the stairs, across the gangplank and onto the cinnamon sands that framed the Naihl.

Dalia stood alone on the beach in a flowing emerald tunic and robe, warm for the first time in four years. Her neck and arms were unadorned with the jewelry that was her right by rank, and she was bareheaded with her black glossy hair loosely pulled back away from her face. She had a small half smile that barely tipped the corners of her mouth, and her eyes held Atvasfara's with greeting and depths of hidden message.

"Welcome home, Dalia, Priestess of Nut."

"I trust the sincerity of your welcome, Atvasfara, High Priestess of Isis. We shall see if that welcome extends into the court of Pharaoh, eh?"

Atvasfara looked at Dalia carefully and saw that the years abroad had not aged her. Still small of stature, her skin had lightened with the years of no strong sun. She had fewer lines of stress around her eyes, and an ease in her limbs that had not been present before her scholar's journey.

"The North seems to have been kind to you," Atvasfara said as she stepped closer to embrace Dalia. As their two heads came to rest beside the other, Dalia whispered in Atvasfara's ear.

"I bring to you your sisters of the vision. The Goddess made it clear to me that now was not the time to avoid my own nightmares of the past. The future must take care of itself."

Atvasfara pulled back and looked deep into Dalia's black eyes, "For whatever comes next, I shall be grateful for your company and your courage. Now, where are these sisters you speak of?"

Dalia gestured with her arm, up and over the high dune directly lining the shore. The women began to walk along the path and Dalia said cryptically, "Open your eyes and your heart, my friend."

"I have seen their faces in my dreams," Atvasfara said with a tinge of irritation in her voice.

"Well, yes, but in the flesh… Let's just say, it may be louder and smellier than your dreams gave you hint!"

As they crested the top of the dune Atvasfara came to a sudden stop. Arrayed before them was a crescent moon of people and creatures with colors and clothing and body art and weapons and demeanor unlike anything she had ever seen before. There was an elephant – she had seen only paintings of those – with an elaborate floating platform on its back. There was a huge woman – taller than any man in Egypt – with long flames of red hair and festooned with swords and knives and leather armor. Seven women, tall and lean seemed to flitter in and out of focus, wearing robes of shimmering amethyst that seemed to obey winds that weren't blowing. A giant black cat, a woman with elaborate bright feathers in her hair, two young girls with feral eyes, a woman of middle years wearing shorn off trousers had one hand on the elephant's trunk. There were more folks, women and men. Was that massive thing a dog? All seemed to be held in a suspension, in silence, waiting to see what Atvasfara would do. And for once in her life, Atvasfara didn't know what to do.

Dalia broke the spell by drawing Atvasfara by the hand, down the far slope of the dune, taking her to meet each of the other vision carriers, one by one, telling her their names and home places and the Goddesses they served.

"All these twelve received the same vision of what is to come. Their friends and families and companions travel with them," Dalia said and broadly indicated the women and men standing behind the twelve. "They ask entry into the Land of Egypt and the protection of the Temple of Isis."

Atvasfara caught the hidden message. Asking for the protection of the Temple of Isis, indeed. Placing these travelers outside the jurisdiction of Pharaoh's court. Strategic of Dalia. Atvasfara knew that whatever happened next, whatever was actually unfolding today, had been set in place moons before, perhaps eons before: Goddess foretold, Goddess directed, and hopefully, Goddess protected. She looked at

each vision carrier in the eye. Uxua, Awa, Badh, Parasfahe, Maia, Tiamet, Driftwood, Ni Me, Silbara, Autakla, Kiyia, Io. And now herself
as the thirteenth. The Sisterhood was complete.

"I, too, received this vision, my sisters. I extend to you the most
heartfelt greetings, and all the sanctuary of the Temple of Isis. Welcome to Egypt!"

AT THONIS

With their journey at a hiatus, Io was bored. She wandered aimlessly and watched with vague curiosity as the Egyptians and travelers had met and begun to make a connected camp. Never being very comfortable with small talk, or most conversation truthfully, she hung back and listened from a slight distance as the older women met and initiated friendships and shared stories.

Feeling lonely, she went looking for Kiyia who had become the closest thing she had ever had to a friend, but stopped short when she saw her leg wrestling with the wild haired woman, Badh. Those two, powerfully muscled and less than skilled in social graces, had an instant affinity. A small group was clustered around them, laughing and cheering them on. Io stood at the edge of the group, and noticed that the young man with auburn curls who traveled with Badh had a look of mingled consternation and forlornness. He and the giant hound turned and walked to the tables of food and drink, and he placed a large bowl of fresh water down for the dog, who gratefully and sloppily drank deep.

She moved away from the noisy crowd, instead looking for Pel. The older girl had been a steady and concerned presence on their journey southward and Io had secretly enjoyed the big-sisterish bossiness that Pel had in organizing their travels and tending to Io's needs. Not that she would ever let Pel know that. But right at this moment, Io was uncomfortably alone in the midst of all these people, and she looked through the company to find her. She found her standing close, too close, to that extraordinarily beautiful young man with the copper skin and starburst tattoos across those ridiculously high carved cheekbones. Talo was a few inches taller than Pel, and was looking down into her eyes, standing closer than was necessary. Why this bothered Io so much was a mystery to her, but she found it enormously irritating. The giant jaguar that had been standing at his side must have found it annoying too, for the cat left and walked over to the hound and the water bowl.

Io, edgy and adrift, went to sit at the edge of the encampment in the shadow thrown by the sand dune. She felt a jolt of surprise, not alarm really, just surprise she told herself, when the hound and the cat came to join her and sit, one on either side. *Well, at least they'll be quiet,* she thought gloomily. The hound nudged her elbow with his long snout and lifted her arm so it draped over his thick neck. On her other side, the jaguar did the same. The trio sat like that for quite some time, silent and at rest, watching the swirl of people and hearing the rivers of laughter and speech.

As shadows lengthened into deep mauve elongations of forms, the young fellow with the curly head came to the three carrying a plate of food.

"I thought you might want something. Don't worry, Dog and Cat won't want your food. They look down their long noses at human food. I'm sure they will go off hunting for themselves any moment," he said with cheerfulness.

Said Dog and Cat granted him a sideways look and resumed their perusal of all the goings on. The young man squatted down in front of Io, and flashed a quick, sweet smile that lit his face all the way to his tawny eyes.

"Aren't you hungry?" He handed her the plate and looked over his shoulder at the mingling of people. "I don't like crowds much. Do you?"

Io shook her head and mumbled a smattering of sounds that he took to be a thank you.

"You are welcome, little Curly. We fuzzy heads have to stick together, eh?"

He ruffled his own curls, and then reached out a hand to ruffle hers. She pulled back a fraction, and then allowed his hand to shift her hair with a gentle touch like one would handle a wild creature.

$$) \bigcirc ($$

"Ready to call it quits, old woman?" Kiyia taunted Badh who growled in response.

"That's it! That's it! Use your right leg!"

In his exuberance in the wresting match, Smith the Younger forgot for a second who he was supposed to be rooting for and shouted out support for the wild-haired woman from Eiru. His slip earned him an elbow in the ribs from Misi, close by his side.

"Better cheer on the Guardian," she advised under her breath. "I'm sure she is paying attention."

"Oh, I'm not afraid of her anymore," he replied, and half believed it.

The crowd around Kiyia, Guardian of Epona, and Badh, of the Cailleach, the Keeper of Wild Spaces had grown to include Smith the Elder who seemed to be taking particular delight when Kiyia took a hit, Tiamet's servants, Yan and Shema, the calm and observant man from Calanais, Malvu, and the Sumerian guide they had acquired in Canaan, Uluf who was a bit flummoxed by women in such undignified positions. Kiyia and Badh were circling each other, spinning a cocoon of dust and sand as they threw out feet trying to trip the other.

"Oooohhh!" a collective cry of triumph and empathic pain as Kiyia hit the ground hard. She sprang to her feet like a cat, and lunged forward with a feint to the right and a swooping leg from the left, bringing Badh down onto her knees with a thud.

"Ooooooooooohh!" responded the crowd.

Sweating and panting, Badh brushed a hank of hair out of her eyes with a forceful forearm and ran straight at Kiyia's midsection, aiming her shoulder low at Kiyia's belly. The younger of the two wrestlers flew backward and landed on her rear, sliding a few feet in the sand.

"Who did you call 'old woman'?" Badh roared with arms lifted high like wings.

Kiyia took three gasping attempts at breath to no avail, then with a light-headed rush, felt her lungs fill up again.

"You, old woman…" Kiyia rasped, with a slight grin breaking, "help me up!" she said reaching a hand up to Badh who was standing looming over her.

"Do you concede?" Badh said as she stretched her arm forward to assist.

"Never!" Kiyia howled as she yanked on Badh's arm and flipped her over her head to land on her back in the dirt beyond.

The crowd hushed, waiting to see if Badh was hurt, waiting to see if she moved, waiting to see what the repercussions of that trick would be.

Badh lay as if stunned for a long moment, then began to laugh from deep in her belly, so contagious a sound that Kiyia and all the spectators joined in. Kiyia sat on the ground next to Badh with a thump and the two continued to cackle and howl with dust and tears of laughter flowing down their cheeks.

Misi and Smith the Younger slipped away to find some private moments. "I think the Guardian has found a playmate," the young man whispered in her ear. "I don't believe she will notice us gone for a bit."

$$\text{)} \bigcirc \text{(}$$

Talo of the Land of Ix Chel, brother of the Divine Embodiment of the Goddess, knew himself to be of great physical beauty. He was usually, along with his sister Uxua, far and away the most beautiful creature in any gathering of people. But he found himself struck to the core by the perfection of the young woman standing before him. He had seen her the night before, when their two parties had met up by the village of Thonis, and he had found himself tracking her movements, knowing always where she was in the crowd, feeling her absence if she went out of sight as a physical ache. Now, standing close enough to see the sharp spikes of her surprisingly black eyelashes, he felt his heart speared by the clarity of those sapphire eyes. Guileless and direct, she too was suspended in the power of their connected gaze.

"How do you come to be on this journey? And whence do you

come?" he asked, feeling less graceful and composed than he would in normal conversation.

"I am a Dedicant of Artemis from our Mother Temple in Ephesus. I was tasked with the role of protector and companion for Io when she received the fateful vision," Pel replied.

She stood, tall and lithe with her wheaten hair in the elaborate seven strand warrior braids that denoted her status. She still wore the fawn tunic and leather leggings of her Temple with her bare arms now a deep golden tan from their journey southward. The blue sickle moon tattoo at her third eye seemed more muted than before she had faced many months of travel and increasingly hot suns.

"We met up with Kiyia, the Guardian of Epona, and her band over two moons ago and have traveled with them since," she continued, feeling a blush begin to blossom in her face from the intensity of his gaze. "And you? What are you called and whence do you come?"

"Me? I am Talo, the twin of Uxua, the Divine Embodiment of Ix Chel. We come from across the ocean, in the land of Yucatan," he said, gesturing with his arm toward his sister who was standing some thirty feet away in deep conversation with Maia of Kali Ma. "Where she goes, I go."

He was vaguely aware that his heart was beating quickly, and that the rest of the commotion around them had fallen away till all he saw, all he heard, all he could feel was Pel.

"What is a dedicant?"

"Hmmm?" she said, adrift in a sea of emerald eyes.

"A dedicant? What does it mean?"

"Oh. We who are born on the full moon are chosen to come to the Temple to train when we are quite small. We train till age nine when we may be selected to join a Wild Hunt pack of nine girls. If our pack is successful in bringing down a stag, we are allowed to train for nine more sun cycles. And then we decide. Do we become a Dedicant who lives in the Temple or a Trainer who lives in the village and comes and goes in the outside world?"

"And you decided."

"Yes. I was content to serve the Goddess, more than content, fulfilled. And then. Well, then, She had other plans for me," Pel explained, drawn closer and closer to him like filings to a magnet.

"Yes," he said softly. "Nothing is as it was before."

$$) \bigcirc ($$

"You are a most exquisite creature, aren't you?" Autakla stroked the long trunk and marveled at the ripples of skin that covered the powerful muscles underneath. "So beautiful, like a land whale, eh?"

Savi seemed to understand the joke and lifted his trunk to let out a trumpet that sounded a lot like laughter. He gently wrapped his trunk around Autakla's hips and lifted her up above his head and around onto his back. The harness he had worn with the floating platform for Parasfahe had been taken off, and Autakla sat on his warm broad neck and felt the leathery skin against her thighs. She leaned forward and said, "Shall we swim in this sea of sand?"

Savi ambled away from the camp and took the path over the dunes toward the River Naihl. The servants of Atvasfara took a prudent step back when he approached, and clapped and laughed as he lifted a giant spout of water from the river and sprayed it over his back onto Autakla.

She, the child of Seal Woman, tilted back her head and spread her arms wide, thrilled to feel the flow of water on her face.

"More, my Land Whale! More!"

$$) \bigcirc ($$

"Wrapping, I think. Swollen painful joints benefit greatly from a wrapping of the affected areas in seaweed. Have you tried that?" Celebi, the Brighid from Calanais asked.

"Yes!" Dalia of Egypt exclaimed. "Of course! The seaweed and the outer layer of oat straw. That worked well for the older fisher folk at Calanais. I brought oat straw with me in my medicine trunk. We just need the seaweed." She and Celebi dove into a discussion of types of seaweed and the benefits thereof.

Parasfahe of Sumeria was usually violently opposed to anyone looking at her tortured body, much less poking at it and making medical suggestions. But for some reason, she was oddly comfortable with Celebi and Dalia. Maybe it was because those two women didn't appear to pity her. If anything, they observed her with a kind of professional detachment that was still kind and not overbearing.

"You know, after all these years and all those treatments, I don't believe anyone has suggested seaweed," Parasfahe conceded.

"Wonderful!" Dalia jumped up and called for an Egyptian servant. The girl came and stood before Dalia, about the same height and with downcast eyes and a catarrhal mouth agape.

"Look up, little fish," Dalia gently commanded. "I won't eat you. Run to the shore and procure several baskets of dulse and laver. Make sure it is still damp. Have them pack it in leaves to stay supple. Well, what are you waiting for?"

The girl slipped away like the minnow Dalia had called her.

"The seaweed shall be excellent, Celebi. Well done!" Dalia looked delighted and turned her gaze back to Parasfahe with a hint of glee. "Now that that is in process, let us talk about your monthly bleeding cycles."

Parasfahe resigned herself to these curious ministrations, as Celebi and Dalia questioned her with the avid focus of a mother hen watching a chick. It looked like she was going to get better whether she wanted to or not. She allowed herself a gossamer wisp of hope. Maybe she could be well!

☽ ○ ☾

Under an awning fronting her luxurious tent, Atvasfara of the Temple of Isis sat with three other brilliant scholars of astral observation. A slight breeze rustled the silk hangings, keeping the afternoon comfortable and warm but not stifling. They watched as Autakla, waving a hand in joyful greeting, rode by on Savi the elephant. The four women heard the laughter and cheers from the wrestling match across the encampment and a loud victorious roar. All of the travelers were learning of each other, enjoying the respite from weeks on sea or land, and resting up for whatever was to come next. And these four were looking at the forces that had moved them all here.

Silbara of Calanais had spent her time in training, observing the moon's complete nodal cycle of eighteen and a half sun cycles. The Priestesses of Brig had, since time before memory, held that to be their sacred task. They knew in the deepest parts of their beings, where She was in that long ellipse, and counted themselves truly blessed if they could see more than one of the complete lunar node cycles in a lifetime. Though she was still young, Silbara was steady, and had a perfect memory of all the astral events from during her time at the Mystery School these last fifteen turns of the solar wheel.

Ni Me, one of the Seven Sisters of Malta who had come originally from the Pleiades, had spent her time on Earth tracking the movements of all the planets and suns. The Seven kept perfect records of these planetary mappings, and sent a continuous stream of information back to their home world. Tiamet from the Roof of the World had spent her very, very long lifetime in meditation and prayer, staring at the sky, and had a particularly precise catalogue of eclipses, both solar and lunar.

An astral chart on papyrus was spread out before them on the low table. Atvasfara's three attendants were seated on low stools nearby, and her servants kept a constant and yet unobtrusive supply of refreshments coming. Chilled hibiscus juice was Tiamet's new favorite, and Silbara had discovered the perfection of a ripe fig.

"We see here the alignment at the Winter Solstice, the night we all received the vision," Atvasfara pointed out. Tiamet, whose faith in written maps and charts was limited at best, grunted and reached for a date filled with pistachios and spices.

Ni Me sang under her breath as she contemplated the chart, and then turned it around so that the angle of the alignment became clear.

"And see, here at the Summer Solstice! See here the pattern will be the eight-pointed Star of the Goddess!"

"I stood witness to a full lunar eclipse on that fateful night of our vision," Tiamet said around a mouthful. "And there will be a full solar eclipse on the longest day."

Silbara looked pale and excited, "That longest day will also be a dark moon. With eclipse and dark moon we will have a darkened day and an even darker night. And it is a sacred time, the last fourteen days of the lunar node cycle when She will have completed Her journey! All the factors: planets, sun, moon, they all reach a peak at that time!"

The four astronomers shared a look of the deepest knowing. The stars and the Beings of Light were directing them toward that auspicious day. The celestial bodies would be doing their work, and now the Thirteen knew when to do theirs.

$$\text{☽ ◯ ☾}$$

"Bloodroot. And then we set the dye with horse urine," Yollo said.

"Ah yes, and this deep purple? It looks like the amethyst gems. How do you achieve this color?" Ndeup was fingering Yollo's shawl, marveling at the intensity of colors and high degree of skill in the weaving.

"Well, we have a berry, we call it elderberry. It fruits late in the summer. And if you let it sit, and let the juice ferment, it sets this deep purple and resists all fading."

"We use ground shells to achieve a red like you achieve with the bloodroot. Again, set with urine, but we use goat."

Ndeup, the mother of Awa, and Yollo, who had been kidnapped by Kiyia, the Guardian of Epona, settled in to share weaving techniques, oooing and ahhing over the patterns in each other's work. They discussed tightness of weave and the benefits of sheep over plant fibers. And as with all of the distaff arts, the deeper links to the realm of the spirits quickly became the focus of their conversation.

"Well, yes, the weaving of prayers is vital for the integrity of the fabric. But I have found that the pattern can create a map for the community," Ndeup explained.

"Show me!" Yollo replied with eagerness.

"Well, see here, in the pattern of my turban, I have the lines of color that signify all the priestesses in my lineage. This black line is my great-great-great grandmother. The deep brown is her daughter. The red is her daughter. This yellow is my grandmother. The blue is my mother. And the green is myself."

"There are two black lines side by side here," Yollo pointed out.

"Ah yes, that second line is my girl, Awa. When she was born the ancestor spirits told me she was my great-great-great grannie reborn. So, we added her color again. Then we repeat the pattern, until she has a daughter and another color is added. This is our lineage, and I wear it on me always. But you could do any community that way. Use colors and patterns to represent the health and longevity or strength that is desired."

"All of those who received the vision are doing some weaving together of their own, yes?" Yollo said softly, as an idea bloomed in her mind.

"Yes, the vision carriers need to be a new tribe, I think, to do whatever it is they are called here to do." Ndeup agreed. "They need to feel a part of each other."

"And those of us who traveled with them, we need to do some weaving together too." Yollo could see the patterns necessary being drawn quickly and sharply in her mind's eye.

"And we all need to wear the pattern of this group, to make it whole!"

Ndeup was right there with her, excitement building. For them both the reason and rightness of their participation in the journey was suddenly revealed. They could envision all the assorted members of this group wearing cloaks or tunics or shirts or turbans of a pattern that spoke of their mission and their connection. The weaving needed to be done on all levels in the physical and spiritual realms. As above, so below. As within, so without.

"Sister Weaver, we have some work ahead of us, yes?"

"Yes! They will weave the magick and we will weave the cloth!"

$$) \bigcirc ($$

"Uxua," the beautiful young woman said, nodding her head in greeting and introduction.

"Maia," the older woman replied with a hint of a smile as she looked at the creature before her who was much, much more beautiful than anyone had a need to be. "I have seen you with a man and a cat, haven't I?"

"Yes," Uxua acknowledged with a trill of musical laughter. "My brother Talo and the jaguar, my familiar. And you have an animal companion as well, I believe."

Maia gave a snort of a laugh.

"Yes. Savi. You could say he serves as both familiar and brother too."

"Well, that certainly makes it easier to keep track of their whereabouts, doesn't it?" Uxua said in her deep voice, with a sliver of her dry wit.

She shot a quick look over her shoulder at her brother, Talo. He stood a short distance away, rapt in conversation with one of those two Hunters of Artemis girls. He looked very rapt indeed. Uxua felt a twinge of something that might have been concern, or even jealousy, and then quickly pushed it aside.

"Am I correct that you, too, come from a land of jungle?" Uxua asked.

"Yes! And by the Goddess I could wish us there in a heartbeat! This air is so dry, and the heat sears my throat," Maia exclaimed without thinking.

How astonishing, this was the first time she had felt any homesickness at all. She and Uxua took a stroll over the dune to the river. The air was a bit softer here, and the two women, who had always been so busy leading their worlds, stood together and acknowledged how very odd it felt to have absolutely nothing to do at that moment. They watched the servants of Egypt carry food and cushions back over the dune. They saw the black-headed heron diving to catch the small fish in schools near the center of the river. They laughed as Savi sprayed water over the selkie girl. And they stood in stillness, feeling the current of the river and the deepening shadows of the afternoon.

"I always dreamed of what it would be like to not have everyone needing me," Maia said, her words coming slowly, as if from a dream itself.

"I, as well. To be free of responsibility. How lovely that sounded," Uxua agreed. "But in actuality, I am finding it stultifyingly boring."

"Exactly! I could do with someone to boss around!" Maia turned to her glamorous new friend with a wide smile across her face and her slanted eyes alight with mischief. "Let us go find someone to give orders to."

"What a delightful idea!" Uxua replied. And the two turned to go back over the dune, and find a way to be in charge of something again.

THE CIRCLE IS CAST

Young Awa had spent the afternoon and early gloaming floating between the small groups of travelers, watching the hearing folk, gleaning what she could from their lips and their bodies. She saw her mother speak with great animation to a thin pale woman wrapped in a beautiful shawl of magenta and amethyst. Weaver had clearly found weaver. She saw the tiny girl, Io, seated between the giant hound and huge black jaguar with an arm around each one's neck. Dalia of Egypt and Celibi, the Brighid from Calanais had settled next to Parasfahe of Sumeria.

All seemed to be well enough, but Awa felt some disquiet that she couldn't name. *Go to the trees,* she thought. So, she found the small cluster of palms a quarter mile away and began to introduce herself to the spirits that lived there. Gentle *how do you do's* and exchanges of names unfolded as Awa sat in the arms of the ancestor spirits, and told the tale of her journey thus far.

"There is one of your folk in much distress. Can you help her? We have offered to connect her with the trees of her homeland, but she refuses," the spirits said.

"Can you guide me to her?" Awa asked.

And she felt herself handed from one spirit to the next, tenderly passed through the trees till she saw the huddled back of the one called Driftwood who was sobbing into a deep green cloak. Awa stood in indecision: should she step forward to help or honor the girl's privacy? A not-so-gentle nudge at her back shoved her forward as the trees decided for her. She moved silently, her long, thin, high-arched feet barely troubling the sand, and sat down next to Driftwood.

The girl didn't look up. The only clue Awa had that her presence was even noticed was a slight tightening and subtle shifting away of Driftwood's shoulders.

They sat, alone and yet together, for a long time as the sunkissed the western horizon and shot brilliant arrows of scarlet in a half circle of dying light. Gradually Driftwood's sobs subsided, and eventually she lifted her grief-ravaged face and wiped her nose on the green wool. She stared straight ahead and said nothing. Awa, intimately comfortable with silence, stayed still beside her.

The light was now so diminished that the trees threw no shadows, and bats whipped through the twilight sky.

"Why are you so sad?" Awa asked in her flat intonation that made the question sound like a statement.

"Because the wrong woman died," Driftwood replied, equally without inflection. She continued, "Alama, my mentor and teacher would have been so thrilled to be here and see all of this unfolding. She could have met the others and represented our traditions with grace and wisdom. But instead, it is only me to speak for all the beauty of the North Woods and the greatness of Nematona."

And she continued to tell the story of Alama's death and her being taken into the realm of the Fey, "There were hundreds of the Fey there, the Queen and all her court. They stood and sang and opened their arms. I watched as Alama's body completely disappeared and was absorbed by the trees, and saw her spirit take form as one of the Fey. And then they all were gone in the blink of an eye, and I was alone."

"Why won't you let these trees connect with your home forest? They might send a message to Alama for you," Awa said gently.

"I am not worthy," Driftwood replied morosely.

"That's camel spit!"

"What did you say?" Driftwood snorted, with the tiniest hint of a turn up at the corner of her mouth.

"You heard me. I said that's camel spit!"

Both girls began to giggle, then laugh, then howl with gulps of air until they wept tears of relief and absolution. They sat together as complete darkness fell, and Awa could no longer read Driftwood's lips. She turned to her and let her fingertips gently dance over Driftwood's face, feeling the trails that tears had run down her cheeks, "Well, if you don't deserve to talk to her, you do deserve to mourn her properly. Come with me!"

Awa grabbed Driftwood's wrist and pulled her to her feet. The grove of palm trees seemed to part and make an avenue in the semi-dark, and Awa raced back to the camp, tugging Driftwood along behind her.

Back where the Egyptians and the travelers had conjoined, as evening drifted down upon them, all the vision carriers and their companions gathered, settling into groupings that were not defined by geography but rather by friendships weathered or newly formed. The servants and attendants of Atvasfara had set up an elaborate temporary village along the riverside of the dunes. A constant stream of women, rivulets flowing back and forth over top the sand ridge, brought food and drink along with cushions and benches, setting everything around a giant stack of cedar and acacia wood that was ready to be set ablaze.

The two girls burst into the assemblage, and Awa ran straight for Ni Me. On the sail from Malta to this shore the two had discovered that they could speak directly to each other's minds, a joyous find for Awa who still found vocal speech very taxing. With gestures and thought forms Awa was able to communicate how Driftwood had never had the opportunity for a formal leave-taking of her mentor, *"The trees and the Fey did it all. Quite wondrous, I'm sure, but it left no place for our Driftwood to act."*

"Ah, how wise you are, my little bird. What shall we do?" Ni Me replied.

"Perhaps tonight, with us all holding space for her, she can speak a memorial." Awa gestured to the wood standing ready to flame right behind her. *"A fire to honor a great priestess?"*

"Yes! A fire so that we may all honor a great priestess. And ask her blessings upon our endeavors." Ni Me smiled, and her amber eyes lit with a fierce intensity. *"Yes, a funeral fire! And a ritual created by the Thirteen!"*

So as the evening progressed and food was had and stories told, they passed the word that they would make a ritual circle tonight, their first one with all the Thirteen together. And that ritual would honor the lineage of Driftwood and her Alama, and they would honor the lineages of all the women who had stood before so that they could stand here now, ready and able to work the greatest magicks yet seen.

$$\text{)} \bigcirc \text{(}$$

When the time was right and the desert sky was filled with a multitude of stars, Awa stood up and came to stand on the west side, close to the fire that had settled down to a steady, even burn. One by one the others of the Thirteen came to stand and complete the circle, holding the energy of the direction whence they had come. Ni Me and Atvasfara were on Awa's right and Uxua on her left. Across from Awa, on the north side of the fire, Autakla and Badh stood side by side. Kiyia took Parasfahe's arm and helped her to stand in the east, and Io and Tiamet flanked them. Around the Thirteen, forming an outer Circle, stood the companions of their journeys and the familiars to form the outer boundary of the sacred space. Now the work could begin.

Silbara of Brig and Maia of Kali Ma led Driftwood closer in to stand as near as she could bear to the heat of the flames. Their Goddesses had particular affinity with fire, and they began to move moon-wise around this pile of wood and flame, calling the element of Sacred Fire, summoning it to be present, and witness their work. All of the Thirteen, and many of their companions making up the outer circle, could feel the exact moment when Fire in Her divine presence entered their Circle and it was cast. A collective *ahh* in exhalation, and Silbara moved to the north, and Maia to the east, stepping back into the Circle of the Thirteen. There was an audible 'click' as the women held the energies of their directions, and their working Circle began to hum in a low frequency that was more discernible in their bones than in their ears. They caught each other's eyes in recognition of something extraordinary happening, then let their lids drift closed so as to see better with internal vision.

"I come to speak of Alama, the First Among Equals," Driftwood began in a halting voice. She took a deep bracing breath and began again.

"I come… to speak… of Alama, the First Among Equals!" her voice rang out into the desert night, so strong and filled with love that the palm trees and the river and all the spirits of that land could hear her, and all attended to what she had to say.

"I come to speak of Alama, beloved of all the priestesses of her Grove, beloved of all the priestesses of all the Groves of the North Woods!"

A shot of flame reached upward, blue and orange.

"I come to speak of Alama, teacher and mentor and Keeper of the Ways!"

The wind began to whip tiny curls of sand around their feet.

"I come to speak of Alama, daughter of the Fey!"

Shooting stars fell across the dome of sky above.

"I come to speak of Alama, generous of heart, so generous that her heart split open as she saved my life!"

A keening floated from the mouths of the women there.

"I come to speak of Alama, beautiful and graceful, the mother of sisterhoods!"

The fire grew and danced.

"I come to speak of Alama, most worthy, most honorable, most cherished, never to be forgotten!"

And Driftwood swept the green cloak of Alama off her shoulders and threw it into the blaze.

"I am Eiofachta, of Nematona, the soul daughter of Alama! I come to speak of her and for her and for the Goddess that she adored. I am Eiofachta, and I stand in the footsteps made by Alama, forever the First Among Equals!"

The wool caught and the fire roared. Sparks shot up into the firmament. The driftwood girl faced her fears and her responsibilities and was transformed. The woman that she was meant to be now stood in her place.

The smell of moss and ferns and moist forest soil filled the Circle.

Each woman of the Thirteen felt the gentle touch of dew on her face, and saw, in her mind's eye, the sharp blue eyes of Alama surrounded by her thick auburn hair. It was a face filled with compassion and forgiveness and intelligence and peace.

"Alama! Alama! Alama!" the Thirteen chanted, raising the sound in a cone of energy that touched those falling stars. The Seven Daughters of the Earth sang her name. The jaguar screamed. The hound let loose a single deep bray. The elephant ripped the night with sound. And when the last thread of Alama's cloak was consumed by the flames, the fire folded in on itself and was immediately extinguished.

☽ ○ ☾

They all stood in the instantaneous darkness, listening to the particles of silence, breathing in the smell of gravity that kept them grounded on the Earth. Eiofachta felt oceans of tears streaming down her face, as if she had been anointed and made free of guilt by the enormity of Alama's forgiveness. Finding her way to the north side of the Circle, she stepped between Silbara and Io. The Thirteen, together in Circle. As the silence deepened, stretched, became eternal, each woman of the Thirteen placed her right hand on the heart of the woman to her right, and then placed her left hand atop the hand now resting on her own heart. They all began to chant, one voice first, that of Awa, the most generous of them. Then additional voices joined her flattened song. Then all the voices with the glorious harmony from Ni Me floating above and below and around all the other voices.

"Welcome to my heart. Welcome to my heart. Welcome to my heart."

Over and over and over, until there was no singular voice, just the united voice of the Thirteen raised in divine song.

The companions who had been standing witness in the outer circle began to drift away, some to sit some distance farther to watch and protect, some to settle into the arms of a loved one, most with tears of their own for the beauty and the stunning power of what they had just seen.

The Thirteen, connected in body and mind, and now in magick, sang and sang and sang until the first sounds of pre-dawn birds filled the night. They sang until the first glimpse of coral lit the eastern horizon. They sang until the Sun in all Her glory rose molten and regal. And with one joined breath they sank down onto the sand, exhausted bodies making a boundary around where their sacred fire had been, where their magickal Circle had been created. They rested then with arms holding and laps accepting heads. They stroked each others' hair and rubbed each others' backs. They held each other in such exquisite tenderness that the Goddesses, seeing this, were pleased.

$$\text{)} \bigcirc \text{(}$$

As the sun rose in the sky it turned from red to apricot to sunflower yellow. By three hands past the horizon, the companions of the Thirteen and the servants and Temple officials of Atvasfara had created a shaded pavilion where the Thirteen could retire. They had combined the awnings of several tents and covered the ground with layer upon layer of carpets and cushions of every hue of gem and flower. Gently they then went to assist the Thirteen to their feet and guide their wobbly walk toward the pavilion. Each of the Thirteen, even the most seasoned ritualists among them, the most learned in gramarye, felt scooped out, hollow, and empty of thought. Their magickal Circle of the night before had exceeded anything any of them had before experienced. It would be necessary, when thought was again possible, to be very careful in the construction of their ongoing work together. Their spirits were very willing; they must be prudent with their bodies.

$$\text{)} \bigcirc \text{(}$$

"Papa, how do we explain what we saw?" Smith the Younger was standing with his father at the charcoal remains of last night's ritual fire.

"There may be no explanation but that we have been gifted with a seeing that defies our understanding. I never, in my wildest dreams could have even thought to see and do and hear what we have seen and done and heard since Kiyia forced us into that boat at the point of her sword. I never, in my most vivid imaginings would have even thought to ever leave the Sea of Grasses. But here we are," his father said contemplatively. He looked at his son with a slight tinge of disorientation. "I feel like the earth is trembling beneath us. For the first time I am beginning to understand the panic I sometimes see in Kiyia's eyes, the tremble in Io's voice, the nightmares that haunt Parasfahe. And I have no words of comfort for you and your safety. May the Goddess protect you, my boy, for I fear that I have not and cannot."

The younger Smith shook his head once with vigor, "We will survive this Papa. Together!" He looked intensely at the ashes. "Pa! See. Something still burns!"

The older Smith followed the direction of his son's outstretched finger and saw that, indeed, some embers were still smoldering.

"How can that be? We saw that fire involute and be extinguished!"

The two men, so alike in physicality, so bonded in love and loyalty, crouched down to see the embers more clearly. Flaxen head near the one softened with gray. Strong arms covered in the tiny scars from their trade. Necks now deep red brown from months of travel in an ever-stronger heat. As they stared, they saw that sure enough, a tiny flicker of red moved at the very heart of the ashes, and a thread-like rise of smoke showed the life still of the Sacred Fire.

The father looked into his son's identical pale blue eyes, "I feel the call to save these embers. We could make a small box to hold them. But before we go anywhere near touching them we had better get permission."

With determined and yet apprehensive gait, the two went in search of one of the Thirteen. Or some of the Thirteen. Or all of the Thirteen. It was clearly a hive mind at work there. No one woman seemed to be the leader, or expert. From whom should they ask permission?

As they approached the pavilion, they saw the Thirteen all together, some reclining, some propped up with cushions, some languidly eating small bites of roasted lamb and lentils. The two men stood in the sun a few feet from the awnings that snapped in the quickening breeze. They waited with deference till Uxua noticed them there and called to them.

"What do you require?"

"Exalted One, we have seen some life still in the fire. We hear the command to save these embers. We are smiths and could craft a suitable receptacle, if the Thirteen so desire." Smith the Elder lowered his gaze as he finished speaking and waited.

Silbara and Maia stirred. They carried the fire wisdoms of their Goddesses and their peoples, and the others of the Thirteen looked to them for a decision. They gestured for the two Smiths to come into the shade and then settled down onto the carpets with easy grace, motioning for the two men to sit as well.

"We do this at Calanais. We save ash from one Fire Feast to seed the next," Silbara said.

"I am moved by your connection to the Fire and your listening to Her," Maia directed her words to the Smiths. "Perhaps we need to ask the Fire what we should do," she said to Silbara.

So, the two priestesses and the two Smiths walked over the now hot sand to stand around the remains of last night's ritual fire. The wind was rising more and whipped tendrils of hair into Silbara's face and tugged at their tunics. They stood in stillness, listening, and as they looked the tiny glimmer of fire became a long tongue of flame.

"She intends to live," Maia said.

"Can you make a small ember box with thirteen sheets of very thin metal?" Silbara asked the men.

"One with thirteen clasps," Smith the Younger slowly replied.

"With thirteen interlacing spirals in hammered copper," Smith the Elder added.

The men turned to rush off and begin the project, and then together, remembered with whom they were in audience, halted, pivoted on their heels, bowed, and asked permission to leave. Silbara laughed easily, and Maia smiled her huge wide smile.

"Proceed with haste. And may the Goddesses guide your work," Maia told them. "May They guide us all."

☽ ○ ☾

Four companions, Talo of the Yucatan, Domnhu the companion of the Keeper of Wild Spaces, Malvu the Chief Observer from Calanais, and Misi the girl who herded pigs, sat around a small bowl of lentils and roasted lamb. They ate without much consciousness, shoveling food in without tasting it. Their minds were elsewhere. They had witnessed a ritual of extraordinary power last night. As observers and protectors, they had known themselves to be essential in the event even as they watched the Thirteen create a shaft of energy that had connected the center of the Earth to the farthest stars. But they all felt twitchy, as if something much more needed to happen.

"I must do *something!*" Talo brusquely swiped at the fly buzzing his ear. "I feel that I will explode with uselessness."

"We *were* in service, my young friend. You felt how we held the outer circle for the Thirteen," Malvu of Calanais said calmly. He was rattled too, but so expert at carrying authority that none of his inner qualms rippled the surface of his outer demeanor of steady surety.

"That was then!" Domnhu almost shouted. He jumped to his feet, pumping slightly on the balls of his feet, his face pale with a slash of crimson across his cheeks. "We could hold the outer circle then. But next time? I don't believe these magickal workings are going to get anything but more and more powerful. These women, the Thirteen, have come from across the world, been called to do this. And then, you saw them this morning. Badh could hardly walk! Badh, stronger than mountains, all done in! We have to protect them better."

"So, let's do that," Misi said flatly.

They all turned to look at her in curiosity. She looked sturdier and more self-assured than at any time since she had been kidnapped by Kiyia and dragged into a leaky boat to come to Goddess knows where. Her life before had been one of sheer survival. Mourning the loss of her family in one fell swoop from disease, the need to feed herself, even her work herding those smart and stubborn pigs, it all had been to simply see her way to the next day. This journey had shown her her strength, and she had found a family of sorts, odd in appearance but bound together. They were a unit of support for each other. She and Smith the Younger had become friends and lovers. Yollo, still weaker than they all liked, but improving daily was a gentle and quiet maternal presence. And Smith the Elder was their rock. They had been dragged halfway around the world by Kiyia, the Guardian of Epona, and had found a comfort together that defied their circumstances. And Misi had found how to speak her mind.

"How do we do better?" she asked.

Talo thought for a moment, and decided that his people's Mysteries, the ones he had been taught in secret and into which he had been initiated, were not useful if kept from these folk. These were his people now. He needed to teach them.

"The Form," he stated.

"What form?" Malvu asked.

"The Jaguar Dance," Talo replied. "No one from the outside has ever been taught this Form. It is one of our deepest Mysteries. If we were in my Temple, you could be punished for even watching this Form being practiced. But I think, perhaps, we are all very far from our Temples now, eh? I believe that my ancestors will approve if I teach you the Jaguar Dance."

"A dance?" Domnhu snorted. "How is that going to help?"

"Stand up, boy, and prepare to be proven wanting!" Talo snapped back.

Malvu stood up abruptly and stepped between the two younger men, placing a hand on each chest.

"Mayhaps our energies can be better used preparing to be aimed *not* at one another."

Like two dogs meeting and, after sizing each other up, choosing not to fight, Domnhu and Talo leaned back slightly and cut glances toward Malvu, but remained poised, with Malvu's hands separating them.

"You are right, of course," Talo conceded. But he didn't break the tableau.

"Oh, by the sun and the moon! Will you two stop, and let's learn this dance then," Misi stood and brushed the sand off her bottom.

Chagrined, Talo and Domnhu took two steps back from each

other, and Talo began their instruction.

"The Form begins like this. Start with your feet slightly apart and your knees softened. Weight on the balls of your feet. Lower yourself to the ground. Swing the right leg out to the side and forward."

The sun swept higher and higher in the sky and the teaching continued. Malvu was breathing heavily, and Misi's face was pomegranate red.

"Straighten your knee!" Talo barked.

Domnhu refused to give Talo the satisfaction of seeing him falter, and though his muscles were trembling he kept apace.

"If you fall get right back up!" Talo's voice was inside their heads.

They kicked high above their heads. They turned and struck with both hand and foot. They slid to their knees and jumped back to their feet. They tipped to one side and, after placing a hand on the ground, sprung over, feet overhead. It was an elaborate sequence. It was beautiful. It was intricate. It was brutal. After the peak of midday, Talo brought them to the end of the sequence of movements, and directed them to take three deep breaths as they returned to their starting posture.

"That is the first section of the Form. The ones to follow aren't easy like this one," Talo said. He wasn't even breathing hard and only had a slight sheen of sweat across those ridiculously carved cheekbones.

"No one as pretty as you should be so competent," Misi gasped and sank down as her legs turned to water. "Out of interest, after you 'Jaguar Dance' all our strength away, how do we protect the Thirteen better?"

Malvu was bent over, hands on knees and trying very hard to get the sound out of his tortured lungs, "That is a fair question, young Talo."

Domnhu stood and stared at Talo with a defiant glint in his eyes. But then he slowly gave him a single nod.

"It will make us warriors though, won't it?"

Talo looked at them and saw past the dripping faces and heaving chests. He saw people who loved and feared for those they loved.

"Give me a moon's length, and I will turn you into warriors like no one has ever seen before. Get some water, and then we begin again."

$$\text{)} \bigcirc \text{(}$$

Across the camp, Pel, the Dedicant of Artemis found herself sitting with six of the Seven Sisters who had traveled from Malta. She felt a pressure, a warmth, and turned to see Talo looking at her across the distance. She gave him a slow smile and turned back to hear the one called Ni Mu say, "We have made these bold and irrevocable changes, all on faith. But for the first time, this morning, I feel fear."

"What shall we do? What shall we do?" The round of voices began the chorale as the women of the Pleiades sang their concerns.

To Pel's ear, their song was eerily beautiful. She didn't understand the language of the music, but she found that she understood the emotional truth in the melodies. Rather than feeling left out, she felt as if they swept her into their song, brought her with them into the uncertainty for their futures, and she let her heartbeat and breath be a harmony to theirs. Their bodies swayed gently, arms and hands making tiny floating gestures as they moved like clouds and clung to each other and pulled apart effortlessly.

As their song came to a slow quieting, she spoke her truth.

"In my Temple we are taught that fear must transform to action, or else it becomes a poison to the soul."

The one called Ni Ma, the elder of the Sisters, gave her a tender look, "What action do you propose, young hunter?"

"Well," and here Pel took a long pause and an even longer leap into the unknown, "Well, there is the Form."

The six of the Seven Sisters sat quietly, watching what was obvious to them to be her inner struggle. They waited and listened to the silence between her breaths.

"We… it is one of our Sacred Mysteries, but we have something called the Dance of the Wild Hunt."

She looked at them with a countenance of perhaps having taken one step too far, said one word too much. So, patiently, they waited till the young woman resolved her qualms and spoke now with resolution.

"It is the way we are trained, to be prepared in body for the Hunt, to become still whilst in action, to breath as one, think as one, hunt as one. We are all sworn to protect the secrets, but somehow, I don't believe that I will be forsworn if I teach this to you."

"Is it strenuous?" said the one called Ni Mou with a languid wave of her hand. Her sisters chuckled, and Pel gave her a gleeful grin.

"If you learn the Form you would work till your eyeballs sweat. Does that sound strenuous?"

"You then have your tasks ahead of you, young hunter, to see if you can move this lazy bunch!" Ni Ma replied.

Pel's face lit with a lightning bolt of a smile, "On your feet then, my willowy friends. Begin by placing your feet slightly apart and gently softening your knees."

She led them through the lunges, the crouches, the leaps up and out. They kicked high above their heads, they tipped to the side and placed one hand on the ground, they sprang forward and rolled to their feet. At one point, Pel looked across the camp and saw Talo doing remarkably similar movements, cajoling and berating his group of three. He felt her stare, looked up and flashed her his astonishingly beautiful smile with teeth snow white against his copper skin. She felt it then, the rightness of her being here, the measure of her worth, the value of those companions, herself and the others who had accompanied the Thirteen. They had purpose here. They were needed. And everything was perfectly revealed exactly as it was.

A FIERCE, DARK NIGHT

T he day was spinning to its end, and the light grew thin. Thousands of white slashes, ibises coming to roost, filled the bushes along the river, and the sky held black swirls of the millions of migratory birds heading north along the Naihl. The kitchen servants had been working through the latter part of the sun to complete an evening meal for the Thirteen and all of their companions. All of the company had started to gather by the pavilion that had been created for their comfort.

The sun disk, palest yellow as it rested on the horizon, seemed to hesitate, and then plummeted out of sight as the world plunged into darkness.

"What just happened?" Celebi exclaimed. "Night has no patience here. The darkness falls in an instant."

She shivered with the sudden drop in temperature, and Malvu stepped close to wrap his arm around her shoulders.

"Yes, it is the sunsets here that remind me we are in a foreign land," he agreed.

He heard, or thought he heard a low, almost subterranean, grumble, and all the hair stood up on his arms.

"Beloved, did you hear that?"

"I hoped I hadn't," she whispered in reply.

Suddenly the black jaguar and the silver hound raced past them a few yards and stopped, staring into the undefined space beyond what light the central fire threw. Their ears were held forward, and the hair bristled on their necks.

"What is it, boy?" Domnhu came to stand by the hound, and Talo emerged in the half-light to position himself next to the jaguar. They placed their hands on the animals' necks and felt the tremor of thinly reined vigilance.

Again, the barely perceptible rumble came out of the dark.

"Stay!" Domnhu said with quiet urgency. "Stay!"

Like a gust of wind, Atvasfara swept past them. The rest of the Thirteen came behind like the ripples on water following a swan. They moved a few feet past the circle of firelight and were swallowed up in the silk of night. Within heartbeats, all of the rest of the companions clustered with Celibi and Malvu and Talo and Domnhu, poised at the edge of the light, peering with concern into the impenetrable night.

"What is happening?" Pel said as she stepped beside Talo and let her arm rest against his.

"Something really big is out there," Misi said in a very small voice and slipped her hand into the hands of Smiths the Elder and Younger.

For the Thirteen the darkness felt alive with unseen eyes, the air quivered with danger. A growling, lower and longer than any thunder they had ever heard, emerged. The ground itself vibrated with it. Fear rippled from body to body in the thick darkness.

In the density of the darkness a form, solid yet amorphous was suddenly visible. It was giant and black, yet seemed to be lit with some source of light. The earth shook beneath and Io and Eiofachta gasped. The rumble that had been indistinct subtly began to take form, larger and larger until it enveloped them, greater and greater until they could feel nothing else in the cells of their bodies and still it grew. And grew. Gradually, almost imperceptibly moving from an echoing roar into words:

"AHHHHHHHHHIIIII…

"AHHHHHIIII AM…

"I AM… I AM HERE.

"I AM FOR YOU.

"I AM THE LOVE OF THE MOTHER. I AM THE COURAGE OF THE MOTHER. I AM…"

The Thirteen heard Her voice in their hearts and in their wombs.

"It is the Lion Goddess! Can it be?" whispered Awa.

"Yes, it is Sekhmet!" Atvasfara confirmed, almost breathless with awe. "It is Sekhmet, She is here."

The Thirteen reached out to touch each other, a cohort of intention and common purpose, receiving all the strength and bravery that Sekhmet had to give them. The very air seemed to be saturated with the presence of the Great One, and as they breathed in, they drew Her into themselves, feeling the shimmer of the divine in the very marrow of their bones. At the edge of their vision was movement, and in the dim light of the emerging stars they could see lions, this world lions, standing in the sand, surrounding them. The primal panic of coming face to face with the queens of the wild froze the blood of the Thirteen.

"DO NOT FEAR. MY BELOVEDS WILL FOLLOW YOU AS YOU DO YOUR SACRED WORK. THEY WILL STAND GUARD WHEN YOU NEED IT THE MOST."

From the cluster of women, first Ni Me, then Silbara, then Uxua began to slowly walk forward, hands extended low in front of their bodies. The lions watched with calm curiosity and then stretched their necks to smell the extended hands. Gently, inexorably, the women's hands came to rest on the lions' heads. A shiver, like star lightning ran up their arms, and the rest of the pride moved like lava, forward, to surround the others of the Thirteen. Io sat on the cooling sand and a young lioness put her head into her lap. Tiamet began to croon to the eldest lion and run her hands over the thick scratchy fur from neck to tail, "Oh, my lovely. Oh, my lovely."

Maia and Atvasfara helped Parasfahe to walk toward the Presence that was Sekhmet. The three raised their arms to salute the Great One, arms shaped like the cup of a sickle moon. A song emerged, and the rise of three notes, held, then the descent of four tones, and the three women lifted arms, formed a circle above their heads with their hands and let the music guide their movements. It became a dance, a dance to Sekhmet, the Dance of Sekhmet. Some of the Thirteen danced with the lions, some came to join the trio before the Presence in the darkness. And the song built and built and built, a sacred container of sound and timelessness. Eventually all the women and lions formed a circle around the Presence that shone in the blackness leaning in like flower petals pulled to the center by the source of life's energy. The moment seemed to be eternal, crystallized in pure love.

"I AM. YOU ARE. AND YOU WILL ALWAYS BE."

Some small thing seemed to break in Atvasfara's heart. She felt the tears stream down her face, from a place of grief and sadness that was ages old or had not yet been seen. And the Presence that was Sekhmet began, imperceptibly, to not be, like the wisps of dream held tightly upon awakening.

When the Thirteen looked up, the blanket of stars looked like the face of Sekhmet, the sad warm eyes, the whiskers, the noble forehead. The lions, weaving through the women like fingers gently stroking through hair, walked gracefully deeper into the night. As one, the Thirteen turned to walk back across the now cold sand, toward the light of the fire and the warmth of their companions.

Maia sat nestled in Savi's trunk as he lay with his back against a sand dune. She pressed her cheek against the dry wrinkles of skin and whispered to her dear friend.

"The lions danced with us! What an incredible place this Egypt is."

☽ ◯ ☾

Awa was wrapped in her mother's arms and a soft cotton blanket surrounded them both.

"It was the Lion Goddess, Mama. And I saw Her! And heard Her!"

"What did she say, precious?"

"That She was our protector, and that we would always be. What does that mean, Mama?"

"I wish I knew, my love."

☽ ◯ ☾

Kiyia and Io sat together close to the fire. They spoke softly though no one was close enough to hear.

"When lions choose to be your guardians, it looks like the days ahead may indeed be perilous. I'll stay close, Little Sister."

"And I will have your back, Big Sister."

$$\mathbb{) \bigcirc (}$$

Badh was lying across Domnhu's chest, inside the small tent they shared. They had made love fiercely, as if their lives depended on it. When her breathing slowed closer to normal, she let her lips move like falling snow across his neck and whispered in his ear.

"No matter what may befall us, I will remember this."

His only response was to tighten his arm that was draped across her back, as a single tear slipped from the side of his eye.

PRIESTESS OF NUT

D alia was seated cross-legged on the sand as the Thirteen and their companions began to filter back into camp. She was deep in the prayer practice of her Goddess, but could hear their voices and was aware that something of some great magnitude had happened.

Later, she said to herself, *I'll know soon enough*, and settled back down into the deep inner quiet that was required of all Priestesses of Nut. This was a precious delight, to be again under the darkest blue of the Egyptian night. Dalia drank it in, thirsty for the still point that came with the hours of night prayer.

Yes, Egypt was the place where she could find this sublime bliss. And it was also the place where she could experience the most discomfort. Here she found her truest purpose. And here her life was always in danger.

When she was a child, the palace of Pharaoh had been a place of turmoil and the constant thrum of human interaction and friction. Dalia's mother, Medrona, She who was Pharaoh, had been on the throne for many sun cycles, and was the mother of four daughters, a sign of great blessings and approbation from the Goddess. The royal daughters were in constant training and education. Not to mention the never-ending conniving and maneuvering that went on between factions of cousins and half-siblings. There were the four royal daughters from two consorts, and everyone's position in the hierarchy was always in flux. The eldest child, Maysa was bright and cunning, but her mother felt little affection for her. The next daughter, Petrinh, had a different father, and a sweetness of nature that helped her develop a coterie of supporters in the court. Dalia, fathered by this man as well, was the smartest of them, but she found the intrigue and competition tiring, and early in her childhood had espoused a desire to be a priestess and not vie for the throne. The baby girl, Maisoun, full sister to Maysa, was born with defects, slow of mind and not quick of body, but a patience and open-heartedness that made her their mother's favorite. But perhaps it was because Medrona could simply love her, and not need to consider her in the contest as her successor.

Dalia had entered the Temple of Nut there in the royal city of Thebes at her menarche at the age of twelve sun cycles, and had found a beauty and peace in those walls that nourished her soul. On her infrequent visits back to the palace she could almost taste the enmity between her two older sisters. Once she spoke to their mother about the rancor, and Medrona only sighed and said, "You are so much better situated my love, to be away from here. I can only hold back the clash between them for so long. And whichever I choose to follow me, there will be a chorus of unhappy voices in disagreement with my choice."

"Mother, how will you choose?"

"I will choose for Egypt, my little dove. It is always what will be best for Egypt."

So, with no further insight into her mother's decision making, it was with some surprise that she heard one day, several sun cycles later, that Medrona was announcing her successor on the morrow.

The event was splendid and crowded, and the wide streets of Thebes hummed in anticipation. Representatives of the noble class, the merchants' guild and the royal army filled the outer chambers of the palace. Dalia and the other Priestesses of Nut came in their midnight blue robes. The High Priestess of Isis, newly appointed, and many believed too young for the job, Atvasfara, arrived with her Temple's contingent in their bedazzling gold and azure. The smell of myrrh and spikenard was thick, and the smaller groupings of priestesses of Ma'at and Sekhmet made splashes of scarlet and jungle green.

Medrona entered on a high platform, and stood in shimmering splendor. It looked like she wore all the gold of Egypt in her hair and around her neck and arms and waist. A hush fell, and with great dramatic instinct, Medrona let the pause and silence build.

"I, Medrona, fifty-seventh Pharaoh of my line, ruler of Upper and Lower Egypt, mother of daughters, faithful to my lineage, will now pronounce who the Goddesses will anoint as my successor when I am called to the next world. I want my daughters to come to me."

With a start, Dalia realized that that meant her too. She moved warily up the stairs to join her sisters who had emerged from a door at the back of the platform. They stood in a formation around their mother that revealed all anyone would need to know about the alliances that had formed within the palace. Maysa stood on her mother's right, with a false humility barely covering a smug air of victory. Petrinh stood on their mother's left and looked at their mother with a smile of blinding sweetness. Dalia was a half-step behind Petrinh, holding onto Maisoun's hand and gently stroking her hair.

"After deep reflection, and with the guidance of the Oracle of Isis, the High Priestess Atvasfara, I have reached a decision for the good of Egypt. Whenever I am called into the arms of the Great Mother Hathor, I will be followed on the throne by my daughter... Petrinh."

Medrona continued talking, but few could hear her. There were gasps of surprise from Petrinh's admirers. There were muffled exclamations from those who had positioned themselves in Maysa's favor. Maysa herself seemed to compress into solid marble, devoid of expression with only her eyes slicing through the crowd to pierce into Atvasfara's eyes. In that moment Dalia thought, *Ah, the new High Priestess has made a serious enemy today. I hope she is prepared for the poison that can be Maysa.*

The feast that followed that pronouncement was a study in genuine versus forced frivolity. Maysa froze a smile on her face and kissed her sister on both cheeks.

"Blessings on your good fortune, my sister."

"Thank you, Maysa. You know I always treasure your goodwill."

Dalia heard all this and wondered if her sister Petrinh was guileless or a masterful manipulator. Either way it was all exhausting, and she wove her way through the crowd to take her leave of their mother.

The two locked eyes, both pairs a deep nut brown with an abundance of black lashes.

"You are the wisest of them all, my little dove. I would council you to get as far away from the coming storms as you can."

"I wish I could help you, Mother, but me being here would only make it worse."

"Get away, my love. And stay away if you can. I would not have you in the middle of this contest, even if I could. Find peace in your Goddess. For truth, there is none here in this palace."

It was with great disquiet in her heart that Dalia left the palace to return to her sanctuary and the still beauty of the practices of Nut.

Four sun cycles later Medrona, She who was Pharaoh, succumbed to the fever she caught during Inundation. All the royal daughters performed the required three days of chanting before their mother's body was prepared for the afterlife. Little Maisoun wept without ceasing, and Maysa and Petrinh circled each other like roosters in a fighting ring. Dalia left to return to her Temple as soon as possible after Petrinh was hastily crowned Pharaoh, and an uneasy mood fell over the palace.

Five sun cycles passed. The seasons rolled on: Spring, Inundation, Winter. Followed by Spring. Inundation. Winter. And again. And again. Eternal like the Naihl. And most treasured the stability in Egypt. Most.

Then came the morning when the giant gongs that announced the births and deaths of the royal family clanged throughout Thebes. Dalia sat bolt upright on her bed and broke out in a cold sweat. The gongs split her head with sound and panic. No woman was expecting a child, so who had died? Ripping herself free of her bedclothes, she had dressed and run through the streets to the palace. The wails and screams that poured from Petrinh's chambers told the story.

Dalia saw Maysa walking in her direction down the corridor, looking down, preoccupied with adjusting her stole. When Maysa looked up and spotted Dalia, she also adjusted a look of grief on her face.

"Oh, Sister! Such a dire calamity! Petrinh has died from an asp's sting!"

Dalia raced in to the bedchamber and saw Petrinh's body, bloated and purple, with arms and legs askew. All sound fell away as she turned slowly to see the look of sheer triumph on Maysa's sharp fox face.

The day after the funeral rites were completed, without waiting for Maysa's coronation, Dalia sailed from Thonis to the Mystery School at Eleusis for a stay of several seasons. The priestesses there welcomed her warmly, and the Mysteries were deep and inviting, but it all felt a little too close to Egypt and Maysa's reach. In search of peace and safety she then traveled through the Middle Sea, along the Tin Trail, and far to the north to the Mystery School of great repute at Calanais, where she had stayed for four cold but happy sun cycles. She had missed the cloudless skies of Egypt where it never rained, and the night sky that was always open and available. But the mists and liminal gray of the Outer Isles had been a perfect solace. She had vowed never to return to her home where asps found their way into certain women's beds as if by accident.

But the Goddess had put this great plan into action, and Dalia, a priestess trained and ordained, had put herself into the river of this transformation to be in service to the Great Mother. And now, here she was, loving and hating her homeland. Thonis was only a brief span of days' journey to Thebes in the south. To the place of her birth. To the palace. To her sister, the Pharaoh. To the Temple of Isis. And to the destiny of all the Thirteen who were Goddess called. With the rising of the sun, she ended her prayer practice, stood in one easy movement from her perch on the sand, and brushed off her cloak. Time to see what had happened while she prayed. Time to help these women prepare for their Goddess fate. Time to face her own fate here in Egypt as well.

PREPARATIONS FOR
THE BATTLE AHEAD

Over the next half moon the work to be done became apparent. The company of the Thirteen, their companions, and the entourage from the Temple of Isis began to build a coherent community. Each morning Talo and Pel led their respective trainees in their versions of the Form. On the second day Eiofachta and Autakla had come to practice the Jaguar Dance with Talo. The next day Io, Silbara and Kiyia joined in the Dance of the Wild Hunt with Pel. As the days rolled on, others of the Egyptian Temple inhabitants as well as a few others of the companions joined in. A pattern emerged. Talo and his trainees filled an open space on the western edge of their camp. Pel and her group used a smoothed sandy surface on the eastern side. The two groups began to face each other across the tents and cook fires, practicing their respective Forms, gently but insistently challenging the other in a call and response of movement and effort.

☽ ○ ☾

Standing on a gentle rise of sand dune some distance from the camp, three women stood watching: Atvasfara, Maia, and Uxua. They were the authorities of their worlds, strong in their ability to lead. They had formed a strategy team, mapping out how and when and to what purpose this combination of people and animals would move up the Naihl toward the Temple.

The three watched with silent appreciation as the figures below kicked and lunged and swung with greater and greater precision.

"We are building an army," Uxua said with a hint of a question in her voice.

"Yes! Yes, we are," Atvasfara replied.

"I take it, then, that we will need an army," Maia chimed in.

"Yes! Yes, I fear that we will," Atvasfara said, almost under her breath.

The three walked down the slope and went to the shaded pavilion where Yollo and Ndeup were overseeing the weaving of fabric on the four looms that had been brought from the nearby village of Thonis. The two weavers had explained the mystical purpose behind their design, and shifts of Egyptian women worked most hours of the day and far into the night to create reams and reams of cloth. The pattern held thirteen colors of alternating silk and linen and cotton with vertical stripes of white and black that held the thirteen colors in shapes of squares and rectangles. With each throw of the shuttle the weavers called the names of the Thirteen, to summon the strength and essence of those women into the cloth, to make a magickal weave that would connect them all and unite them in purpose. And here too was a call and response.

"Atvasfara," called Yollo.

"Atvasfara!" the rest replied.

"Awa," and the shuttle was thrown.

"Awa!" the shuttle was caught.

And the Song of the Names continued through Uxua, Autakla, Silbara, Badh, Eiofachta, Ni Me, Kiyia, Tiamet, Io, Parasfahe, and Maia. And then it began again. And again. And again.

The chorale of the camp, the commands and grunts of the Form dancers, the singing of names of the weavers, the peal of an elephant's trumpet became the sound fabric of their days.

☽ ○ ☾

Parasfahe sat with Celebi and Dalia. Their remedies and treatments had eased her discomfort almost immediately. The once constant roar of pain was now a low rumble with occasional shouts of sharp heat in her joints. The three sat under an awning of scarlet silk, grinding herbs with mortar and pestle, melting beeswax over a low flame, straining rose petal infusion though fine cloth Their voices were soft and intermittent. Bits of instruction to Parasfahe on the next step in the making of an ointment. Bits of memories from their lives. Bits of laughter as they watched the hound and the cat wrestle in the center of camp.

"Will we need honey-infused bandages, do you think?" Celebi asked with a studied air of casualness.

"Well, they could be very useful in preventing the infection of wounds," Dalia replied without answering the unspoken question.

"We are supposing that there will be wounds, then?" Parasfahe asked.

"Oh, knowing my sister, and the way she views the world, I think it is safe to say that this collection of powerful women will not move though Egypt without challenge. Atvasfara has offered us the protection of the Temple of Isis. That is all well and good. But there are many miles of river between that Temple and us. The wise woman would make honey-infused bandages."

"Bandages it is, then," Celebi said, and Parasfahe nodded in agreement and set her eyes down to her task.

$$) \, O \, ($$

A half moon followed in relative contentment. Everyone seemed to find a set of tasks to prepare, but no one would actually say aloud what they were preparing for. At some point in every day, the Thirteen would meet and practice magick. Each day, one of them would set the work, describe the parts from her tradition, and they would come together in that common purpose. They developed their own short-hand shared language, a way of communicating to each other that needed only a word or a sound or a look. To an outside observer, their practices looked like very little was happening. But in the realms of magick and energy and the otherworlds, they were as busy and working as strenuously as the students of the Forms and the weavers and the healers.

On one day, "Call the energy of the trees into your feet and then up and out of your fingertips." Eiofachta instructed. And the palm trees waved in response.

And on another, "Summon the creatures of the water and the water itself." Autakla demonstrated at the edge of the river. Tiny waves began to form, whipped white peaks on the otherwise calm surface, and the hooded eyes of crocodiles lifted above the surface of the water to watch and wait for further instruction.

And on yet another, "Pull the power of the waxing moon into your third eye and push it out your palms," Tiamet coaxed. And Savi sneezed a mighty sneeze as the breeze they created blew dust up his nose.

They began to appreciate and trust the wisdom of each of the traditions that they represented. They each could now resonate with Earth, Water, Air, Fire, the celestial bodies, the plants and animals and all the beings of the otherworlds. As cultivated and as proficient as they had each been individually in their own worlds, they now forged a combined consciousness that surpassed all known wisdoms.

As the waxing moon came full, the Thirteen and their familiars came to form a circle around the central fire. In the next ring came their companions, with new friendships and bonds clear from the linked arms and clasped hands. And in the outer ring, the company of priestesses and artisans and servants from the Temple of Isis settled into comfort on the sand.

Atvasfara, Uxua, and Maia stood and addressed the gathering.

"We have found welcome here on the banks of the Mother River. We have built community and relished the solace of this interlude." Maia had lifted her voice to be heard by all. She nodded to Uxua who then continued.

"Our vision has led us here, but we know our work is not yet done. And so, we have set upon a plan of action," at this both Maia and Uxua turned to Atvasfara.

"Tomorrow we begin the construction of barges to accommodate our new friends. The craftswomen and men of Thonis will arrive with their heritage of boat building to make our flotilla. We will move upriver at the next dark moon, stopping only to moor up at night. With the blessings of Amaunet, the Wind Goddess we will reach Thebes and the Temple by the next dark moon that follows. Are there any questions?"

Total silence held for a span of five heartbeats. And then, an avalanche of words flowed from each of the circles.

"Can the boats be built that quickly?"

"Will everyone travel by water?"

"What is the 'work' you speak of?"

"Must we go to Thebes?"

And more and more, all wrapped together, indiscernible as individual queries, but impressive in the tumult of perplexity. Above it all came the thunder call of the elephant. All heads turned to Savi and his mistress who stroked his trunk and, with a half-smile, said, "Savi hates boats. He will walk."

ONCE THE STORY IS TOLD

"**I**t occurs to me that we know that each of us received a vision, but that we don't know what those visions were."

Atvasfara sat upon ruby cushions under the gently lifting canopy of amethyst and turquoise cotton. All the Thirteen were resting there after today's magick practice in which Kiyia had taught them to taste soil and predict the weather. Most of the Thirteen were now sipping from chilled glasses of tamarind juice to clear out the taste of dust and drought. A clear cascade of laughter, like water down mountain stones, floated from Atvasfara as she continued, "We are either an extraordinarily prescient gathering of women, or a most gullible bunch!"

This statement was met with soft chuckles and giggles and a snort of what could be called laughter from Tiamet that sounded like the earth was cracking open.

"A less foolish group I have never before seen in my eons of life," Tiamet cackled. "Although, those two over there did believe me when I said I slept on clouds and farted stars."

The laughter swelled as Tiamet pointed to Silbara and Autakla who were reclining on a cushion, arms wrapped around each other's waists, exchanging kisses.

"We never," Autakla blushed as she attempted a false vehemence in her reply. "Well, perhaps for the briefest of moments did we believe that."

"The impossibly Old One toots, all right!" said Parasfahe. "But I can attest that it isn't stars that come out her backside!"

The rest of the Thirteen turned to look at Parasfahe, held their breath for a fraction of a moment, and burst into raucous peals of whoops and guffaws. Parasfahe, the distant. Parasfahe, the aloof. Parasfahe, who, up until this moment, had wrapped her conversational responses into monosyllables and undefined grunts of assent or refusal. Tiamet's laughter became the sound of a mountain avalanche, and she bent over double at the waist till her tiny body looked like a ball of white fur. The Thirteen were holding their sides, wiping tears from their faces, gasping for air. As soon as the tumble of laughter quieted down, one would catch the eye of another, and the peals of sound and mirth would pick up again. Small clusters of servants had come to stand just outside the shade of the pavilion, concerned that something was wrong. Atvasfara waved them away, and wiped her eyes on her sleeve, leaving a trail of wet across the gold silk that looked like darkest amber, saying, "It is good that we have established who among us is gullible, then," and the laughter erupted again.

"I would hope that if I live that long," Silbara said archly, "I would develop an interesting talent. It would be good to have something to show for all those sun cycles!"

This was met by more whoops and shouts of, "That's a good one!" and, "She got you there!"

Tiamet jokingly waved a fist in Silbara's direction. This led to a spate of shared jokes and tales of dubious talents. It culminated with Awa in her endearingly flat-toned voice demonstrating the array of sounds she could make with her hand in her armpit. It was even more outrageously funny to the others because Awa couldn't hear how fartlike those sounds were.

"And it always comes back to farts!" Kiyia shouted, and the Thirteen collapsed in howls. They gradually quieted, with little hiccups of giggles and wheezes of final laughter. The shared humor had swept the pavilion clean of any lingering distance or doubt between them. They passed around platters of dates and olives, filled each other's glasses with more tamarind juice. Io brought Parasfahe another cushion, and Maia placed a small stool under Tiamet's feet. They settled and looked at each other with an affection that was building into love. They settled and let the disappearing light of the end of day line each face with silver and mauve. They settled and waited for the tale of each woman's vision to be revealed into the midst of them.

"I was sound asleep," Eiofachta said, dropping her words like small stones into a calm pond. Uxua, Atvasfara, Badh, and Parasfahe nodded in agreement of the common state of how things were.

"I was awake, doing astral observation," Silbara said, as if from a distance in her memory, and Tiamet and Ni Me looked to her and remembered how they had been doing that as well.

"I was hiding in a tree, avoiding ceremony," Awa confessed, and the rest of the Thirteen looked at her and smiled.

"I was stinking drunk," Kiyia said, just a little too loud. And the group chuckled as Maia clasped the warrior woman's hand and gave it a squeeze.

"I was hunting the Stag," said Io.

"I was swimming free in the sea," said Autakla.

"I was the embodiment of Kali Ma, dancing for my people for the last time," said Maia with a slight catch in her voice. And Kiyia squeezed her hand back.

Slowly, quietly, almost reverentially the images and sounds and emotions from those visions began to spill out from the mouths of the Thirteen. As the complete picture started to emerge it was if they had been standing at thirteen different points around a Circle, the circle of the world as it was. And they had each seen the same things from their different points in space, the same and yet specific to where they were standing in the dreamscape that the Goddess had sent them.

"I saw Temples pulled to the ground, with fire burning all that is sacred."

"I heard screams, such screams, of women being raped and slaughtered."

"I saw priestesses, shackled in a line like cattle, being led into the mountains."

"I saw creatures with long legs and hooves, Silbara says they are horses, I saw them trampling the beautiful and the precious, the paintings, the diadem, the offering bowls…"

"I heard the rending of fabric and flesh."

"I saw the Groves burn and the bodies of those who honor the Goddess burning too."

The details, once allowed to come to the surface, kept pouring out, a purging of the acid and the toxins that the Thirteen had experienced and carried these moons, with such a momentum that they couldn't be stopped.

"Statues of the Goddess toppled."

"Devotees hunted down like rabbits."

"Cries for life and mercy."

"Cries for mercy and death."

"It was men."

"Fueled by the desire to dominate."

"Fueled by the need to dominate."

"Fueled by the rage to destroy."

When, finally, the reliving of the vision had stopped hemorrhaging out from the memories of the Thirteen, there was a hush. They all now looked squarely at the world that was to come. The sight of this oncoming debacle had driven them all here to this place, to be together, to combine their wisdom and their strength. But the questions hung in the air like an oily fog.

Why did we need to come to this place?

Why Egypt?

And what, in the name of all the Goddesses, are we to do now that we are all here?

In the way of this land, night descended in a moment. Servants tentatively approached, and in the silence they lit lamps and brought cloaks and wraps to combat the desert chill that fell like stepping off a cliff. The Thirteen could see the cook fires being roused and the torches brought to blaze by the tents that were scattered around the camp. They saw their companions and familiars moving, in and out of light, as they walked and talked and ate by the fires. And from all of this, the Thirteen felt distant, removed, as if encapsulated in amber.

Io, the youngest amongst them, stood and posed the first question that burned in their minds, "Why did we have to come here? What is it of this place that makes it necessary to be here? Why this Egypt?"

All eyes turned to Atvasfara, as if she, of this place, could answer the *why this place* question. She hesitated, with the need to have some answer swelling in her throat. Before she could find words, each of the Thirteen felt a shift, a tremor, and tingling in the center of their knowing. And one by one they stood to form a Circle, with arms at their sides and hands low with palms facing inward to the center. Eyes rolled upward as lids gently closed, and a voice, a Voice, spoke to each one in the privacy of her own mind. Yet they knew that all of the others heard the same Voice, the same message.

"MY DAUGHTERS. I HAVE BROUGHT YOU HERE TO MAKE USE OF THE FOMENT, THE TENSION, THE DISSONANCE THAT THE HUMANS HAVE MADE IN THIS LAND. THERE IS CONFLICT HERE. THERE IS GREED. THERE HAS BEEN MURDER. THE ABSOLUTE FORBIDDEN HAS HAPPENED HERE: ONE HUMAN HAS TAKEN ANOTHER'S LIFE. THIS HAS MADE A RIP IN THE FABRIC OF THE WORLD, A RIP THAT WILL TEAR MORE AND MORE OF THE WORLD APART. AND IN THE RIPPING THERE IS FRICTION AND AN ENERGY THAT WE CAN, YOU MUST, TAKE AND USE AND TRANSFORM. IN THIS DISHARMONY YOU CAN MAKE GREAT MAGICK. AND SO, I BROUGHT YOU FROM YOUR HOMES, THE PLACES OF PEACE AND BALANCE AND RESPECT FOR ALL LIFE, TO THIS PLACE WHERE LIFE HAS BEEN HELD CHEAP. I ASK OF YOU A GREAT SACRIFICE TO MAKE A GREAT MAGICK. DO YOU SEE IT?"

They all saw and acknowledged the truth of what they saw. They saw what they might be asked to give.

"YOU WILL NOT BE ABLE TO SAVE THE WORLD THAT IS. BUT YOU MAY, IF YOU GIVE ALL YOU HAVE, BE ABLE TO HIDE THE DEEP WISDOMS UNTIL, ONE DAY, IT WILL BE SAFE FOR THEM TO EMERGE."

They could envision it, the condensing of all they knew, all the wisdom of their traditions, all the knowledge of their lineages. They could bury this treasure of how a world might be; they could hide it till the world could be made anew again.

"NOW THAT YOU HAVE SEEN THE SACRIFICE ASKED OF YOU, IF YOU CHOOSE TO LEAVE HERE NOW, YOUR CHOICE WILL BE HONORED. THERE IS NO DISGRACE IN THE USE OF YOUR OWN FREE WILL. IF YOU LEAVE, YOU GO WITH THE LOVE OF ALL HERE AND THE LOVE OF THE GREAT MOTHER. IF YOU STAY, YOU MUST HOLD THE SECRET WITHIN THE THIRTEEN. THOSE OUTSIDE THIS CIRCLE MAY NOT KNOW WHAT FUTURE BEFALLS. THE SECRET IS HEAVY. NOW, KNOWING ALL THIS, WHO WILL REMAIN?"

Uxua thought of her brother, their paradise in the jungle, the bond between them, and yet, she stepped forward into the Circle and said, "I remain."

Awa wept at the thought of her mother and the ancestors in the trees at home, but she too stepped into the circle and said, "I remain."

Badh realized that she actually loved that confounded boy, Domn-hu, and yet she stepped into the circle and said, "I remain."

Autakla and Silbara clasped hands and stepped and spoke together.

Maia wondered who would care for Savi, and yet she still stepped and declared she would remain.

One by one each woman weighed the choice, and stepped into the circle and said, "I remain."

WHEN AT THEBES

*T*he moon just past had been a focused chaos. The boat builders from Thonis had arrived and worked night and day crafting the sailing ships needed for the Thirteen and their companions. Every day held more weaving, more medicine making, more practicing of the warrior Forms. The Thirteen increased the hours of their magickal instruction together. And now, every day Dalia, Priestess of Nut and next in line for the seat of Pharaoh, taught them about the intricacies of the court and the web of connection and manipulation of power that resided there.

At the next dark moon, the flotilla left the delta and began the journey upriver. Egypt was full into the harvest season, but farmers would stop and stare at the curious procession. Women, men and children ran down to the riverbank to ululate at the grand barge of Atvasfara, their representative of the beloved Isis. They gaped at the massive number of small, one-sail craft and the multiple other two-masted dahabiyas. They stepped back in caution and awe at the giant cat, hound and elephant that coursed the side of the water.

It took seven days to move past Memphis where the west bank was dotted with tombs and the east bank held a flourishing market town for trade between the Upper and Lower Naihl lands. Another fourteen days took their company past luscious mile after mile of sugar cane, flax, and wheat. The sky turned black from the clouds of hundreds of thousands of migratory birds, swooping down in funnel clouds to enjoy the leavings from the harvested fields.

One day out from Thebes they made camp near sunset on the east bank. Everyone got down to the serious business of cook fires and the evening meal, as cat and hound slipped into the nearby woods to hunt for their dinner. Maia stood at the riverbank with Savi, and waited for Autakla to emerge from the water. The shapeshifter had found that as each day progressed, she needed more and more time in her water form, drawing her sustenance of soul from the sweet, silted Naihl. She would be sitting with her dear love, Silbara, laughing or sharing tales from their youth, when she would hear the call, feel the tug in the waters of her human body, the thirst to be in the water, of the water, Water itself. She would need to go, be at the river, in the river, of the river. And so, giving Silbara a gentle kiss on the lips, she would slip away from the hubbub of human activity and run to the riverbank. And the Thirteen would take turns gathering her clothes and waiting for her return later in the day. Now, Maia saw the ripples begin and then build into a churning as Autakla transformed from seal to woman.

"I'm here, Little One. I have your clothes," Maia called softly into the deepening gloaming. One needed to speak gently to Autakla now, as each transformation of shape seemed to be more and more tangled and laborious for her. Maia saw the brown, round fur back shiver and become skin and spine. She tenderly took Autakla's newly emerged hand and helped her into a tunic and soft jacket of indigo cotton.

As if emerging from a fog, Autakla's eyes became sharp and focused, locking on Maia's face as an anchor in the world of land and air. She seemed to be struggling more than usual with her integration back to human form. Her mouth began to twist and lift as words, painfully formed, floated out past her lips.

"The Wa… the Water says… the sound… many… human feet… coming this way," with each utterance her speech became more distinct, the words flowing more fluently.

"People are coming?" Maia sounded worried. "How many? How fast?"

"The Water said, 'like a herd of four-leggeds'. And they come quick and hard," Autakla replied.

"Then we'd best spread the word that we will be having visitors," Maia took off at a half-run up the slope out of the falling dark and toward the camp. Autakla took three ragged steps and then found the rolling rhythm of her human legs as she followed toward the firelight with Savi walking patiently beside her as guardian and companion.

Back in camp, Maia was on one knee, leaning into Atvasfara who was seated at a stool near the central fire. Mouth close to ear it was clear that the message was urgent, and Atvasfara stood immediately, summoning the Thirteen to come close to hear the news. Cat and hound appeared as if they too had heard the news, sliding from the shadow of the papyrus field into the warmth of the camp. Orders given, the people of the camp moved with purpose to form concentric circles around the Thirteen. From the nearby shadows came the sound of the low rumble of lion growls, invisible in the growing darkness but on guard. The lions had been traveling, unseen and unheard, with them up the Naihl since the night Sekhmet had given them to the Thirteen as guardians. But tonight, they were on full alert and making their presence known.

"I had wished to be inside the Temple before they came," Atvasfara said to no one in particular. A horn sounded in the distance, a halloo that prompted a response in kind from Savi. Talo and Pel moved forward with their trainees right behind them, settled into their breath, and waited with their weight on the balls of their feet.

In the final fragments of dim daylight, a form could be seen riding hard on a camel from the south. Dressed in the livery of Pharaoh's court, the messenger stopped fifty feet from the outermost circle of the Temple contingent.

"Oh, Most High Priestess Atvasfara, I come in welcome from the Pharaoh, to greet you in your return to the Temple of Isis!" he shouted into the growing darkness.

"How generous," Atvasfara's voice lifted from the middle of her company, sounding calm and in full authority though her heart was racing. She glided forward, moving through the circles of companions and priestesses and servants and familiars.

"Please tell Pharaoh that we are well met, and in no need of escort."

"But, the escort is already here, my Lady." The messenger sounded unsure, caught off guard, trapped between the entourage of Pharaoh's 'welcome' and the implacable force that was Atvasfara.

"Then you can tell them to turn around and go back to Thebes," Atvasfara said in a steelier tone.

"Pharaoh was insistent that you must be given the honor due you, my Lady."

"How generous," she said again, this time with asperity and sarcasm dripping from the words. "Pray tell me, who heads the welcome party?"

"The captain of Pharaoh's Guard, my Lady," the messenger said in a wilting voice. This was not going as well as he had hoped or been led to believe. He could feel the intensity of Atvasfara's gaze, though the limited light made her form vague before him. He could hear what sounded like, but surely couldn't be, the deep throated rumble of something very, very big in the black folds of night nearby.

Atvasfara bit the inside of her lip in utter frustration: the captain of Pharaoh's Guard! By the moon, this was a military foray not a welcome escort. Pharaoh meant to interfere, to stop them, to set the stage for her own purposes. Time. They needed time, and to choose their own ground. Not here. They must get to the Temple!

"You may tell the captain of the Pharaoh's Guard that he may visit our camp tomorrow at two hands after sunrise. We will be most pleased to greet him then."

"Uh..."

"You may tell him now!"

"Yes, yes, of course, my Lady." And the messenger turned the camel's head abruptly and with deepest relief rode straight back to the Pharaoh's Guard camp some three miles still upriver.

Atvasfara spun on her heels and sped back into the circle of the Thirteen.

"This is not to our advantage, is it?" Tiamet stated in her abrupt way.

"No, it most certainly is not," Atvasfara snorted in reply. "But we make our own advantage then, do we not?"

With whispered orders and directions, the assembled company from the Temple and the Thirteen began to break down their camp in complete silence. All the campfires were built up, stoked to burn all night long to give all appearances from a distance that the camp remained here. The tents and pavilions, so recently unloaded, went back on the boats. The Thirteen came together and wove a glamoury, a powerful spell of invisibility around the people and the boats so that the captain and the two dozen encamped up river would see only fog and mist on the water. As if a silent graceful dance, the flotilla set sail, running with no lights, floating soundlessly in the dark and past the encampment of the Pharaoh's Guard. The animals all slipped into the water, and traveled across to the west bank, paddling and swimming hard against the current, coming up on the shore and moving like wraiths.

The odd grouping of lions, hound, jaguar and elephant padded quietly through the night, keeping apace of the boats until, at sunrise, the entire company came to the egg-shaped island in the center of the river whose high rocky walls held the Temple of Isis. The hound bounded joyfully toward his mistress, shaking water off violently, and Badh bent to greet him, not even complaining about the dousing she received. Smiles broke the tension of the night and the silent journey. Shoulders relaxed and the servants of the Temple set about to show the visitors to private quarters. As everyone disembarked, Atvasfara and her three heart companions went directly to the most sacred chamber where the most sacred statue of Isis stood, cut from alabaster and radiating power and love. They bowed before Her and announced their return, "Source of All Life, we are here. We bring with us the others who were called to a sacred mission. We also bring trouble on our heels. We ask for your protection."

And as the sun rose, light flooded into the deepest recesses of the chamber illuminating the statue and the wall behind so that the drawings and markings came to life and the voice of Isis filled the chamber, filled their minds, filled their hearts. They absorbed Her presence and felt the grace of Her wisdom.

"I AM. I AM HERE. I AM THE SOURCE OF ALL LIFE. LIFE IS ETERNAL. LIFE FLOWS LIKE THE RIVER. I AM HERE. I AM."

When Atvasfara and her attendants walked from the inner chamber a short time later, they were met in the outer courtyard of the Temple by the others. The soft light of dawn made the limestone pillars shimmer, and painted each tired face with streaks of gold and rose.

"We managed to avoid confrontation last night, because of all of your efforts to travel through the night. I thank you," Atvasfara was imbued with a radiant glow, a form of certainty and divine love that erased fatigue and worry. "Pharaoh will try again to impede our mission, for that is who she is and what she does, but we are now on the Goddess' land, the home of Isis, The Source of All Life. Pharaoh has no power here."

PHARAOH'S PALACE

Several days passed as the retinue settled into their new quarters, one eye always on the palace, another on the river bank… watching, waiting… for what exactly they did not know. The Longest Day was fast approaching, preparations were being readied. The Thirteen spent nearly all their time sequestered in the Inner Chamber of the Temple together.

When the Eve of the Solstice arrived, and all remained quiet, Dalia, wearing the diadem of Nut, a spilling of stars made of diamonds and silver, and the midnight blue robe of the priestess class, knew she could put her visit off no longer. "The day has come. I believe that it is time for me to see my sister. When she looks upon me, she will have few thoughts to spare for you and your mission. You will be free to continue your work here unimpeded."

"I shall give you a blessing before you leave for the Palace," the High Priestess said formally. And then, as if speaking past her own reservations, she continued in a rush, "You don't have to do this, Dalia."

Dalia reached up to gently touch Atvasfara's cheek, "The Goddess told me I was needed on this journey, and so I came. When I left Egypt, I turned my back on the damage my sister had done. I ran away from the responsibilities of my lineage. We have never spoken of this, you and I. But I must say the words aloud: my sister Maysa, She who is Pharaoh, was responsible for the death of Petrinh, She who was Pharaoh. It is an abomination, the most forbidden of all things. And it was done. One woman took another's life, the life of one of her bloodline, her very own sister."

Atvasfara paled to the color of new papyrus. She had tried very hard to not suspect the very thing to which Dalia had just testified. To take a human life! Unheard of! Unforgivable! This must be what the Goddess had meant when She said that the fabric of the world was ripped. And the Crones of Atlantia had prophesized the rending asunder of the world, the irrevocable tearing of the physical and spiritual wholeness of the planet. All made chaos by the greed of one woman.

Dalia looked at Atvasfara with compassion and resolve.

"I chose to run away. I might have stopped the avalanche of consequences, but I ran away. Now is the time for me to be a tribute to my foremothers. I need to make them proud of me."

"I should come with you!"

"No, dearest. You know that you and the rest of the Thirteen have the bigger goal. Stay. Stay and prepare. Be ready for when the Goddess gives the final call."

"I am frightened for you."

Dalia gave a bark of a laugh, "I am frightened for me too."

She lifted up on her toes and gave Atvasfara a gentle kiss on both cheeks, then turned and walked past the column and down the wide stone steps that led down to the river. When she arrived at the small boat waiting to ferry her to the eastern bank she saw that Celebi, she who had been the Brighid, and Malvu, he who had been Chief Observer of Calanais, stood hand in hand at the bottom of the steps.

"My dear friends, come to bid me safe journey?"

"No, you silly fool. We have come to try and talk you out of it, or if that fails, to go with you," Celebi said with more than a tinge of exasperation in her voice. Malvu spoke into the fraught silence that stretched between the two women.

"Of course, we don't think *you* a fool, Dalia, but perceive this as a foolish venture."

"Oh no, she's a fool alright," Celebi shot back. "What do you hope to achieve? Your sister is a scorpion. You think she will greet you with kisses and wine?"

"The odds are not favorable for either kisses or wine that I feel safe to drink," Dalia retorted.

"Let us come with you, sister," Malvu said gently. "Perhaps she won't sting if you have witnesses."

Dalia looked up at these two who had welcomed her to their Mystery School with open arms. They had been fellow scholars and had become her friends. She knew she could trust them, but wondered if she should put them at any more risk than they had already suffered on this journey. Celebi, as if reading her mind, reached forward and grasped Dalia's forearm, and held her gaze. Those pale green eyes, the color of shallow seas peered straight into Dalia's heart.

"We are Goddess-directed too, my dear. It appears that finding our love and making the Sacred Marriage is not all She needs from us. Trust that our purpose supports yours. Let us come with you."

Dalia tilted her head slightly, and wiped her eyes with a knuckle, "Ah, this sun in my eyes." Clearing her throat, she said, "Would you like a tour of Pharaoh's palace, then?" And she smiled as Celebi and Malvu were helped into the boat by the waiting riverman.

The trip to the eastern bank was quick and a window of tranquility. The sun, directly overhead, made the ripples on the water look like ribbons of green and gold, and ibis dove for fish closer to the shore.

On a normal day the dock should have been a hive of activity. But there was not a single soul there now. As the riverman jumped up onto the dock to secure the ropes, Dalia said, under her breath, "Curious."

The river was at its lowest level now during the harvest, and the Temple was built just a short stone's toss from the edge of the water. There were lines of black and brown some nine or ten feet above the ground along the walls and the pillars that made up the entrance portico.

"What are those?" Malvu asked, pointing up at the sequence of parallel lines.

"Those are the water marks from Inundations," Dalia replied.

"How often is this Inundation?" Celebi queried.

"Every year," Dalia said.

"And for how many days does the flooding last?" from Malvu.

"Moons, not days." Dalia said.

"For how many moons?"

"Three or four."

"And then why, in the name of Brig, do you have a Palace here? Are you fish?" said Celebi with asperity.

Dalia began to laugh softly, "It must seem mad, yes?" Malvu and Celebi nodded. "There are two palaces, identical, one behind the other but on higher ground, for in Egypt Pharaoh must abide where her toes can touch the water, to be in communion with the Naihl and the Source of all Life. So, there are two Temples, one for flood and one for spring and winter."

"And does your royal sister spend much time communing, do you think?" Celebi asked.

"The odds are not favorable," Dalia said slyly.

The three walked up the steps that faced the river and into the Grand Chamber. Again, there was no one there. Or rather, no one visible. There should have been dozens of people, bustling about, doing work or trying to curry favor. But it appeared to be a deserted vaulted space. The midday sun cast no shadows into the chamber, and the only sounds were the chirping and rustlings from the small songbirds that lived on the outer friezes.

"More curious still," Dalia said.

"Does no one know you are coming?" Celebi's voice bounced off the limestone pillars.

"Oh, they know. I sent word this morning. What is Maysa playing at?"

The three stood in the center of the Chamber for what seemed like long minutes waiting to be greeted. After some time, Dalia turned to her friends, deep brown eyes flashing, "I think we should just walk on in. This *is* my home after all." She abruptly walked off down a long corridor to their right, with Celebi and Malvu, again hand in hand, right behind her. Dalia walked speedily and with a focused purpose.

"Where are we going?" Malvu asked.

"To see my baby sister."

She led them around several corners and down more columned corridors to a suite of rooms that opened onto a central garden. Sitting in the shade was a very old nursemaid, spinning wool from a drop spindle. Next to her, on the floor playing with carved wooden animals, Maisoun, with the body of a woman and the mind of a child, sat with legs splayed wide wearing a tunic stained with sweat and food. Dalia gave a small cry of heart pain and dropped down next to her sister.

"Hello, my beautiful girl! What are you playing?" Maisoun looked up from her toys and her wide, slanted eyes took on a sharper attention of memory.

"Are you my Dalia?"

"Yes, my dearest, your very own Dalia."

"Are you really?"

"Yes, most really," and Dalia stroked Maisoun's hair in the way she had always done.

"Maysa said you were dead like Mama and Petrinh. She said she was all the family I had now."

Dalia gave a brittle smile and stroked her sister's hair again. She shot a sharp glance at the nursemaid who had milky eyes and was missing several teeth.

"Who has the charge of my sister?"

The nursemaid dropped her spindle and gasped. "Are you she, Dalia, returned from the dead?"

"Yes! I mean, no! I am Dalia and I have never been dead! Why is my sister in this condition? Her hair isn't brushed; her clothes are dirty. How is this allowed to be?"

"There is only me to care for her, my Lady. I wash her clothes in a basin and heat her porridge on the brazier. Some days go by and we might not receive food at all. I do what I can."

The old woman began to cry. Maisoun, hearing the distress in the nursemaid's voice, leaned into her legs and said, "Nanny alright? Nanny sad?"

"Nanny is fine, my sweet rabbit, Nanny is fine. Don't you worry." And she patted Maisoun's head gently.

"Does Pharaoh know this?" Dalia said in a low steely tone. The nursemaid heard the tone, and only responded with a nod of her head.

"And do you have any idea where Pharaoh might be?" Dalia's voice was terrifyingly quiet.

"In the Birthing Room, I suspect."

"The Birthing Room? Why?"

"She spends much of each day there in prayer, hoping for a daughter. Your sister has born three stillborn girls and only one living child, a boy. She is desperate for an heir. Or so it is whispered along the halls."

"No daughters?"

"Not a single living one."

"And that makes me her heir."

"Yes, my Lady. May the Goddess help you, uh, bless you." The nursemaid coughed to cover her misspeaking, and bent to pick up the drop spindle again, hands nervously seeking business.

Dalia took a few more moments to stroke and kiss Maisoun.

"I will be back, my beautiful girl. I will bring you something delicious to eat. What would you like?"

"Pomegranates?" Maisoun asked hopefully. "Mama let me have them sometimes. If I promise not to stick them in my nose."

"Yes, dearest, and your Dalia will let you have them too."

Dalia stood and looked at her companions. Her face was set in a fury Celebi had never seen in her friend before. "How could she?" was all she could say.

They followed her out the room, down several hallways and back to the massive kitchens that served the Palace. Here the flurry of activity came to sudden halt at the appearance of Dalia and her friends from Calanais, and then the sounds of food preparation cautiously began again.

"Who is in charge?" Dalia said in a most imperious tone.

"That would be me." A servant in a simple but elegant tunic of bronze raw linen stepped forward, her black hair streaked with white.

"I know you, you are Enphiesus, am I right?"

"Yes, Princess. I am she. I served your mother and your sister Petrinh, They who were Pharaoh, and now I am Head of Household for your sister Maysa, She who is Pharaoh."

"Enphiesus, why is my sister Maisoun sitting in filthy clothes with little food?" Dalia's nostrils were flaring and she barely held onto the rage that splintered through her voice.

"It is as Pharaoh has decreed, Princess. She required the servants that had served your sister for her ailing son."

"Pharaoh begrudged our baby sister food and succor?" Dalia's voice was rising to an angry pitch that cut above the sounds of chopping and slicing going on behind.

Enphiesus looked down and spoke very softly, "It is as Pharaoh has decreed, my Princess, not as I had wished."

"You call me Princess. You recognize my royal birth?"

"Yes, my Princess."

"So, you shall be in compliance with my wishes?"

"Yes, my Princess." And Enphiesus looked up.

"Then there will be a lavish meal, including pomegranates, sent up to my sister Maisoun, along with water for bathing and some clean clothes. And there will be maids present at all times to assist the nursemaid. Is that clear?"

Enphiesus's solemn face lit up, and a wide smile turned her austere features into beauty.

"Most clear, my Princess!"

Dalia whipped around, more running than walking, and Celebi and Malvu rushed to follow.

"Dalia! Dalia! Take a moment to come into yourself! Do not play into her hands by giving your power to rage." Celebi caught up with her friend and gently held her shoulder. "Dalia!"

Malvu had stopped just behind and to the left of Celebi, so that when Dalia looked at them, she saw their two dear faces framed in light coming into the covered walkway from the kitchen garden. She looked into their eyes, wise and kind, with her best wishes held there. She felt her rage slowing, coming from the stampede to a measured, tamped down fury. She felt herself gather inward, calm her breath, and become poised, ready to pounce, set for the hunt. Celebi and Malvu saw, and nodded their approval.

"Now, let us go find Pharaoh."

THE BIRTHING ROOM

D alia led her friends through the maze of corridors and walk-
ways, back to the vast Grand Chamber that was still oddly
and ominously empty of human activity.

"We shall find my sister far back in the Palace temple, in the Birthing Room," Dalia explained to her friends.

"An actual room in which to give birth?" Celebi asked.

"It can be that," Dalia said. "But it is adorned with the paintings
and carvings that tell the story of Isis and the other Goddesses giving
birth to the world. It is a place to encourage fertility and safe birthing, a holy place. And my sister, the Pharaoh has taken to ensconcing
herself there, asking for divine intervention." Dalia looked resolved
and composed, with only the slightest tremor in her hands giving
sign of her inner fury.

The three began a measured pace through the Grand Chamber,
then through the Advisors' Chamber which was a slightly smaller
replica of the one before, and then into the Counselors' Chamber, a
third and slightly smaller version still. The gold paint and vivid colors
of the wall carvings shimmered, and the figures seemed to awaken
and turn their attention to the three humans below. Celebi and Malvu kept up a continuous flow of hand movements drawing sigils and
whispered incantations to create wards of protection around them,
building layer upon layer of magickal shields. At the entrance to the
Throne Chamber, Dalia turned to the left and strode down a small,
dark hallway to the Birthing Room. The large doors were closed, but
the three could hear the sound of chanting coming from inside the
room.

Dalia hesitated a single heartbeat, and then pushed the large double doors in, and walked into the round Birthing Room with the force of the floodwaters of the Inundation. All of the dozen or so women in the room cut off their chanting abruptly save for one: Maysa, She who was Pharaoh. She kept chanting as if nothing had happened, though the slip of her gaze told that she knew full well that Dalia and her companions had entered the room.

Dalia stood in her full power and waited her sister out. After several minutes, a couple of the women attending the Pharaoh began to giggle nervously, and still Dalia and her sister kept their positions with Maysa's chanting sounding more and more desolate in its solitude. As the chant circled around to its final chorus, Dalia joined in in full voice.

"You are the Source of All Life,
Flowing and Giving and Birthing now.
You are the Source of All Life,
Flowing and Giving and Birthing now."

As both women finished the last line of the chorus, the sound continued to wash through the room, wave after wave of devotion hitting the walls and rushing back. Pharaoh turned slowly and looked straight at her sister, Dalia. As children they had looked alike, both taking after their mother, Medrona. The two women still had eyes the same deep brown with hair that curled around their temples. But there the similarities ended. The lives they had led, the desires of their hearts, the dreams they had sought had formed them in very different ways. Dalia's skin was unlined and smooth after years of peaceful study and contemplation in the soft, moist land of the Standing Stones. Her desire for inner truths and harmony in her life had created a body that was supple and responsive, and a mind that could find rest. Maysa had sought power and dominance, and her face was lined with a deep, double furrow between her eyes and those lines led down to a high-bridged nose with an imperious curve. Her lips were thin and bracketed with more deep lines that pointed down to her chin. Hers had always been a sharp face, and was now carved severe by avarice and obsession. The curly hair was streaked with gray and her form was bloated from multiple pregnancies and, perhaps, ill health. Those brown eyes flashed malice and were met with Dalia's, which held banked rage and condensed resolve.

"Sister," Dalia said, with the first verbal sword slash, placing Maysa as her family member not as her sovereign.

Maysa took a sharp intake of breath, and cross-slashed. "Sister! So, you do indeed live. You had disappeared so precipitously and were gone for so long we supposed you dead."

Dalia stopped herself from a backward step to avoid the cut her sister intended to give her. Steeling her spine, she responded, "I am most definitely alive, Sister, and intend to stay that way. You need me, no? I hear that you have no daughters to take the Throne after you, so the title goes to me as our mother's other daughter. Whenever the Goddess takes you, in the natural course of events, of course. We would not want that a moment sooner, surely."

Maysa bared her teeth. "Why are you here? I thought Egypt was not to your liking."

"I travel with friends," Dalia said, gesturing to her right and left toward Malvu and Celebi at her shoulders. "And, as I am sure you know by now, we come with many others to attend to the business of the Goddess at the Temple of Isis."

"What business?" Maysa hissed. "Pharaoh must know!"

"As I said, Sister, Goddess business and none of the Pharaoh's."

Two verbal swords met and straining, neither giving way. Everyone in the Birthing Room held their breath.

"*All* that occurs in Egypt is Pharaoh's business!" Maysa's voice began to rise.

"Ah, Sister, you know that is not so," Dalia chided as one would a child. "Pharaohs serve at the pleasure of the Goddess, yes?"

Maysa's face turned the shade of ripe plums, and her voice exploded in a screech.

"I am Pharaoh! *All* of Egypt serves at my pleasure!" The words rang out in the room, and it seemed that the very carvings in the wall tilted their heads in disbelief at the hubris. "I am Pharaoh! *I am Egypt!* I am greater than the Goddess!"

A stunned gasp filled the room and a deep, cold chill began to seep from the carvings, from the truths painted on the walls.

Dalia looked at her sister, at what remained of the girl she had known all her life. She saw greed and delusion and madness staring back at her from the eyes that they had both inherited from their mother. Those eyes no longer held a sense of relatedness, now only the stench of rapacious hunger. Very sadly and softly she said, "Ah, Maysa. You don't mean that. Take back those words, Sister. Take them back before it is too late."

Maysa was trembling and spitting froth.

"I mean every word! I am Egypt! I am great beyond all things! Your Goddesses have no power. They cannot even give me a daughter!"

Dalia saw the specters of their mother and all the foremothers, all the Pharaohs standing in the room, watching, witnessing. And she saw and heard as her sister ripped herself from the embrace of the women who had gone before, as her sister tore loose and ravaged the lineage of wisdom by her actions, by causing the death of their sister Petrinh, by subverting the balance between the human and the divine. And she heard the foremothers weep. She started to reach out to Maysa, but felt the ones who had gone before gently wrap their ghost fingers around her arm and pull her back. *So, this is it*, she thought. *This is the unraveling. This is the step beyond the step too far.*

She looked at the faces of all the women standing in shock there in the Birthing Room. Some met her eyes; some looked down and refused to acknowledge what was happening. Years ago, as a child, she had relinquished this destiny and found refuge in the stillness of the Temple. But now she decided to step out of the shadow of her own making. She decided to stand for the sanctity of life and the relationship of balance and stewardship that had held the line of Pharaohs since before memory. She spoke as their mother, and her mother before, and all the mothers before that, feeling their voices course through her and fill up her resolve.

"By taking the life of another, Sister, you have cut the fabric of the world. And a weaving, once cut, will rip and tear more and more easily. You have done this. I accuse you of the murder of Petrinh, she who was Pharaoh. And I will stand against you."

She turned and felt Celebi and Malvu's hands on her shoulders as she walked from the room. She felt rather than saw that many of the women there followed her. The screams of her sister rang along the corridors and through the chambers as she left the Palace.

"*I am Egypt!* Do you hear?! I am! I would see my son on the throne before you! I would see a man as Pharaoh! I would do this! I will do this! It matters not that he cannot give life. Pharaoh is the power!"

Dalia held her bones and flesh together as they wove through the corridors of the Palace picking up speed. Racing half-blinded to the garden courtyard, she grabbed her younger sister with one hand and the nursemaid with the other.

"It is time, we must go!" she said, breathless. And flocked by many of the Temple servants, Dalia emerged, stunned, into the sunshine, her sister's voice echoing and echoing behind her.

"*I am Egypt!*"

She kept her spine strong as they sat and watched as the court women in their wake, now some three dozen more, filled the remaining boats at the dock and slipped their moorings. She looked straight ahead as this small collection of crafts moved west into the current of the river and came to on the island of the Temple of Isis. She led the group up those wide, smooth stone steps to the Temple itself.

Atvasfara and her beloved companions, flanked by all the Priestesses of Isis stood waiting to greet them. The High Priestess took one look at Dalia and signaled the chorus to begin the Song of Glory, the song traditionally sung when a Pharaoh came to the Temple.

> *"She has come to greet the Dawn.*
> *She is splendid in the glory of the Sun.*
> *She who holds the key of Life,*
> *Comes to meet the One."*

Dalia, numb and glazed, felt the meaning of that song deep in her being. The Temple was doing the unprecedented thing of taking sides and declaring her Pharaoh. It was unheard of. It was ugly. It was inevitable. Dalia felt the gentle kiss from the foremothers on her lips. It was clear. The Goddess and Her vow to protect the sanctity of all life here in Egypt would not go down without a struggle royal. Atvasfara stepped forward and lifted her hands, both palms up.

"Welcome, Dalia, She who is Pharaoh!"

Everyone in the courtyard, the Priestesses of Isis, the Thirteen and their companions, the newly arrived courtiers all called out together, "Dalia, She who is Pharaoh!"

And from across the water could still be heard the crazed screams of Maysa, *"I am Egypt! I will do as I wish! I am greater than any Goddess! Pharaoh is the power!"*

The lions of Sekhmet began to roar, the ground began to quake, the Temple stones shook, a storm of dust rose and the sun, high in the sky, went black.

AND THE EARTH ROARED

*T*he three Crones of Atlantia stood on the high plateau of their island near the mouth of the mother volcano. Naked but for the yards of white and silver hair that struggled around them in the wind, they vibrated roughly. These three women, who could read the movements of the Earth and all her inhabitants through the energy as it rolled up through their feet, were positioned in a circle, clasping hands, with the power of the tremors coursing up and exploding the thin web of connections holding the cells of their bodies together. They had foretold this day. They had been successful in having the people of Atlantia evacuated and sent to all the far-flung edges of the world to spread and save the wisdom of Atlantia. They had offered sacrifices to the volcano in supplication, at first to ward off the coming cataclysm, and then when it became apparent that the inevitable would come, to ask for more time to get their people off the island and safe far away. They had offered chickens and then goats. They had thought that the offering of the magickal deaf girl who had appeared several moons before could be a precious enough gift to hold things at bay, but she and her companions had escaped, and the opportunity was lost. They fed horses and harvest to the volcano. But they knew, in their deepest knowing, that the fulminating energies of the Mother Earth Herself could not be stopped. And now the time was here.

Miles below the surface the massive titans of rock crashed together with the force of a tidal wave. Three plates of stone, from three directions, smashed into one another and split the surface of the Earth high above. The sound was beyond sound; the force was beyond description. The volcano erupted, shooting molten rock miles into the air, and creating mountains of smoke and cinder that floated on the prevailing winds and coated the lands to the west. The three Crones of Atlantia became the molten rock, their bodies incinerated, their spirits clinging to each other until the force from below finally hurled them apart.

"Sisters!" they cried with their last human breaths.

"DAUGHTERS!" came the reply from the Mother Earth Herself.

Atlantia splintered and sank, almost in an eye blink. All trace of her existence was swallowed into the maw of the volcano. As the island disappeared, the ocean surrounding her drew back, like a giant curtain of water being pulled away by an unseen hand. For miles and miles, the water was sucked away. It stopped, poised, in a heart-breaking stillness, and then roared back into the empty space, toward what had been the island of Atlantia. Billions of tons of water crashing and exploding. The ocean was a tumult, a churning tempest of water and sea creatures and rock tossed up from the deepest seabed. And as water will, it found its way. It raced northward and drove a channel that split the lands of Standing Stones into three separate parts. The people at the Mystery School in Calanais felt the tremors and saw stones tilt off their alignment. In the wild places of Eiru, the hawks and falcons huddled together in the crags of mountains. The Great North Woods felt the salt spray from the ocean far away. The shapeshifters of Seal Woman had moved their folk inland long before, and the selkies rode the massive waves in their seal forms, tossed and churned all about.

The water raced westward and tore land from land until the western shore was strewn with tiny islands where once there had been a contiguous whole. The people of the Land of the Jaguar saw massive blocks from their pyramids jostle and tumble. And along the coast of the Land of Yemaya, a giant wave raced inland and toppled the star-given statue of the Goddess, dragging it back into the sea.

The water overcame the Straits of Gaia, turning what had been a narrow stricture into the Middle Sea into a wide gaping mouth through which the ocean poured. The Middle Sea flooded. The shoreline was erased; cities were swept away. The people of the Basquela, high in their mountains, felt the earth tremors and took to their ready refuge hidden by the magick of the Sacred Marriage. On Malta, the folks had been well prepared by the foresight of the beloved Seven Sisters. They had moved high up the mountainside and now clung to one another and watched as the land below was ripped off and pulled deep into the sea.

Walls of water, mountains of water pushed east and overcame the lands of Artemis, roared into the Inner Sea, drowning thousands of miles of grasslands and farms and towns. The earth rumbled and cracked and in Babylon, the massive columns of the Temple of Inanna smashed to the ground and women ran through the corridors, wailing for their loved ones. The mountains that formed the Roof of the World were pushed up higher and higher, jagged crevices forming and tearing villages apart. Farther east, the Land of Kali Ma felt the rolling earth like waves of the sea, and jungle creatures ran pell-mell up into the hills.

In Egypt that night was one of terror. The animals had begun to whimper and pace as soon as the sun had gone dark. On the island of the Temple of Isis, Savi began to trumpet loudly, desperately seeking his mistress, anxious to run and escape what he was feeling under his feet. The wind picked up to a ferocious pace and began to bring sand from the desert and droplets of salt water that formed sharp crystals that hit and sliced the skin.

Inside the Inner Chamber, the Thirteen were immersed in their deepest meditation yet. Day had turned to night. Dark and moonless. They had forsworn food for two days past, and now only existed on a liminal plane of minds that connected to the universal intelligence of the Great Mother. They knew when the earth split. They were aware when the oceans overflowed their edges and mountains tumbled. They went down deeper and deeper into the knowing of all things until their separate selves were disintegrated, and the sound of the Goddess in their ears was all they heard.

Outside their chamber chaos was running rampant. The three companions of Atvasfara clung to each other as the Temple swayed like a sheet in the wind. The hound and cat clawed at the doors to the Inner Chamber, frantic to find their women. All of those who had traveled with the Thirteen, raced into the Temple to rescue their beloveds.

"We must get them out of here!" Celebi shouted above the roar of the wind.

"Onto Atvasfara's barge!" Talo yelled. "The river is safer. This Temple could tumble at any minute!"

The three companions guarding the entrance to the Inner Chamber held each other's eyes, and then nodded.

"Yes! Outside will be safer," the eldest companion agreed.

They threw open the doors and found the Thirteen, standing in readiness, eyes focused down, standing in a V-shaped formation like wild geese in flight. Atvasfara led the way and the rest streamed behind her. They didn't look to their friends and families with a glance or touch, they simply moved quickly out of the Temple, into the courtyard and down the wide, stone steps to the river. The Naihl looked whipped and frothy, and the barge, well tied, was tipping wildly from side to side. The sky was black and silver with slashes of lightning rending the western horizon.

Standing at the edge of the ramp leading into the barge, the Thirteen turned as one, and like a single organism with twenty-six eyes they stared deep into the eyes of all their beloveds. As one they lifted their right hands and sent a blessing, an anointing of rain and sand, to the new Pharaoh, Dalia, who stood looking at them with despair. With the internal cue that only they heard they went up into the barge wearing the clothes fashioned for them with the cloth that bound them together as one, and with Kiyia carrying the beautiful ember box that had been crafted to their specifications. They had individually been the vessels for the wisdom of their peoples; now they had woven all that into a singular unit to hide and protect the paths to the Goddess.

When they were well aboard, the servants slipped loose the ropes and let the barge float out into the current.

"Let us get back up to higher ground," Dalia mouthed, her voice ripped away by the screaming wind.

She motioned, and all those remaining scurried back up the steps to stand at the cliffs and watch the barge as it settled into the center of the river. Talo held Pel tightly in his arms as they watched the boat, looking tiny and fragile, bob in the waves, "No matter what, I am glad that I found you," he spoke into her ear. She nestled closer.

Celebi and Malvu stood with Dalia, each holding one of her hands,

"We stand with you in the days to come." Celebi struggled to get the words out past the worry and fear that choked her throat. "Whatever may come."

And as if the very fabric of Egypt was tearing, there was a terrible sound of pain, as if the Earth was giving birth. Everything tipped sideways. The western shore fell. The eastern shore rose up as high as the uppermost level of the island. Rock abrupted from rock.

And in the very middle of the River Naihl, a chasm opened up, a canyon of nothingness. The barge of Atvasfara with all the Thirteen on board disappeared into it.

With an indescribable sound, the hound and cat and elephant who had been standing faithfully on the shore hurled themselves into the river to follow their women. Those standing high on the island that housed what remained of the Temple of Isis had been thrown to the ground, and when they clambered to their feet all they could see was the slow folding inward of the deep slate waters of the Naihl. A wail of the most profound pain was ripped from those that remained.

"Do you see them?"

"Where is the barge?"

"They are gone!"

Ndeup collapsed weeping, "My baby! My baby!"

More tremors shook the ground, and rain fell so heavy as to obliterate the landscape entirely.

The tumult was unending, and the blackened sky obscured day and night for hour upon hour. Time seemed to stand still.

High atop the island, Dalia, the companions of the Thirteen and the lions of Sekhmet held vigil, waiting and hoping beyond hope that the barge would appear from the confusion below. They held to the frantic prayer that the Thirteen would come back. They chanted and sang and keened and wept, but there was no sign.

Just more rain, more darkness, more shaking.

They stood and watched as the Palace of Pharaoh on the eastern shore tipped and slid silently off the land into the dark water.

When the last stones had tumbled, the sun began to break through. The watchers were soaked and cold, with cracked lips and desperate eyes. The light shone peach and pearl as the extent of the devastation was exposed. Nothing below looked as it had before. No Palace, no Thebes. The river had carved a wide course to the west and the Temple of Isis now formed the eastern shore of the new Naihl.

The survivors faced the raw open space of an Earth where the connections that had held them all together were ripped asunder. On the high ground of the eastern shore Dalia could see a frantic wave of cloth, a distress call. The small, sickly son of her sister Maysa, She who had been Pharaoh, had been carried up to the safe ground by his nursemaid, and a bedraggled contingent of Palace folk stood there signaling for help. The students of Pel and Talo, trained in the arts of martial practice, formed a protective circle around Dalia as the remnants of the once thriving city pledged allegiance to their new leader.

That day and the ones that followed took shape, as they labored to instill order and safety, to quell panic, and fairly distribute food.

The world at large took on its new struggles. New powers fought for ascendency. The weather became winter and harvests were lost. Peoples wandered to find safety and sustenance. What had been sacred could now be diminished and reviled. The pendulum swung.

The combined wisdom of the Goddesses had been submerged into the deep waters to be held safe until it could emerge and reinvigorate the world again. But until then, the children of the Goddess were orphans without a Mother. New gods arose, some bringing comfort, some bringing pain and shame. Suns and moons shone light across the sapphire and jade, the topaz and pearl of the Earth as worlds were born and died, as the truth of what had been became myths and fairy tales to amuse children... Atvasfara, Awa, Eiofachta, Silbara, Uxua, Maia, Tiamet, Parasfahe Io, Autakla, Kiyia, Ni Me, and Badh. The souls of these Thirteen sought each other, sought Her, over and over again. And in between the heartbeats of the Earth those who listened deeply, those who found comfort in the wild places, those who felt the searing loss could hear...

I. I AM. I AM HERE.

ABOUT THE AUTHOR

*G*ina Martin is a founding mother and High Priestess of Triple Spiral of Dún na Sidhe, a pagan spiritual congregation in the Hudson Valley. She is a ritualist, teacher, healer, mother, wife and writer of sacred songs. She has helped to create RISE (Revivers of Indigenous Spiritualities and Eco-systems), an organization dedicated to protecting and promoting indigenous and pagan belief structures and the lands that support them.

Gina is a practitioner of Classical Chinese medicine and a Board-certified acupuncturist.

She lives as a steward of the land that previously held a village of the Ramapough Lenape where people can come together now to remember the Old Ways. She is kept company by her husband and dogs, as well as the Sidhe who live in the hills.

www.ginamartinauthor.com

COMING SOON...

WALKING THE THREADS OF TIME

GINA MARTIN

Book Two of the *When She Wakes* series

I n lifetime after lifetime, she who was Atvasfara, High Priestess of
Isis, seeks the others of the Thirteen.

In this gripping sequel, the thirteen vision carriers first intro-
duced in *Sisters of the Solstice Moon* face death and danger to serve
the Goddess in the times when She is forbidden. Travel with them
as they navigate through patriarchal history, seeking to save Her wisdom in the darkest of times.

ABOUT THE ARTIST

Iris Sullivan was born in Australia, lived in the UK and settled in California to raise her four children. She now lives on Maui teaching art therapy, and the understanding of color in relation to the soul to international groups. Iris strives to reveal the invisible transparent soul movements through her art.

movingthesoulwithcolor.com

ABOUT WOMANCRAFT

Womancraft Publishing was founded on the revolutionary vision that women and words can change the world. We act as midwife to transformational women's words that have the power to challenge, inspire, heal and speak to the silenced aspects of ourselves.

We believe that:

+ books are a fabulous way of transmitting powerful transformation,

+ values should be juicy actions, lived out,

+ ethical business is a key way to contribute to conscious change.

At the heart of our Womancraft philosophy is fairness and integrity. Creatives and women have always been underpaid. Not on our watch! We split royalties 50:50 with our authors. We work on a full circle model of giving and receiving: reaching backwards, supporting TreeSisters' reforestation projects, and forwards via Worldreader, providing books at no cost to education projects for girls and women.

We are proud that Womancraft is walking its talk and engaging so many women each year via our books and online. Join the revolution! Sign up to the mailing list at womancraftpublishing.com and find us on social media for exclusive offers:

 womancraftpublishing

 womancraftbooks

 womancraft_publishing

ALSO FROM
WOMANCRAFT PUBLISHING

THE OTHER SIDE OF THE RIVER:
STORIES OF WOMEN, WATER
AND THE WORLD

Eila Kundrie Carrico

Rooted in rivers, inspired by wetlands, sources and
tributaries, this book weaves its path between the
banks of memory and story, from Florida to Kyoto,
storm-ravaged New Orleans to London, via San Fran-
cisco and Ghana. We navigate through flood and drought to confront
the place of wildness in the age of technology. A deep searching into the
ways we become dammed and how we recover fluidity. A journey through
memory and time, personal and shared landscapes to discover the source,
the flow and the deltas of women and water.

BURNING WOMAN
Lucy H. Pearce

A breath-taking and controversial woman's journey through history – personal and cultural – on a
quest to find and free her own power.

Uncompromising and all-encompassing, Pearce
uncovers the archetype of the Burning Women of
days gone by – Joan of Arc and the witch trials, through to the way
women are burned today in cyber bullying, acid attacks, shaming and
burnout, fearlessly examining the roots of Feminine power – what it
is, how it has been controlled, and why it needs to be unleashed on
the world in our modern Burning Times.

*A must-read for all women! A life-changing book that fills the reader
with a burning passion and desire for change.*

Glennie Kindred, **author of** *Earth Wisdom*

CREATRIX: SHE WHO MAKES
Lucy H. Pearce

"Creatrix is a more accessible identity for us to claim, especially as women, than the archetype of Artist, which has been forged in the male image for so long.

"To live as a creatrix is to dedicate your life to nurturing and sharing your creative gifts, using them in every way you can to imbue the world with greater colour, beauty, joy, understanding, playfulness, daring, rebellion…"

From bestselling author of *The Rainbow Way* and *Burning Woman*, Lucy H. Pearce, comes *Creatrix: she who makes* – a soul-full companion for the road less-travelled, to support the life that unfolds when we say YES to The Creative Way.

This definitive guide covers vast territory, from owning our creative gifts and our voices, claiming space and time to create, the dynamics of the creative process, to the key parts of Creative Entrepreneurship from marketing to building soul-led communities.

Featuring the lived wisdom of dozens of creatrixes from around the world, including: singer-songwriter Eleanor Brown; artist Lucy Pierce; sculptress and author Molly Remer; doll maker Laura Whalen and many more.

shop.womancraftpublishing.com

Made in the USA
Las Vegas, NV
11 December 2023

82567842R10163